Dear Target Reader:

What a dream to have my novel chosen as a Target Book Club selection! The idea that *Keeping Lucy* will sit on the shelves next to so many of my own favorite writers' books in one of my favorite stores feels like some sort of magic. They say that Disneyland is the Happiest Place on Earth, but I would argue that *Target* is that place for me. (Seriously, sometimes I'll wander around Target for hours just to shake away the blues.)

I am grateful, as well, to be given this opportunity to reach out to you. The reader! The *reason*.

I always tell my students that writing is about communicating. It is about distilling your ideas and dreams and fears into a narrative and sharing them with an audience. A novel without a reader is like that proverbial tree falling in a forest. And so, a writer's first responsibility is to *you*, the reader who is there in that quiet forest, listening.

I knew that in this book there were some things I wanted to communicate. I wanted to talk about what it meant to be a woman in the early 1970s. I wanted to explore the life of a young woman living on the edge of the women's movement: straddling the conventions of her mother's generation and the ideals of her own. This story is about Ginny finding her voice. Her agency. I wanted to examine the life of a woman who, denied access to a higher education, finds herself trapped in the roles prescribed for her (rather than those she has sought out). A woman who has no voice when the biggest decision of her life is made.

The very first image I had of Ginny was of her empty arms after her daughter, born with Down syndrome, is whisked away. That emptiness, that betrayal, that *theft* was the heart of what I wanted to convey.

And I knew I wanted to communicate to my readers that finding your voice is not impossible, no matter the obstacles that stand in the way. While Ginny must struggle against a system that seems hell-bent on keeping women under the thumbs of men, on keeping "imperfect" children out of sight, and on maintaining an archaic status quo, she rises to the occasion with the help of her best friend.

This novel is set in 1971. The world is, thankfully, a different place today. But the themes of this book—I hope—transcend time. This is, in so many ways, a love story. Between a woman and a man, between best friends, and between a mother and her child.

Part of communicating is finding common ground, something to which the reader can relate. My hope is that you, my readers, will find yourselves in Ginny. Or maybe in Marsha, her fiercest ally.

But most of all, I hope that this story *speaks* to you. Thank you so much for reading my work. And thanks to Target for giving it a wider audience.

Happy reading!

T. Greenwood

keeping lucy

Also by T. Greenwood

Rust & Stardust

keeping lucy

T. Greenwood

ST. MARTIN'S GRIFFIN
NEW YORK

Published in the United States by St. Martin's Griffin,
an imprint of St. Martin's Publishing Group

KEEPING LUCY. Copyright © 2019 by T. Greenwood. All rights reserved. Printed in the United States of America. For information, address St. Martin's Publishing Group, 120 Broadway, New York, NY 10271.

www.stmartins.com

THE LIBRARY OF CONGRESS HAS CATALOGED
THE HARDCOVER EDITION AS FOLLOWS:

Names: Greenwood, T. (Tammy), author.
Title: Keeping Lucy / T. Greenwood.
Description: First edition. | New York : St. Martin's Press, 2019.
Identifiers: LCCN 2018055449 | ISBN 9781250164223 (hardcover) |
    ISBN 9781250164247 (ebook)
Classification: LCC PS3557.R3978 K44 2019 | DDC 813/.54—dc23
LC record available at https://lccn.loc.gov/2018055449

ISBN 978-1-250-16423-0 (trade paperback)

Our books may be purchased in bulk for promotional, educational, or business use. Please contact your local bookseller or the Macmillan Corporate and Premium Sales Department at 1-800-221-7945, extension 5442, or by email at MacmillanSpecialMarkets@macmillan.com.

First St. Martin's Griffin Edition: 2020

10 9 8 7 6 5 4 3 2 1

For my daughters

The Moon for all her light and grace
Has never learned to know her place.

—Robert Frost

We'd never know how high we are, till we are called to rise;
and then, if we are true to plan, our statures touch the sky.

—Emily Dickinson

It might be miles beyond the moon,
Or right there where you stand.

—"Never Never Land," from the musical *Peter Pan,*
lyrics by Betty Comden and Adolph Green, music by Jule Styne

Prologue

℘

Later, she would blame the moon. That full blood moon that pierced the night sky like a bleeding bullet hole.

Of course, Ginny had heard the old wives' tales, about hospitals filling with pregnant women on the night of a full moon. Her mother had called her just that morning and warned her to pack her overnight bag. Ginny still had two weeks to go, but Shirley had insisted she be ready. *That baby won't wait for you to find your slippers,* she said. Ab had seemed doubtful of Ginny's mother's predictions but cheerfully complied, loading the small blue train case with Ginny's night clothes, toothbrush, and tiny receiving blankets into the back of the Galaxie before they drove to his parents' house for her baby shower that afternoon.

And sure enough, just as the shower was coming to an end (the paper plate hat covered with bows firmly affixed atop her head, the pristine bibs and layettes folded and stacked), she felt the first pains. Then, only moments later, as her mother-in-law Sylvia's housekeeper cleared the empty cups and half-eaten finger sandwiches from the coffee table, she felt the hot rush between her legs. As Sylvia's friends and their daughters bustled about, gathering their pocketbooks and coats, Ginny sat motionless on the sofa, praying she'd only tipped over her punch. But Rosa had already cleared away her crystal punch cup, and Ginny's bottom was soaked.

Mortified, she'd remained silent for ten minutes as the shower guests motioned for her to *No, no, stay put,* bending over to kiss her cheeks and say good-bye. And, *What a lovely shower.* And, *Let us know as soon as the baby arrives!* She sat still as stone and sodden as her best friend, Marsha, leaned over and whispered, *I heard that screwing will get things started, if you're ready to get that baby out.* Ginny had blushed and swatted at Marsha's arm but then embraced her tightly.

"Thank you for coming," Ginny whispered. "I hope it wasn't too terrible."

Marsha had come all the way from their hometown in western Massachusetts, enduring nearly three hours of cucumber and cream cheese sandwiches and silly shower games with women who usually held nothing but disdain for girls like them; even Ginny's own mother had refused to make the trip, citing some vague ailment as an excuse.

It was a Sunday, and after dropping Ginny off at his parents' house, Ab had taken Peyton to see a matinee of *Peter Pan.* He was only four, and Ginny had worried he was too young and squirmy to sit through a whole movie, but when she glanced at her watch, she saw that the film was likely over and expected they'd be back any minute. She'd asked Ab to please come straight to the shower as soon as the credits rolled to rescue her.

"She's just trying to be nice," Ab had said of his mother.

"I know. But I hardly even know these women."

"You should at least *try,*" he said. "They're our neighbors, too."

They'd moved to Dover from their tiny house in Cambridge as soon as Ab graduated from law school when Peyton was still a toddler. He'd started working for his father's firm in the city before he'd even passed the bar exam. The down payment on the home in Dover was a graduation gift from his parents. The fact that the house was only a half a mile away from his parents' house didn't seem to bother Ab, despite all their early dreams of a quiet, simple life, raising their children in nature rather than in these stuffy suburbs. "Come on, Gin. It's not so bad. *I* grew up here," he'd argued. "And I turned out okay." But it had been two years, and she still felt about as welcome in this world as a skunk at a lawn party.

Her abdomen cramped, and she gasped, causing Sylvia, who was wiping a paper napkin feverishly at a watermark left by Marsha's cup on the end table, to look up.

"Virginia?" she said. "Are you okay?"

Only then had Ginny dared to stand, using the armrest for leverage. She glanced nervously down at the spot where she'd been sitting, confirming it was, indeed, not simply a puddle of strawberry and ginger ale punch.

"I think my water broke. I'm sorry about the sofa."

"Oh, my goodness," Sylvia said, forcing a smile as she glanced at the wide stain on her divan and then glanced out the window and nodded her head. "Full moon tonight. I suppose we should have expected this."

Ginny felt a surge of hopefulness—for the first time, Sylvia and Ginny's mother agreed about something, though, sadly, neither one of them would ever know.

Ab arrived only moments later, Peyton slung over his shoulder like a tiny sack of potatoes and fast asleep. Rosa appeared like magic to take Peyton upstairs to the guest room. Ab looked frazzled but excited as Sylvia relayed the news of the impending baby to him, and he led Ginny out to the car, the canvas top still down.

It was cool out, just a few weeks until Halloween. The ground was littered with fallen leaves, and the grand homes in the Richardsons' neighborhood were alight in an autumnal glow.

Ab grinned at her as he opened the passenger door. "I hope he waits until we get to the hospital."

"What makes you think it's a . . ." Another contraction seized her, and she trailed off, grabbing onto the open car door to steady herself. When the pain had passed, Ab situated her in the passenger seat, then hopped into the driver's seat, his grin wide and dimples deep. "We're having a baby tonight!" he said and howled at that bloodred moon punctuating the sky, then peeled out of the circular driveway onto the road that would take them to the hospital.

When the next contraction came, she glanced up at the moon and made a wish, as if it were a star. "Please, let everything be okay."

But later, at the hospital, as she surfaced from the ether stupor, her throat raw and her stomach roiling, Ginny knew that something was terribly wrong. The room was quiet. There was no sound of an infant's healthy wails, only the hush of whispers between the doctor and nurse who stood, heads bent together like schoolgirls.

The doctor came to the bedside, and she felt a wave of nausea, acid burning her throat. He had a gentle face, but his voice was firm.

"Mrs. Richardson, I know you're feeling groggy still, but I need you to listen to me."

She nodded, and it felt as though her head weighed a hundred pounds. There was fire between her legs. Everything ached.

"I'm so sorry."

She opened her mouth to cry out, but as she did, she retched and covered her mouth with her hands, vomiting into her palms.

"Oh, *dear*," the nurse scolded, coming over. She grabbed a cloth diaper from a stack on a rolling table and handed it to Ginny, who wiped at her mouth and her hands and tried to sit up.

"Mrs. Richardson, it's important you understand . . ." the doctor started. "Your daughter . . ."

"My *daughter*?" Ginny cried, the words burning her throat. A *girl*. "Is she okay?"

The nurse moved toward a bassinet across the room. Ginny watched through rheumy eyes as she briskly lifted the small bundle and cradled it in her arms before heading to the door.

"Please, give me my child," Ginny snarled, barely recognizing her own voice, and the nurse stopped, looking at the doctor for direction.

He took a deep breath and nodded, and the nurse returned to Ginny's bedside and reluctantly handed her the parcel.

The baby was not crying; she was still and silent in her arms. Dark eyelashes like a doll's. She was beautiful. *Lucy,* she thought. Like a radiant bit of light. Ginny peered into the face of her child, her *daughter,* feeling overwhelmed with nothing but love. Her chest ached with it. The doctor's words felt far away, as if he were speaking under water.

"Mrs. Richardson, this condition, it comes with many, many challenges," he said as though he were speaking to a child. "Heart defects, hearing and vision problems. Thyroid malfunctions."

Defects? Ginny shook her head. No, the baby was perfect. She knew this, even through the hazy ether scrim.

"She may never talk. She will never, ever live on her own. She will never be a normal girl, Mrs. Richardson. You must understand."

"You've made a mistake," she said in disbelief, peering at her perfect child.

She touched her finger to Lucy's soft, round cheek.

The doctor continued, relentless. "She's *mongoloid.* Which means severe mental retardation. She'll be feeble-minded, no more intelligent than a dog. The hardship she will bring to your family—women never realize the impact that raising an imbecile has on a marriage. On the other children. You must think of your son."

"Where is my husband?" she said, wincing at the fire between her legs.

"After you've had some rest, after the anesthesia fully wears off, it will be clearer. I'll speak to your husband. Now get some sleep," he said. "Doctor's orders."

When he left the room, the nurse leaned over Ginny to take the baby, but she held on tight.

"Please let me hold her," Ginny pleaded. "Just a little longer."

"*Blood moon* tonight," the nurse said, shaking her head sadly, a look of pity on her pinched and bitter face. "My grandmother said never, ever look at the blood moon when you're pregnant."

Another wave of nausea rolled in Ginny's stomach, and she held back tears. She stroked the soft skin of the baby's cool cheek.

"*Did* you look at it?" the nurse asked, reaching for the infant again. Ginny's arms felt weak, her eyes heavy as she fought sleep. "Did you look at the moon?"

Ether dreams. Like Alice falling down that rabbit hole, tumbling, end over end. Sleeping and waking, waking and sleeping. Somersaulting between wakefulness and consciousness, tumbling through a fitful slumber.

When she woke again, she couldn't tell if it was dusk or dawn, but the room was filled with a sort of dreamy half-light. For a moment, she thought the chirping was of a bird, but realized then, it was the sound of an infant's cry.

Her baby. Her little girl. Where had they taken her? She struggled to remember what the nurse had said, something about the moon. The blood moon. Her voice filled with accusation. And she recalled the softness of Lucy's cheek. The flutter of her eyelashes. Or had that been part of the dream? That twilight sleep the doctor had promised as the needle slipped into flesh, that delicious amnesia. The forgetting. But she *recalled*, she remembered his words like the prick of that needle, the sting of bees.

"Well, I see someone's finally awake," the nurse said cheerfully as she entered the room now. Thankfully, it was not the same nurse, not the one who'd offered her prophecy. Her curse. "Good morning!"

Morning. That glow was from the sun, not the moon.

"My baby," Ginny said, her words like dry puffs of cotton in her mouth.

The nurse's face was gentle, her eyes kind. She reached for Ginny's hand and squeezed it. "The doctor will be in to see you in just a little bit, sweetheart," she said. Then she handed her a pack of ice. "Put this between your legs. It will help the pain. You've got quite a few stitches."

"Lucy," she said. "I need to see my baby."

"Can I get you some breakfast? Maybe some grapefruit juice and buttered toast? Coffee?"

Ginny shook her head, though her stomach rumbled angrily.

"Is my husband here?" she asked, wondering where he could be.

She thought of Ab waiting in the other room, pockets stuffed with the last of his father's Cuban cigars he'd been keeping in the glove box of their car for this occasion. She thought of his wrinkled trousers and messy hair. He'd probably made friends with every other waiting father, maybe even sharing one of those precious Cubans. She wondered if he'd slept at all, if he'd eaten. A *daughter*. He'd chosen the name *William* for a boy, convinced he was about to have another son, but she'd decided on *Lucy*. She'd known all along it was a girl.

She tried to smile; this nurse seemed friendly enough, maybe she would bring her daughter to her. "Ab—my husband—he wanted another boy, of course, but I told him it would be a girl. I just knew. Do you have children?"

The nurse sighed, her eyes glistening. "I'll get you some Cream of Wheat, a little butter and maple syrup. It'll settle your stomach. Sometimes the medicine can make you queasy."

An hour later, when the Cream of Wheat had congealed in the bowl and her coffee had grown cold, Dr. Wells arrived and brusquely examined her before folding his arms across his chest. Bedside manner was best left to the nurses, she supposed.

"Please, where is my husband?" she asked. It had been so long since she'd seen him. Not since they'd whisked her into the delivery room. "I'd like to go to the nursery now," she said, sitting up. The tray with her breakfast tipped over, and the bowl clattered to the floor. "Is Ab with her?"

"Now, now, Mrs. Richardson," the doctor said. His voice was gentle, but his hands were firm as they gripped her arm and pushed her back onto the scratchy pillows. "I think maybe you need to get a little more rest. Nurse?"

The nurse reappeared like magic, holding a syringe this time and smiling apologetically as she plunged it into Ginny's arm.

When Ginny woke again, it was dusk. Ab was sitting at her bedside, holding her hand and smiling sadly. He was wearing his favorite tweed jacket and a chocolate-colored sweater beneath, the same clothes he'd had on the night before. His eyes were soft and warm. She felt such relief seeing him finally that she let out a little cry.

"Where is she?" she asked, sitting up, wincing at the pain in her bottom. It felt as though someone had taken a baseball bat to her tailbone. The ice the nurse had given her had melted. She was swollen and sore, and she nearly cried out at the pain. "Where is the baby, Ab? Why won't they left me see her?"

Ab squeezed her hand, stroked it with his thumb.

"Gin," he said and held her hand to his cheek, which was warm and scratchy. Unshaven. He looked as though he hadn't slept.

Suddenly, there was a brisk knock at the door and her father-in-law, Abbott Senior, pushed the door open and leaned into the room.

Startled, she clutched at the thin blanket to cover herself.

"Hello, Virginia. You look well," Abbott Senior said to her but nodded at Ab, who squeezed her hand again.

"Why is he here?" she whispered.

Ab took a deep breath. "Dad knows the state mental health commissioner personally. He's a friend from Harvard." He looked to his father for affirmation, confirmation, something, then turned back to her. Ginny's skin prickled. His eyes were imploring, but what did he *want*?

"He's found a place for her," Ab said, nodding.

Abbott Senior, still standing, tall and somber as always, nodded. "It's called Willowridge School. Out near where your mother lives, actually. She will be loved and cared for there."

"That's ridiculous. We will care for her. *I* will care for her." She shook her head, trying to understand what they were telling her, but the words felt loose, like pearls slipping off a string.

"Gin . . ." Ab's chest heaved, squeezing her hand. "The doctor says there could be a problem with her heart. These children, sometimes they don't live but a couple of years."

"This is all a terrible mistake," she said, yanking her hand from his and swinging her legs over the edge of the bed to get up. Her head felt swimmy and she could still taste the acrid vomit at the back of her throat. "Let's just go see her. I'll *show* you."

"Virginia, please," her father-in-law said, approaching the bed. "Dr. Wells says you need to rest."

"I *need* to go see my baby," she said to him, bending over to search for her slippers. "Have you been to the nursery?" she asked Ab.

He closed his eyes, ran his hand through his disheveled hair. "She's not there."

"Of course she is," she said, irritated. When her bare feet hit the cold linoleum floor, a jolt ran up her spine.

Ab shook his head and reached for both of her hands, gripping them between his own. He peered out the window at the sky, where the moon was now just a pale scar. When he looked back at her, his eyes were glossy with tears.

"Ginny, honey, she's already gone."

One

❦

E verything hissed.

The roast in the oven, the steam from the iron heating on its board, the katydids in the trees as the sun set. Ginny felt the buzz and hum, that endless drone, in her blood, and it made her anxious. She fiddled with the radio on the kitchen counter, hoping to mask the insidious hiss, but the reception was terrible, and even the music was threaded with static.

Ab had called earlier as she was putting the roast in the oven to let her know he'd be late. Apologetic, as always, though it hardly classified as "late" given that he'd been "late" every night for the last six months. Still, she went through the motions, setting the table with three settings as if he might just walk through the door, hat in one hand and bouquet of flowers in the other. That goofy Dick Van Dyke grin on his face, and her, his Laura Petrie, in her ballet flats and capris, standing on tiptoes to give him a kiss before ushering him to the table, where the pot roast and their freshly scrubbed son sat waiting.

But tonight, like nearly every night lately, she and Peyton sat at the table alone. She cut Peyton's meat for him, sopped up spilled milk with a napkin when he inevitably knocked over his cup, and nodded and smiled as he recounted the injustices committed against him by their next-door neighbor's son, a towheaded monster named Christopher. The two boys would be in the same first-grade class at St. Joseph's this fall, and Ginny was dreading the unavoidable daily interactions. It was hard enough simply living in such proximity. She tried to prevent the inevitable front-yard skirmishes by sending poor Peyton to the backyard to play most days. But cooping them up in a classroom together every day would be like caging a hungry cat with a defenseless mouse.

Now she tried to focus on his story—something about stolen Hot Wheels cars and a sabotaged dump truck. But even his impassioned babbling couldn't mask the underlying sizzle, the crackle and spit.

After dinner, she put together a plate of food for Ab, wrapping the entire thing in aluminum foil before putting it in the still-warm oven. She washed the dishes, noting the whine of the faucet, the low groan of the pipes behind the walls.

Upstairs, she knelt on the furry blue bath mat and gave Peyton a bath, those pipes clamoring, restless. He was six now, able to bathe himself, but he struggled with his hair, and so she helped him, careful not to get soap in his eyes. She was mystified by his ability to get so dirty in such a short period of time, the water turning a weak brown around him. Afterward, she helped dry him off with one of the fluffy towels she'd just washed and folded this morning, then handed him a pair of clean and pressed pajamas.

He didn't bother to ask when his father would be home anymore. She feared Ab was becoming little more than a kiss on the cheek in the morning and perhaps the feeling of his blanket tightening as he dreamed his little boy dreams at night after Ab finally came home. He was an idle threat as well, *Wait until I tell your father,* an admonishment that meant nothing at all, since Ab had never so much as raised his voice to his son.

Ginny put Peyton into bed, the fresh *Fantasia* bedsheets tucked in tight, the soft glow from the matching Mickey Mouse lamp, the bulb illuminating an endless parade with Mickey's marching band on the lampshade. She knew he would outgrow the cartoon mouse soon, in favor of superheroes or cowboys or astronauts, but for now, he was only six. Still just a little boy.

"Goodnight stars," she said, as she always said.

"Goodnight air," he recited, one stubby finger dancing in the air.

"Goodnight noises everywhere."

Downstairs, the iron was waiting, the bottomless basket of Ab's dress shirts expectant. *Hiss.* The iron exhaled its exasperated sigh. *Sssss,* the spray bottle of starch expressed. She lifted one of his shirts, each of them nearly identical, and stretched it across the ironing board. She always started with the collars and cuffs before tackling the front, carefully nosing the hot iron between the buttons. She saved the large swath of the back for last; there was something satisfying about the sweeping motions across the expanse of fabric. A small freedom. A bit of grace.

The TV was on, *The Carol Burnett Show.* But the audience's laughter sounded sinister somehow, so Ginny reached for the knob and turned the sound down. *Hiss,* the iron exhaled furiously.

When the phone rang, it startled her, and she ran to the kitchen to answer it before it could wake Peyton up; he was a light sleeper and did not go back to sleep easily once woken. She figured it was Ab calling to say he was leaving the office soon.

"Richardson residence," she said softly.

"Gin?"

It was Marsha. She still lived in Amherst, where they had grown up. Usually, she called on the weekends when the long-distance rates were lower. She worked the swing shift as an ER nurse and almost never called at night. Ginny held her breath. *Please don't let it be Mother,* she thought. Shirley had been suffering some shortness of breath lately but had been dismissive when Ginny suggested she see a doctor. She was overweight, had always been overweight, and insisted she, like Ginny herself, just needed to lose a few pounds. But Shirley shared a duplex with her sister now; certainly, if something had happened to her, then it would be Aunt Bonnie who called, not Marsha.

"I take it you haven't seen the papers this week?" Marsha said.

"The *papers*?" Ginny tried to imagine what she could have missed. As a rule, she ignored the newspapers, the news. The Russians could have invaded the country, and she would be entirely oblivious. This willful ignorance was irresponsible, she knew. Foolish, even. But really, what could she do about an unjust war? She couldn't even keep that little monster Christopher from tormenting Peyton; what could she possibly do about nuclear tests in the desert, bombings in Ireland, or earthquakes in Peru? The only thing she had power over, the only change she could reasonably and predictably effect, was the removal of wrinkles from shirts, of mildew from tile, of dirt from her child.

"No. What happened?" Ginny asked.

"No one's told you? About the report?"

Ab was constantly buzzing and talking about reports, briefs, affidavits, and subpoenas. His briefcase was overflowing with them. He was still working for his father's firm, but she knew the plan was to eventually become an assistant district attorney, a DA. Maybe even run for office one day. His life was mapped out in an endless stream of papers.

"I don't know what you're talking about, Marsh."

"There's a local reporter, here in Amherst," she said. "He's written a— damn, what do they call it—an exposé? There's been an article in the paper every day since Monday. I just sat down tonight to get caught up."

"Exposé?"

"The *school*, Gin. The reporter, he went in undercover and took photos. Of course, it's the newspaper, so the pictures are kind of grainy . . . but, Gin, it's so awful. I read the parents have filed a lawsuit."

"The parents?"

"Yes, of the children there. A class-action lawsuit. Gin? Listen. Will you be home tomorrow? I'll drive over."

"I don't understand. You mean . . ." Her voice trailed off. She could imagine it like steam slipping away.

"Yes, Gin," Marsha said. "It's *Willowridge*."

Willowridge. The hum and buzz were now filling her ears, she could see the hiss, taste it. Smell it burning.

"I'll be there by noon. . . ." Marsha said.

"Oh, no!" Ginny dropped the phone and ran to the living room, where the iron was breathing smoke and Ab's shirt, the gingham ironing board cover, and the pad underneath were scorched. The smoke alarm began to ring out then.

"Mama?" Peyton said as he came padding down the stairs, covering his ears with his fat fists. He was crying, his voice a high whine.

"Stop!" Ginny said to no one. To everyone. To the world. She pressed her hands against her ears to still the deafening noise.

She heard a car door slam and Ab flew through the door, wide eyed, frantic. "What's going on? Is there a fire? I could hear the alarm all the way down the street!"

Normally, when Ab finally arrived home each night she'd feel an odd calm descend upon her, the ceaseless buzzing beginning to quiet. But tonight, it persisted. Even after Ab reached up to the wall and extricated the battery from the alarm, even as he hung up the dangling phone and scooped Peyton up in his arms, nuzzling him before playfully swatting his bottom and sending him back upstairs. Even as he tossed the singed Brooks Brothers shirt into the sink, took her in his arms, and teased, "Hey there! You tryin' to burn the house down?" Normally, when he held her, he could somehow contain the thrum and hum. But now that incessant whisper would not fade.

"Your dinner's in the oven," she said, her own voice buzzing. "It's still warm."

Willowridge.

"Marsha's coming by tomorrow," she said, her body still vibrating as he released her. The aftershock of an earthquake, the relentless shiver.

"Oh?" he asked, distracted, as he opened his briefcase and set it next to the plate at the table. He pulled out a stack of briefs, a yellow lined pad. He looked tired. His hair was messy, and there were shadows beneath his dark eyes. The carefully ironed shirt he'd left wearing this morning was now a wrinkled mess. Something about this nearly brought tears to Ginny's eyes. He sat down, loosened his tie, and sighed, exhaling in one long exhausted hiss.

"Coming for a visit in the middle of the week? Everything all right? Your mom okay?"

"Yes," she said, the words like bees at her lips. "Everything's fine."

That night, Ginny watched Ab sleep. At thirty, in sleep at least, his face was still boyish. Untroubled. She'd once marveled at the ease with which he fell asleep at night, able to slip into a peaceful slumber while her own mind whirled with whatever had consumed her day. She used to think it was affluence that assured his easy departure from the world, but even after they'd married and she herself no longer had to worry over finances, she was often turned away at the gate to Dreamland. Now, his ability to shut out the world with the flip of the light switch filled her with a quiet sort of rage. And tonight, while he took his solo flight to oblivion, Ginny was left alone again with thoughts of Lucy.

Ginny studied Ab in his blissful quiescence, the silence of his absence nearly deafening. She wanted to scream, to shake him from his willful slumber. But she feared that if she were to open her mouth, no sounds would come out.

Two

❧

October 1969

She left the hospital three days after Lucy was born, wheeled out in a wheelchair like all the other new mothers, but her arms empty, save for the little blue train case, the tiny layette still nestled, unused, inside. She'd been sedated again, after her realization that her baby girl had already been swept away. She could recall nothing of those three days besides a prevailing ache that started deep in her chest and emanated outward. It wasn't until she and Ab arrived back at home that the haze lifted, however, and that ache became the sharp bite of an open wound.

"Mother's sending Rosa over tomorrow to stay with us for a bit. To help take care of Peyton and the house while you get better," Ab had said as they walked down the upstairs hallway to their bedroom, where she wanted to do nothing more than fall asleep and never wake up again. But she stopped at the open door to the nursery. When Ab reached to pull the door closed, she pushed it back open.

"I have someone coming on Tuesday to paint. I thought we could turn it into an office. At least for now? A place for your books?"

They had painted the nursery a butter yellow, the exact color of buttercups reflected on the underside of one's chin. She had sewn the crib bumper and matching eyelet dust ruffle herself. The small stuffed animals still sat inside the caged crib, like a miniature zoo, waiting for the arrival of the baby. Their faces—button eyes and embroidered mouths—looked at her expectantly. She felt a fresh swell of sadness threatening to overcome her. The room smelled of talcum and starch, two of the best smells in the world, she had once thought. Now the scent burned her eyes and seared her throat.

"Where's Peyton?" she asked.

"He's at my parents' still. Rosa is taking him to pick out a Halloween costume at the Woolworth's today. He says he wants to be Peter Pan. Here, let's get you back to bed." Ab steered her past the nursery door to the bedroom, which seemed arranged for an invalid. Funny word, that was, she thought. Invalid. *Not valid*. Null and void.

He'd brought the television up from the living room and piled a stack of novels next to the bed, along with a glass pitcher of water sweating in the unseasonable heat. Indian summer. At the end of October.

Suddenly exhausted, she slipped off her heels and climbed into the waiting bed without even taking off her clothes. Ab sat down at the foot of the bed, and Ginny winced. He reached for her hand, studying it as though he had never seen it before. He turned the wedding band so that the diamond was facing outward, ran his thumb over and over the three-carat stone. The ring had belonged to his grandmother, an heirloom no one in Ab's family was happy about her wearing. Ginny had cut herself on it more than once and took to turning the stone inward whenever she was out in public. This kind of display made her feel uncomfortable.

Ab shook his head, looked down at her hand. "I don't know what to say to make this better," he said. "I really just don't have the words."

Ab's honesty, his sensitivity, was something that had endeared him to her when they first met. But now she didn't want his weakness, didn't want his beating, aching heart laid out before her. She wanted him to undo this damage. To tell his father that they'd made a terrible mistake and that they would like their daughter back. She wanted him to drive to that school, *Willowridge,* and sign their daughter out, bring her *home.* Let her live here, God, *die* here with her family. She wanted him to make this right.

"When do we get to see her?" she asked, clenching her jaw to keep the words she wanted to say *(to spit)* from forming.

Ab took a deep breath.

"When can we go to the school?" she said, louder this time.

"They don't allow visits at all for the first thirty days. It's too difficult otherwise."

"*Difficult?*" Her voice felt like a balloon, rising, rising.

"The doctors say that the transition is easier this way."

"Easier for *whom?*" she asked.

"For her?" he said. "For us, I suppose."

"Well, that's ridiculous. As soon as my stitches are healed, I'd like you to take me to her. And we will visit her every week. And eventually, I'd like her to come home. What did you tell Peyton?"

Ab's head dropped to his chest. His eyes were filled with tears when he looked up at her again. Softly, he said, "Mother explained to him that she's with the angels."

"*Angels?*" she said, her chest crushed with the weight of this.

"Gin," he pleaded and reached for her, but as he leaned down, she slapped him. Not once but twice, three times, until her arms ached and her palms stung, and hot milk leaked from her breasts, soaking her blouse and his shirt as he pressed himself against her whispering his futile apologies.

The only people who knew the truth about Lucy were her in-laws, her mother, and Marsha. Abbott Senior and Sylvia hadn't wanted them to tell anyone at all, but Ginny lashed out angrily and said she refused to lie to her mother. To her best friend. She had no siblings; Marsha was all she had.

The Richardsons told friends and extended family that the baby had been born with the umbilical cord wrapped around her neck like a noose. That she had been blue. That there was nothing anyone could do. There was no funeral, of course, the baby *having not breathed a single breath,* and the shower gifts were all returned. Flowers had arrived at the hospital and, later, at the house in a steady stream: sickening bouquets of gladiolas, lilies, white roses, and chrysanthemums. The sympathy cards that arrived in the mail spoke of *angels* and *heaven* and *God's will.* Ginny burned everything in the garden incinerator, all that misguided sympathy turned to ash, floating like snow in the autumn air. She knew that if she didn't destroy everything, she might begin to believe the lie, might let grief overwhelm her, might even one day let go.

She refused to let go. Thirty days, in thirty days they would be allowed to visit her. She clung to this; it was the only thing that pulled her from the hazy depths of slumber each morning. The only thing that enabled her to rise from the bed and the sheets (the ones she refused to change— stiff and sour with the milk that continued to leak from her breasts). When sorrow overwhelmed her, pulled her heart in its relentless undertow, it was the only thing that saved her from swallowing that sorrow whole.

She rose because she had to. Rosa stayed with them for a week, taking care of the household chores Ginny was unable or unwilling to perform. But soon she was needed back at the Richardsons' house. Sylvia was hosting the annual Children's Hospital fund-raising event this year, with Thanksgiving following not long after. She would need Rosa round the clock until after the holidays.

Autumn fled, the last vestiges of fall disappearing as the air turned cold and the trees bare. Each day bled into the next. Ginny moved through the world, through what used to be her life, feeling numb. She made coffee and cooked breakfast, washed dishes, took care of Peyton who, at only four, was too young to understand. She kissed her husband good-bye each morning and waved as he drove to the train station where he caught the train into Boston. She walked with Peyton to the park and sat alone watching the other mothers, her eyes drawn to the ones pushing strollers, cradling infants, trying to manage a rambunctious toddler while comforting a wailing baby in their arms.

Her breasts dried up, the stitches were removed, the pouch of fat at her belly receded. In only a month, other than her weight gain, there was little physical evidence that she had recently carried a child, given birth to a daughter.

A body forgets, but the heart remembers. And no matter how hard Ginny tried to let Lucy go, to surrender the idea of ever holding her child again, she was still with her. Lucy was inside her chest: a beating, pulsing thing. She carried the memory of her just as she had carried her inside her womb.

Ab never spoke of her, of Lucy, never again allowed tears to spill from his eyes. Instead, he disappeared, slipped away into the ether. He blamed work, apologizing that it was demanding so much of his time, but she suspected work was simply a convenient excuse for retreat from this palpable heartache. And on November 5, twenty-nine days after Lucy's birthday, he had made no mention of a visit to the hospital.

That night, they sat in bed reading, as was their habit since the earlier days of their lives together. When they were first married and living in Cambridge, he used to read to her, reciting poetry, tracing the words across her bare flesh with his finger.

That night Ab was reading a new biography of Bertrand Russell, but Ginny couldn't seem to focus enough to read anymore. She could have been holding her novel upside down and she wouldn't have even noticed. She wasn't sure he would have, either. They were distracted. Both of them.

The book she'd plucked from the nightstand tonight was *Valley of the*

Dolls. Total trash, but something Marsha had sent her in the mail along with a pound of the drugstore chocolates Ginny loved. Marsha somehow always knew exactly what Ginny needed.

"So, we should get an early start tomorrow, I imagine," she said quietly, without looking up from her book. She'd been gathering the courage to speak this single sentence all day.

"What's that?" Ab asked, setting that giant tome in his lap.

"To the school," she said, the word like a tumor in her throat. "Willowridge?"

Ab winced.

She carefully creased the top right corner of the page into a perfect triangle, marking her spot, and put the book on her nightstand. Her heart was beating hard beneath her nightgown.

Ab rubbed his face with his hands, stopped and studied her.

"It's been thirty days," she said, feeling anger welling up inside her. Hot. "They said we're allowed to visit after thirty days."

Ab reached for her, put his arm around her, pulled her close. She could smell the Listerine on his breath, the sharp scent of detergent from his freshly laundered pajamas. He kissed the top of her head and cradled her face in his hands, peering into her eyes in a way that used to make her feel so loved. Safe. He was searching for something now, though.

She shook her head, and he lowered his hands from her face.

"If we leave after breakfast, we can get there by ten o'clock. I want to bring something for her. Maybe we could swing by the Square and pick up a special stuffed animal?"

"I was thinking," he started, stroking the back of her hand with the soft pad of his thumb. "I was thinking maybe we should try again."

She scowled, confused.

"The doctor said that he's ninety-nine percent sure this won't happen again. You're young. We're young. It was just an accident. A genetic accident. The chances of it happening again are practically nonexistent."

"You want another baby?" she said in disbelief.

Hopeful, he smiled. "Just imagine," he said. "By next summer, we could have another son. Or a *daughter*."

"We *have* a daughter," she said and felt like she might vomit. "Her name is Lucy, and she is four weeks old. Why don't you say her name, Ab? Why don't you ever say her name?"

Ginny was trembling; the old house was drafty and winter was coming.

Ab took a deep breath, summoning courage perhaps. But when he spoke, it was his father's words she heard. "The school discourages visits for the terminal cases. They say it's detrimental not only to the parents but to the child. It's too confusing for everyone. How would we even explain this to Peyton? To our friends? It's better to grieve now."

Grief? Was this what she'd been feeling since the minute Lucy was taken from her arms? No. Grief was transient, something that eventually subsided. She knew, as Ab did, that grief, like a wound, healed over time, until nothing remained but a faint scar, a reminder of pain. She couldn't imagine this feeling ever subsiding. True grief came only with death. And Lucy was not dead. And Ginny knew that so long as Lucy was alive, so too would be this excruciating ache.

"We have to choose, Gin. Between the past and our future. Because we can't have both."

"What are you saying?" she said.

"I'm saying," he said, "we can either cling to this sinking ship, or we can swim."

All breath and air were knocked out of her. She was drowning.

"I love you," he said, his voice breaking, filling with sorrow. "Please, Gin. I'm so sorry. But for Peyton, for *us*. We have to let her go."

He said they had to choose, but she knew the choice had already been made.

Three

꩜

The next day, Marsha arrived just after lunch, as Ginny was sending Peyton out to play. She hoped to keep him confined inside the fenced backyard to avoid contact with Christopher, who she suspected was scheming acts of terror even as they ate their lunch. Peyton hadn't wanted to go outside at all given the latest harassment, but she'd plied him with fresh-baked cookies and the promise of *Gomer Pyle* later. "Play on your swing," she pleaded. "In your fort."

"It'll be just like *The Swiss Family Robinson!*" Ab had said when Peyton was still a baby, not even crawling yet. He had spent every Saturday for a month making trips to the lumberyard, sawing and hammering, and stifling a host of expletives as he attempted to follow the plans in the book. But earnestness did not necessarily translate to mastery, and he'd eventually had to hire someone to come complete the backyard project for him. No matter, the end result was truly magical: a double-decker tree house high up in the branches of a seventy-five-year-old red oak, complete with a tire swing and a pirate's lookout. It was every little boy's—including Ab's—dream. Before his brother Paul died, he and Ab had practically lived in the woods behind their parents' home, building their own forts out of sticks and bricks.

She'd caught Christopher trying to climb over the fence once (having stacked two or three milk crates on his side of the fence), but his plan was foiled when Arthur, the Richardsons' Newfoundland, was waiting on the other side. Arthur was harmless, of course, but enormous, and Christopher was afraid of him. This afternoon Arthur had bounded out into the backyard after Peyton, hopefully ensuring a respite from Christopher.

Ginny peered out the window when she heard Marsha pull into the circular driveway out front. She watched as Marsha slammed the car door shut and marched up the steps. She knocked only once before opening the door and storming into the foyer.

Marsha gave Ginny a terse hug and then held on to her shoulders, studying her face. "You okay?"

"Come into the kitchen," Ginny said. "Peyton's in the backyard, and I want to be able to keep an eye on him while we chat."

Marsha wore a pair of knee-high suede boots, a mustard-colored corduroy miniskirt, and a tight cream-colored sweater, her long curly black hair parted in the middle and nearly to her waist now. Ginny had dressed as she did most days, in a turtleneck and wraparound calico skirt (which she appreciated for its adjustability depending on her fluctuating waistline as well as to hide her dimpled knees). She'd always felt like the homely stepsister next to Marsha, though she never begrudged Marsha her beauty. "Beauty and the Brains" was what their high school classmates had called them.

Marsha followed Ginny down the long, newly carpeted hallway.

"I'm sinking," Marsha said and stopped, unzipping each soft suede boot and wriggling her toes. "There, that's better."

"You want some lunch? I made tuna salad," Ginny offered. She and Peyton had already eaten before he went out to play.

"No, but I'll take a cup of that coffee." Marsha gestured to the percolator bubbling on the gleaming counter and plopped down at the dinette set.

Ginny poured them each a cup of coffee, adding creamer and sweetener to her own, leaving Marsha's black. She checked on that evening's pork shoulder, which was slow-roasting in the oven. The kitchen was warm and smelled wonderful. There would be pineapple upside-down cake for dessert.

She thought, for a moment, that this could be like any other visit with Marsha. Gossip about their former classmates. Updates about Marsha's love life. Talk about books or TV or movies. Nothing of import. Nothing that would rattle the tenuous walls of this world she'd made. But then Marsha pulled the papers from her purse and laid them on the table like a fortune-teller laying down a pack of tarot cards.

Ginny sat down and Marsha pushed the first one toward her.

There were four papers, with four separate articles. Each one took up nearly the entire front page before directing the reader to turn to a page later in the paper. The reporter who wrote the exposé had visited every corner of the facility. He'd spoken to the students, the attendants, the staff. He'd photographed the rooms: the bathroom without stalls. The sleeping quarters' walls smeared with human waste. The kitchen with its cockroaches. As she read about the vats of slop meant to pass as sustenance, as food, her stomach turned. The rich scent of the roast in the oven filled her eyes with tears. Broken elevators filled with dirty laundry. Sewage spills. And the children, God, the children huddled into corners. Alone.

"It says a child nearly *died* last year," Marsha said, her voice hushed.

Ginny sucked in her breath, the current buzzing and hissing in her veins again.

"He wandered off but nobody noticed. They found him three days later. He'd crawled into one of the washing machines in the laundry. He's lucky he didn't suffocate."

"Oh, my God," Ginny said. She felt oddly numb, her skin almost prickly, the way a limb feels when it falls asleep. She was gripping the newspaper so tightly her knuckles ached.

"You okay?" Marsha said, reaching for her. "Let me get you some water." She stood and started to make her way to the sink, but Ginny felt acid burning her throat and rose quickly from the table, trembling, and rushed back down the hall to the powder room where she vomited the tuna salad she'd had for lunch. When she looked at her face in the mirror, she barely recognized herself. Her blond hair was still perfectly coiffed: freshly trimmed bangs and ends flipped hopefully upward. Her makeup was still clean and bright, but her eyes looked haunted. She splashed cold water on her face, swished her mouth with water, but nothing could take away that look in her eyes or the red splotches, like a disease, that bloomed across her pale chest, climbing up her neck.

Marsha knocked gently on the bathroom door before pushing it open. "You okay, hon?" Ginny shook her head.

Back in the kitchen, Marsha lit a cigarette, the paper crackling and hissing as it ignited.

"Well, I can't imagine they'll be able to keep it running after this," Marsha said. "The state will have to shut the facility down. You and Ab really need to talk to the parents who've filed the lawsuit. Find out what they plan to do about their children. There must be other schools, better schools."

"I need to go talk to Ab, to show him these," Ginny said. The newspaper was one that she and Ab did not get in Dover, and one her mother had stopped subscribing to years ago. Shirley, like Ginny, lived with her head firmly embedded in the sand. If not for Marsha's call, Ginny realized, she might never have found out. She was sure Ab had no idea, either. "Can you drop me off at the train station in Needham and then stay here with Peyton until I get back?"

"Of course," Marsha said and reached for Ginny's hand.

"Ab can fix this," Ginny said, though she wasn't sure whom she was trying to convince.

Ginny brought the newspapers with her, folded neatly in her purse. She couldn't bear to look at them again, but Ab needed to see. If he had any idea what was going on at the school, he'd have to do something. Still, it was the rage of betrayal that informed every muscle in her body as the train hurled along the tracks. She felt like an angry lover preparing to confront her cheating husband, his mistress's love letters in hand, as she marched into the building and ascended the elevator to Ab and the elder Richardson's firm's offices.

It was just a forty-minute train ride to Boston, but she rarely left Dover. She'd been to the firm only a handful of times in the last five years of his employment: once when he first started working there, and later only for the annual Christmas parties. As the elevator doors opened, she felt overwhelmed by all that she did not know about her husband's life. Day after day, he took the train into the city, rose into the sky on this elevator, and exited these same doors to a world so far beyond her own, it might as well have been the moon.

No one recognized her as she walked toward the gleaming reception desk. She was a stranger, an alien having landed on a new planet. She half expected when the receptionist opened her mouth that some peculiar language would come out.

"Good afternoon," the receptionist said, and Ginny sighed in relief. The girl was pretty, though she wore heavy makeup, including a spider-like pair of false eyelashes. Her hair was short, in a pixie cut, like a boy's, but she wore large hoop earrings. If she were to stand up, Ginny was sure her skirt would be a good eight inches above her dimple-free knees.

"I'm here to see Mr. Richardson," Ginny said.

"Junior or Senior?" the woman asked, picking up the phone next to her.

"Junior," she said. Ab would hate that. Ginny wondered if he knew this was how he was referred to here.

The woman smiled a white-lipstick smile and tapped at the numbers on the phone. "May I tell him who's calling, please?"

"Tell him it's Ginny," she said.

The woman cocked her head expectantly.

"His *wife*?" Ginny had no idea why she said it like this, as if there were any uncertainty about her relationship to him. She was Ginny Richardson, Abbott Richardson Jr.'s wife.

"Oh!" the receptionist said, clearly surprised, though Ginny wasn't sure if it was because she was the wife or that he had one at all. Neither option left her feeling very well. "So nice to meet you, Mrs. Richardson. My apologies. I've only been here a few months. I'm Sissy." With that, she extended her hand out across the reception desk, and Ginny noted a flawless manicure, her nails the same color pink as her flushed cheeks.

"Is this an emergency?" Sissy whispered, covering the mouthpiece with her hand.

Ginny shook her head, *No*, even as her heart reverberated in her chest.

"She says no," Sissy offered into the phone, and then as she hung up, "He said to give him five minutes. He's with a client. You can have a seat if you like. There's coffee over there as well." She gestured to a small console table in a waiting area. A large silver urn like the one her mother-in-law put out when she had her bridge parties. "There's some Sweet'N Low if you need it. Or I can bring you a Tab?"

The suggestion that Ginny might need an artificial sweetener, that she might be "watching her figure," stung. Though truth be told, she'd ballooned up fifty pounds when she was pregnant with Lucy and, even two years later, had yet to fully deflate. She *was* watching her weight. She was always watching her weight.

The sofa was sleek and uncomfortable, the glass coffee table before it covered with careful stacks of magazines. She sat down, straightened her skirt, and let her eyes wander across their covers: *Life, Look,* and *Time*. She reached for the *Time* magazine, on the cover the crew of the Apollo 15. She recalled the night of the moon landing a couple of years before, when she was pregnant with Lucy. Ab had been at work late, working on a case around the clock. Peyton was asleep, despite her efforts to keep him up to witness the moon landing, and she had sat alone in the living room, riveted by the jumpy images on the TV. But once the *Eagle* had landed, for some reason, she'd felt consumed by an unexpected emotion. While the rest of the country rejoiced, Ginny felt overwhelmed by the *arrogance* of it all, the audacity, and found herself weeping as these men staked their claim on the luminous moon.

She startled when the receptionist, *Sissy*, said, "Mrs. Richardson? You may go in now."

Ginny set the magazine down and watched as a man in a heavy overcoat walked past her and out the lobby door. Ab's client, she imagined.

Clutching her purse, she made her way down the hallway to where Ab was standing in the last doorway, hand on the jamb, eyes wide and expectant. His dimpled smile betrayed his obvious confusion as to why she would be here, in his office, late on a Thursday afternoon.

"Hey, Gin," he said, his dark eyebrows furrowing in concern when she did not return his smile. "Come in."

Her throat ached as he kissed her cheek and ushered her into his office. She'd been in this room exactly once, when he first started working at his father's firm right after he graduated from Harvard. The framed photo of them on their wedding day remained where he had first placed it on his desk, next to a photo of Peyton smiling wide, showing off the dimples he'd inherited from his dad.

"Where's Pey?" Ab asked, gesturing for her to sit down in the chair across from his desk, as if she were a client.

"Marsha's with him at the house," she said, still standing.

His eyes narrowed. "Are you okay? Sissy said it wasn't an emergency. Is something wrong? Your mom's okay?"

But when he reached for her, she grew rigid.

"Hey," he said, holding onto her stony shoulders and looking at her quizzically. "What's going on?"

Her stomach tightened as she reached into her pocketbook and pulled out the newspapers. Wordlessly, she handed them to him.

"What's this?" he asked, as if she were still about to spring some wonderful surprise on him. Ab lived his life always expecting the best. What a uniquely fortunate state to be in, she thought, trusting that every surprise is a good one.

He took the papers from her and moved to a small sofa across the room. He sat down and scratched the back of his neck before reading the headline: TRAGEDY AT WILLOWRIDGE.

His face blanched.

"I need you to get her out of there," Ginny said.

Ab didn't look up from the papers. His hands were trembling as he rustled through them, one horrifying photo after another. He wasn't reading them, though, and something about this made her furious. She wanted him to read each word; to know what kind of place Abbott Senior had convinced them to deposit their daughter.

"Ab," she said. " You need to fix this. Your father was wrong about this place."

He set the papers down and rubbed his temples, then his chin, before looking up at her.

"My father," he started, and she felt like she might scream.

"Is he here? He should see this, too."

"No, he had a late lunch meeting with a client. Listen, my father—"

"Your *father*," she said. "Your father is wrong. This was a terrible mistake. It's been almost two years, Ab. Two years our daughter has been in that horrible place. There are parents, other parents of these children, that are filing a class-action lawsuit. Against the school."

He took a deep breath and set the papers down on the end table next to the sofa.

"I *know*," he said softly.

She felt her body go cold. "You *know*? How do you know?"

"I told you. Dad and the state mental health commissioner went to Harvard together. They were both in the Spee. They've been friends for *thirty years,* Gin. But you have to understand, this isn't the school's fault. It's a state-run institution, and it operates on state funding. The funding has been cut . . . and when funding gets cut, conditions can suffer. They're just understaffed."

"You *knew* about this? You knew that Lucy was living like this? In this *cesspool*?"

Ginny felt as though she were lifting out of her body, rising, rising upward toward the ceiling. Air was thin, she could hardly breathe.

"Ginny," he said. His voice swam to her, from below, like smoke rising.

"You *knew* this," she said, though it was no longer a question but a horrible, awful truth.

"Listen," he said, his eyes gentle. Apologetic. "The reporter, this guy Banks, he has a reputation for creating scandals. It's all about selling papers. He did a so-called exposé about a local dry-cleaning business being a front for money laundering a few years ago. Turns out his unnamed source was a con man. It ruined an entire family's livelihood."

"There are *photos*, Ab."

"Gin?" he said and moved toward her again, but when he reached out for her, she yanked her arm away.

"No," she said. *"Don't touch me."*

Ab stumbled back as if she'd just shot him.

"Ginny," he said. "I'll talk to Dad. But I still believe we did what was best for her. For us. For our family."

Ginny studied Ab's face for some sort of evidence of the man she'd married, the boy she'd fallen in love with all those years ago. But he was gone. Swallowed whole by this man before her. This callous man. This *stranger.*

She turned to the door and walked toward it, shaking her head.

"Please, Gin. Let's talk this through. We can take the train home together. . . ."

"Who *are* you?" She hadn't meant to say this aloud, but there it was between them: this question she was sure neither of them could answer anymore.

Four

꩜

W ho are *you*?" the boy standing at the circulation desk asked.
Ginny was confused. The endless stream of Amherst boys
who came through the library's doors rarely, if ever, spoke to her other
than to offer a sleepy *good morning* or ask an anxious question about a
book's availability. Every now and then, she might get an apology for a
book being returned after the stamp's mandate.

"Excuse me?"

"Your name," he said. "I'd like to know what it is."

"Oh," she said. "It's Ginny. For short. Virginia for long."

"Well, *Virginia for Long,* I'm Abbott for Long. But you can call me Ab."
But rather than grabbing his teetering stack of books and turning to go,
he continued to stand there, looking at her thoughtfully.

"Can I help you with something else?" she asked, studying his face for clues. He had the same easy, breezy composure that so many men here had, particularly the affluent upperclassmen. But there was something else: a hint of mischievousness, a certain sparkle in his big brown eyes.

Without losing her gaze, he plucked something from his shirt pocket and set it down on the counter. At first it looked like a library card, but when she picked it up, she realized what it was.

Admit One to
Convocation to Honor
The President of the United States
Saturday, October 26, 1963
Indoor Athletic Field, Amherst College

"How did you get these?" she exclaimed, losing any sense of occupational propriety.

"Would you like to go with me, Virginia for Long?" he asked.

"To see John F. Kennedy?" she said, still in utter disbelief.

"Well, I understand Kennedy's still the sitting president."

"My girlfriend Marsha and I were planning to go to the groundbreaking," Ginny said, nodding and studying the ticket. "Try to catch a peek of him there." The president's visit had been all that anyone was talking about since the semester started. He was coming to receive an honorary degree and then to attend the groundbreaking ceremony for the Frost Library, named after the college's beloved poet, who had recently passed away. "These tickets are for the actual convocation?"

He cocked his head and grinned. "Front row and center."

"But why me?" she asked, peering around as if there might be another girl he had meant to invite. But unless he'd had his sights set on old Mrs. Beasley, with her cotton candy hair and moth-eaten sweaters, she was the only girl around.

"I've seen you reading Frost, for one," he offered. In the fall, she often sat outside on the front steps of the library, back against one of the giant columns, reading while she ate her lunch. Had he been spying on her?

"Well, it's not exactly as though Frost *himself* will be there," she said, and then thought better of her gallows humor. Robert Frost was a minor god here. While poor Emily Dickinson had spent her years in Amherst holed up in the second story of that big yellow house on Main Street, Mr. Frost had spent his tenure teaching here. His name was uttered with the hushed respect usually reserved for Jesus Christ himself.

Ab lowered his voice and leaned across the counter, whispering conspiratorially. "Also, I think you're pretty."

No one besides her father had ever called her "pretty," and no one had *ever* gazed at her with any sort of interest before now.

So they went together to the convocation, listened as the president spoke of poetry. *When power corrupts, poetry cleanses,* he promised. Afterward, as they walked across the leaf-strewn quad, Ab explained that he was graduating that spring and heading to Harvard to follow in his father's footsteps.

"My father wants me to run for office one day," he said. "Law school is just the first step. Then practice for a few years before running for assistant DA or local government. Mayor, maybe. Or state representative. He has me running for president by the time I'm forty."

"Wow," she said. The presumptuousness of such a dream was what struck her, the assumption that one could simply *decide* to hold the highest office in the country.

"One fundamental problem with the plan, though," he said.

"Oh? What's that?"

"I hate the law," he said. He chuckled, but his eyes belied something like fear. As if he'd spoken a secret aloud and wanted to take it back. "Of course, I don't have much say in the matter."

"What would *you* like to be?" she asked. "When you grow up?"

"Well, I do like the idea of helping people," Ab said. "That part of politics appeals to me. But so much of it seems self-serving. I prefer to have my boots on the ground. I've got a friend who's joining up with the IVS. Have you heard of it?"

Ginny shook her head.

"International Voluntary Services. A bit like Kennedy's Peace Corps. Volunteers who go to third world countries—help the people build houses, get clean water, farm their land."

"How noble," she said.

Ab shrugged. "How about you? Do you plan to stay in the stacks at the Converse forever?"

"Well, I've always thought it would be nice to be a poet," she said boldly, realizing she had never articulated this to anyone before, her chicken scratches in her leather-bound journal safely locked away with a tiny tin key.

He grinned suspiciously, as if he couldn't tell if she was pulling his leg or speaking in earnest.

She continued, "You know, like Frost. To live in a little cabin in the woods and sit around thinking big thoughts. Studying the birds and trees."

"*Yes!*" he exclaimed and slapped his thigh. "To take the road less traveled by," he said.

"Exactly."

"Though I do hear it's a hard road to walk alone," he said.

"Is it, now?" she asked, feeling her heart quicken.

"Yes, it's always a good idea to travel in pairs."

She'd fallen in love with Ab in that moment, despite the chasm that existed between their worlds. She was a townie, and he was an Amherst man. She'd grown up in a clapboard house near the railroad tracks, and he'd been raised in a tony suburb of Boston. Her widowed mother had toiled away as a cook in the Amherst dining hall, while his mother played bridge and hosted charity events. But they both loved books, and she later learned they had both suffered a huge loss when they were children; she had lost her father, and he his older brother. They were bonded by those old sorrows and by dreams of a simple, meaningful life. At twenty-two years old, they'd been stupid and hopeful and blind enough to believe this was enough.

They couldn't see the future then, of course. They didn't know that within a month that handsome, hopeful president would be assassinated by a gunman's bullet. That Ab's dream of a life spent in service of others was just that—a dream. They also didn't know that there would be a whole series of roadblocks on that road less traveled, all of them put up by his father.

Five

❦

September 1971

Abbott. Of course, Abbott was behind all of this. He had proactively convinced Ab that the exposé was a farce. But to what end? To protect the carefully crafted fiction of their perfect family, of his perfect son. At the cost of his granddaughter's safety. She was livid: at Abbott for his callousness and Ab for his compliance.

When the train finally arrived at the station in Needham, it was nearly dusk. Ginny grabbed a cab, which dropped her off in front of her house. Peyton and Christopher were in the front yard, Christopher about to pocket Peyton's newest Hot Wheels car. She paid the cabbie and slammed the door shut.

"Listen here, you little thief," she growled at the towheaded child. "That does not belong to you, and if you don't give it back this minute, I'll sic Arthur on you." Arthur, as if on command, barked on the other side of their front door.

Startled, Christopher threw the tiny car at Peyton and scrambled to his feet, running across their wide front lawn to his own home, and Ginny ushered Peyton inside. Marsha was at the kitchen stove pulling the roast from the oven. The smell of it stung Ginny's eyes.

"Can I get a ride with you back to Amherst?" Ginny said. "Tonight?"

"Of course," Marsha said.

Ginny wrapped the roast in foil, fed Arthur, and left Ab a note that she was taking Peyton to Amherst for the long weekend. Told him she needed time to think about everything that had transpired. To see her mother. Marsha would drive them there, and they'd be back by Monday afternoon. She hurriedly packed a small suitcase for herself and one for Peyton, making sure to include his favorite blanket and Brownie, his teddy bear.

It was the Thursday before Labor Day weekend, the last weekend of the summer. Most traffic on the road was headed in the opposite direction: east toward Boston or south to the Cape. Before Peyton was born, Ginny and Ab often made the journey from Cambridge to Cape Cod, where his family had a rustic little beach house they rarely used. But the last two summers, Ab had spent at least one day of the weekend working. He'd suggested she and Peyton go alone, enjoy the peace and quiet of the quaint cottage with its cedar shakes, climbing roses, wooded yard, and private beach. But Ginny didn't drive, and the elaborate use of public transportation it would require to get there was daunting. Besides, what sort of family getaway was it without Ab?

It was eight o'clock, dark out, when they arrived at Marsha's apartment, one she shared with her younger sister, Melanie, who went to UMass Amherst but worked as a waitress at a local steak house in the summer. She was at the Cape herself, soaking up the last bit of summer before classes started again after the holiday. Ginny would have stayed with her mother, but her duplex apartment was too small for all of them.

"Peyton can sleep in Melanie's room," Marsha said. He stood groggily swaying in the doorway, clutching both blanket and bear. "You take my bed, and I'll crash on the couch."

"I don't mind the couch," Ginny said.

"Don't worry about it," Marsha said. "My sleep schedule's all out of whack because of work. On my nights off, I stay up half the night watching TV anyway."

After high school graduation, Marsha, like many girls in their class, went to nursing school. After her training, she'd gotten a job at the hospital in Holyoke. Marsha's dream, however, was to one day save enough money to move to Florida, where her older sister, Theresa, worked as a "mermaid" at a roadside attraction near Tampa. Theresa sent Marsha postcards from Weeki Wachee Springs, which Marsha had pasted over her bed in a collage of fins and tails. Marsha said she figured she could get a job at a retirement home. "Everybody down there's a hundred years old. If I've got to be changing some old lady's bedpan, I might as well be doing it somewhere with a little bit of sunshine," she said. Even though they hadn't lived in the same town together since she and Ab got married, Ginny hated the idea of Marsha leaving Massachusetts. Luckily, this dream—like so many local girls' dreams—had not yet come to fruition, however, and Marsha was still here.

Ginny was wondering if she should call home and let Ab know she and Peyton had arrived safely, but the fury of their conversation rekindled. She felt the anger igniting again, burning hot.

Marsha put her arms around Ginny and squeezed.

"We'll figure this out, Gin. Everything's going to be okay. We've got the whole weekend before you need to get Peyton back for school. I'm not on at work again until Monday night, either. Maybe you can reach out to that parent group? I think they published the guy's name in the paper. The one who's heading it up? Maybe you can even contact the reporter. I dated a guy who wrote for the *Gazette*. I can ask him if he knows him?"

But that night as she tossed and turned in Marsha's twin bed beneath the mermaids' tails, she tried to imagine what she would say to the other Willowridge parents, to these mothers and fathers who had been fighting tirelessly for their children while she had been ironing shirts and cooking pot roasts in Dover, pretending she hadn't abandoned her child two years ago. Hadn't allowed her husband and her father-in-law to convince her that Lucy was somehow better off with strangers for the rest of her life, regardless of how brief that life might be.

The room was hot, an old electric fan spinning the stale air around and around. The buzz of it crept under her skin, pricking at her.

What would she ask of the reporter, the one who had exposed the school for what it truly was: a prison, a torture chamber? *Did you see my child?* He would want to know what she looked like, and Ginny didn't even know. She wouldn't know her own child if she was standing in front of her.

The next morning, Ginny woke with a start, drenched in sweat, her nightgown twisted about her legs. She'd been dreaming of the ocean, of being caught in a fishing net. She sat up and flicked on the light, still gasping for air. She was disoriented, expecting when she clicked the light on to see the familiar expanse of her own bed, Ab's body next to her. She expected the golden fleur-de-lis wallpaper, the heavy gold drapes blocking out the sun. But instead, she found herself tangled up in softly worn daisy-printed sheets, under a faded patchwork quilt, and with nothing hanging in the window but several strings of glass beads. Somewhere a wind chime tinkled.

It was Friday. She imagined Ab waking to an empty house. Normally, she rose at least an hour before he did during the week, relishing the peace of the sleeping house. The thick shag carpeting made stealth easy. She would pee without flushing the toilet and wait until later to wash her face and brush her teeth. She could navigate the labyrinthine house's twists and turns without turning a light on.

She always stopped at Peyton's door to peek inside, where she invariably found him sprawled out across his bed, flat on his back with his arms and legs spread wide, before making her way down the hall.

Ab had, as promised, turned the nursery, that tiny room near the top of the stairs, into a study for her. He had ordered a desk from Design Research in Boston as well as the most comfortable chair, brought her an electric typewriter that was being disposed of at his office. He had the walls painted a soft mauve and hired the same man who built Peyton's tree house to install floor-to-ceiling bookshelves. He'd been so proud of himself when he presented the transformed room.

"The *other* Virginia says a woman should always have a room of her own," he had said and kissed her softly at her temple.

He'd meant well, but she couldn't imagine sitting at that desk, sinking into that overstuffed chair, looking out that window without thinking of Lucy. And though he didn't say so, she knew he'd been hurt when she sat down in the chair at the desk, ran her fingers across the keys of that hulking Selectric. As she stared blankly out the window at the giant oak that would have been the first thing Lucy saw each morning from her crib. But his disappointment slowly turned into resignation, and he stopped trying to get her to use the room and, instead, simply closed the door. She went in only if she was looking for a book or when she needed the Electrolux, which they kept in the room's closet.

At home in the mornings, she made coffee and, weather permitting, took a mug and a book outside onto the screened-in back porch, where she read and watched the sun come up, relishing the last few minutes of solitude before her husband and son awoke. It was here where Peyton would find her most mornings, still rubbing sleep from his eyes as he tugged at her arm to pull her from her reverie and into the kitchen to make him breakfast. "Mama! Pan-a-cakes?"

The moaning of the pipes would signal that Ab was in the shower. By the time he came downstairs, she'd have breakfast cooking on the stove: eggs and pancakes and sausages sizzling in a cast-iron skillet. His clothes were ironed, his shoes shined, his lunch packed so that he needed only to get dressed and eat before heading out the door to catch the train.

Without her there, she had no idea what Ab would do, nor what she herself should do here at Marsha's.

She pulled on a filmy pink robe she found hanging on the back of the bedroom door, noting the musky scent of Marsha's Styx perfume, hoping Marsha wouldn't mind, and padded down the short hallway to the kitchen, where there was a large box of doughnuts open on the counter and a cigarette burning in the cut-glass ashtray. Peyton was sitting on one of the barstools, munching on a maple bar, his plastic tumbler of milk sitting dangerously close to the edge. Ginny pushed the cup to safety and ruffled his hair, kissing the top of his head. He smelled like shampoo and maple.

"Marsha says I can have three doughnuts," he said, licking the frosting from his stubby fingers.

Marsha was also sitting at the kitchen counter, smoking and reading the paper, and Ginny's heart sank.

"Is there another article today?" she asked.

Marsha nodded and slowly pushed the paper toward her. The final installment of the exposé covered the entire front page: THE TRAGEDY OF WILLOWRIDGE: THE FORGOTTEN CHILDREN. Ginny quickly scanned the article, but tears filled her eyes, blurring the words. *The children, of course, are the worst casualties. Retreating into their imaginations to escape the horrific reality.*

Yesterday, she hadn't thought much beyond simply getting home to Amherst. But now she knew exactly what she had to do, perhaps what she'd known all along.

"I need to go," Ginny said. "To Willowridge. To see if it's true."

Marsha took a long drag on her Virginia Slim and exhaled, the smoke curling like an apparition toward the popcorn ceiling. "Okay," she said, nodding. "I'll take you."

Six

~

September 1971

"M y tummy hurts. Where are we going?" Peyton asked as they climbed into Marsha's car, a blue Dodge Dart parked in the alley behind her apartment building.

Marsha looked at Ginny, eyebrow raised.

Ginny took a deep breath and peered into the backseat at Peyton. "We're going to go see your sister," she said, trying the word for the first time, relishing the sweetness of it, the delicious *s*.

"My *sister*?" he asked.

"Her name is Lucy," she said. How could they have lied to him, this little boy? Did Ab really think that a secret like this could be kept? Peyton had a right to know that he had a baby sister. It was ridiculous.

But when he peered back at her with confusion, she felt her heart squeeze. Maybe she shouldn't have said anything. Maybe it was too soon. Regret snagged in her chest like a hook.

"She lives at a special school, and we are going for a visit today."

Ginny had been too nervous to call the school to find out about visiting hours, so Marsha had called for her. She had taken the phone down the hallway, the cord curling like a snake behind her. When she came back, she was smiling.

"Will they let me see her?" Ginny had asked, her words struggling past the lump in her throat.

"How would you like to have her for the whole weekend?" Marsha asked, reaching for Ginny's hands and pressing them in her own.

"Really?" Ginny asked, her eyes brimming with tears, her heart brimming with gratitude. It seemed too simple. All it took was a phone call? "They'll really let me take her for the weekend?"

"I think with all of this publicity, with the lawsuit and all, they know they can't afford to anger any more parents."

"But she won't even know me. What if she doesn't want to go?"

Marsha smiled. "She'll know that you're her mama. I guarantee."

Ginny wanted to believe her, wanted nothing more than to take Lucy into her arms, to hold her and comfort her the way she did Peyton when he was hurt or scared. If even half of what was written in the papers was true, then she must be terrified. The photo of the little girl curled up in the corner on the floor, knees to her chest, had disturbed her terribly. Thankfully, she looked too old to be Lucy, but she was *someone's* daughter.

She'd read an article just last year about a little girl named Genie who'd been confined by her own father for nearly eleven years, caged like an animal. When she was rescued at thirteen, she still wore diapers, couldn't speak, and crawled on all fours. The article had haunted Ginny. She'd had to convince herself that this was not the same. That she and Ab were giving Lucy the best life they could. But the exposé in the papers changed all that. The children at Willowridge were no better off than that poor neglected child, and Ab and she were no better than that awful father who caged his daughter and the mother who turned a blind eye.

As they hurtled down the country road toward Willowridge, she tried to conjure the words she might say to Lucy. The explanations, the apologies. But for once, words seemed inadequate.

In town, they stopped at a five-and-dime to pick up diapers, bottles, and other items she thought she might need for a weekend with a two-year-old. She also picked up a couple of jumpers and blouses, a pair of Mary Janes, and two pairs of pajamas. She felt giddy as her fingers skipped across the beautiful girls' clothing. She had avoided the girls' department for the last two years. But now she delighted in the tiny pink things, the bows and barrettes. The tights and dresses and ruffled socks. She could easily spend her whole wad here if she wasn't careful.

"Do you think she's walking yet?" Marsha asked, looking at the tiny pair of shoes in Ginny's hand.

"I have no idea," she said.

Ginny thought of the milestones that a normal child reached in the first two years of life: walking, talking, feeding oneself. She had no idea what milestones a two-year-old child with Down syndrome would have met. By two, Peyton, with his quick little mind and his strong legs, was running, singing, identifying colors even. Before he turned three, he could ride a tricycle and had started to potty-train. Lucy, she suspected, would still be in diapers. Would she drink from a bottle? She wondered if she had even said *Mama* yet, and then she realized the absurdity of this. Why would she give a name to something that, as far as she knew, did not exist?

"Do you think it's really as bad as the reporter says?" Ginny asked as they turned down the road to Willowridge. "Maybe Ab's right. That it's a scandal just to sell more papers."

Marsha reached for her hand without her eyes leaving the road.

"That article said that most attendants don't last more than six months," she said. "One of them hung himself from a tree on the school's property."

Ginny felt sick. She hadn't been able to make herself read much beyond the first article in the series.

"What about the other employees? Why would they stay?" Ginny asked. "If it's so terrible?"

"One of the nurses the reporter interviewed said she can't leave them," Marsha offered. "The babies. She says she hears their cries in her dreams."

Ginny covered her face with her hands.

"I'm sorry, honey," Marsha said. "I only meant there are people there who care for them. People just as upset as you are."

Ginny tried not to think about the doctor's warnings. That Lucy had health issues, heart issues. Her father-in-law had cautioned that many mongoloid children die as infants from their damaged hearts. At this, Ginny had felt a distinct pain in her chest. She thought of those children's poor, broken hearts. Dying alone in that awful place. Did they just go to sleep and never wake up? Did anyone mourn them?

Mourning, this was exactly what the last two years felt like. Ginny had been asked to accept the loss of her daughter the way one would mourn the loss of the dead. To pretend she had died. But she was *not* dead, and so this was a special kind of grief. An endless sort of sorrow.

"Where should we take her?" Marsha asked brightly.

Ginny hadn't thought beyond going to the school, seeing her daughter with her own eyes. She certainly hadn't imagined getting to take her off campus. And definitely not overnight. She hadn't seen her in two years. Despite Marsha's assurances, Lucy likely *wouldn't* know Ginny, but worse, Ginny wondered if she would even know *Lucy* anymore, if she would be able to recognize her own daughter.

"We could go to Look Park, to the petting zoo?" Marsha suggested. "Maybe to McCray's for some ice cream cones? So the kids can see the cows?"

Ginny shook her head. It was a dreary day, not a day for ice cream.

"No," Ginny said, shaking her head. "Let's just get her first and then we can decide."

The winding road was lined on either side with trees, the leaves still lush and green despite the slight crispness in the air. As Marsha sped down the road, Ginny rolled the window down and felt the cool air on her face. She leaned into the wind, closed her eyes.

WILLOWRIDGE SCHOOL FOR THE FEEBLEMINDED, the sign at the entrance to the campus read. Ginny felt a wave of nausea overwhelm her.

She looked at Marsha.

"You okay?" Marsha asked.

Ginny nodded, and Marsha pulled in through the open gates onto a long gravel driveway.

Seven

❦

They could have been driving onto a college campus. It looked surprisingly like Amherst's campus. She even felt an odd ping of nostalgia, of longing. What had she imagined? Certainly not this. For some reason, she'd pictured a hospital, like the one in which Lucy was born. She'd never dreamed it would be so beautiful. Perhaps she had been worrying over nothing. Ab had promised that his father would make sure Lucy was in the best possible facility, that she was cared for. Perhaps Ab was right all along; this was simply an eager reporter's attempt at scandal.

Marsha pulled up in front of what appeared to be the main entrance, a large ivy-laced brick building with white pillars and a sign that said ADMINISTRATION.

"It's going to be okay," Marsha said.

Still, Ginny felt paralyzed, unable to reach for the car's door handle. Maybe coming here was a mistake. Maybe Ab was right, Lucy was better off without them. But when she closed her eyes and took a deep breath, the words from the news article swam before her eyes again: *cockroaches, slop, solitary confinement. Filth.* She simply needed to see for herself. And if all was well, no harm done.

"Do you want us to come with you?" Marsha asked.

Peyton had fallen asleep in the backseat. He was snoring softly under the worn blue blanket her mother had crocheted for him, clutching Brownie.

She shook her head. "No," she said. "I'll be fine."

Ginny got out of the car and straightened her skirt. It was overcast and chilly out, but she still felt flushed. She worried she might be perspiring through her sweater. She made her way up the steps to the heavy front door, which took both hands and all her weight to open. Inside she was greeted with slightly warmer air, though it carried the scent of something faintly sickening.

The receptionist was severe looking, with jet-black hair in a dramatic bouffant, thick liquid eyeliner making her look more feline than human. She peered up at Ginny over a pair of cat's-eye glasses, missing a rhinestone on one side. This, along with the dirty linoleum and a large water stain on the ceiling, contributed to a nagging unease.

"Can I help you?" the woman asked.

"Yes," Ginny said tentatively as she stepped forward. "My daughter is a resident here. I've come to check her out for a visit."

"Name?" the woman said.

"Richardson. Mrs. Richardson? I called earlier. I'm Lucy Richardson's mother." As she spoke this sentence, she realized it was the first time she had said her daughter's full name aloud. As the woman reached for a clipboard, Ginny nervously added, "My husband, he couldn't get away from work."

"Is this your first visit?" the woman asked, but her tone wasn't accusatory.

"Yes. We would have come sooner, but my husband . . . he thought it best we wait a little longer. But now, with . . . everything . . . she's nearly two years old . . ."

Ginny felt her words trailing off, even as she tried to make sense of the fact that she had never been to visit her own child.

From somewhere came a low moaning. At first Ginny thought it was only ancient pipes coming alive; their house in Dover was nearly a hundred years old. If someone flushed a toilet on the second floor, the pipes in the kitchen lamented. But when it came again, Ginny felt her skin prickle. It was human, this keening.

"Is that . . . ? Should someone check?" she started.

The woman let out a sigh, followed by a knowing, smug little chuckle.

"Ma'am," she said, shaking her head, "I take it you've never been to an institution before?"

Institution. The word felt so clinical, so terrible.

She shook her head. "My husband, my father-in-law . . . they said this is a *school.* The sign outside . . ."

"For the retarded, they're called *schools.* For the mentally ill, they're *hospitals.* But they're the same thing, sweetheart. What did you say your name was again?"

"Richardson," Ginny said. "Virginia."

"Oh, yes," the woman said, tapping one bloodred nail at a clipboard. "Here you are. We have you on the visitor list today. You're aware of the rules?"

"No," Ginny said. "I'm sorry."

"You can check her out for the weekend, through Monday if you like, since it's a holiday. But you must stay in Massachusetts, no crossing state lines. And I'll need your identification, of course."

"Oh," she said. "I don't . . ."

"Driver's license?"

"I don't drive," Ginny said, feeling panic start to creep up her back. She never needed identification in Dover. All the shopkeepers knew the Richardsons; she could write a check without providing anything but her signature. And often she simply charged purchases to Ab's tab or paid in cash.

"Passport?" the woman asked impatiently. "Social Security card? Birth certificate?"

Ginny shook her head. Ab kept all their important papers in a locked safe in his office. She hadn't planned on this. She wasn't prepared.

"You got anything at all with your name on it?" the woman asked.

"I . . . I . . ." Ginny said and reached into her purse, digging through her cosmetics. There were a handful of rocks—gifts from Peyton, who could never leave anywhere without some sort of souvenir. Finally, near the bottom of her purse, she found a letter from her mother. It had her name and address in her mother's wobbly handwriting.

The woman studied it and then handed it back to her.

Ginny felt her knees go soft. The woman wasn't going to let her take Lucy. She knew it. What on earth would she do now? How could she have been so stupid?

"I guess this will do," she said, and Ginny's breath hitched.

"Oh," she said, "thank you. Thank you so much. I came all the way from Dover. I didn't know I'd need anything."

"Well, next time, make sure you have the proper paperwork. I could get in a lot of trouble for this, but I understand. I've got two kids of my own." She stood up and motioned for Ginny to follow her. "My name's Penny, by the by."

They walked out a side door and across the sprawling campus toward another ivy-covered brick building. The desolate campus looked just like Amherst's campus over holiday breaks. There was no one on the grounds, not even a caretaker; the grass was high, the hedges untrimmed. There was a sort of wildness to the landscape, despite the rather dignified architecture of the school itself.

"Normally, I'd have called to have someone bring her over from the children's ward, but we're short-staffed today. One of our attendants just left."

Ginny thought of what Marsha had told her about the attendant hanging himself in these woods and felt queasy. Then, as they approached the children's ward, she saw the strangest thing in the distance. Right in the middle of an overgrown field.

"Is that a *carousel*?" Ginny asked.

"Oh," Penny said, as though she had forgotten something. "Yes. Some local millionaire who had a son here back in the twenties bought it for the children."

Ginny thought what a lovely gesture that was, but as they got closer, she could see that the carousel was inoperable. Weeds were growing through the platform. The paint had worn off the horses, and the mirrors and glass bulbs were shattered. It too had been left to weather the elements, neglected.

Ginny followed behind Penny to the large building, where Penny unlocked the heavy front door with a key from a large ring at her hip as though she were some sort of prison warden. This, like everything else here, gave Ginny pause.

Inside, she followed Penny down a hallway, through an empty reception area, and on to a shorter hallway, studying the crooked seam at the back of the woman's hose.

"That's the nursery," Penny said, gesturing to a room to the left with at least a half dozen rows of cribs, inside which twenty or so infants appeared to be in varying states of distress. The walls practically reverberated with the sound of their crying. Inside the nursery, she saw a solitary nurse in her whites, sitting in a rocking chair, feeding the bundle in her arms.

Ginny's breasts tingled with heat, and her arms flew reflexively to her chest, pressing against them. The shock of her body's response surprised her. When she pulled her arms away, she could feel her blouse was wet with milk beneath her jacket. Her milk had dried up nearly two years ago; the doctor had given her medication to trick her body into believing there had been no baby. But biology was clearly stronger than any chemical deception, even after all this time.

Ginny felt her stomach turning. Her daughter was *here*? Somewhere in this strange steerage of human infancy?

"Where is she?" Ginny asked. She didn't know where to fix her gaze, her eyes searching desperately for the child she'd only seen once, only held for a few moments.

"Oh, no," Penny said, clucking her tongue. "She's with the older children. Follow me."

They passed through another set of doors to a long hallway, which ended at another empty waiting area: a vacant reception desk, a battered brown couch, and a sign hanging crookedly on the wall saying that visitors were not allowed beyond this point. The black-and-white linoleum floor was filthy and scratched, and the smell was oppressive. Like rotten meat. Like excrement.

"Oh, dear," Ginny said, her eyes stinging.

"No real ventilation's the problem; can't open the windows. You'll be surprised how fast you get used to it, though," Penny said. "Stay here. I'll go get her."

Penny disappeared through the swinging door. Ginny heard her footsteps grow fainter and fainter on the other side. She looked around the small room. Glanced out the barred window. Eight hundred residents lived at Willowridge, but there was still not a soul outside. She wondered if she should sit and wait or continue standing. She opted to sit, hoping to quiet her trembling knees.

When she heard a piercing scream, she startled. When it came again, she jumped to her feet and looked around the empty room, feeling helpless. It was not the sound of an infant this time, but a child.

She went to the door, peering through the round smudged glass window: a porthole. A portal. The light behind her reflected brightly in the glass, so she cupped her hands around her eyes, though she still couldn't see much but a corridor on the other side.

At the next howl, she pushed the door open gently; peering behind her to make sure no one would see her trespass.

The hallway was long, with closed doors lining each side. Nervously, she began to walk slowly down the corridor, noting that each door was secured shut with a padlock. The walls were filthy, and the smell was pervasive. She covered her mouth and nose with her hand, her eyes burning.

This time the cry sounded animalistic, primal. Her steps quickened. Her wooden Dr. Scholl's sandals echoed loudly against the tile. She didn't know where she was going or what she would do when she got there, but her body moved forward despite any reservations she had.

Finally, near the end of the corridor, she saw an open door. Quietly, she walked toward it and placed her hand on the jamb to steady herself. It was a bathroom, likely the origin of that smell. But instead of stalls, there was a line of ten toilets next to each other. Just as she'd seen in the newspaper. At the farthest commode was a little girl, kneeling on the floor, howling.

At first, she thought the girl might be sick. She began to move toward her, to offer help, but then she realized the child wasn't vomiting, rather scooping the water from the toilet and drinking it in her cupped hand. Crying all the while.

Ginny stumbled backward, her breath catching. Regaining her composure, she stepped slowly toward the girl.

"Hello there," she said, her own voice sounding strange to her.

The girl looked up from the bowl, her eyes wild and scared. She was emaciated, her milky eyes bulging with fear. She was all angles, elbows jutting out, hips and knees bent sharply.

Despite her good sense telling her not to, Ginny squatted down next to her on the grimy floor.

"Oh, sweetheart." she said. "Are you thirsty?"

The girl looked at her, her eyes unfocused.

"I can get some water for you," Ginny said softly. "I can find someone to get you something to drink." She reached out and gently touched the girl's shoulder, but when she did, the girl fell backward onto her bottom and scurried away from her, pushing herself backward into the corner.

"I'm sorry," Ginny said, her heart tolling in her chest. "I'm sorry."

Ginny scrambled to her feet and hurried back to the door, peering out into the desolate hallway, unsure if she should leave the child here or try to get her to come with her. But to where? Penny had said that there was only one attendant on duty. Maybe the nurse in the nursery? But no, she was the only nurse in charge of all those babies. She wouldn't be able to leave her station.

She needed to find Penny. She raced down the hallway, nearly running into a young man who was exiting one of the rooms. He was tall and thin, with a thick beard and thick glasses, an intense gaze behind them.

"Ma'am?" he said.

"Oh, thank God," she said, her heart pressed against her racing heart. "There's a girl—"

"You're not supposed to be back here," he interrupted. "This area's for staff and residents only. Didn't you see the signs?"

"I just, I heard someone crying . . . there's a girl . . . in the powder room," she started but the ridiculousness of the term struck her like a punch. She gestured down the hallway from where she'd come and then turned back to him.

Behind him, at the far end of the corridor, she saw the dark silhouette of a woman, carrying something.

"You need to go back to the waiting area," the man said, reaching for her elbow. His bony fingers dug into her skin.

"Excuse me!" she said, her voice tight and high. She yanked her arm away, and she began to walk briskly toward the woman. Perhaps she could help.

It took a moment for it to register that this was Penny. And the shadow she was holding was *Lucy*.

Ginny couldn't move. While her body had brought her here, now it seemed rooted in place. She was unable to even lift her arms from her sides.

"Mrs. Richardson, what are you doing back here?" Penny said, smiling but stern, as she approached.

"I told her," the man said and then scolded her again. "Visitors aren't allowed back here."

"It's okay, Robert," she said. "I'll take care of this."

Robert scowled.

"Go on," Penny said, and he finally disappeared back into the room from which he'd emerged.

Ginny couldn't take her eyes off the child, the two-year-old little girl, clinging to Penny, her face pressed against Penny's chest, her small body trembling.

"Lucy," Penny said sternly. "This is your mother. She's going to take you for a visit today."

The little girl, face still turned, shook her head.

"Come on, now," she said, pulling her gently but firmly away from her body. "Be a good girl." Lucy cautiously turned to look at Ginny.

Of course Ginny knew her. How could she forget this child's face? She would have been able to pick her out of a crowd of a million little girls; of this she was certain. Her hair was a mop of golden ringlets. Ginny ironed her own curls straight now, but when she was a little girl, she too had a lion's mane. Lucy's forehead was broad, and her eyes wide set and almond shaped, of course, like all children with Down syndrome, but they were also the most beautiful amber, her eyelashes long and dark. The dimples in her round cheeks belonged to Ab. Her tongue protruded slightly through Cupid's-bow lips.

"Hi, Lucy," Ginny said softly, her body flush with warmth. "Would you like to come with me on a visit?"

Lucy tilted her head curiously.

"She doesn't talk," Penny said.

"Oh?" Ginny said, peering up at Penny. Then she looked back down at Lucy and smiled. "Well, that is just fine. You don't need to say a word if you don't want to."

"Okay," Penny said. "We should be getting back. I don't like to leave my desk unattended for long. Here you go," she said and started to pass Lucy to Ginny. Lucy let out a little cry.

"It's okay," Ginny said, the words struggling past the lump in her throat. She put her hands under Lucy's arms, lifting her. Lucy's body stiffened reflexively, resisting Ginny's touch. But once she had her securely on her hip, Lucy's tiny hands clung to Ginny's neck, her legs circling her desperately.

Ginny was surprised by how heavy she was. She hadn't carried Peyton for at least a year, but her body remembered this delicious burden.

"May I?" Ginny asked, her voice cracking. "May I take her now?"

"You'll need to sign her out in the main office. But yes," Penny said.

"Is there anything I need to know?" Ginny asked. "About her health issues?"

Penny looked confused.

"Her heart, I understand there is a defect?"

"I don't know anything about that." Again, she looked at Ginny blankly.

Confused, Ginny started to ask if maybe they should consult with the school's doctor before she took her, but just as she was about to suggest this, they walked past the bathroom, the little girl still sitting in the corner. She had her bony knees to her chest now and was rocking back and forth.

"There," Ginny whispered to Penny. "That's the child I was concerned about. She was drinking . . . from the *toilet*. Should you let someone know?"

"Oh, that's Miriam. She's fine. She's just being difficult."

"Oh," Ginny said, feeling sick. "Does anyone know where she is?"

"Of course. Robert knows; he's on duty," Penny snapped. "Come on now."

Ginny signed the logbook in the administration building, and though Penny searched through Lucy's admission file, she couldn't find anything regarding a heart defect. As far as Ginny could tell, Lucy might be a little delayed physically and developmentally, but she didn't appear *sick*. Could this have been a mistake?

"Remember, you'll need to have her back Monday by five o'clock," the woman said. "Enjoy your holiday weekend."

Marsha was still parked in front of the main administration building when Ginny emerged, holding Lucy in her arms. Lucy sucked in her breath and shivered as the breeze blew through the air. Ginny wondered how often the children were allowed outside; Lucy's skin was pale, almost translucent, as if it had never seen the sun.

Marsha's window was down, and she was smoking a cigarette. The smoke curled up into the air. Ginny could see Peyton in the backseat, his face pressed to the glass, studying them. Marsha put out her cigarette and leaned out the open window, waving.

Lucy dug her fingers into Ginny's neck as she began to descend the steps.

"I won't let go," she said, and as she made her way slowly down the stairs so as not to scare Lucy, she felt tears on her cheeks. "I promise, I won't let you go."

Eight

❦

Lucy was afraid to get in the car. Ginny tried, at first, to put her in the backseat next to Peyton, but she only clung harder to Ginny. Her eyes filled with terror, and she wouldn't let go of Ginny's neck.

Peyton looked aghast at Ginny, as if she were trying to put a wild animal in the backseat with him. Ginny had a momentary flash of anger and indignation. *This is your sister,* she thought. *Your flesh and blood.* But then she chastised herself. He was six years old, and he had never seen this other child before. Never laid eyes on her—sister or not.

"It's okay. Just hold her on your lap up front," Marsha said.

Ginny nodded and circled around to the passenger's side, slowly lowering herself into the seat with Lucy still clinging to her. Lucy buried her face into Ginny's neck and trembled. They had Peyton's old safety seat in the garage at home, but the Dart only had seat belts. She supposed it would be okay if she just adjusted the seat belt across them both.

"Well, where should we go?" Marsha asked brightly, as if this were any other weekend outing.

Ginny shook her head, attempting to shake away what she had just experienced inside that dormitory. The smell, the keening, that poor child drinking from a filthy commode.

"Away," she said, shaking her head rapidly as tears burned trails down her cheeks. "Just away from here."

Marsha nodded and put the car in gear. Lucy startled a bit when the engine came to life, and clung to Ginny, but she turned her head and her eyes widened in both fear and wonder as they rolled down the long driveway. Soon her body began to relax, and Ginny pressed her tightly against herself.

They drove quietly, no one saying a word, not even Peyton, who was generally a real chatterbox. Like Ab, he was almost always effusive. Boisterous. He was a child so full of life and wonder, but now he sat quietly in the backseat, staring out the window. Marsha looked up at the rearview mirror.

"How about Mountain Park, Pey?" Marsha asked.

"We haven't taken him there yet," Ginny said, turning to look back at him. "Would you like to go to a special park?"

Peyton nodded, but then leaned his head against the window again.

The back of Ginny's throat ached. *He'll be okay,* she assured herself. Though maybe she should have dropped him off at her mother's instead of bringing him here. Of course this would be confusing. A shock even. Why hadn't she thought this through? He was just a little boy; how could she expect him to process any of this, when she herself hardly knew what to feel, what to say, what to do?

"Mind if I put on some music?" Marsha asked.

"Please," Ginny said, suddenly desperate to fill that silent void.

Marsha reached for the radio knob and turned it on. "Joy to the World," which had been playing nonstop all summer, came on the radio, and Ginny turned around to see Peyton smile a little. Ab had taught Peyton all the words to this song; Ab made fishy faces and swimmy hands and danced around the living room, Peyton mimicking behind him.

"Joy to the fishes in the deep blue sea," Marsha sang, reaching behind her and tickling Peyton's feet.

Peyton was clearly resisting the urge to sing along. Ginny looked back at him and made fishy lips, and his mouth twitched as he tried not to smile.

Marsha wiggled in her seat, shoulders jumping up and down with the music. She pulled the visor down to shield her eyes from the bright sun ahead, and then looked over at Ginny.

Lucy had sat up and was pressing her palms to her ears, but she didn't seem upset. Slowly, she lowered her hands and leaned forward a little, pushing her chubby palm against the speaker, as though trying to touch the music. Her breath quickened and she squealed. The sharp sound of her voice startled Ginny, but Lucy was smiling. Smiling and squealing, wriggling in Ginny's lap now.

"Oh! Turn it up!" Ginny said, and Marsha reached for the knob again, but the song had ended and the DJ came on hawking mattresses. Lucy scowled.

"It's okay," Ginny said. "There'll be another song in a minute."

Sure enough, when the commercial ended, James Taylor came on, singing "You've Got a Friend," but now Lucy's mood shifted. As he sang those sweet sorrowful notes, promising that no matter the season, all you had to do was call his name and he'd come running to see you, Lucy started to cry. Was it the words? Or was it just the soft, gentle music? She didn't look sad, so much as *moved*. Had she ever even heard music before? Ginny knew there had been no lullabies for Lucy. No one singing to her.

Ab and Ginny's house was always filled with music. All kinds of music. The Rolling Stones and Bach. Folk music and rock music and jazz. Ab had a zillion albums; there was always something on the hi-fi. Ab liked to sweep Ginny up off her feet and dance her around the living room. Once, when they'd tripped, he'd joked that this must be where the expression "cutting a rug" came from. They'd made sure that Peyton had toy instruments: drums and tambourines and a maraca. He liked to shimmy and shake along with them. Ginny never felt quite as happy as she did in those moments when her whole family was sharing a song. Ab wanted Peyton to take piano lessons as soon as he started school.

School. Peyton was starting first grade in just a few days.

Ginny clutched Lucy tightly and whispered the lyrics into her hair, "Winter, spring, summer, or fall . . ." and soon she'd stopped crying. And then her body became heavy in Ginny's lap. She was asleep.

Marsha clicked the radio off. She reached over and tucked a stray strand of Ginny's hair behind her ear. Her face was filled with concern. "You okay?" she asked, and Ginny nodded, though her heart felt cleaved.

Nine

ভ

January 1964

*D*ance with me, Ab had said, reaching for Ginny's hands and pulling
her up the stairs of the old Summit House onto the wraparound
porch.

It was late January, snowless but cold. He'd just gotten back to campus
after winter break, and he'd driven her to the top of Mount Holyoke,
parked under the stars. During the day, the view was of the mountains
and valley below, the winding Connecticut River snaking between them.
But tonight, there was nothing but inky darkness stippled with light.

He'd left the keys in the ignition and tuned in to a local station. He
told Ginny that his mother, Sylvia, in her younger days, had been a singer.
Before she met Abbott Senior, she'd left her small town in Vermont and
moved to New York, where she sang with the house band at Nick's Tav-
ern in Greenwich Village before a brief stint on Broadway in *Much Ado
About Nothing*. But then she'd met Abbott Senior, gotten married, and had

his brother Paul and him in quick succession. Now she only sang with the church choir.

"Blame It on the Bossa Nova" filled the quiet night. "It all began with just one little dance . . ." Eydie Gormé sang. "But then it ended up a big romance."

Ab shimmied and shuffled and Ginny rolled her eyes, swatting his arm when he tried to get her to move along with him. She'd danced with a boy exactly once, at her high school prom, before sitting out the rest of the night, eating stale cookies and drinking punch. Now she felt awkward and clumsy and self-conscious. She wished she could be like Marsha, able to let go. To enjoy herself for once.

When the song ended and "Blue Velvet" came on, he hung his head and looked up at her with his basset hound eyes.

She sighed. *"Fine,"* she said and moved toward him, stringing her arms awkwardly around his neck. Her stomach growled. Since he'd started coming by the library, she'd been trying to lose some weight, skipping breakfast and bringing only an apple and a hard-boiled egg for lunch. Tonight, she'd pushed her food around her plate at the fancy restaurant where he'd taken her for dinner.

He smelled like licorice and soap, a heady combination that, as he drew her closer to him, had a dizzying effect. She couldn't tell for a moment if the constellations were in the sky or in her eyes.

"You okay?" he asked as she stumbled, her knees quaking.

"Yeah," she said, feeling the earth tilt back to level. "Just swooning here. *Literally.*"

"Well, lean in. I'll hold you up."

"Do you have this effect on all the girls?" she teased.

"Only on the pretty ones," he said, and as he said it, she felt herself transforming from the homely, thick-waisted girl she'd always been to a woman of grace and loveliness.

Together they swayed to the music, and soon she began to warm up.

He nudged her under her chin, lifting her face to meet his. "Can we stay here?" he said.

"On the mountain?" she asked, smirking. "It's awfully cold up here. Once it snows, we'd need snowshoes, and I'd definitely need warmer boots. . . ."

"No. Just *here*," he said and pulled her closer. "Wherever you are, Virginia for Long."

Ten

❧

September 1971

Marsha and Ginny arrived at the amusement park situated on the top of Mount Tom just after noon. From the summit, you could see all the way across the river to Mount Holyoke, where Ab had once danced with her under the stars. She ached with the memory, with how it felt as far away as that mountain. As that night.

Both kids had woken up as they climbed to the summit, and Peyton seemed surprised that Lucy was still there, as if he'd only dreamed her.

"Where are we, Mama?" he asked.

"You'll see," Ginny teased.

Ginny and Ab had talked about bringing Peyton here when he was a little older. There was a fun house, roller coasters, a carousel. At night, there were concerts. It was just twenty minutes from her mother's house, but it was an entirely different world. Like Disneyland, but practically in their backyard.

They drove through the entrance, a huge checkerboard archway with a clown smiling down at them. Lucy looked up, mouth gaping. They parked the car in a crowded lot and once they were out of the car, Peyton ran ahead, Marsha scurrying after him. Ginny hoisted Lucy up on her hip again, and they made their way into the park.

Ginny had brought along the cash she kept in the bread box, the weekly allowance Ab doled out, a practice that had initially made her feel strange, but to which she'd gradually grown accustomed if not resigned. When she'd still lived at home with her mother, she'd overseen their finances. She'd done the bills, written checks for all their monthly expenses. She was used to budgeting—if only for the two of them—and accustomed to having her own money. And while Ab was always generous, she could never quite get past the idea that she had to ask him for money simply for the things their family needed. She'd told him once how uncomfortable it made her, and the next day he'd offered to let her determine the amount. "Whatever you need," he'd said, missing the point entirely.

Now, she unrolled a five-dollar bill from the wad in her pocketbook and paid their admission, brushing Marsha's hand aside when she reached into her own pocketbook.

"Then the cotton candy is on me," Marsha said and winked before grabbing Peyton's hand and skipping ahead.

Lucy was too afraid to pet the animals at the petting zoo, though she watched in wonder as Peyton turned the knob on the dispenser and a handful of pellets poured into his tiny palm. He raced over to the baby goats that bleated and begged, nudging their snouts through the chain-link fence. She was also too little to go on any of the rides, so Marsha took Peyton into the Pirates' Den and on the little roller coaster.

"Let's go ride the merry-go-round!" Peyton said excitedly, tugging at Ginny's hand.

"Okay." She nodded; she thought she might be able to hold Lucy up on one of the beautiful painted ponies. But as they approached the carousel, Lucy began to shake her head and her whole body started to tremble. She was practically convulsing, and soon her body's anguish was released in a loud wail.

"Are you afraid?" she asked. "Of the horses?"

Lucy continued to scream as if she hadn't heard anything that Ginny said.

Ginny thought about that decrepit carousel at Willowridge. This one must have reminded her of those battered and broken ponies. How stupid she had been to think this was a good idea.

Marsha motioned to Ginny that she was taking Peyton onto the carousel, and Ginny nodded gratefully as she attempted to maneuver Lucy away from the ride to one of the benches near a large shady tree.

A woman in a bright red-and-white polka-dot dress was sitting on the bench, grinning and waving at a little boy on the carousel.

Ginny smiled apologetically at her as she sat down and tried to soothe Lucy, who was still crying, face pressed into Ginny's chest.

The woman reached into her large tote and pulled out a sandwich in a baggie.

"Would she like a Fluffernutter?" she asked. "Whenever my little guy pitches a fit, I give him one of these. It's hard to cry with peanut butter and marshmallow in your mouth."

Lucy's cries were, finally, subsiding, and she turned to look at the woman, who, at the sight of Lucy's face, stiffened, her own face turning nearly as red as the polka dots on her dress.

"Oh," the woman said, half of the sandwich dangling between her fingers. "I, I didn't know . . . I didn't realize she was *mongoloid.*"

"She's *fine,*" Ginny said, grimacing. "And no, thank you."

The woman straightened her shoulders and stood up from the bench, waving furiously at her son on the carousel as it came to a stop.

"It's okay," Ginny whispered, more to herself than to Lucy.

Lucy sucked in a few breaths, shuddering in the aftermath of her tantrum. With her hand under Lucy's bottom, Ginny realized that she had soaked through her diaper. She glanced at the carousel, where Peyton was gleefully riding a rearing black stallion, its mane festooned with red roses. Marsha caught her glance and waved. She'd go change Lucy and get back before the ride ended.

She glanced around, looking for the nearest restroom, and finally spotted one near a concession stand not far from the carousel. She carried Lucy there, hoping there would be a large enough private area where she could change her. Luckily, there was no one else in the restroom, and she closed herself in one of the stalls. She sighed and sat down on the toilet lid, Lucy balanced on her lap.

"Okay, sweetheart," she said. "Let's get you dry."

Lucy was wearing a dress, a worn gray gingham jumper with a button missing at her belly. Ginny unpinned the soaking wet diaper and let it fall to the floor. Lucy's chin quivered.

"It's okay," Ginny comforted her. "I have a nice fresh diaper in my bag. You'll feel so much better soon."

She reached into her bag and pulled out a diaper, along with a small container of talcum powder. It would be no small feat to affix a diaper on a two-year-old in this cramped space, and she suddenly wondered if maybe she should have just tried to find a secluded spot behind one of the many trees outside. She certainly wouldn't want her to lie down on the floor here.

She lifted Lucy's jumper, tucking the hem into the collar, exposing her bare bottom, and Ginny's hand flew to her mouth.

Raw. Her skin was completely red and raw. A diaper rash like Ginny had never seen before. It had spread even beyond her private area to her buttocks and her belly.

Ginny rifled through her purse for the new tube of Desitin she'd bought, but when she went to apply it, she realized that no one had wiped or cleaned Lucy up in some time, old feces dried between her legs, the angry rash likely in response to this festering filth.

Ginny's eyes burned with rage as she opened the stall, and carrying Lucy, wet a bunch of paper towels and attempted to clean her. Lucy screamed, likely in agony from the blistering rash, and Ginny could do nothing but cry along with her. Finally, she was able to get the area somewhat clean (she just wanted to put her in a bathtub, to wash it all away), smeared with ointment, and powdered. She also somehow managed to get the fresh diaper on her, and when it was all over she held her and rocked back and forth.

She gathered the soiled paper towels to toss in the trash can when she saw something moving on the towel. She felt bile rise to her throat, and it took everything she had not to vomit. A *maggot*.

"Everything okay in there?" a voice asked as a fist knocked on the stall door.

She shook her head. *No, no, no.* "Yes," she said weakly. "Thank you."

When Marsha and Peyton stepped off the spinning carousel, Peyton clutching the brass ring Marsha had managed to snag for him, Ginny said, "We need to go."

Marsha nodded, no questions asked.

"Come on, Pey," Marsha said. "Time to go home. I'll buy you a snow cone on the way out, okay?"

When they finally made it to the car, Ginny realized that Lucy had fallen asleep in her arms, and she was able to lower her into the backseat next to Peyton, who was contentedly sucking on a blue snow cone, his lips ringed in a halo of blue.

"What's going on?" Marsha whispered.

Ginny peered ahead, her jaw set but tears streaming down her eyes.

"Should we take her back?"

Ginny looked at Marsha, feeling her rage and defiance like a fist in her gut.

"No," she said. "She is *never* going back there."

Eleven

❧

Do you want to go to your mom's?" Marsha asked, serious now and gripping the steering wheel with two hands. Ginny noticed that her red nail polish was chipping on one finger.

Ginny rubbed her temples. "I don't know." She hadn't told her mother she was going to Willowridge. She hadn't even told her she'd come home to Amherst yet.

Marsha nodded. "Listen, how about we go back to my apartment first and figure things out? We've got the whole weekend. They said you don't have to have her back till Monday at five, right?"

"Yes, five o'clock Monday," Ginny said. But even as she tried to imagine pulling up to that building again, relinquishing Lucy to that school, she knew she couldn't. She needed to speak to Ab, to plead with him to get their daughter out of there. There had to be another option. Someplace safe.

"What's going on?" Marsha whispered, glancing in the rearview mirror at the two sleeping children.

Ginny shook her head and felt her chest heave at the thought of the filthy diaper, the violent rash between Lucy's legs. That filthy, squirming *worm*. She wondered what other things Willowridge had neglected: bathing, feeding, God, had they even been giving her water? She recalled that poor child drinking from the toilet bowl.

She looked out the passenger window at the bright sunny day and wondered how the world could appear so beautiful when there was such ugliness hidden inside it. The burden of the last two years during which her child had been a prisoner inside that horrific place weighed on her. While she had been going about her life—raising her son, reading books, and having tea—her daughter, her flesh and blood, had been ignored. Imprisoned. And she was the one who held that key. She'd been holding it the whole time.

Ginny's heart ached behind her ribs. She thought about the days when she, herself, had forgotten Lucy. The hours when she could be completely engaged in one thing or another, ironing Ab's work shirts (that starch-scented hiss) or pushing Peyton in the swing, and she'd realize she hadn't thought of Lucy for hours. Then the thoughts would consume her, swallow her. She felt the same way after her father passed. The first time she realized that she'd gone an entire day without him entering her consciousness, the guilt had consumed her, like a tide that slipped away and then came back with tsunami force.

Her chest pitched as she turned to look at her children in the backseat. Peyton slept with his lips slightly parted, his arms and legs splayed. Such exquisite trust. Lucy had finally allowed herself to be seat-belted in the back without much complaint; however, she was now curled into a little ball. Like a pill bug tucked into a protective shell.

"I don't know what to do, Marsh," Ginny said.

"What do you need from me, hon?" Marsha reached out and took

Ginny's hand in hers. Squeezed, forcing Ginny to look at her. "Because I'm here. You know that, right?"

The whole way back to Marsha's apartment, Ginny once again formulated her argument. Like a law student, she pondered the debate tactic that would be most effective with her husband. She figured she'd appeal to reason first, to logic. To logistics. That would be where she'd start, before any sort of emotional plea.

Money. She considered first the resources they had at their disposal, the elder Richardsons' vast wealth. They were not some destitute family who could simply not *afford* to care for a disabled child. Her heart ached for those families whose finances would have been taxed by the need for constant care.

Time. Peyton was six years old, starting school full-time on Tuesday. What would she do now with her day besides putter around the empty house?

Last, the foundation upon which the decision had been made: the doctor's ominous threats that Lucy's health was somehow precarious. The woman at Willowridge had seen nothing in her chart to indicate poor health. The damaged heart the doctor threatened, the whole premise upon which they'd based their decision to put her in someone else's care. And regardless, even if she *was* sick, even if Lucy's time with them was limited, didn't she deserve to be someplace where she was cherished?

The swell of love Ginny felt as she held her was undeniable. But so too was the love she felt for Ab. He was a good husband, a good man. He truly thought he was doing what was best for their daughter. If he had any idea that the reporter's assessment had been 100 percent true, he certainly wouldn't let her stay there. Maybe a petition to him as a father would be enough.

As they descended the mountain, she was overwhelmed with all the ways in which she had, in the past two years, failed her child. But she would fix this. She would talk to Ab, convince him that Lucy would be better off with them, and then she would bring her home.

Back at Marsha's apartment, the one near the railroad tracks, which shook and swayed each time a train passed, Ginny gave Lucy a bath in the dingy claw-foot tub, taking great care to gently clean her infected bottom using a soft washcloth and a fresh bar of Ivory soap.

"That feels better, doesn't it?" she cooed to her.

Immediately, Lucy seemed happier, more content. She even babbled and played with a couple of aluminum tumblers Ginny had brought in from the kitchen, splashing and squealing as Ginny made a waterfall spill from the shiny blue cup. Lucy wouldn't allow Ginny to touch her hair, though, the wispy curls matted and tangled. The moment Ginny started to work one knot free, she splashed and squirmed and fussed. Ginny finally gave up, figured getting her body clean was top priority; she'd contend with her tangles later.

Afterward, Ginny laid her gently on the fuzzy green bath mat and lathered on some more Desitin, sprinkled her with powder, and gave her a fresh diaper. She dressed her in one of the new pairs of pajamas she'd picked up earlier that day on the way to Willowridge. Lucy looked happier now that she was clean, but Ginny also knew she needed to do something to clear those horrifying parasites out of her system.

When her poor old cat, Fleming, had worms, her mother had given him castor oil. Luckily, Marsha had some castor oil in her medicine cabinet. She carried Lucy into the kitchen to find a spoon. Marsha was at the stove, phone cradled between her chin and her shoulder.

"I can't really talk now," Marsha said to whoever was on the other end of the line. "I'll call you later. When is your shift over?" She pulled a pot out of the cupboard and began to fill it with water, still talking. Her cigarette was burning in the ashtray.

"I've got a friend staying with me. We're about to have supper. I'll call you later. I promise."

She rolled her eyes at Ginny and sighed.

"You, too," she said and hung up.

Marsha set the pot on the olive-green electric stovetop, turned on the burner, and retrieved her cigarette. She inhaled glamorously and exhaled a gorgeous plume of smoke.

"Gabe," she said, gesturing to the phone with her chin, answering Ginny's unspoken question.

"The X-ray tech?" Ginny asked. She had a hard time keeping track of Marsha's various love interests. The turnover of men in Marsha's life was pretty fast.

"EMT," she said.

"Oh, that's right," Ginny said. "You've been seeing him awhile, right?"

Marsha shrugged. "Six months?"

"Wow!" Ginny said. "When's the wedding?"

Marsha flushed a little but then scowled.

"Oh! You *really* like him," Ginny marveled.

"Little bit." Marsha pinched her fingers together and winked. "What's the castor oil for?"

"For Lucy. I think she has *worms*," she said, mortified.

Thankfully, Marsha was a nurse, unflappable, apparently even when it came to parasites. She simply nodded and reached for a little terra-cotta pot on her windowsill. "Add some thyme," she said and then grabbed a bulb of garlic from a little wooden bowl. "And garlic. If that doesn't work, apple cider vinegar is a good remedy. But she really should see a doctor, Gin. Can you take her to Peyton's pediatrician?"

Ginny knew Marsha was right, but the logistics of all of this baffled her. Getting Lucy to a doctor meant getting Lucy home, getting her added to their insurance policy, making an appointment. Meanwhile, there were *worms* in the poor little thing's digestive system. What she needed was immediate relief. She prayed this home remedy would do the trick.

Ginny crushed the garlic and tore the thyme into bits, mixing it with the castor oil. She filled a spoon with the mix and attempted to feed it to

Lucy, who was sitting on the floor, playing with an empty pot and a wooden spoon that Marsha had given her. Lucy resisted, of course, shaking her head and refusing to part her lips, but Ginny scooped her up, held her tightly.

"You need to take this, sweetheart," she said softly. "I promise it will make your tummy feel so much better."

"Maybe we can mix it with something?" Marsha reached into her freezer. "What about ice cream?"

Lucy initially rejected the spoonful, but as soon as the sweet concoction met her lips, she began to nod. She lapped it up and then lurched forward as if she wanted more.

Ginny complied, though without the medicine this time, and Lucy ate and ate until the ice cream was gone. There was melted ice cream in a ring around her mouth, her little pink tongue still sticking out. She clapped her hands together, smiling widely, and Ginny noted that her front teeth were badly decayed. She'd need to see a dentist as well as a doctor, Ginny thought. Thankfully, these were just her baby teeth.

"Hey!" Peyton said. He'd wandered into the kitchen, tearing himself away from the TV. "Can *I* have some ice cream?"

"Oh, honey," Ginny said. "This was the last bite. And look, Aunt Marsha's making spaghetti."

Peyton's lip began to quiver, but he didn't give in to his tears.

"I'll go get some more ice cream after supper, okay?" Marsha said. "Whatever flavor you want."

Peyton scowled and sat at the counter, arms crossed.

As Marsha assembled the pasta and jar of sauce, Ginny realized that she was, indeed, starving. Other than a doughnut that morning, she hadn't eaten anything all day, though truthfully, she was surprised she had any appetite at all given everything she'd seen that day.

They sat together at Marsha's kitchen island, eating. Lucy couldn't hold a fork or feed herself, so Ginny cut the pasta into pieces and fed it to her as though she were an infant still.

Afterward, she got the kids settled onto the couch in front of the TV and returned to the kitchen, where Marsha was finishing up the dishes.

"Can I use your phone to call Ab? I'll call collect," Ginny said.

Marsha shook her head. "Just call directly. It's on me," she said. "I'll go to the market around the corner and grab that ice cream for Pey."

Ginny recalled her plan to lay out the facts first. Then make the appeal. She knew she first had to confess that she'd gone to see Lucy. He'd be angry, of course, that she'd lied about what she was doing in Amherst. But once he knew that the reporters had been right, that everything in that exposé had been 100 percent true, he'd have no choice but to bring her home. If he knew the horrifying evidence of the school's neglect, there was no way he would insist that Lucy stay there. Even if she couldn't bring her home right away, certainly there had to be better institutions, better *schools* where they could enroll her.

She also had to believe that once he saw her, actually *saw* Lucy and held her in his arms, there would be no way he could do anything but love her. Suddenly it felt simple, easy even. She went from feeling hopeless to hopeful in a matter of seconds.

The phone cord was long and stretched nearly the length of the tiny apartment. Ginny dialed and then walked all the way down to the end of the hall, where she sat on the floor with her back against the wall.

She glanced at her watch. It was nearly six o'clock, though in the life of an aspiring attorney the end of the workday, the end of a workweek, signaled little more than a possible break for a vending machine sandwich or a fortifying cup of coffee. She hoped to catch him when he had at least a minute to hear her out.

As the phone rang, she recited her pitch in her head. She expected Sissy to answer and was startled when her husband's voice greeted her.

"Ab?" Her own voice suddenly sounded like it belonged to someone else.

"Hey, Gin, oh, my God, I'm so glad you called. But listen, I am swamped here, can I give you a call right back? I want to be able to talk, but my father dumped a whole bunch of stuff on my lap, and I am drowning. . . . Give me an hour and I promise I'll be all ears—"

"No," she said firmly, surprising herself.

Silence. Then, *"No?"*

"No. I need you to hear me out. Now."

She heard papers rustle, but nothing else on the other end of the line. Not even the typical exasperated sigh she'd grown accustomed to lately. He was listening, at least. She had his attention. "Okay?"

"I went to Willowridge today," she said, feeling as though she were floating away from her body. "I'm sorry I didn't tell you. But I needed to see for myself."

Still nothing on the other end. She could hear a clock in Marsha's hallway ticking.

"Did you . . ." he asked finally, softly, ". . . did you see her?"

Ginny's chin began to tremble and tears welled up hotly in her eyes. She needed to keep it together, though. She took a breath.

"Everything they said is true, Ab. Every single thing in that article; you wouldn't believe what I saw. The neglect. She's been sitting in her own waste. She has some sort of parasite. Her teeth are rotten. She needs to see a dentist, a doctor. They didn't even know anything about a heart condition. There was nothing in her record. I think it was a mistake. And if not, then nobody is monitoring it."

She continued, Pandora's box opened, all those wicked things flying out now. Escaped and dangerous.

"Gin," he said.

"Please, just listen," she said, summoning every bit of courage she had. "She's safe with me now. I signed her out—"

"You did *what?*" he said, the softness in his voice replaced by disbelief.

"I'm supposed to take her back on Monday. But you need to figure something out before then. We can't make her go back there. Those parents? The ones who've filed suit? They're just trying to *protect* their children. I can't just sit by; *we* can't just let this happen. Not to our daughter, and not to anyone else's child. We have plenty of money to take care of her, and with Peyton in school, I will have time to care for her. . . ." Her plea came in a rush, and then she waited for his response, but he said nothing.

"Ab? You can't possibly think we should leave her there. Now that we know it's as bad as the paper says?"

"Oh, Ginny, you don't understand," he said. "It's more complicated than that."

"I understand *completely*. I saw it with my own eyes. What they are allowing to happen to those children, those *human beings*, is criminal. Even if she weren't our daughter, even if . . ." Frustration and fury were like fire in her shoulder, in her hand as she gripped the telephone. "Please, ask your father to talk to his friend. The mental health commissioner, you said? Tell him that it's all true, everything that reporter said. He can do something. He *has* to do something."

"Gin, it's . . . my father. The firm . . ." His voice grew weak, and then there was nothing but silence. She thought for a moment he'd hung up on her when he finally spoke again. "We're representing the school."

She felt as if someone had just punched her in the throat.

"What?"

"In the class-action suit. We're defending Willowridge."

She felt dizzy, trying to put together exactly what he was saying. The firm, his firm, was the *defense team* in this lawsuit? They were fighting against the parents who simply wanted a safe place for their children? It was absurd. *Unfathomable.*

Ginny felt faint and was glad she was already sitting. Her heart was thrumming in her chest, banging against her ribs like someone trying to break down a locked door.

"Ginny?" he said, but his voice trailed off as she lowered the phone from her ear. His voice grew farther and farther away. She stood up and made her way back to the kitchen, where she clicked the handset down, cutting off the call.

"You okay?" Marsha asked as she came in the front door, clutching a half gallon of Rocky Road.

Ginny looked at Lucy sitting, eyes bright, mesmerized by the TV.

"What happened?" Marsha said. "What did he say?"

She shook her head; she couldn't articulate anything she was feeling. The betrayal was like a bomb had gone off, her body buzzing in the aftermath.

"What did Ab say?" Marsha said. "Are you taking her home?

She shook her head. She only knew she was never taking Lucy back to that place. And that now she couldn't take her home, either.

Twelve

༒

September 1971

Ginny called her mother after getting Peyton settled into bed. As always, he fell asleep quickly and easily after only a few moments. She had put Lucy into the second bedroom, where Ginny planned to sleep with her that night, before returning to the telephone.

"Mama, I need to tell you what happened today. At the school . . ." she started. She hoped that her mother would have some advice. Shirley, while not always the warmest woman, was logical. Reasonable and rational to a fault. If Ginny could count on anything, it was this.

She relayed the conversation with Ab, explained the awful predicament she was in. She told her about Lucy, and her mother listened, withholding her thoughts. At least for the moment.

"I know you don't have room for all three of us. We'll stay at Marsha's," she offered, anticipating her mother's concerns about how she might accommodate them all. "For the weekend anyway. I'll need to go back to the school on Monday to get her discharged." She had no idea what that would entail, how complicated it would be to get her released from the school. Without Ab's help, she imagined, it might not be as simple as a phone call saying they no longer needed the school's services.

She'd need to get her to a doctor, of course. A dentist. She thought about asking her mother if her pediatrician, the boisterous and friendly Dr. Rogers, who had seen her through childhood bouts of measles and mumps and various and sundry poxes, still made house calls.

But after that, she had no idea what she should do. Pray that Ab came to his senses? She tried to imagine what he would do if she just returned home with their daughter. Would he really turn them away? Imagining that scenario made her stomach turn.

She had hoped, quietly anyway, that her mother might offer her a solution. She was nothing if not pragmatic.

"Ginny," her mother said, her tone somber.

"Yeah, Mama?"

"Ab called here about an hour ago."

Ginny's heart flew to her throat. She knew he would come around. That he would see how crazy this was. Defending the school that had allowed their own daughter to suffer this sort of neglect was *unconscionable*. The heaviness in her chest lightened, and for the first time since she'd spoken to him she felt like she could breathe.

"He said to tell you he'll be here in the morning," her mother said.

Tears filled her eyes. He was coming. To see Lucy. To fix this awful mess. How could she have doubted him?

"He *and* his father," her mother added.

"What?"

"His father. They're coming tomorrow to pick you up and to bring the baby back to Willowridge."

"No," Ginny said, shaking her head slowly. Like Peyton at the beginning of a temper tantrum, she felt the hissing rage, the seething, steaming anger rising to the surface. "What did you tell him? What did you say?"

There was silence on the other end of the line, and for a moment Ginny worried the connection had been cut.

"I told him maybe he should talk to his wife about this first."

"And?"

"And he said he and his father would be here by ten tomorrow."

"What do I do, Mama?"

"You want my honest opinion?"

"Of course," Ginny said, though she knew exactly what her mother would say before she said it.

"I think you should go home. These are powerful people, Ginny. And he's your husband. Peyton's father. He loves you, but this is serious. Take the baby back to the school. Go home."

Ginny felt sick, swallowing past the aching, swollen lump in her throat.

"I'm sorry. I can't do that, Mama."

Thirteen

ॐ

February 1964

G inny should have known it would be a disaster.

But Ab had pleaded with Ginny to come home with him over the long holiday weekend that February. He wanted her to meet his mother and father. "They'll love you as much as I do," he said. "Please?"

She finally agreed, but as she got dressed that morning, she worried over every detail. Ab had told her not to change a thing, to wear what she would normally wear. Assured her that they would love her even if she arrived in a potato sack. She thought a potato sack might be better than her worn woolen skirts and moth-eaten sweaters. Her pearl necklace was made of paste, and every pair of stockings had at least one snag and run, tracks stopped only by sticky globs of nail polish.

"You look *stunning*," he said as he rushed to open the car door for her.

The drive to Dover normally took only a couple hours, but she'd had to stop to pee three times, the skirt, a size too small, squeezing at her bladder. By the time they pulled up the long drive to the house, she felt like she might burst.

The house. It was unlike anything she'd ever seen. It was twilight, but she could still make out the grand Colonial with a hundred shuttered windows and two large columns flanking the doorway. It could have been Gatsby's house. It could have been Tara in *Gone with the Wind.* Each window glowed with the warmth of light, chandeliers glittering through the glass.

Ginny sat staring through the passenger window, gaping at the architectural wonder before her, for at least a minute before Ab nudged her gently and said, "It'll be *fine.*"

"Come in, Mr. Abbott," the housekeeper, Rosa, said, ushering them in.

"Rosey Posey!" Ab said, squeezing the small woman, kissing her cheek with a loud smack.

Rosa gently cuffed the back of his head. "You're late. Your mother is having a, how you always say, conniption?"

"Yes! A *conniption* fit. The best kind. Which way to the gallows?" he asked and winked.

"I no understand *gallows.* Missus is in the kitchen."

Mrs. Richardson was fussing over a glass bowl, plump shrimp clinging to the side like children at the edge of a swimming pool. She was just as beautiful as Ginny had pictured her. She was at least five or ten years younger than her own mother, with shiny black hair streaked with one silver strand at her temple. She looked like an older Anne Bancroft. Wide-set brown eyes and a square jaw. Clearly, Ab had gotten his good looks from his mother.

"I ordered these shelled *and* deveined," she said accusingly, looking quickly up from the platter to Ab.

"Mother," Ab said, squeezing Ginny's hand. "I want you to meet Virginia."

Virginia. No one in the whole world called her Virginia except for her dentist.

"Call me *Ginny*!" she said, thrusting her hand out as Mrs. Richardson finally looked up.

But Mrs. Richardson did not accept her handshake, as her own hands had just been worrying over the, apparently, *fully* veined shrimp.

"Sorry," Mrs. Richardson said, gesturing with her chin to her hands. "It's a pleasure to meet you, Virginia."

Ginny slowly lowered her hand to her side and tugged at her skirt, which suddenly felt not only too tight but too short as well.

"Your father was supposed to be here. To meet your girl," she said. At this, Ginny's heart fluttered a bit. "But he's stuck at the office. Virginia, don't ever marry a lawyer. You'll spend your whole life alone."

Ginny's mouth twitched. She didn't know whether Mrs. Richardson was teasing or dead serious.

"Why don't you have Rosa show Virginia where she'll be sleeping," Mrs. Richardson said to Ab. To Ginny, she said, "And you can freshen up before dinner."

Rosa led her to a dormered bedroom at the top of the stairs. The walls were a slate blue, and there were two twin beds with identical red-and-blue plaid spreads. Two matching desks faced the windows, though there was no paraphernalia to indicate recent usage. Unlike the rest of the house, the wooden floors here were scuffed and scratched. It struck her that this had likely been Ab's childhood room, perhaps the one he shared with his brother, Paul, before he passed, though why two boys would share a room in a house with so many bedrooms (six or seven was Ginny's guess) was beyond her. Marsha and her sisters had shared a room growing up, purely out of necessity, but given a choice (and amenable real estate), they would gladly have separated.

Ginny looked at the closed door, listened for any sounds of life outside, and, hearing none, tiptoed to the closet, turning the glass knob carefully in her hand. The door opened with a slow groan and she winced, furtively glancing back at the door.

She didn't know what she was expecting. Ab's dead brother's clothing, still hanging from the rod? A baseball uniform still smudged with grass and dirt? Or maybe banker's boxes filled with all the history of his life, filed by year?

The closet was empty. Just a half dozen wire hangers, some with the paper dressings of the dry cleaner, Lewandos, still affixed. The shelf above the rack was empty, save for a stack of extra blankets. The floor was clear as well; not even a neglected dust bunny huddled in the corner. Not a bit of evidence of the room's former inhabitants. Not a scrap of proof that two boys once shared this space, maybe even searched the sky through that window looking for constellations. Something about this weighed heavy on her, a sorrow more profound than if the room had been preserved, their childhood entombed inside.

They ate dinner quietly, though Ginny could hardly eat, her stomach was in such knots. Somehow, while they were sipping on glasses of chardonnay, Rosa had magically shelled and deveined each shrimp as well as prepared beef Wellington and the creamiest mashed potatoes Ginny had ever eaten.

Mrs. Richardson asked polite questions about what it was like growing up in Amherst and asking if she enjoyed her work at the library. But she was clearly distracted, looking at the empty chair at the head of the table every few minutes before glancing toward the foyer and the closed front door.

And then, as if conjured by Mrs. Richardson's sheer will, the front door opened and Mr. Richardson entered. From her spot at the dining table, Ginny had a full view of the foyer and Ab's long-awaited dad.

What struck Ginny first was his size. He had to have been six feet two or three inches tall, broad shouldered and looming. He filled the foyer as he removed his hat and coat, depositing them in Rosa's arms. Even after a full workday, his clothes were immaculate, his shoes gleaming.

"Dad!" Ab said. "Come meet Ginny."

Mr. Richardson came into the dining room and Ginny didn't know whether to remain sitting or stand. She opted to rise, the china before her rattling as she bumped the table's edge to stand up, reaching across the table, hand extended.

"Pleasure to meet you, Virginia," he said, nodding at her, then gruffly taking his seat at the empty head of the table. "Sorry," he said to Mrs. Richardson. "Burning the midnight oil again."

"We'll wait for you to finish before we start dessert," Mrs. Richardson said, and Rosa appeared with another steaming Wellington.

Soundlessly, Mr. Richardson ate while the rest of them waited. Luckily, he devoured the entire meal in just a few awkward minutes, before wiping the cloth napkin across his lips and sitting back in his chair.

Rosa scurried in, removing the dirty dishes and quickly replacing them with dessert plates, each holding a teetering slice of a four-layered pastel-pink cake with white frosting.

"Pink champagne cake," Rosa said to Ginny. "It's Missus's favorite."

"So you're the one who's been keeping our son occupied this year," Mr. Richardson said, abruptly breaking his silence.

Ginny smiled but wondered what on earth this meant. Had someone else been occupying Ab's time last year? Ab hadn't mentioned other girlfriends, though there must have been some. Or did *occupying* mean *distracting*?

"You a Smith girl? Wasn't the last one a Smith girl?" he asked Mrs. Richardson.

"Ginny works at the library," Ab said. "She grew up in Amherst."

"Ah, a local girl," he said.

Again, she couldn't ascertain if this statement had any judgment associated with it or was simply a statement of fact.

"So what does your father do for work?" Mr. Richardson asked.

"My father's passed," Ginny said. "Car accident when I was ten. My mother works at the college, too." She didn't mention that her job was in the dining hall kitchen, then felt guilty for feeling this to be a shameful thing.

"Just a few months left until graduation," Mr. Richardson said, leaning forward and resting his elbows on the table. He peered at Ginny with a new intensity, as if she were just now coming into focus. "This book's due date is coming up, so to speak. Time for it to be returned."

Ginny felt her breath catch, her jaw drop.

"I'm glad you're here, Dad," Ab said suddenly, setting his fork down on his empty dessert plate. "I actually have some really good news to share."

Mrs. Richardson looked up from her cake, which she'd been studying with the intensity of a surgeon. Ginny looked at him, too.

"I've been accepted to Harvard. Law school."

Ginny felt the champagne cake turn from bubbles to lead in her stomach. She knew of course, that he had sent his applications out. All the Ivy League schools had received his LSAT scores and transcripts. But he'd avoided talking about what would happen when one of these schools offered him admission.

"*But,*" he said, "I've decided not to accept their offer."

Ginny sucked in her breath, and Mrs. Richardson's spoon clattered from her hand to the floor. Rosa swooped in like a seagull going after a sandwich.

"What are you talking about?" Mrs. Richardson said. "Of course you'll go to Harvard. Your father, your grandfather . . . you're a *legacy.*"

Ab rolled his shoulders as if he'd just been spared an enormous burden. "I've joined up with IVS, a group of aid workers. They're sending me to Southeast Asia. Vietnam. In the fall. I'll only be gone six months. Harvard isn't going anywhere."

"Vietnam?" Mrs. Richardson said incredulously. She turned to Mr. Richardson and asked, "Isn't there some sort of civil war going on there?"

Vietnam. Ginny couldn't even begin to place the country on a map.

"I suppose this is *your* doing?" Mrs. Richardson said, suddenly turning everyone's attention to Ginny, who felt her eyes widen at this odd accusation, especially given that the rug had just been pulled out from under her as well.

"I . . . *no* . . ."

"Because Abbott has wanted to be an attorney like his father since he was six years old."

Really? What sort of six-year-old aspires to be an attorney?

"Ma'am," Ginny started and then realized it wouldn't matter what she said. She would forever be linked in Mrs. Richardson's mind with Ab's decision not to go to law school. There was no taking back this moment. It made her angry at Ab, almost angrier than the fact that he was leaving her to go to some remote corner of the earth to be some sort of do-gooder.

Mrs. Richardson continued, "His whole life, he's been studying, preparing for this, and suddenly, he meets you and everything goes out the window."

Mr. Richardson, who had remained silent, shook his head. "Your brother wouldn't have gotten caught up in such foolishness."

At this the color drained from Ab's face.

Mr. Richardson's demeanor, however, was calm, scarily so.

"How do you know that, Dad?" Ab said. "Really. He was twelve years old."

"You're right," Mr. Richardson said. "We never got a chance to know what he could have become."

Ab was quiet now, his face completely impassive.

Mrs. Richardson pushed her full dessert plate away from her. "Well, you'll just need to tell those IVS people that you've changed your mind. Your father will call them tomorrow. Figure out how to undo whatever it is you've done here. We'll figure this out in the morning after everyone's had a good night's sleep."

"Actually, I think we better just head back to Amherst tonight," Ab said, pushing himself away from the table. "I'm sorry, Ginny. I shouldn't have brought you here."

Ginny nodded silently and cast her eyes down before looking up at Mrs. Richardson. But Ab's mother refused to return her gaze. Mr. Richardson stood up and without a word disappeared down the hall.

Ginny felt duped. Just as blindsided as his parents were. Here, she'd been falling head over heels, and Ab was surreptitiously making plans to move to the other side of the world. He'd effectively chosen a village of strangers over her.

They gathered their things and silently loaded them back into the car. Rosa walked them out, and Ab kissed her on the cheek. "Bye, Rosey Posey. Dinner was lovely. I'm sorry."

"I'm sorry," he said to Ginny after nearly thirty minutes of silence in the car. "I didn't mean to spring it on you like that. But I knew if I talked about it with you, I'd never be able to go through with it."

"Well, good thing, then," Ginny said, peering out at the night.

"It's just six months, Gin. I don't even leave until September, and I'll be home by Valentine's Day. A year from now, I'll already be home again. You need to understand, this was the only way I could get out of law school. The only way to get my father off my back. I've bought myself a year to come up with another plan."

"But what about us? Do you just want me to twiddle my thumbs while you're off milking cows or digging ditches or whatever you plan to do?"

"No," he said. And then he steered the car over to the shoulder of the dark road. He put the car in neutral and idled for a moment. He took a deep breath and turned to her. A shiver ran through her body, and she pulled her sweater around her tightly. "While I'm gone, I was thinking you could plan our wedding."

"*What?*"

"Our wedding," he said and pulled a ring from his pocket. It was large. Dazzling. "This is part of the reason I needed to go home. It's been sitting in our safe since I was sixteen. My grandmother's. She gave it to me, and now it's yours, if you'll have it."

She gawked, speechless.

"Is that a yes?"

Her eyes filled with tears.

"Yes," she croaked.

Ab hit the steering wheel with the palm of his hand and whooped. He looked at her, checking as if he might have made a mistake. When she nodded again, saying "Yes!" he rolled down the window, leaned his head out, and hollered out at a passing car, "She said *yes!*"

Instead of going back to Amherst, Ab drove them an hour southeast to his family's little cottage on Cape Cod. He found the key hanging behind a battered shutter and opened the door. Inside the musty living room, he started a fire in the fireplace while she studied the ring on her finger, trying to figure out how a simple trip to meet Ab's parents had turned into *this*.

When the fire finally caught, he came to her where she was sitting on a lumpy down-filled sofa and knelt on one knee before her, proposing properly this time.

Then, in the firelight, he undressed her as if she were a gift. He kissed her stomach and neck and hair, and every follicle sang. *Wild nights, wild nights!* she thought. *Oh, Emily, if you could see me now.*

Afterward, they lay breathless, watching the flickering flames.

"My brother and I used to come here," he said. "In the summers. The woods on one side of us. The beach on the other. It was like our own magical world."

"What happened?" she asked. "To Paul?"

"Influenza," he said. "Then pneumonia."

"What your father said . . . that wasn't fair."

"Yeah, well." Ab shook his head and propped himself up on his elbow, studying Ginny's face. "What about here?"

"What?" She was still breathless, her heart a ragged thing. Her bones and brain felt happily bruised.

"We'll move *here*. In exactly one year. When I get back. I'll make you fires, and you can read your poetry to me."

In the firelight, Ab's face was as bright and sincere as the snow that had started to fall outside the little paned windows.

"Promise?" she said holding out her pinky, hooked and awaiting his.

He linked his pinky with hers. *"Promise."*

Fourteen

ɞ

September 1971

I think we should just get out of town for the weekend," Marsha suggested. "We can drive to the beach. Think this through without worrying about your asshole father-in-law. Willowridge isn't expecting Lucy back until Monday night. We can leave early tomorrow, have a couple of days to think about it, and be back here in plenty of time. It'll also send a message to Ab that you're serious about this. That you won't just go along with whatever plan his father dreams up."

Maybe they could take the kids to the little house on the Cape. But then again, her father-in-law could easily find her there. She was livid that Ab had gotten his father involved; he was no longer playing fair. It was cowardly. Lucy was not Abbott's daughter; she was *Ab's*.

The children were still asleep, and Marsha and Ginny were sitting at Marsha's little red Formica table, drinking coffee and smoking. Ginny didn't generally smoke, but she needed something to do with the nervous energy that was running through her like an electric current.

"I don't know. Ab will be furious if he gets all the way here only to find that we're gone. And who knows what Abbott will do? Probably sic the hounds on us," Ginny joked, but her heart felt heavy with all that Abbott Richardson might be capable of. He was a man who got exactly what he wanted. Always. There was no negotiating with Abbott Senior. He was a lawyer, but with him, there was no reasoning. No compromise. She'd witnessed her husband's multiple failed attempts to confer with Abbott— on everything from what to have for dinner to what house he should buy. Abbott won every time.

"Where would we go?" Ginny asked, with the Cape out of the question and exactly $150 in her purse.

"I don't know," Marsha said. "Where would be a good place to take the kids? Someplace we can drive to in a few hours? Someplace Abbott wouldn't think to look?"

Ginny shrugged. The idea of getting in the car and driving anywhere with her children but without her husband seemed like a betrayal.

"God, maybe I should just stay here. See what their idea is."

"Their *idea*?" Marsha said, snorting. "Their idea is that you should never have gone to the school. That you should have left Lucy there. That you should have just kept pretending that everything was okay. That she was *dead*. That is what their idea is. And that is exactly what Abbott is going to make you do."

Ginny dragged deeply on her Virginia Slim and then exhaled. She knew Marsha was right. If she stayed, Ab and his father would convince her that it was better for all of them. Better for Lucy, even, to go back to the only home she'd ever known. But she also knew that something had snapped inside her. Something had shifted, broken, even, and like the ceramic lamp that Peyton had once knocked over, there was no putting things back together again. Not without visible evidence of those fissures.

"*I* know!" Marsha said suddenly, clapping her hands together.

Ginny looked at her, waiting.

"Atlantic City!" she said. "The beach for us, and the boardwalk for the kids. We'll find a cheap place to stay."

"The school says I'm not allowed to take her out of state," Ginny said, shaking her head.

"How will they know?" Marsha said.

She had a point. If Ginny returned her by Monday, there was no way they'd know where they'd gone. It wasn't as though Lucy would say anything.

"What do I tell Ab?" she said.

"You tell Ab to hold his damned horses."

They left just after seven-thirty the next morning, settling the children into the backseat of Marsha's car, the Dart with its tattered upholstery and squeaky brakes. Ginny had done the laundry that night, so the clothes she'd brought for Peyton and bought for Lucy were clean. Enough to get them through the weekend, she hoped. They swung by the supermarket as soon as it opened and picked up a package of Pampers, baby wipes, and a couple more plastic bottles. Lucy really was much more infant than toddler. She still drank from a bottle, something Ginny couldn't bear to take away from her, though Peyton's doctor had cautioned that bottles caused teeth not only to rot but to buck outward. Besides, Lucy's baby teeth were already ruined; she figured the damage was already done.

The last stop was at a gas station just outside of town where Marsha had the attendant fill up the tank, refusing Ginny's money when she reached into her pocketbook.

"Please," Ginny said. "It's the least I can do."

"Save your money for the shore," she said.

Marsha kept insisting that Ginny consider this a vacation. And while this seemed ludicrous to Ginny, the notion that this was some sort of holiday from her life, the word itself—*vacation*—was oddly fitting. That was exactly what this felt like; she was vacating. Vacating her life, vacating the world she'd been residing in for the last seven years, a world not much bigger than the four walls of their home, the four square blocks of their neighborhood. The idea of going to the beach, of checking into a hotel, of walking in the sand, seemed scandalous but also tempting.

Marsha said she'd been meaning to go to Atlantic City forever. She'd gone there once when she was a little girl; it was the first time she and her sister had ever seen the ocean. After that, they were both smitten. Now she finally had an excuse.

"Won't it be expensive? Atlantic City's a resort town, isn't it? God, it's a holiday weekend, too. We might not even be able to find a room. Should we call someplace and make reservations?" Ginny had asked.

"You worry too much," Marsha scolded. "We'll find someplace cheap to stay. "

It was almost nine o'clock before they finally got on the road, and Ginny glanced at her watch, feeling sick. Ab had told her mother he and his father would be pulling into Amherst at ten. She had no idea what he would do when they discovered she wasn't there.

The highway was filled with bumper-to-bumper traffic. It seemed that every person in Massachusetts had decided to get away for the weekend. A car behind them blared its horn, and Marsha reached out the open window, flipping off the angry driver who passed her. Ginny glanced quickly in the backseat to see if Peyton had any reaction, but he was looking dreamily out the window, clinging to his teddy bear. Lucy was asleep but stirring. She'd been less afraid of the car this time, hadn't resisted when Ginny buckled her into the backseat. Peyton was still leery of Lucy, the way he'd been when they first brought Arthur home. They'd expected him to be thrilled by the big-pawed puppy, but instead he'd run to his room and had to be coaxed out again. She hoped he'd warm up to her, the way he eventually had to Arthur.

"Do you think I should call Ab once we get there? Let him at least know we're okay?" she asked.

Marsha took a deep breath and sighed. "We don't have to do this," she said. "You can call Ab and just have him come get you."

Ginny felt a ping in her chest at the thought of Ab coming, of his bringing her home.

"But if he comes for you, Lucy will go right back to Willowridge. You know that, right?"

As much as Ginny would like to protest, to argue that Ab was a good man, a rational, kindhearted man, she knew that when it came to Lucy, there was something in him that was proving immovable. He was a good father to Peyton, the best. But to Lucy, he was nothing. Nor she to him.

After a roadside picnic lunch, as they crossed the George Washington Bridge, Lucy got carsick. It came without warning. No crying or moaning in anticipation, just the animal-like sound of her vomiting and then the awful, sour stench.

"It's okay," Ginny soothed Lucy, who seemed unaffected by the whole incident. She was wide-eyed but silent.

Peyton had pulled his T-shirt up over his nose. "She stinks, Mama," his muffled voice said.

Ginny grabbed a handful of napkins she'd stashed in her purse earlier and turned around to assess the damage. They were at a standstill, stuck between, behind, and in front of several semis, and so she climbed into the backseat, which was a tricky maneuver given the tiny confines of the car. Situated between the kids, she pulled Lucy's soiled shirt over her head. She'd have tossed the whole thing out the window if they'd had more than a couple of clean shirts remaining. She patted at Lucy's neck and hair with the dry napkins, but what Lucy really needed was another bath. Ginny brushed a wet strand of Lucy's hair from her cheek. Poor little thing.

"How bad is it?" Marsha asked.

"Pretty bad. I think we'll need to stop somewhere to get her cleaned up as soon as we're out of the city."

Ginny searched for something to sop up the mess. Finally, she located a beach towel shoved beneath the passenger seat.

"I'm sorry," Ginny said to Marsha. "I had to use one of your towels. Maybe we can find a Laundromat in Atlantic City so I can wash all this stuff. Maybe a car wash, too."

She wrapped Lucy's soiled T-shirt in the beach towel and rolled it tightly before shoving the whole horrible bundle back under the seat. As she bent down, she felt something tickling her neck. It startled her, until she realized it was Lucy. Her tiny fingers were stroking Ginny's hair the same gentle way Ginny had just touched hers. She felt her heart swell, and tears filled her eyes.

Ginny sat back up and took that tiny hand in her own and kissed her fat, sweet palm. "It's okay," she said, though she wasn't sure if she was talking to Lucy or to herself. "Everything is going to be okay."

The traffic snaked the entire length of the New Jersey Turnpike, and it was nearly twilight when they finally reached Atlantic City. They'd all gotten accustomed to the sour smell of the car, but they were also tired and hungry, and Ginny wanted nothing more than to simply be clean. For her children to be clean. For this godforsaken car to be clean.

"Oh, my God! I can smell the ocean!" Marsha said excitedly, leaning her head out the open window. "Can you grab the map? I need you to navigate."

Ginny reached for the glove box, but it was locked.

"Oh, the atlas is under the seat," Marsha said.

Ginny reached under the long bench seat and found a road atlas along with some fast food bags, a tube of lipstick, and a single foil-wrapped condom. She left everything but the atlas under the seat. She located the New Jersey page and the Atlantic City insert.

"Turn here," Ginny said. "That'll take us close to the boardwalk. That's probably where the motels are, right?"

They found the blinking neon lights of a motel not far from the beach, and Marsha pulled into the parking lot. It was in a well-lit area and seemed safe. The motel was pink and white, almost cheerful. Welcoming.

"I'll go check us in," Marsha said. "Should I maybe use a different name?"

Ginny shrugged. Her mother had insisted she wouldn't tell Ab where they'd gone, only that Ginny needed some time to think. He would never guess they'd have gone to Atlantic City, of all places, but it couldn't hurt to be cautious. She was still nervous the school might find out she'd taken Lucy across state lines, though given how lax they'd been about handing her over to somebody whose identity was based on an envelope in her purse, she doubted they'd care. "Yeah, that's a good idea."

Ginny watched Marsha walk toward the motel lobby, admired how she held her head so high, her confidence, as if two women going to get a motel room for a weekend vacation was the most normal thing in the world. After she disappeared inside, Ginny observed the people walking up and down the neighboring streets, mesmerized by the colorful crowd. Most of the women wore short skirts and tall boots. The men's pants were tight and their hair was long. There were black men and women, nearly in equal proportion to the white people in the crowd. Since she and Ab moved to Dover, she'd yet to see a single black person other than the men and women who worked in the restaurant kitchens and kept houses. Several of Sylvia's friends had Negro maids, women who silently and stoically went about their business of cleaning and cooking and caring for her neighbors' children. Ab had suggested exactly once that they hire a girl to come in and help with the housework, and Ginny had politely said, "That won't be necessary." The whole business of it made her feel uncomfortable.

ჟ

Ginny rolled the window down farther and stuck her face out. The air did indeed smell of the ocean, and she could even hear the roar of the surf, though they weren't close enough to the beach to see it. Perhaps this was exactly what she needed to clear her head, to come up with a plan. Clean, salty air. The calming sea.

Marsha emerged from the motel office and made her way back to the car, shoulders slumped now, sighing.

"No room at the inn," she said. "Don't worry, though. There's a whole strip of motels just a couple blocks away."

But as they drove down Pacific Avenue, every one of the motels' signs was blinking NO VACANCY.

When Marsha came out of the last motel on the strip, she said, "The clerk told me to go to Pleasantville. That we should find a room there. It's just a quick drive from there to the shore. It's the holiday. Everything close to the beach is booked."

As promised, there were plenty of motels along Black Horse Pike, most of them advertising either weekly or hourly rates.

Finally, at a small, squat motel, Marsha came out of the office dangling a key ring from one finger, waving it like she'd won a prize.

They drove the car around to the other side of the L-shaped motel and pulled into the parking space right in front of their door. Number 111. That had to be lucky, Ginny thought, and, like a child, made a wish.

Marsha unlocked the room door as Ginny got the kids unbuckled, discovering as she did a missed pool of vomit underneath poor Lucy. While she got her out of the car, Peyton ran straight into the motel room and jumped onto one of the double beds. Lucy, however, clung like a monkey to Ginny's neck and did not want to be put down.

"I'll go get the car cleaned out and pick up some food," Marsha said. "Why don't you give Lucy a bath, and once she's cleaned up, then we can eat."

❧

The motel was shabby but clean, with a rust-ringed toilet and sink, a yellowed popcorn ceiling, and faded drapes. The distinct scent of cigarettes permeated everything.

The water was blessedly hot at first, but after the pale pink tub was filled only about halfway, it began to run cold. She'd need to put both kids in at once. Who knew how long it would take for the water to heat up again.

She undressed Lucy first; her little dimpled bottom already looked a thousand times better than it had just yesterday. She'd seen no sign of the awful tiny worms she'd seen in her diaper at the amusement park. She'd be sure to give her another dose of the castor oil concoction before bed, though, just to make sure.

"Peyton," she hollered, leaning toward the open bathroom door.

When he didn't answer, she stood up from the bathtub's edge where she'd been perched and poked her head out of the bathroom.

"I'm watching *Bewitched*," he said, his eyes not leaving the TV.

"Come have a bath," Ginny said, motioning for him to come to her when he finally looked away from the screen.

"That baby is in there," he said.

"That's all right. You can both be in the bathtub."

He shook his head. "She's a girl."

"She's your *sister*."

He stubbornly crossed his arms and shook his head again.

Normally Ab dealt with Peyton when he was being like this. When Peyton was cross, Ab was silly, and could coax him out of his willful defiance with tickles or playfulness. Ginny lacked the requisite patience and good humor, however, and felt herself growing from impatient to angry.

"You need a bath, and there's no more hot water. Unless you want to soak in a cold tub, you'll need to share a bath with your sister." As if logic and reason meant anything to a stubborn six-year-old.

"*No!*" he said and reached for the knob on the TV, making it even louder.

If she had more energy, she would have simply gone and scooped him up. But she was exhausted, her back aching.

"*Fine!*" she said. She needed to figure out a way to wash Lucy's hair. It might be easier without Peyton there anyway.

She turned back to the bathtub, and there, floating in the water, was a turd. A worm-riddled turd.

"Oh, my *God!*" she said, feeling like she might throw up.

Lucy's face fell, and she started to cry. She squeezed her eyes shut and shook her head.

"Oh, no, no! I'm sorry. I'm not mad at you," Ginny said and quickly pulled Lucy out of the water—she'd deal with the poop later—and wrapped her in a threadbare but clean towel. She sat on the toilet seat with Lucy on her lap and sighed into her hair.

Marsha returned just twenty minutes later with a paper bag with four burgers and some greasy fries as well as two frothy chocolate shakes for the kids, which was perfect to help disguise the flavor of the castor oil and thyme. Lucy happily drank it down without any prodding. They sat together on the beds to eat, beach towels spread out beneath them.

"What's this, Mama?" Peyton asked, leaning across the bed to a contraption on the nightstand.

Marsha raised an eyebrow at Ginny, who was mystified.

"It says two five cents!" he said. "Mama, do you have two five cents?" Ginny had been working with him on his numbers.

"That means *twenty*-five cents," she corrected. "A quarter. I think I have one in my purse."

"What is it?" Ginny whispered to Marsha.

"Your mama ever let you ride one of those rides out in front of the Big Y?" Marsha asked Peyton, jumping up from the bed and pulling a coin out of the tiny pocket in her hip-huggers.

"I rode the fire truck once!" Peyton exclaimed.

Marsha handed him the quarter and he clumsily put it in the coin slot. Suddenly the whole bed began to rumble.

"Oh!" Ginny said, gasping as it rocked beneath her. Lucy squealed, with fear at first and then delight as the bed vibrated. Peyton stood up as the bed tried to buck him off.

"It's Magic Fingers!" Marsha said gleefully. She hopped on the bed, too, and they all trembled and shook and laughed.

When it stopped, Peyton hollered, "Again!" and Lucy's lip began to quiver, and so Ginny stood up and went to her purse, where she had a stash of quarters for the tolls. After they'd enjoyed three rides on the magic bed, Ginny felt like her teeth had been rattled loose and the burger and fries were unsettled in her stomach.

"That's enough for tonight, I think," she said, breathless.

She situated both kids in the now still bed, pulling the orange-and-yellow paisley spread up to their chins. A lazy ceiling fan spun overhead, rocking on its mount, making her worry that the whole thing might come tumbling down.

"Goodnight stars," she whispered into Peyton's ear.

"Goodnight air," he said, yawning, worn out.

"Goodnight noises everywhere."

"I need a shower," Marsha said.

"Shoot," Ginny said quietly, rummaging through her bag and pulling out Lucy's last two bottles of milk. "I need some ice to keep Lucy's bottles cold. I'll be right back."

She grabbed the plastic bucket and locked the door behind her. Outside she saw a group of women congregating in the parking lot. They were dressed in tight miniskirts, breasts spilling out of bikini tops. Chunky heels and fishnet stockings. A car pulled up, and one of the women leaned in to speak to the driver. Ginny felt her face grow hot. *Prostitutes.* As she watched one woman slip into an open door on the ground floor of the motel, she thought, *No wonder they have Magic Fingers in the rooms.*

As she quickly filled the bucket with ice at the machine, Ginny could now see how seedy the motel was. The dimly lit street, the dingy curtains, the carpeted floor gritty with sand. How had she not noticed this before? The realization that her perspective could be so skewed made her feel uneasy, sick even. If she had been wrong about this, she could be wrong about so many things. Weren't mothers supposed to have heightened instincts? Apparently, she had none.

Back in the motel, Marsha was in the shower. Ginny double-bolted the door and strung the chain across, pulled the curtains tight, and put the bottles in the ice bucket. She quickly changed out of her clothes into the only nightgown she'd brought and slipped under the covers next to Lucy, trying not to think about who had last slept (or done whatever) on this mattress.

She watched Lucy sleep, the barely perceptible rise and fall of her round chest. The little lift of her dimpled chin, her tongue, as always, peeking out between her lips. Her clenched hands. She'd forgotten the simple pleasure of a child's warm body next to hers. Lately Peyton wanted her affection only on his terms. When he pushed her away, she would ignore the sting and back off. Ab, however pushed harder, wrapping Peyton in a hug and squeezing him until he giggled and relented.

She leaned over Lucy to kiss Peyton's sweaty forehead and then pressed her hand against Lucy's chest, confirming the beating of her heart, her gentle breath. *Mine,* she thought. *This child is mine.*

And before she could begin to worry about what had caused that enormous stain on the ceiling, exhausted, she fell asleep.

Fifteen

꩜

Ginny awoke the next morning to commotion outside the motel window, rattled from her dreams as though the Magic Fingers were stuck in overdrive.

"What's going on?" she asked, bolting upright.

Marsha was at the window, peering out. "I'm not sure. Looks like some sort of parade?"

"A parade?" Peyton said sleepily. His favorite book was the Seuss book *And to Think That I Saw It on Mulberry Street*. Ab read it to him nearly every night that he got home from work before Peyton was in bed. This year, Ab had promised they'd drive down to New York City and see the Macy's parade on Thanksgiving. Peyton's favorite balloon was Underdog.

Ginny quickly checked on Lucy, who was still sleeping, then scurried out of bed to join Marsha at the window.

A crowd of women was congregating at the corner. Not hookers this time, thankfully, but women of all ages, carrying signs. They were a bit

far away, but Ginny could make out a few. WELCOME TO THE CATTLE AUC-
TION! and ALL WOMEN ARE BEAUTIFUL. Another had a photo of a bikini-clad
woman, her body marked off in parts: LOIN, RUMP, RIB, ROUND.

Of course, she'd read about the protests. Just last summer, there was
the women's strike for equality. She'd spent the day tending to Peyton,
who had been sick with a summer flu, and so she'd propped him up on
the couch and given him Popsicles to try to bring his fever down. She'd
caught up on her ironing as he convalesced. She understood the irony of
this, but seriously, if she'd gone on "strike," who would have taken care
of her child? Certainly not Ab. Besides, what would she have done with
that spare time if not attempt to make a dent in that bottomless basket of
wrinkled clothes?

Marsha went to the door, unlocked the chain and two dead bolts, and
swung the door open. A rush of salty air blew into the room. She cupped
her hands around her mouth and hollered, "Free our sisters, free our-
selves!"

"Marsha!" Ginny reprimanded, as Lucy stirred.

Beaming, Marsha came back into the room. "I think they're here to
protest the Miss America Pageant."

"The Miss America Pageant? Why?"

Ginny and her mother used to watch the pageant religiously each year,
always rooting for Miss Massachusetts, who never seemed to get a break,
though she often got close. Just last year a girl from Foxborough had gotten
second runner-up.

Ginny tried to imagine what it must be like prancing across the stage
in a bathing suit and couldn't. Ginny couldn't remember the last time
she'd even been in public in a bathing suit. Probably not since junior high
school. Even then it had been just horrifying. She'd gotten breasts in the
fifth grade and had spent the next two years attempting to hide them as
the other girls caught up.

"We should go march with them!" Marsha said.

Ginny shook her head. Of course, she believed in women's rights, in equality, but she wasn't someone who liked to call attention to herself. Crowds made her nervous, and who knew what sort of trouble they might stir up. The last thing she needed was to get hauled off in a paddy wagon. Wouldn't her father-in-law love that?

"I promised Peyton we'd go to the beach today. The boardwalk?" Ginny said, trying to reel Marsha back in.

Marsha's eyes were wild; she was energized. "Oh, sure. Sure! Of course."

Peyton grabbed a quarter from the nightstand and set the bed to rocking again, shaking Lucy awake. When she started to cry, Ginny scooped her up and sighed.

Peyton was scratching his head. "I'm itchy, Mama."

"God, I hope there aren't bedbugs," she said. "Are *you* itchy?" she asked Marsha. Marsha shook her head.

"Let me see your back," she said to Peyton. He bent over and she lifted his pajama shirt, revealing the knobby bones of his spine. His skin was unmarked.

"It's my head," he said.

"Let me see?"

He bent his head to her, and she inspected his scalp. It took about two seconds to locate the sesame-seed-size louse. Then another and another.

"Goddamnit," she said. "He's got lice."

"Oh, man," Marsha said, coming over to inspect. "Do you think it's from the motel?"

"Let me check Lucy," she said. She scooped Lucy, just waking up, into her arms and ran her finger gently through her hair. There, beneath her curls, was an infestation; her scalp was riddled with scabs.

Ginny's hand flew to her mouth. No wonder she hadn't wanted Ginny to touch her head. Lucy hadn't been itching at all, but she'd clearly been hosting this insect party for some time. That place, that awful place had left her *infested*. Like a piece of meat left out in the sun. She felt suddenly overwhelmed. This was all too much. She wondered why on earth Lucy hadn't complained. Was she just so accustomed to feeling awful that she didn't bother to cry?

Marsha turned away from the window and plopped down next to Peyton. "Well, I saw a barber shop around the corner. We can take Peyton there and just get his head shaved. We could do that to Lucy, too, but she's got such gorgeous curls." Marsha tapped her finger to her lip, thinking. "Mayonnaise works. That's what my mother did the one time we all got lice."

"Mayo?" Ginny said.

"It smothers them. You put mayo on the hair and cover it with a shower cap. It makes the nits slip off, too."

"Nits?"

"The eggs."

"Oh, my *God*," Ginny said, shoulders slumping. "This is so disgusting."

"It'll be fine," Marsha said. "I'll take Peyton to the barber and grab some mayo from that little market on the way back. You stay here."

"Thank you," Ginny said.

"It's just a haircut and some condiments," Marsha said, shrugging.

"No, for everything. This was supposed to be your holiday weekend, and you wound up with this," she said and gestured to everything. The crappy motel, her two lice-infested children.

"It's nothing," Marsha said and winked. "Let's go get you a buzz cut, Peyton."

They returned an hour later, and while they were gone Ginny had combed through Lucy's hair, eliminating as many lice as she could. She put her hair up into a ponytail to avoid any that might try to hitch a ride on her own head. Marsha gave her some little mayonnaise packets, the kind you get at a deli. Remarkably, there was a plastic shower cap and a couple of small shampoo bottles in the motel bathroom. Tonight, she'd put the mayo in Lucy's hair and seal it all shut inside the shower cap. Smother those horrid little buggers. She and Marsha checked each other's scalps, and by some small bit of grace, neither one of them was infested.

The beach was teeming with families trying to soak up the last bit of summer. Ginny, of course, had not thought to bring a bathing suit when she left Dover, and one of Marsha's would never have fit anyway. Marsha's two-piece was hot pink, leaving very little to the imagination, and she wore a matching pair of big round rose-colored sunglasses. She could have easily been mistaken for a contestant in the pageant. As always, Marsha managed to look completely glamorous, while Ginny felt like a *mom* in lime-green pedal pushers and a loose embroidered smock top. She'd brought shorts for Peyton that worked as trunks, and she figured Lucy was little enough that she could get away with just wearing her diaper. With her blond curls, she looked almost like that little girl on the Coppertone billboard overlooking the boardwalk, the one with the dog pulling her bottoms down to reveal a tiny white heinie.

They bought a couple of beach towels at a boardwalk souvenir shop as well as a big tube of suntan lotion. Settling on a rare open swath of sand near the water's edge, Ginny felt her body relax for the first time in days. She tried not to think about Ab, or what might be hatching on Lucy's scalp or in her intestines. As Marsha walked both children down to where the waves lapped the shore, she lay back, closed her eyes, and tried to let everything go.

They spent the whole day at the beach, taking turns running to the boardwalk for snacks and drinks for the kids. Marsha's skin turned a deep gold, but the exposed parts of Ginny only burned pink. Peyton contentedly dug holes and gathered shells and built castle after castle, only to pillage and plunder them with his tiny bare feet afterward. Lucy was more cautious and seemed tired, so she curled up next to Ginny on the beach towel and fell asleep. She slept on her back, legs splayed open like a frog ready for dissection; her joints seemed loose, her legs hyperflexible. Perhaps this was why she wasn't walking yet; her muscles were simply too slack to hold her up.

Ginny knew she needed to call Ab, to let him know that she was okay but that she was also serious about this. She had to believe that if he could just meet Lucy, just hold this sweet child in his arms as he held Peyton, that he would love her. That he would feel the same swell of emotions she had. That he would see how wrong his father had been and figure out a way to make everything right with the people at Willowridge. But even as she tried to imagine the conversation they would have, she could anticipate his arguments, how calculated he could be when he was trying to prove his point. Or, in this case, she suspected, his *father's* point.

She hated that he was so spineless against Abbott. That he hadn't ever really wanted to be a lawyer, that he hadn't wanted this life, and yet here he was, here *they* were, living it. She also knew that she was never going to bring Lucy back to Willowridge, that unless someone came and tore her out of her arms, she would never let go of her again.

"How about we take you on that Ferris wheel?" Marsha said to Peyton, gesturing to the pier where a tall Ferris wheel spun.

"Yes, yes, yes!" he said, jumping up and down, sand flying everywhere.

They packed up their things and walked along the boardwalk until they got to the entrance to the pier.

Ginny had never liked heights, and so initially she declined when Marsha asked if she should buy her a ticket, but then she felt a surge of bravery overwhelm her. She was different now, in some fundamental way she couldn't describe, and so, just as Marsha was turning away from the ticket booth, she said, "Actually? Can you get a ticket for me, too?"

All four of them fit into one of the ride's buckets. She held Lucy tightly on her lap, and Peyton sat next to Marsha. Ginny felt her heart flutter like something winged in her chest as the vessel rocked back and forth and the ride operator pulled the lever, which made them start to slowly rise.

As they lifted off the ground, a hush fell over them all as the world below them slipped away.

When Lucy pointed at the sky, at first Ginny figured she was gesturing to the beautiful lights flickering below, but then realized it wasn't the earth she was concerned with, but the moon, just shy of full. Waning, she figured, since last night it had been bright as the sun through the crack in the motel drapes.

"That's the moon, Lucy," she said, her throat feeling thick with the recollection of the night she was born. That blood moon and the nurse's cruel accusations.

Lucy's face was aglow with delight. *My God,* Ginny thought, *has she never seen the moon before now?*

"Moon," Ginny said again and pointed.

"Moon?" Lucy said.

Lucy. *Said.*

Ginny caught her breath.

Marsha, who had been peering over the edge with Peyton, turned around. Ginny's heart pounded in her throat.

"Did she just say 'moon'?" Marsha asked.

"Moon!" Lucy said again, her voice like the wind chimes on Marsha's back porch. Sweet and high, like tinkling glass. Breakable.

"Yes!" Ginny said, holding her tighter and peering at the moon through tear-filled eyes. "That is the moon."

They made their way back to the motel room, and Ginny got Lucy's hair slathered with mayonnaise and covered with a plastic shower cap. She was pretty sure she'd pulled every living critter from her scalp earlier, but this would ensure the demise of any she'd missed. The kids were exhausted from the beach; even Peyton, who, after excitement like this, usually fought sleep like a mortal enemy, was snoring within minutes of his head hitting the pillow.

"I should call my mother," Ginny said.

Marsha nodded. "And I could use a drink. There's a liquor store right around the corner. What's your poison?"

Ginny shrugged. Ab drank whiskey, neat, and would take any brand you had to offer. Abbott Senior's drink of choice was Maker's Mark, one ice cube. She thought of the way he swirled the viscous liquid around in his glass before drinking it. *See this?* he'd said to her once. *These drips here, after you give it a spin? They're called legs. The older the whiskey, the heavier and slower moving the legs are. Just like a woman,* he'd added and winked at her.

"Vodka? Or maybe gin?" Marsha prodded.

"You choose," she said. "Just no whiskey."

"You got it!" Marsha said and slipped on her sandals and opened the door.

"Shit," Marsha said, standing under the buzzing light over the doorway, hands on her hips, staring at the car. "SHIT!"

"What?" Ginny asked, walking to the door to join her.

"How did I not notice this?"

"What?" Ginny asked again.

"Look!" she said, pointing to the front of the car. "Somebody stole my goddamned plate."

"Your plate?"

"My license plate," Marsha said as they circled around to the back of the car. "Both of them."

Sure enough, both the front and rear license plates were completely gone.

"What do we do?" Ginny asked.

"I don't know," she said. "It must have happened when we were at the beach."

"Is there somebody we can call? We probably shouldn't drive back to Amherst without license plates."

Marsha ran her hands through her hair and sighed heavily. "How are we supposed to get Massachusetts plates in New Jersey?"

"I don't know," Ginny said. "But this can't be the first time this has happened."

"You're right. I'll get the DMV's number and we'll call in the morning." Marsha brightened.

"Oh, crap," Ginny said, feeling her heart sink.

"What now?" Marsha said, almost laughing.

"It's Labor Day tomorrow. The DMV won't be open."

"Goddamn!" Marsha said. "Well, fuck it in a bucket. Let's get sauced then."

Ginny borrowed Marsha's blue bottle of Noxzema to lather on her sunburned arms and face. She turned the TV on low. It was Jerry Lewis's telethon weekend. Barbra Streisand was singing. When she was finished, Jerry brought out a child in a wheelchair and beamed as he told his story and pleaded with the audience to contribute.

Of course, Ginny had watched the telethon before. It was an annual event. But she had never thought before about the families he was helping. It also made her angry, once again, at Ab. Raising children who were "damaged" somehow was not *impossible*. Not shameful. Jerry Lewis had raised eight million dollars so far to help the families of these children who were suffering from this debilitating disease. She wondered how many of the children at Willowridge were also afflicted with muscular dystrophy. How many of those parents, like Ab, gave up on them?

She picked up the motel phone and dialed the operator, asked to make a collect call to her mother, who accepted the charges.

"Hi, Mama," she said. "I just wanted to let you know we're in Atlantic City for the weekend. Everything's going fine, but we ran into just a little trouble. No big deal, but I think we may need to call the school and get them to extend the visit with Lucy."

"What kind of trouble?"

"Oh, just some car trouble," she said. "Listen, I'm just checking in. I know this is expensive. Did Ab and his father show up yesterday? Did you send them back home?"

"Honey?" her mother said.

"What, Mama?" Ginny said, feeling her heart start to race.

Her mother was quiet on the other end of the line. "How is she? Your baby girl?"

The fist in Ginny's chest opened, and she felt tears welling up in her eyes. "She's perfect, Mama. She's just perfect."

"Virginia," her mother said, and Ginny held her breath. She never called her by her given name. "You need to get her back to the school tomorrow. There can't be any delay."

"I'll call Willowridge, Mama. If Ab won't. I'll take care of it."

She heard her mother draw a deep breath.

"You okay, Mama?"

"Did you sign any papers?" she asked. "At the hospital?"

"At Willowridge? Just a logbook. I checked her out, just like I was supposed to." She wondered if the receptionist had gotten in trouble maybe for her not showing proper ID. That woman, Penny, had been so helpful and understanding. She hoped she hadn't caused her any problems.

"No, honey," her mother said. "At the hospital when she was born."

That night was still such a blur. The blood moon, the cruel nurse, the baby whisked away before Ginny even came out of her ether fog.

"I didn't sign anything," she said.

"Well, Ab did."

"I've got booze!" Marsha hollered outside the door.

"What kind of papers, Mama?" Ginny asked and unlocked the door to let Marsha in. Marsha shrugged and mouthed an apology when she saw that Ginny was on the phone.

"He signed Lucy over," her mother said. "To the state. He said it was the only way they would take her."

Her words felt like a fist to Ginny's chest that knocked the wind out of her. She couldn't speak. She sat down at the foot of the bed.

Marsha raised an eyebrow in concern. Ginny shook her head, and her brain seemed to clang inside her skull like a loose marble.

"He gave up your rights to her. Your parental rights. When she was committed."

"*Committed?*" He'd said she was going to be *enrolled*. Enrolled in a special school.

"You don't have custody of her, Ginny," her mother said. "And if you don't get her back to the school by tomorrow, they can arrest you for kidnapping."

Sixteen

ৼ

The kids were both asleep, but Ginny was afraid they might wake them up, so she and Marsha huddled in the Pepto Bismol–pink bathroom, where Marsha poured the gin in the motel's plastic cups. She'd also bought some tonic water, a plastic squeeze bottle of lime juice, and a bag of ice, which she dumped into the plugged sink. Ginny sat on the closed lid of the toilet seat, head in hands.

"Bottoms up," Marsha said, handing Ginny the makeshift cocktail.

Ginny felt tipsy after only a single drink, but she allowed Marsha to pour a second for her.

"What are you going to do?" Marsha asked softly after Ginny explained the conversation with her mother.

"I don't know," Ginny said. "Ab told my mother they won't discharge her. She doesn't even belong to us anymore. We gave her up."

"She's your daughter," Marsha said. "You never consented; if you'd been *conscious,* you never would have agreed to this. *You* didn't give her up; Ab did."

Ginny sucked in a deep breath as if she were about to go underwater.

"But if I don't bring her back tomorrow, I could . . ." she started. "Ab told Mama I could be *arrested.*"

Marsha turned to her. "And if you *do* bring her back?"

Ginny shook her head. The idea of returning her to that place now was inconceivable. "I can't."

"Then don't," Marsha said, not bothering with tonic water this time. Instead, she just threw back a hefty shot of gin, grimaced, and shook her head.

Ginny followed her lead and relished the heat in her chest. It seemed to embolden her. Empower her. She felt suddenly invincible. Rage at the injustice of everything turning into kindle for a new sort of fire.

"I'll call my sister," Marsha said. "Theresa."

"In Florida?" Ginny asked. "Why?"

Marsha paced back and forth across the small space, thinking aloud.

"We'll drive to Weeki Wachee, stay with Theresa. In case they send someone after you."

Ginny shook her head. This was ridiculous. All of it.

"What about your job?" Ginny asked. "Don't you have to work tomorrow night?"

"Somebody's always breathing down my neck, hoping for overtime. I can get somebody to cover my shifts this week."

Despite the booze, Ginny felt remarkably sober, her head clearer than it had been since they first got to Willowridge, if that was possible.

"But then what?" Ginny asked. "After we get to Florida?"

"Then Ab knows you are serious. That you didn't fucking sign up for this shit, and either he'll do what's right and get her out of that school or . . ."

"Or?"

"Or . . ." Marsha said and trailed off. "Let's not think about 'or.' Let's think about sunshine and oranges and Disney World. Did you know that Disney World is opening in the beginning of October? We'll take the kids. Peyton would love it! To see Mickey Mouse in person?"

"*October?*" Ginny snorted, and the gin burned in her nostrils. "He's supposed to start school on *Tuesday*." The momentary fantasy slipped away, replaced by the reality of Catholic school: of bake sales and homework and bullies like Christopher.

"It's first grade," Marsha said. "What's he going to miss if he doesn't start right away? Coloring? Some cutting and pasting?"

"Marsh," she said and sighed. She set the plastic cup on the counter. She did not need another ounce of booze.

"I need to think about Lucy. I still don't know what her health status actually is." This, of all things, scared her the most. While there had been nothing in Lucy's file, the fear of some lurking heart defect troubled her. She knew so little about this disability. About what, besides the mental and developmental delays, Lucy might suffer from. Once, not long after Lucy was taken away, she'd gone to the library and asked for a book on Down syndrome. But she'd read exactly three pages before her eyes filled with tears and she felt faint. She'd left the book on the table where she'd been sitting and cried all the way home.

"I'm a *nurse*," Marsha said. "And believe it or not, I can do more than change bedpans and use a thermometer. I'll keep a close eye. She'll be fine."

Ginny nodded, the alcohol now making her feel sleepy. The fatigue of the day, of Willowridge, of everything consuming her. "I think I need to lie down."

"We'll leave early tomorrow," Marsha said somberly. "My aunt Pepper lives in Virginia. We can go there first."

"But what about the missing plates?" Ginny asked. "We'll get pulled over the second we get on the road. Maybe we should stay here until Tuesday, when the DMV opens, so we can get temporary plates at least?"

"Plenty of time for Ab to figure out where we've gone. I have a better idea. Give me that?" Marsha said, gesturing toward the bottle of gin. She poured a couple of fingers into her empty cup and threw it back. "Can you hold down the fort for a few minutes?"

"Where are you going?" Ginny asked, suddenly awake again. Drunk, but buzzing and alert.

"I'll be right back," she said.

"It's not really safe out there," Ginny said, thinking of the hookers, of whatever other illicit things might be happening under that brilliant moon.

"It's fine. I'm fine. Plus, I've got *this*!" she said, grabbing a metal emery board from the counter, holding up the daggerlike nail file. "I'll be back in ten minutes." With that, she slipped out the door.

Ginny, spent from the sun and the gin, had little energy to protest. She felt woozy when she stood up, and realized she'd probably had far too much to drink. She stumbled and bumped across the room and peered out through the space between the drawn curtains. The moon was still there, illuminating the parking lot. No sign of Marsha anywhere.

She sat down on the bed and watched Jerry Lewis for a few more minutes, and then she lay down next to Lucy in the kids' bed. Lucy's hair was still wrapped up inside the plastic shower cap, and she smelled like a turkey sandwich. She stroked Lucy's back and despite her best efforts to stay awake, she found herself dozing off just before a loud banging startled her awake.

Her first thought was that it was Ab. That he'd found her. Her heart sank again. *The police. Dear God, Willowridge must have called the police already.* But how had they figured out where she and Marsha were?

Feeling like she might be sick, she crept to the door and peered out the peephole. Marsha was standing in a pool of light, a halo of yellow surrounding her, like an odd sort of angel. She banged again, and Ginny quickly unlocked the dead bolt. Marsha rushed into the room and slammed the door shut behind her, breathless. She leaned her back against the door, and a slow grin spread across her face as she held up a Virginia license plate.

"What is that?" Ginny asked stupidly.

"What does it look like?" Marsha said, tossing it onto the bed and pressing her hand to her chest.

"Are you okay?" Ginny asked, motioning for Marsha to sit down. Marsha plopped down and flopped backward on the empty bed. Then she laughed and sat up.

"What did you do?" Ginny asked.

"When I went out earlier, I noticed a Dodge Dart just like mine parked out in front of another one of the rooms. Same exact color, even, but with Virginia plates."

"Oh, my God, Marsha!"

"I figured it probably belonged to the people staying in the room in front of where it was parked, so I went to see if the room was dark, and it was. I used the nail file and helped myself to the rear plate. I was going to try to get the front one, too, but a light came on in the room, and I freaked out. But now at least we'll have a plate on the rear of the car. Most cops won't pull you over as long as you have rear plates."

"But it's not a Massachusetts plate."

"No, but it was on a blue Dodge Dart, so if we do get pulled over and they call in the plate number, the car will come back as a match."

"But you have a Massachusetts driver's license!" Ginny said.

"Because I just bought the car from my sister in Virginia, Officer," Marsha said, batting her eyelashes. "God, Ginny. I just crept around like a fucking cat burglar and stole somebody's license plate. You could at least be grateful."

Ginny felt queasy. Her lip quivered. She could count the arguments she and Marsha had had over the years on one hand.

"Unless you have a better idea, I think maybe we should just try not to worry. I promise I'll drive like your grandmother so we don't get pulled over to begin with, and if we do, we'll figure it out then." Marsha looked suddenly exasperated, frustrated with Ginny.

"I'm sorry, Marsh," Ginny said. "Thank you."

Marsha's mouth twitched, but she nodded. "No problem. But we really should get out of here early tomorrow. Before those folks wake up and realize that they've only got one license plate."

When the buzzing alarm clock went off at 4:30 A.M., just three hours later, Ginny felt like a small animal had curled up inside her mouth and died. Her head was almost too heavy to lift from the hard motel pillow, and her stomach turned.

Marsha bolted out of bed and flicked on the small lamp on the nightstand, the bright light making Ginny's temples pound. No wonder she never drank.

She thought she would just roll over and go back to sleep. The conversation from the night before, the plans to flee, felt almost like a slippery dream in her memory.

She felt Marsha's hand on her shoulder. "Hey, sleepyhead. Let's rock and roll."

Ginny opened her eyes, the pounding above her brow now nearly audible. She rolled over and saw Lucy next to her, her eyelashes brushing her soft cheeks, and the nausea became a wave of love, and she knew that Ab had left her with no choice. This was not a decision. This was nothing but a mother bear's efforts to protect her young. That urge she felt, that deep protective rumble, was undeniable.

Silently, they dressed and packed up their belongings. Marsha loaded the car in the dark and affixed the new plate to the rear of the car, and then they each carried one of the sleeping children, settling them into the backseat. Peyton woke briefly, mumbling a little before settling back into his dreams. The shower cap on Lucy's head had come off, and her curls, greasy with mayo, were matted around her face.

"Maybe I should rinse her hair first?" she said to Marsha.

"You should let her sleep. And besides, the sun will be up in just a little bit," Marsha said nervously. "Can we do it on the road? Or maybe once we stop tonight?"

Marsha was right. It could take them an hour to leave if she had to wake Lucy up and coax her out of the car and into the tub. Ginny would just need to give her a nice long bath when they got settled again tonight.

"Ready, Freddy?" Marsha asked. Ginny looked back at the empty room they were leaving behind. At least in there they had been safe. The idea of heading out on the road with a stolen license plate and a stolen child filled her with fear, but she nodded. "Yep," she said. "Let's go."

Seventeen

૨

September 1971

The highway was blessedly free of cars this early in the morning (or late at night, depending on how you saw it): this exquisite limbo between midnight and dawn in which the rest of the world slept. Ginny's headache dissipated with the fog that had settled over the highway, and after about an hour her shoulders began to relax, the muscled knots in her back to untangle.

They planned to stay just outside Roanoke that night with Marsha's aunt Pepper, her mother's sister. Marsha assured Ginny that they would be safe there. That her aunt had no idea that they were on the run. The very idea of this made Ginny almost laugh. Two days ago, she'd been a housewife, and now she was a fugitive? It all was so ridiculous, absurd.

Pepper apparently had a big farmhouse with plenty of rooms, and when Marsha called her from a pay phone along the Jersey Turnpike, she said she was happy to host her favorite niece for the night.

Ginny had heard Marsha talk about her aunt Pepper before, but she'd never met her.

"She's a lesbian," Marsha said. "Just so you know."

"Oh," Ginny said.

"I mean, in case you were wondering."

"Okay," Ginny said.

Ginny didn't know any lesbians. At least she didn't think she did. There was one girl from their high school class that students had whispered about. She refused to wear skirts and kept her hair short. She was on the track and field team and could throw the javelin farther than any of the boys. But Ginny wasn't athletic and didn't have any classes with her, so she'd never even spoken to her. That probably didn't count.

"Does she have a girlfriend?" Ginny asked. Was that what a lesbian's lover was called?

"Yes," Marsha said, checking her reflection in the mirror. "Her name's Nancy. They live together."

Ginny tried to imagine what it would be like being in love with a girl instead of with Ab. What a day would look like in a household run by two women. Would one of them play the part of the man: going off to work, coming home after a couple of drinks at the bar, expecting dinner on the table? Or would they both putter around the house all day? Housework would certainly get done faster if there were two women running things. And child care. Already, she'd noted how much more of a help Marsha was than Ab had ever been with the kids, and Marsha didn't even have children of her own. It seemed to Ginny that women just seemed to have a natural affinity for that: for knowing when to coddle, to discipline, to soothe. Marsha also seemed to intuit exactly when Ginny needed her to step in, particularly with Peyton, whom Ab just seemed to get more riled up. She had felt many times that she was raising *two* boys, the way they both misbehaved. Sometimes, he even seemed more playmate to Peyton than father, than husband, even. Yes, certainly, raising children would be easier with another woman.

But when she tried to imagine what happened after the lights went off each night, her mind drew a blank and her cheeks flushed. She tried to think about how two similar bodies might find happiness together, but the logistics of it felt confusing and a little shameful.

She was so self-conscious about her body, especially after her pregnancies, the embarrassment keeping her from enjoying sex the way she had early on. No matter how many times Ab told her he loved her curves, the extra weight she'd put on made her feel as if she'd somehow failed. She insisted on having the lights out and refused to remove her bra, afraid for him to see her now heavy breasts that were at the mercy of gravity. He was earnest in his lovemaking, but it was, honestly, something she endured rather than enjoyed lately, silently reflecting on those extra pounds rather than on any pleasure she might be experiencing.

She knew there were women out there who loved sex, who felt comfortable in their own skin. Marsha talked about sex the way Ginny talked about food. With desire and longing. Marsha seemed to assess men the way men studied women: their bodies something to be admired or scorned.

"Did you see that ass?" Marsha would say in disbelief at some poor sucker's backside before he was even out of earshot. "I bet he's got a small dick. The ones with big necks always have small dicks."

Boys had been drawn to Marsha ever since sixth grade. And Marsha loved the attention. Reveled in it. Ginny knew Marsha had had at least a half dozen lovers. She'd been called "easy" in high school, though having a reputation never seemed to bother her. "Why eat only vanilla ice cream if you had a choice of all the flavors?" she said. Ginny's mom called her "wild." But as far as Ginny was concerned, Marsha was just a girl who didn't care what anybody thought, a girl who did what she wanted. Did that make her wild? If so, then what was Ginny? *Domesticated*, she supposed. Tame.

Later, after high school and nursing school, the hospital proved to be a virtual playground for Marsha, filled with so many handsome doctors.

Of course, some of them were married, and she drew the line there. But most of the interns and residents were single, having stayed bachelors during the grueling years of medical school. She'd dated at least three residents before she met her current flavor of the month.

"Are you going to call Gabe?" Ginny asked. "Is he going to be upset about you leaving?"

"I am not about to start making life decisions just because a man's good in the sack," Marsha said dismissively.

Marsha had rolled her eyes as she relayed poor Gabe's puppy-eyed pleading, but Ginny also sensed that Marsha might have a little snag in her heart as well, saw her touch the simple gold necklace with a tiny gold heart charm she knew he'd given her for her birthday.

The sun came up just as they were skirting around Washington, D.C.

"The Kennedy Center is opening in D.C. this week," Marsha said. "I heard Jackie O. is skipping out, though."

There'd been a whole lot of clamoring on the news about why she'd chosen to skip the event. But Ginny understood. How very strange to be a woman aligned with such a powerful and beloved man. Now that he was gone, who was she in the world but a ghostly reminder of his absence? That poor ethereal woman carrying the burden of an entire country's grief. Ginny would have stayed home and read a book in her pajamas instead as well.

Marsha did not seem daunted by the city traffic, though it put Ginny on edge. Several times she had to force herself to stop gripping the dashboard as Marsha zipped in and out of traffic. She caught herself a half dozen times glancing in the side-view mirror, hoping there weren't any highway patrolmen behind them.

When the traffic finally thinned and they barreled into Virginia, she started to relax. The kids had woken up by then and Peyton was complaining that he was hungry. If Ginny had been thinking, she would have had Marsha pick up some snacks while she was at the liquor store the night before, but as it was, the only thing resembling food was a mushy apple in the bottom of her purse. Hardly an adequate breakfast.

"We'll stop soon, little man," Marsha said, peering in the rearview mirror at Peyton. "You look like you might need some pancakes?"

"Pan-a-cakes!" Peyton squealed and clapped his hands. Lucy studied him with the same quiet curiosity that she seemed to have about everything. She was a thinker, Ginny thought. An observer of the world.

About a half hour later, the sun crested the Blue Ridge Mountains all around them, and they found a roadside diner, with a sign on the attached gift shop that advertised THE PEANUT CAPITAL OF THE WORLD.

"You hungry?" Marsha asked Ginny.

Ginny was ravenous. The alcohol seemed to have worked its way out of her system, leaving a hole behind. Her stomach growled.

"You?" she asked Marsha. Marsha was always on some sort of diet or another, though she never talked about it with Ginny, who had struggled with her weight since the third grade, when, for some inexplicable reason, her teacher had weighed each child in the class, announcing their weights to the entire class. *Fifty pounds! Sixty-two!* And then a horrified yet oddly triumphant *ninety-six!* as Ginny stood, mortified, on the scale.

Marsha was a fruit cup, cottage cheese, dry toast kind of girl. And it showed in her flat stomach and shapely legs. Ginny admired her self-control; most of her own diets lasted no more than a day or two.

"I'm actually feeling kind of queasy still," Marsha said. "Gin gets me every time. But I could use some coffee."

They got the kids out of the car and made their way into the diner. It appeared to be a locals-only sort of place, and all heads turned as they walked in.

The waitress behind the counter hollered, "Sit anywhere y'all like!" as if they couldn't read the chalkboard sign saying the same thing.

The tables were covered with red-and-white gingham oilcloth, and the seats were upholstered in matching red vinyl. A low-hanging ceiling fan spun the smoky, oppressive air. There was the distinct smell of peanuts throughout.

"Oh, God, that smell is making me nauseous," Marsha said. "I'm gonna run to the little girls' room. Can you just order me a black coffee?"

"Sure," Ginny said.

The sleigh bells hanging on the diner door jingled, and a tall bearded man walked in. He smiled at her and the children and took a seat at the counter.

Peyton was busy stacking creamer packets into a teetering tower, but Lucy was a bit wriggly, uncomfortable. Ginny wondered if her stomach was still troubled. Thankfully, she hadn't seen any more hitchhikers in her last diaper.

Ginny picked Lucy up and put her on her lap, thinking to distract her with the paper place mat that had a map of Virginia to color on it. But there were no crayons and Lucy was starting, for the first time, to really fuss. Maybe her bottom was still bothering her. At least the lice were gone, though her hair was still greasy with mayonnaise. God, what a mess they must all look.

"What's the matter, sweetie?" she said as Lucy thrashed about a bit.

Lucy hadn't said a word since she said "moon" in Atlantic City. If she could talk, at least then she could tell Ginny what was bothering her.

Lucy stiffened and clenched her fists, making a horrible low sound in her throat, almost like Arthur made when the mailman came up the walk each day, and Ginny glanced around the room, smiling uncomfortably, as Lucy was starting to draw the attention of the other patrons. She willed Marsha to come back from the bathroom.

The waitress came over, and Ginny expected to be scolded for the unfolding chaos, but she only pulled out her notepad and said, "What can I get y'all?"

"I'm sorry, I haven't had a chance to look at the menu yet," Ginny said, reaching with one hand for the laminated menu in the center of the table while trying to keep Lucy from squirming off her lap. "Sorry," she offered as Lucy threw her head back and the growl became a howl.

The waitress reached into her pocket and pulled out a cellophane-wrapped sucker, broken at one edge, crushed into orange dust. She squatted down so she was eye level with Lucy and held it out to her.

Lucy stopped fussing for a minute but only looked at the lollipop. She, of course, had probably never seen one before.

The waitress stood up and put the candy back in her pocket, shaking her head. She leaned over to Ginny and said sympathetically, "I got a cousin that's retarded. At least your girl's pretty. I didn't even know nothing was wrong till I got up close. But she needs a good shampooin'. You know, a little dab of that VO5 will go a long way."

Ginny, stunned, gripped Lucy tighter.

"I'll just have two scrambled eggs and toast, please. Two black coffees. The children will each have a pancake and a glass of orange juice. In paper cups, please. With lids and straws if you have them."

"Okay, doll," the waitress said and turned on her heel.

As the waitress walked away, Lucy wriggled out of Ginny's arms and slipped down underneath the table. Ginny checked to make sure Peyton was still occupied. He was still stacking the creamer packets, a tower of Coffee-mate. She bent down and located Lucy sitting on the floor beneath the table, knees to her chest.

"Lucy, honey," she cooed. "Come on up, sweetheart. I just ordered you a pancake. It's going to be so yummy. I promise." Ginny hesitantly reached her hands out, beckoning her gently. Lucy shook her head and tears rolled down her flushed cheeks. She looked scared.

"What's the matter, sweetheart?" she asked. Lucy had, so far, been perfectly trusting. Not afraid at all, and especially not afraid of her.

She sat up to look around the restaurant at what Lucy could possibly be hiding from. The place was filled with people: mostly older couples, a few families with small children. There was a jukebox in one corner playing "I Think I Love You," that Partridge Family song. Nothing scary.

The waitress brought the coffee and said, "I'll be just a minute with y'all's orders."

"Lucy, *please*," she said, starting to wonder how on earth she ever thought she'd be able to do this alone. If Ab were here, he'd at least be able to distract Peyton, to keep him occupied with a knock-knock joke or riddle while she dealt with Lucy. But Ab was not here, and, for whatever reason, Marsha was still in the bathroom. Peyton was swinging his legs under the table, impatiently kicking, kicking. She worried he might wind up kicking Lucy if he wasn't careful. Just then the towering stack of creamers toppled over, half of them tumbling to the floor, under the table, where Lucy remained. Resolute.

"*Peyton*," she said, and, bending down again, she said firmly, "Lucy. I need you to come up. Your breakfast will be here in a minute." She didn't want to lose her patience. The poor thing was clearly already distressed, the last thing she needed was for Lucy be afraid of her. But her patience had been whittled away to a sliver.

The couple at the next table over from their booth were leaning into each other and whispering. The old woman tsk-tsked and shook her head as Ginny tried to pick up the creamers and restore them to their stainless receptacle. She'd deal with the ones on the floor after she got Lucy to come up.

Marsha came back just as Ginny was starting to feel her throat close, choking on her frustration.

"Where's Lucy?" Marsha asked, her eyes widening.

"Under the table," Ginny said, feeling desperate now. "Please, baby," she said again to the shadow under the table, reaching for her with open arms. This time, for some reason, she complied. But once she was back in Ginny's lap she burrowed her head into Ginny's chest. Even when the waitress set down their food, with a pancake that looked just like Mickey Mouse, Lucy refused to unfurl.

"Is she okay?" Marsha asked, reaching across the table and touching Lucy's back gently.

Ginny shook her head. "Something in here is scaring her. But I don't know what it is. Do *you* feel better?" she asked Marsha.

Marsha rolled her eyes a little. "Remind me to never, ever drink again, will you?" she said and took a sip of the steaming coffee.

"I think Peyton needs some whipped cream for his pancakes," Marsha said, and Peyton, who had been scowling, brightened. She beckoned the waitress over. "Ma'am, do you have some Cool Whip?"

Ginny tried to eat her breakfast, but it was difficult with Lucy on her lap, so she asked the waitress to put it in a Styrofoam container for her. She figured she could eat later, once they were on the road again.

Marsha paid the check, and Ginny hoisted Lucy up onto her hip. She could feel her diaper was heavy, but she didn't want to risk taking her to the bathroom here. She just wanted to get her into the car again.

They made their way to the front door, and as they did, Lucy's body stiffened and she dug her sharp little nails into Ginny's neck. That low growl rumbled in Lucy's throat.

The man who had come into the restaurant earlier was still sitting at the counter. Now that she was closer, she could see he was maybe thirty years old, with a dark beard and a slightly lazy eye. As they passed he looked up at them, and Lucy clung onto her for dear life, growling audibly now.

Was she afraid of this man? They'd never even seen him before.

As she rushed her out the doors, Lucy's body slowly, slowly relaxing the farther away they got from the diner, Ginny felt overwhelmed, again, by all that she didn't know about what had happened to this poor child in the last two years. There were ghosts haunting her, ghosts that might *always* haunt her. And it was her fault. Ab's fault.

Marsha got Peyton into the backseat, but Lucy wouldn't let go of Ginny's neck, so Ginny put the food on the dash and settled into the front seat with Lucy still clinging to her.

Marsha rolled down the windows and turned the key. Soon enough the smell of peanuts faded into the distance, and Lucy, finally, finally let go.

Eighteen

❧

September 1971

Marsha's aunt Pepper lived on a farm in the Blue Ridge Mountains, ten miles from civilization in a house she built herself. Pepper worked from home as a tax preparer, and Nancy was a teacher in the local elementary school. They'd lived together for nearly twenty years, though as far as anyone knew (locally, anyway), they were simply "roommates." Nancy would have lost her job if the school administrators caught wind of the truth.

As they pulled up the long gravel drive to their small cabin, Ginny sucked in her breath. The view at sunset was stunning, the mountains in the distance like rolling waves of blue.

The children, groggy in the backseat, woke and silently wondered at the view, like a painting, framed by their windshield. As they pulled to a stop, a woman emerged from the front door of the house, followed by two loping, gray hound dogs.

"Welcome to Paradise!" Pepper said, throwing her arms up and ges-

turing grandly as she barreled toward the car. She was dressed in dun-
garees and a plaid flannel shirt. An Amazonian version of Marsha, she
was at least six feet tall, with broad shoulders and long legs, short black
curls, and a wide smile. Marsha had said she was sixty years old, but she
looked youthful still. Marsha threw the car door open and ran into her
arms.

Ginny tentatively opened the passenger door as Peyton leapt out the
back. Her legs were cramped from the drive, and her spine ached. She
was also hungry. They hadn't stopped since breakfast except for gas, and
all she'd had to eat was a bag of Fritos and part of a little tin can of Hunt's
butterscotch pudding that Peyton couldn't finish.

One dog went straight for her crotch as she moved to the rear door to
get Lucy out. As soon as she opened the back door, the dog leapt into the
backseat. Lucy let out a sharp squeal, and Ginny's heart sank. *God, please
don't let her have another meltdown.* The dog was walking back and forth
across the backseat, slobbering on Lucy, who batted her eyes as if she
couldn't believe what she was seeing. Ginny realized she'd likely never
seen a dog before. She tried to imagine what must have been going
through her mind; so much of the world was completely unknown to her.
A strange and terrifying place. However, it wasn't terror that registered
in Lucy's eyes right now, but rather delight. Lucy reached out at the dog's
wagging tail when it batted back and forth across her face. She blinked and
giggled. Ginny thought of Arthur at home, how gentle and sweet he had
always been with Peyton. She wondered if she brought Lucy home what
she would think of such an enormous (though gentle) beast.

"That's a dog," Ginny explained. *"Dog."*

"That is a *bad* dog," Pepper said. "Come on, June, get yer ass out of that
car right now."

Sheepishly, June tumbled out of the car, leaving Lucy covered in dog
drool and fur.

Pepper squatted to the dog's level and grabbed either side of her jowly
face, frowning. "What am I gonna do with ya?"

The dog looked back at her as if to say, "I haven't got a clue, but whatever it is, I deserve it," her tail firmly between her legs.

"Go on with Johnny," Pepper said. "Git!" The dog bounded off back toward the house, where the other, nearly identical hound dog remained waiting patiently.

"I'm Pepper," the woman said, thrusting her hand into the air between them.

"Ginny," she said. "Thank you so much for having us. I hope it's not too much trouble."

Pepper waved her hand as if swatting a fly. "Hush. Marsha is like my own little girl. Any friend of hers is a friend of mine."

"Where's Nancy?" Marsha asked as she popped the trunk open and started pulling out their bags.

"She's in the kitchen making up some of her famous venison and leather britches. Blackberry dumplings for dessert. You ever had Appalachian cookin'?" Pepper asked Ginny. Ginny shook her head. "Well, yer in for a real treat then. I hope you brought your appetite."

Inside, they met Nancy, a petite woman who seemed older than Pepper by a decade. She had two gray braids wound up into a sort of crown on the top of her head, and a plumpness that comforted Ginny.

The smells coming from the stove were delightful and strange.

"It sure is pretty here," Ginny said, peering out the kitchen window at all that undulating blue.

"Well, too bad you couldn't come a month from now," Pepper said. "It's the prettiest place on earth when the leaves turn."

Peyton stayed outside, occupied with both Johnny and June, throwing a big stick and then watching as the two dogs tumbled after each other for it. Lucy sat in a chair at the kitchen window facing the porch, clapping her hands. When June came up to the glass and slobbered a big wet kiss on the window, she blinked her eyes and laughed.

"Dog!" she said. Clear as the most beautiful bell.

Ginny felt a surge of happiness, and for the first time since they left, she felt a sort of peace descend upon her. They were safe. At least for now. In a warm kitchen with kind people. Family. Far from Willowridge, far from home.

But then, just as they sat down to eat, the tiny wooden door on the cuckoo clock swung open, the little bird popping out to announce the hour.

Five o'clock.

Five o'clock, the time Lucy was supposed to be returned to the school. Ginny was now officially breaking the law. Her body tensed again; she felt as tightly wound as that clock.

Marsha looked at Ginny, concerned. "You okay?"

Ginny nodded, despite the heavy feeling in her chest, the tingling in her hands as she gripped the fork.

Still, the meal was one of the most incredible spreads that Ginny had ever tasted. The blackberry dumplings were so rich and tart, she accepted a second serving with a dollop of sweet cream and a sprig of fresh mint plucked from the front yard, even though her belly was already straining against the waistband of her jeans.

Nancy had cooked the entire meal herself, so Pepper declined everyone's offer of help and excused herself to do the dishes. At home, Ginny did all the cooking *and* all the cleaning. She never once thought to solicit Ab's help; he'd certainly never offered. After dinner, it took her at least an hour to do the dishes and get the children cleaned up. Ab usually retired to the living room, returning to the kitchen only to make a drink or steal a kiss. How had she never seen the inequity in this before? This equal distribution of labor was so simple, so sensible.

When Pepper returned from the kitchen, Marsha opened up the road atlas on the table. "We're trying to figure out where we should stop next. We want to get to Weeki Wachee Springs by Wednesday or Thursday. I figure maybe two more days of driving? Got any recommendations between here and Florida?"

"Well, you said y'all need to stay off the beaten path, right?" Pepper asked, raising her eyebrow.

Marsha had told Ginny that she'd shared just the basic facts with her aunt and Nancy. They didn't know the details of their plight, of their flight, she assured her, but she obviously knew this wasn't just a fun girls' road trip.

Nancy chimed in, "If you aren't in too much of a hurry, you could go by way of Asheville. It's a little out of the way, but sure is pretty."

"Plus, nobody on your tail will expect you to go that way," Pepper added.

Maybe Marsha had told her more than she thought. She wondered about Ab. About Willowridge. She couldn't imagine that Ab would let the school call law enforcement; certainly, he would have spoken to the powers that be by now to ensure that there wasn't any trouble. But assuming the best of Ab was exactly how she'd wound up where she was now. She truly had no idea what he was capable of. The lengths to which Abbott Senior might convince him to go.

She needed to check in with her mother again. Though she was starting to think it was maybe for the best if her mother *didn't* know where she was; that way Shirley couldn't get in trouble for helping her. As of five o'clock, she was a fugitive, she supposed, in the eyes of the law. A kidnapper on the run. It was all so unthinkable.

"Or, you could swoop down to Savannah, maybe stay the night there; it's a straight shot from there to where y'all are headed. Get you there by Wednesday afternoon. You might keep an eye on the weather, though," she added. "Hurricane's coming up from the Caribbean, I believe. Edith, they're calling it. What kind of name is that? Sounds like some fuddy-duddy housewife. If I were the one doing the naming, I'd call it Esmeralda. Now *that's* a storm."

"A *hurricane*?" Ginny said. They didn't get hurricanes in Massachusetts.

"Yeah, I think y'all will be okay. They're sayin' it's gonna hit Mississippi and Louisiana mostly. Might get some rain down there, though," Nancy offered.

Pepper clapped her hands then and said, "How about some Yahtzee?"

❦

After the kids were bathed and put to bed in the guest room, Ginny, Marsha, and Pepper stayed up at the kitchen table rolling dice. Nancy went to bed early. She had to be at school the next morning by seven o'clock. She gave each of them a hug and kissed Pepper sweetly on the cheek before disappearing upstairs.

Pepper was a terrific storyteller and had a sense of humor to match her niece's. Ginny quietly listened to them share jabs and family anecdotes that Ginny, in all the years she'd known Marsha, had never heard.

Marsha started yawning at about nine o'clock. Early for her, but she must have been exhausted from the drive. Ginny wished she could offer to help. It seemed an unfair burden that Marsha had to do all the driving. They might be able to make it to Florida faster if Ginny were able to take the wheel and let Marsha get some sleep.

"I feel like I've been run over by a truck," Marsha said, yawning elaborately again. "I'm gonna head to bed. We should get on the road early."

Ginny nodded. "Yeah, me, too. Plus, I feel like I'm going to burst."

Pepper had gotten the leftover blackberry dumplings out and fixed them each another bowl.

"Thank you again for everything," Ginny said to Pepper as she helped clear the dessert dishes. "I really appreciate your letting us stay here."

Pepper squeezed Ginny's arm as Marsha disappeared up the stairs, as if she wanted her to stay behind a minute. She complied but had no idea what Pepper could want with her.

Once the door to the guest room upstairs clicked shut, Pepper whispered, "That boyfriend of hers, Gabe? He called earlier today."

"He did?" she said. "How did he know we were here?" She knew Marsha had called him once from Atlantic City to tell him she was gone for the weekend. But she hadn't made any calls since they'd been on the road from New Jersey.

"Her sister, Melanie, gave him my number," she said. "They're both concerned is all."

"About Marsha?" she said. Why anyone would be concerned about *Marsha* was beyond her.

Pepper glanced toward the stairwell and leaned across the table, lowering her voice to a hushed whisper. "How far along is she?"

"What?" Ginny asked.

"My niece. How many months along?"

Nineteen

❧

September 1971

Ginny couldn't sleep at all that night. Her mind spun like the lazy Susan she kept on the dining table at home, stopping to serve up something new at each turn.

A *baby*? Pepper was convinced that Marsha was pregnant. But that seemed preposterous. Wouldn't she have said something? Was it possible that Marsha herself didn't know? With both Peyton and Lucy, Ginny had known she was pregnant practically from the moment of conception. Though Marsha had never been pregnant before; perhaps it was possible that she was oblivious? Certainly, if Marsha were aware, she'd never have set out on the road like this. Left her job. Left Gabe, assuming he was the father. Did he know? And what did this mean for the future? How on earth would Marsha be able to both work and take care of a baby?

Spin.

She thought of Ab, of course. Of Willowridge. Of Lucy. Her thoughts lingered at this platterful of possible disasters. She debated for at least an hour about whether she should reach out to her mother again, finally settling on the decision to wait until they got to Florida. With her fickle heart, her mother didn't need the worry. She hoped that Abbott Senior knew better than to keep haranguing Shirley. The less her mother knew about Ginny's whereabouts, the better.

Spin.

She thought about the fact that in just a few hours, she should be rising from her bed in Dover and readying her son for his first day of school. They had purchased his school uniform earlier that summer. She'd washed and ironed the tiny little button-down shirt, the pleated slacks. She'd thought the tiny suit jacket with the school's crest emblazoned on the breast pocket was a bit overkill, but Ab had waxed nostalgic about his own first uniform. He looked exactly like a miniature Ab in his uniform, like a miniature lawyer headed to work. They'd bought him a new lunch pail, a domed tin box that looked like a red barn, the Thermos imprinted to look like a silo. He had a pencil box and a box of fat crayons. They'd even purchased a desk for his room, though she was pretty sure that first grade didn't require homework. There was a part of her that had felt so sad about him being old enough for first grade now. Not a baby anymore.

Spin.

And there she was, back at the first offering. Marsha was going to have a *baby*. Ginny's mind spun in furious circles, settling on nothing at all, as she tried to think about how she might broach the subject with her.

The room was warm, a little too warm, and each time she'd start to drift off to sleep, something would wake her: a sigh from Peyton or a snore from Marsha in the next bed. Or the rasp of Lucy's breath.

She tried to imagine what Ab was doing right now and couldn't. She had been gone less than a week, but that life, her life, felt as far away as the moon, a waning moon, slipping into a dark sky.

She glanced at the glowing clock on the nightstand. It was nearly 5 A.M., and she hadn't slept more than a scattered handful of minutes. It had been twelve hours since she was supposed to return Lucy to Willowridge. How long had the school waited before they called Ab? An hour, two? How long would they wait before they called the police? When he got the call, would Ab have put them off somehow or would he have been angry enough, vindictive enough, to allow them to go after her? What made her chest ache was that she knew it wasn't up to Ab at all. That it was her father-in-law who was likely calling the shots. He was the one, in the end, who would decide if she was a good mother or a criminal. She'd watched him steamroll over Ab for the last seven years. She'd seen Ab try and fail to assert himself against his father. She'd felt both shame and rage at the way Ab kowtowed to him, by the obsequious puddle he became in his father's presence.

Though she was expecting it, when the alarm went off, it rattled her to the core. Because she knew the only choice she had now was to run. To run and keep on running until she couldn't run anymore.

Twenty

❦

Summer 1964

Ginny had known she was pregnant with Peyton long before the doctor confirmed her suspicions. Her already large breasts were even more swollen and tender. She was exhausted, fighting sleep all day at the library (catnapping in a hidden carrel during her breaks), and battling nausea the rest of the time, feeling perpetually like she'd just stepped off a Tilt-A-Whirl ride. It was July, and Ab was oblivious. With so many changes in his life, the change in Ginny's bust size simply hadn't registered.

Abbott Senior had been so furious when Ab decided to forgo law school in favor of the IVS, he and Sylvia didn't even attend Ab's graduation from Amherst. They cut off all financial support as well, so he'd rented a room in nearby Northhampton and took a job working for a produce delivery company. But Ab, ever the optimist, told Ginny he loved the mindlessness of it.

"It gives me time to think! I haven't had time for my own thoughts the last four years," he said. "How ironic is that?"

He said he envied her quiet hours at the library, but that bouncing along the back roads, which connected the local farms to the larger towns, offered a similar quietude for rumination. He also loved interacting with the kitchen staffs at the local restaurants, pulling the truck into the back alleys before the sun came up. Carrying flats of berries or bins of leafy lettuce into the walk-in coolers while chatting with the cooks and bakers, sharing a cup of coffee or being offered a muffin fresh from the oven to sustain him for the next several hours as he made his way from Amherst to Holyoke to Springfield. He drove with the windows down and the music up.

But the best part of the job was that because he started before dawn, he was also finished just after lunch, and he had all afternoon to read or wander as he waited for Ginny to get out of work. He spent much of his free time exploring the woods behind his rooming house. He read voraciously, Ginny greeting him with stacks and stacks of books when he came to pick her up from the library each afternoon.

Most nights, they had dinner with her mother, though on the weekends (finances permitting), he took her out. They went to double features or out dancing. Afterward they'd drive around aimlessly looking for places that offered privacy for more amorous endeavors. He wasn't allowed visitors at his room, so their more intimate moments were relegated to the backseat of his car, in the dark shadows of the movie theater, or (weather permitting) some outdoor venue. Still, they managed, though more than once she had to pluck a twig from her hair, mistaking it for a misplaced bobby pin.

Whenever Ginny expressed guilt about their premarital rendezvous, he said, "We're engaged, Gin. Practically man and wife."

They had planned to move in together as soon as he returned from Vietnam, as soon as they were married, and so each week they both socked away nearly every penny they made. They lived on the leftovers her mother procured from the dining hall and the bruised fruits and wilted vegetables he brought home.

"Someday when we're old, we'll recall these as our Stone Soup years," he said as Ginny stirred a pot full of broth and potatoes she'd had to gore to salvage.

"I'm late," she said without fanfare and without looking up from that steaming, starchy broth. She'd been waiting for the right moment ever since she'd confirmed her suspicions with her doctor earlier that week. Now was as good a time as any, she figured.

"For what?"

She looked up, and her mouth twitched. "Actually, *I'm* not late, my *aunt* is late. For her visit."

"Bonnie?" Ab said. "Doesn't she live down the street?"

She rolled her eyes. "No, Ab. My *aunt Flo*. She usually comes every month?"

Really, for such a brilliant mind, he could be so very, very dense.

He jolted from his seat at the little table in her mother's kitchen, tipping over the weak cup of coffee he'd been drinking. He ran to her and scooped her up in his arms and planted several wet kisses on her cheeks. Her mother, who had been in the other room, watching *I Love Lucy*, came in, hand pressed to her chest, shaking her head. "Jeez Louise, I thought the house was on fire."

"No, ma'am," Ab said, releasing Ginny and turning to her mother, whom he embraced and lifted off her feet. She let out a small squeak, like a rubber toy in the grip of a Doberman's jaw. "How do you feel about being a grandmother?"

Ginny's mother pressed both of her hands against Ab's chest, pushing him back so she could study his face for signs of deception. There were none.

"A baby?" she said, still studying his face. She turned to Ginny, and Ginny shrugged.

Ginny would have been angry at his sharing the news before they'd had even a moment to discuss what it meant, but his wild enthusiasm as he danced her mother across the kitchen floor somehow made her frustration seem silly. Petty, even.

Plus. A *baby*. She'd known for nearly a week but until this moment hadn't allowed herself to ponder the actual implications of this fact. A baby. A living, breathing, kicking, screaming baby!

Her mother was so overwhelmed, she had to go lie down to stop her heart from leaping out of her chest.

"What about the IVS? Vietnam?" Ginny said when they were alone again. "The baby is due before you're scheduled to come home."

"I won't go," he said. "I'll stay."

"I think you should go," she said, shaking her head. "You'll be home right after the baby comes. Wives of soldiers do this sort of thing all the time."

"I'm not a soldier," he said.

"But you've been talking about this for months. You've sacrificed so much already. This isn't the plan."

Ab shrugged. "Sometimes plans change."

That night, after Ab heartily ate three helpings of her pathetic chowder (she couldn't even stomach the thought of a mouthful), and after her mother retired to her room and she sat down, more exhausted than she had ever been in her entire life, Ab sank to his knees at her feet and pressed her hand to her stomach.

"What will your parents say?" she said. "They don't even know we're engaged."

Ab took a deep breath. "I want them to know," he said finally, absently stroking her belly, which revealed no evidence of its new resident. "Because then they'll know this is serious. That this is forever. Maybe then . . ." he trailed off. But she didn't need his words to complete the sentence. Maybe then they'd welcome her into their family. But she knew they'd no sooner accept her than they'd accept the presence of a cancerous tumor. In their eyes, she was the reason Ab had jumped from the moving train that had been his destiny.

"They'll be glad I'm not going overseas," he said.

He was right, though she suspected they'd hardly be thrilled by this alternative.

Twenty-one

ℰ

Marsha gassed up at a station in Roanoke, and Ginny went into the little store and bought them each a sugary cider doughnut, and a cup of black coffee for Marsha. She asked the cashier to break a ten so that she could give Marsha some more money to help cover the expense of the gas.

Marsha kept insisting Ginny shouldn't worry about money, but she did. She had the dwindling roll of bills that Ab had given her the week before. Each Monday he gave her an allowance from which he expected her to run the household. Because she didn't drive, she walked to the market every couple of days and picked up the items she would need to make their meals. If she needed to make purchases for the home, she'd price the items out and then ask Ab for a little extra that week. Once a season, she took the train into the city and purchased clothes for herself and for Peyton or called in an order to the Spiegel catalog. Ab paid the bills, balanced the accounts, and told her not to worry. That all she needed to do was ask if she wanted or needed anything at all.

But now what was she to do? She could hardly call Ab and ask him for a little extra cash to help Marsha pay for gas as they fled down the East Coast. Ginny's name wasn't even on the bank accounts, as far as she knew. Ab had always been so generous with her; she hadn't thought twice about it before. She flipped through her wallet, quietly counting the bills, when she suddenly remembered the Master Charge card he'd given her, told her not to use it unless it was an absolute emergency. She'd tucked it in the back of her wallet and forgotten about it. Credit cards mystified her, scared her a little, even. The idea of essentially having a line of credit at your fingertips seemed dangerous. She wasn't even sure how much money was available to spend. She'd never used it. Perhaps it wasn't valid anymore? She wasn't even sure how it worked exactly.

Once they were on the road again, she handed Marsha the hot cup of coffee and said, "Is this crazy?"

"A little?" Marsha said, taking the cup and blowing across the steaming surface.

"We haven't even thought about what will happen when we get there. How long we'll be gone. About money. And what if Ab won't help me?"

"Then we'll stay," Marsha said, gripping the wheel tightly.

"*Stay?* In Florida?" she scoffed.

"Sure." Marsha shrugged. "Why not?"

"What about your job?"

Marsha turned to her. "I really, really hate the ER. Besides, I've been talking about this for years. Maybe it's a sign that it's finally time."

"What about Gabe?" Ginny asked, thinking of her conversation with Pepper. Thinking about the baby.

Marsha flicked her hand as though dismissing an unpleasant thought.

"He'll get over me," she said and winked, but it seemed like forced cheer.

"I thought things were getting serious," Ginny said, though she stopped short of asking her about the pregnancy. Marsha was wearing a red bandanna-print halter top and a worn pair of hip-hugger bell-bottoms, her flat, tanned tummy exposed. She couldn't be more than a few weeks along.

"Men are like ants. They're everywhere. Even Florida."

Clearly, she did not want to talk about Gabe. And there was definitely not going to be any discussion of a baby.

"What would *I* do for work? If we stayed, I mean?" Ginny hadn't had a job since the library. Her skills were limited to alphabetizing, smiling, and stamping due dates.

"You're so pretty, maybe you could be a mermaid."

"Ha! Maybe more like a beluga whale."

"Oh, shut up."

"Doughnut?" Ginny asked, reaching into the paper bag.

Marsha rolled her eyes and made a puke-y face.

"I think I'm pregnant," Marsha said. Just like that, there it was.

"What will you do?" Ginny asked, though she was afraid of the answer, any answer that Marsha might give.

"My plan right now is to get us to Weeki Wachee," she said, signaling this was the end of the discussion. For now, anyway. But in the dim light of the dash, Ginny could see tears filling Marsha's eyes.

The destination for that night was Savannah, Georgia. Pepper had suggested they go by way of Charlotte, North Carolina. It wouldn't be quite so pretty as following the Blue Ridge Mountains to Asheville, but it was more direct. They could get to Savannah before sunset, and then they would only be a half day's drive to Florida. By Wednesday evening, they'd be in Weeki Wachee. Theresa said she'd procured a place for them to spend at least the first few nights. She lived with a friend whose family owned an orange orchard a half hour drive from the springs; the old migrant farmers' sleeping quarters were vacant. They were welcome to stay there as long as they needed.

Ginny figured by then Ab would realize the gravity of the situation and would, hopefully, be willing to discuss how best to proceed. This is what her optimistic, logical brain told her. However, if she entertained her deepest fears, Abbott Senior had already sent the police after her. Once she was captured, he'd show no mercy. She'd lose not only Lucy again, but her son as well. She couldn't allow these thoughts in; she tried to imagine them behind a locked door in her brain, a chair shoved up underneath the knob for extra protection.

Thankfully, there were only a few other cars on the road that morning, and none of them were police cars. They hadn't seen a single police cruiser since somewhere in southern Virginia. The empty road unfurled in front of them and behind them like a twisted ribbon. The mountains were on the passenger side of the car; it wasn't until they got onto I-77 that they veered away from their rolling blues.

It was beautiful country: so green and lush. So rural and bucolic. Every time they passed an exit, Ginny thought of the lives of the people in those little towns. One after another after another, like beads on a string. They could conceivably just pull off the interstate into one of these villages and start their new life here. She could change her name. Change her history. Start again with a clean slate. She wondered if anyone had ever done that. Just ditched their life when it became unbearable and started again. She leaned her head against the cool window and closed her eyes, tried to dream herself into another life. Into freedom. She drifted, imagining that brand-new life, that dream life, allowing her eyes to close and her body to rest.

Twenty-two

❦

September 1971

She heard the sounds before she understood what they meant: something hitting the front of the car, the screech of the brakes, and the screams.

"Shit!" Marsha said as the car came to a stop in a ditch at the side of the road. "What the fuck was that?"

Ginny had bumped her forehead against the dash and felt dizzy as she whirled around, reaching blindly into the backseat for her children. The children were both crying and crumpled on the floor behind each respective front seat. Peyton was crying the loudest, but Lucy was whimpering as well, a look of terror in her eyes. Ginny couldn't open the passenger door wide enough to get out, so she crawled into the backseat.

"Everybody okay?" Marsha asked.

Ginny pulled Lucy into her arms and helped Peyton up from the floor. "Where does it hurt, Pey?"

"My arm, Mama!" he cried out.

"Sh-sh-sh," she said as he eased himself back into the seat and held out his arm for her inspection. Her heart raced like a hot engine idling in her chest. She examined his tiny arm; thankfully, it didn't appear (at least at first sight) to be broken. No bones protruding through the skin. No swelling. No blood. She studied Lucy next. She, too, showed no immediate signs of distress. She was scared. That was all. Ginny pressed her hand against her own chest as though to still her racing heart, waiting for it to resume its natural rhythm.

Lucy reached out and touched the soft painful bump on Ginny's forehead, and her little fingers came away with her blood.

"Oh, goodness," Ginny said and touched her own fingers to the wound.

"I think we hit an animal, Mama," Peyton said.

Marsha opened the driver's-side door slowly and got out, looking like someone who had just stumbled out of bed, still half asleep. She wondered if Marsha had bumped her head, too.

"Stay here," Ginny said, setting Lucy down next to her brother before climbing out of the backseat.

The car had slid down into a small ditch. Marsha was about thirty feet behind the car, standing over something in the road. Ginny walked tentatively toward her and the animal that clearly had been the cause of their crash.

"What is it?" she asked as she approached.

Marsha's eyes were wide and red.

"It's a fawn," she said.

The baby deer was bloodied, its neck twisted. The body was steaming in the cool morning air, and its chest twitched.

"I didn't even see it until it was too late."

"What do we do?" Ginny asked, feeling her bottom lip trembling as she fought tears. But sadness quickly gave way to fear, and she glanced up the road, terrified that someone would see them here, call an ambulance. Or worse, the police.

Marsha walked back to the car, purposeful. She opened the driver's-side door and leaned inside. When she returned, she had a small revolver in her hand, and Ginny's heart stopped. Now she understood why the glove box was locked. Still, the idea that there had been a gun hidden there filled her with worry. Why hadn't Marsha said anything?

"Where did you . . . ?" Ginny started.

"Go back to the car," she said to Ginny. "Distract the kids."

Ginny did as she was told, the pain in her head pulsing with each beat of her heart. She climbed into the car and turned the ignition so that the radio came on. "Jeremiah was a bullfrog . . ." That damned song again. But when Lucy squealed with delight and Peyton clapped, she turned the music up and started to sing along, turning to the children. Lucy was hugging herself, rocking, and Peyton was cradling his arm.

"Never understood a single word he said . . ." she sang loudly.

Still, the music wasn't loud enough to mask the crack of the gunshot. It took every ounce of self-control she had not to cry out.

Marsha returned to the car somberly, getting in without saying a word. She carefully and quietly slid the gun, which was hot to the touch and smelled like something charred, across the bench seat to Ginny, motioning for her to return it to its hiding place in the glove box. "Lock it," she said. "The key's under the floor mat."

Marsha put the car into gear and revved the engine as she tried to climb out of the ditch. The wheels spun futilely, and Ginny tensed.

"My arm hurts, Mama!" Peyton cried from the backseat as dirt flew up around the car in a dusty storm.

"I know, Pey," Ginny said, trying to soothe him, but her voice felt panicked.

"Come on, you motherfu . . ." Marsha muttered as she revved again.

Then there were lights behind them. The *woop, woop* of the black-and-white police car.

Marsha froze, hands on the wheel. Ginny held her breath, felt her vision beginning to darken at the edges as she watched the officer park

behind the dead fawn, get out of the cruiser, walk past the steaming car-
cass, and make his way to them.

Ginny felt paralyzed as the officer leaned into Marsha's open window
and said, "See you had a little accident here?"

"Yes, Officer. She came out of nowhere," Marsha said. Her voice
sounded otherworldly. Disembodied. Ginny gripped the edge of her seat
so she wouldn't pass out.

"You ladies okay?"

Marsha nodded and Ginny reached for the bump on her head, hoping
it had stopped bleeding.

Peyton and Lucy were suddenly, and thankfully, silent in the backseat.

The officer smiled at Marsha, chewing on something and smirking.
She watched his gaze travel from Marsha's face to her chest and below to
her golden stomach.

"We're just a little shaken up," Marsha said. Ginny wondered if he
could smell the strong scent of gun smoke that still burned her eyes and
made her throat feel raw.

The officer cocked his head and peered into the backseat, and Ginny
felt like she might be sick. If Peyton showed him his arm, then the officer
would want to call for an ambulance. It would all be over.

"Oh! Look at this. You've got a couple of little buggers along with you,"
he said. "You kids okay back there?"

"We're on our way to the new Disney World," Marsha said brightly.
"In Orlando?"

"Driving all the way to Florida on your own?" the officer said, scowling. "What do your husbands think of that?"

Marsha smiled demurely. "What makes you think we've got husbands?" she asked. Ginny felt queasy watching Marsha flirt with him.

The cop cocked his head again, possibly contemplating what she could
be insinuating. His face was host to a half dozen emotions before he finally settled back into one of professional concern.

"Well, if y'all are okay, I'll just give you a little push and get you on your way. Wouldn't want to keep Mickey waiting," he said into the backseat.

"That sure would be kind of you, Officer," Marsha said.

Ginny's heart had to be nearly audible, it was beating so hard. Her head ached.

Marsha raised an eyebrow at Ginny and whispered, "Holy freaking crap," as the cop moved behind the vehicle and hollered from the rear, "Okay, sweetheart, on the count of three give it some gas. One, two, three . . ."

Marsha gunned it, and the car lurched forward, leaving the cop in a virtual tornado of dust. Gripping the wheel for dear life, Marsha got the car out of the ditch and took off down the highway, grinning.

Twenty-three

❧

September 1971

Hundreds of miles later, when they finally felt safe enough to stop for lunch, Marsha double-checked both kids for bumps and bruises and fractured bones. Peyton's arm was sore, but as far as Marsha could see, nothing appeared broken.

"We'll keep an eye on it for swelling, though," she said to Ginny. To Peyton, she said, "You are so brave! I bet you got this owie protecting your sister, didn't you?"

Peyton smiled proudly.

Ginny insisted that she pay for the meal this time. She knew Marsha's own cash must be dwindling as well, though she had insisted that Ginny shouldn't worry, that once they got to their destination, she'd get a wire transfer from her bank. Marsha had been saving for this eventual departure for years and promised she had a pretty nice stash of cash in the bank.

"I have a Master Charge," Ginny said. "By the time Ab gets the bill, we'll already be in Florida."

And so they feasted. The kids had gooey grilled cheese sandwiches and chocolate milk shakes. French fries smothered in ketchup. Lucy delighted at the cold silver canister with the frothy shake inside. Ginny ordered a club sandwich, her appetite the heartiest it had been since they left. But though Marsha ordered herself a large Cobb salad, she did little more than pick at the hard-boiled egg.

"How far along are you?" Ginny asked her softly when the kids were preoccupied.

Marsha's mouth twitched and she shrugged. "Not far."

"Will you . . . do you plan . . ." Ginny didn't know how to ask the questions that had been bubbling up inside her ever since they left Pepper and Nancy's place.

Marsha, like Ginny, had been raised Catholic. Both had grown up going to church. They'd taken their First Communions together, made their first confessions, been confirmed. They'd suffered through catechism classes on Sunday mornings and later, in high school, youth group retreats. Ginny and Ab had been married in a Catholic ceremony in Boston, and the first thing she had done when she finally left the house after Lucy was born was light a candle at their local church in Dover. Marsha, on the other hand, had resisted it all. Fought God, mocked the alcoholic priest (rolling her eyes as he slurred through his sermon on temptation). She'd refused to go to confession, convinced the same priest would blab her transgressions to her father one night over beers at the local pub. By the time they were juniors, she'd stopped going to mass and started sleeping with boys.

Ginny had only personally known one girl who'd gotten pregnant in high school. A freshman girl when they were sophomores. She'd been kicked out of school and had to get her GED. Ginny had seen her sometimes in town, at the market—trying to soothe her crying baby, looking at least twenty years older than her sixteen years. She knew she was likely not the only girl who'd gotten pregnant in high school, however. One girl mysteriously disappeared their sophomore year only to return the fall of their junior year looking hollowed out. The rumors were that she'd been sent away, somewhere in New England, and that the baby had been given up for adoption. She'd also heard about girls who'd gone to see a woman in Boston, a nurse who helped solve the problem of an unwanted pregnancy. She'd heard the stories, whispered like a secret language, of all the ways to take care: *angelica, parsley, pennyroyal tea.*

"That fawn," Marsha said, staring into her salad plate. "It wouldn't have survived, would it?"

"No," Ginny said.

"You would have tried to save it, though," Marsha said, looking at her. "Tried to find its mother?"

Ginny shook her head, feeling Marsha's anguish like something palpable. Like smoke hovering in the air between them.

"You did the right thing," Ginny insisted, though her heart felt heavy. Her stomach was suddenly leaden with the meal. "You did. It was suffering, Marsh."

She thought that Ab too had only thought he was doing the right thing. That sending Lucy away was his way of protecting her, protecting them. Still, the fact that he refused to accept that it had been a mistake angered her. She had no idea what it would take to change his mind.

When they finished their meal, Ginny slid the plastic card across the table to the waitress, knowing she was taking a chance. The card didn't even have her name on it. What if the restaurant refused to take it? Would they call Ab? If Ab knew where they were, he would probably come after her.

"This is my husband's Master Charge," Ginny said. "He gave it to me for our trip."

The waitress shrugged and took it, returning only moments later with a paper for her to sign, the imprint of the numbers in inky blue.

"That's all?" Ginny asked.

"Y'all ain't never used a credit card before?" the waitress asked.

"Oh, of course," she said, backtracking. "It's just my husband's usually the one to get the check."

It was exhilarating, the freedom she felt now. The credit card was like a passport, a free ride. "I'll get this!" she said at the gas station. She came out of the market with dimpled Tab bottles and bags of chips and even a key chain of a Georgia peach, which she presented to Marsha like a gift.

They drove south through Georgia, and Ginny tried to squash the thoughts of where they were supposed to be right now. It was nearly three o'clock. Peyton would have been home after his first day of school. He was supposed to be sitting at the kitchen table having a snack of warm cookies and milk, relaying the adventures of his first day. By the time they got home, how much school would he have missed? And what if . . . what if they didn't go home? Couldn't go home? What if they had to, as Marsha had suggested, *stay*?

"Where's Daddy?" Peyton asked suddenly from the backseat, as if on cue, and she felt her face flush. "Is he coming to Disney World, too?"

So he *had* been paying attention in the backseat. She'd need to be careful about the things she and Marsha talked about. She was actually surprised he'd brought Ab up. He hadn't mentioned him once since they'd left Dover on Thursday.

"Daddy's at home," she said, adding, "He has to work." How many times had this exact sentence come from her mouth? While it had pained her nearly every time she'd needed to use this excuse for Ab's absence, now she was grateful.

"Okay," Peyton said and shrugged.

She thought of her own father: her big, boisterous bear of a dad. Her memories of him stood out in high relief against the flat backdrop of her childhood. Ginny's memories of her father were of piggyback rides and playing horse (of *yee-haws* and his back transformed into that of a bucking bronco). He liked to make things and cook and was the one to teach her a love of books, reading stories to her for as long as she could remember, making up voices for every character in the hundreds of books he collected from yard sales and thrift shops. By the time she was ten, he'd created a home library for her, crafting bookshelves from pallets he brought home from work. He worked for the physical plant at UMass as a custodian. He got up before dawn each day but was always home by the time the bus dropped her off after school. While her mother prepared dinner, he'd take her to the park or on "adventures" in the neighborhood. He was the one who first showed her Emily Dickinson's house, the enormous yellow estate only a mile from their home. He'd recited Emily's poetry to her as they walked down the sidewalk in front of the house. Together, they'd imagine what her life must have been like, living in that upstairs room. They visited her grave as well; she remembered he took his hat off and pressed it against his chest in reverence. It had been autumn then, cold, and he'd carried Ginny on his back the whole way home when she stepped in a puddle and got her feet wet.

When she'd married Ab, she'd expected he'd be a similar kind of father. And, at first, he had been. But after Lucy, he'd slipped away, and she'd been left alone. He blamed work, the demands of a livelihood that depended upon billable hours. She couldn't help but think that for each hour he was away from his office, his mind continued with the same calculations, each hour spent with their family an hour he could not bill anyone for. Each one a loss, creating a deficit in his imagination. She could see it in the way he glanced at his watch, at the way he hurried, harried, when he should have been enjoying himself. It was almost easier, she thought, to just let him go. Let him live inside that office, inside his briefcase.

When her father died, it felt like an amputation, a raw wound. Her life had felt severed, into *before* and *after*. Everywhere she went she was reminded of her father, the silence left in his wake nearly deafening. She'd gone to Emily Dickinson's grave alone and sat on the cold hard ground, imagining his voice booming the poetess's words: *This is the hour of lead, remembered if outlived* . . . Though it pained her, she wondered if Peyton would even notice if Ab were dead. He was already becoming not much more than a ghost.

❧

"Shit," Marsha cussed.

Ginny startled awake. Her eyes shot open, worried that they'd hit another animal. Her heart flew to her throat, and she braced herself.

"What's the matter?" Ginny asked.

"I think it's the radiator," Marsha said. "The car's overheating."

"What are we going to do?" Ginny asked.

"Hell if I know."

Marsha pulled over, this time off the main road so as not to attract any unwanted "help" from a passing police officer. She popped the hood and started fiddling around. As far as Ginny knew, Marsha had no expertise when it came to automotive repair, but then again, she'd had no idea Marsha knew how to shoot a gun, either. Lucy was fussing, so Ginny got her out of the car; her diaper was heavy again. She'd been changing her in gas station restrooms most of the way so far, but the diaper was soaked; she had to be miserable.

"Peyton, you stay here, okay? I'm going to change Lucy's diaper. Come on, sweets," she said. She grabbed one of the beach towels and made her way down an embankment and behind a large tree to a shady area, where she set Lucy down and spread out the towel. Lucy lay on the beach towel, sucking on her bottle, and Ginny unpinned her, preparing herself for the worst. However, the diaper rash was not nearly so angry, and, thankfully, there was no evidence of the parasites, either. She quickly cleaned her up, powdered her bottom, and put on a fresh diaper. She pulled Lucy onto her lap; she smelled clean and powdery with just a touch of milk, and she could feel Lucy's heart beating behind her ribs. She was a stranger, this tiny creature, but Ginny felt connected to her, exactly as she had felt connected to Peyton.

Lucy's chest rattled a little, and she coughed. Then she pointed up, and through the green leaves of the tree, Ginny followed her gaze to a fat peach hanging from a branch.

"Moon," she said.

"Oh, goodness! Look at that," Ginny said and reached up. The peach came free easily, and she held it out to Lucy. "It's a peach."

Lucy looked at her, confused.

"Like this," she said and took a bite from the peach. It was sweet and soft.

She held it out to Lucy again, who leaned forward and took a hesitant bite. She shivered a little, delight in her eyes. She took another bite and then another, the sweet peach juice dripping down her chin and onto her last clean shirt, a ring of the syrupy juice around her mouth.

Ginny looked up again and saw that there were several peaches ripe on the branches, so she gathered a half dozen, tossing them into the beach towel and making a makeshift basket.

She carried Lucy in one arm and held the peaches in her other hand. They walked out of the grove of trees and back up the embankment, where she saw a pickup truck parked behind Marsha's car. *Crap.*

Ginny pressed the baby close to her as she tentatively walked toward the vehicles, noting that the truck was empty. The hood of Marsha's car was still popped, Peyton was still in the backseat, but peering at the engine was a man in faded Levi's and a blue flannel shirt. Marsha was leaning against the car, her hands covered with grease, ponytail loose, and cheeks flushed.

"I think you've got a pinhole puncture in your radiator . . . must have happened when you hit the deer. It's been leaking, and now you're overheating. You're gonna need to get this into a shop." The man stood up and started to say something to Marsha when he startled at the sight of Ginny and Lucy.

"Oh, hi!" he said, smiling. He jutted his hand out toward her in greeting and, seeing the greasy mess, wiped it on his pant leg.

"This is Jesse," Marsha said, unfazed.

"Hi," Ginny said.

Jesse looked to be about their age. His eyes were bright blue against suntanned skin. He was lean but muscular, with long dark hair and a beard.

Ginny felt Lucy stiffen in her arms, then she buried her head in Ginny's chest, hard. She could feel her skull pressing against her sternum.

"Hey, sweetie," she cooed. "You want another peach?" When Lucy buried her head deeper, Ginny looked up at the man again.

"This is gonna sound like a weird question, but any chance you have an egg or some pepper with you in the car?" Jesse asked.

He wanted *lunch*?

"I've got peaches," Ginny said, handing one out to him.

He laughed. "No, not to eat. A raw egg or some pepper will seal the hole in the radiator long enough to get it to a shop," he said.

"Hold on," Marsha said. She leaned into the car again, and for a moment, Ginny wondered if she might be reaching in for the gun. But instead, she came out with a couple of little salt and pepper packets. "Look what I found!"

"Perfect," he said and winked, and when he leaned back under the hood, Marsha looked at Ginny and gestured to his rear end, mouthing, "Nice butt."

The man stood up and released the hood prop, lowered the hood shut, and brushed his hands together. "This should get y'all to the nearest service station. You wanna follow me?"

Marsha nodded and moved around to the driver's side, allowing him to open the door for her, as if they were about to go out on a date. But when he moved around the car and opened the passenger door for Ginny, offering to take the peaches so she could get Lucy into the backseat, Lucy wrapped her legs tightly around Ginny's waist. She could have completely let go of her and she would have continued to cling to her trunk like a monkey. And she made the same low growl she'd made at the restaurant.

"Hey," Ginny cooed, trying to soothe her.

"It's right down here," the man said, gesturing to a dirt road to the right. "I'll pull ahead so you can follow me."

She could not pry Lucy off her, so she pulled her into the front seat, holding her on her lap. Lucy's body was trembling.

"Is she okay?" Marsha asked, starting the engine.

"I don't know what's wrong," Ginny said. "She did this at that diner, too. There was a man there with a beard. Maybe she's afraid of men with beards?"

Jesse pulled his truck up onto the road next to the driver's side and leaned across the seat. "It's about three miles, just follow me!"

Lucy's body trembled, as though she were sitting on the Magic Fingers mattress.

They drove down the dirt road, surrounded on both sides by peach trees making intricate shadows in the waning light. Ginny checked her watch; it was nearly six o'clock already.

"Nothing's gonna be open this late," Ginny said.

Marsha nodded. "But maybe we can at least get the car into a shop, then find someplace to stay for the night? If there's a town?"

It didn't look to Ginny like there was any semblance of civilization, and her skin began to prickle.

"How far did he say it was?" Ginny asked.

"Three miles?" Marsha said, but she looked concerned as well, leaning toward the dash, squinting her eyes.

The truck bounced along in front of them, and when they came to an intersection, the man's arm extended out the window, motioning for them to turn right.

"I don't know," Ginny said. "Maybe we should just turn around. Get back on the highway?"

Marsha's mouth twitched. "What's the worst that could happen?" she said.

Ginny felt her body tense. "Um, the car could break down, and we'd be stuck in the middle of nowhere with some guy we don't know from Adam?"

Marsha gripped the steering wheel and took a deep breath. "Or, we turn around to go back and the car gets so hot it kills the engine and we're stuck in Buttfuck, Georgia, without a vehicle, with a stolen kid and nothing but a bunch of peaches." Marsha looked at her, almost angry.

Ginny winced, her eyes prickling with tears.

"I'm sorry," Ginny said. "I didn't mean to get you into this mess."

Marsha's jaw clenched, which meant she was biting her words.

"Well, look at that," Marsha said suddenly as a small town came into view. Jesse's truck pulled into the lot of a small service station on a street with a motel on either side, a BBQ joint, and a bar, the neon sign flashing a giant peach.

The service station was, indeed, about to close. But the owner, who seemed to know Jesse, assured her that the Dart would be the first job on the docket in the morning, and that it likely wouldn't require replacing the whole radiator. "Leave the car here, and go get a room over at the Island Grove," he said, gesturing with his fat chin to the motel right next to the shop. "They got a pool for the kids. But you're gonna want to get where you're going before the weekend. Storm's coming up through the Gulf, and it's gonna make driving down there pretty dangerous."

"Why don't we all get some supper," Jesse suggested. "They've got a pretty decent pulled pork sandwich over at Ruby's."

Ginny couldn't imagine trying to get Lucy to eat anything with this guy and his ominous beard sitting at the same table. She'd calmed a bit, but was still clinging fiercely to her, her tiny fingers digging divots into Ginny's neck.

"I actually really just want to give both kids a soak in the tub. Looks like the motel has a café attached," Ginny said. Marsha's eyes implored her.

She felt anger welling up in her. Really, was now the time to start taking up with a total stranger they met on the highway? What about Gabe? From what Pepper said, he was really in love with Marsha. Never mind the small issue of her being *pregnant*.

"We've got to get on the road early—as soon as the car's fixed," Ginny added hopefully. "Probably should get some sleep?"

"It's just some sandwiches," Jesse said. "Maybe a beer."

Marsha looked at Ginny, eyes pleading. There was nothing she could say or do that would change her mind.

"You two go on," Ginny said. Resigned.

Marsha leaned into Ginny and kissed her on her cheek. "Go get our room. I won't be late," she said. "Hang something on the door so I know which is ours." With that, she locked arms with Jesse and waggled her fingers at Ginny. Ginny clutched Peyton's hand, hoisted Lucy higher onto her hip, and started walking to the Island Grove's registration office.

The moment she opened the motel room door, she began to regret letting Marsha go. The room was filthy, a spilled soda cup stuck to the floor. The ceilings and walls were stained. There were cigarette burns on the yellowed bathroom counter and matching burn holes in the suspect striped bedspreads. Ginny made Peyton and Lucy sit on top of two towels, which were, thankfully, clean and smelling of bleach, as she plunked down into a chair by the door. The chain lock was broken, she noted, and what she initially assumed was a peephole appeared, instead, to have been made by a bullet.

She peered out the window at the so-called pool: the water murky green, poisonous looking, and the level too low for swimming. A couple of men who looked like they just got off a construction site sat in the plastic chaise lounges at the pool's edge, drinking cans of Old Milwaukee from a cardboard case at their feet and smoking cigarettes. Their gruff laughter put her further on edge.

There were only a few cars parked in the spaces in front of the rooms, most of them banged-up trucks laden with equipment. A rusty Volkswagen Bug and a green Plymouth Duster, its dashboard littered with fast-food wrappers.

"It smells like yucky eggs," Peyton said.

She'd noticed the pervasive scent of sulfur ever since they got off the main highway. She assumed the culprit was a nearby paper mill, as the mills in Holyoke offered that same rotten egg smell, but for as far as the eye could see there was nothing but peach trees.

As she was peering out the window, a man walked past the room, a toothpick working furiously up and down in his mouth, staring back at her as if she were a fish in an aquarium. Ginny gasped a little and drew the drapes shut tightly, the room becoming dark.

She turned on the TV for Peyton, who was restless and hungry. She started thinking maybe she should have just gone with Jesse and Marsha to the BBQ joint. She could have kept an eye on Marsha and actually fed her kids.

"Here," she said, handing Peyton a peach from her stash.

"I don't want it," he said, angrily crossing his arms against his chest. "I want to go home."

Startled, Ginny said, "Oh?"

"I miss my room and my toys," he said. "I miss Arthur. I miss Daddy."

Ginny's heart heaved.

"I don't like it here. I miss Christopher. I want to go to school. Why can't I go to school?"

Lucy was mesmerized by the TV; *The Mod Squad* was on. The lights from the screen flickered across her face.

"When are we going home?" Peyton asked.

"Well," Ginny tried, brightly. "We can't go home until we go to Disney World and see Mickey Mouse."

Peyton was immovable.

"But first," she said, desperate for anything that might sway him, "we're going to see some mermaids."

Peyton's eyes lit up a little.

"Remember, like in *Peter Pan*?" He'd loved that movie, and for a while he was convinced that if he wished hard enough he could fly. She'd caught him about to leap from the top of the stairwell just in time one morning.

Peyton, still skeptical, nodded. "Will there be crocodiles?"

"Maybe," she said, feeling like she might slowly be winning him over.

"When do we bring *her* back?" he said, gesturing at Lucy, who was munching happily on a peach, her hands clumsily grasping the piece of fruit, the juice running down her naked torso, her distended belly.

Ginny felt his words like a tiny fist to her chest.

"Back where?" she managed.

"Back to her school. I don't want a sister anymore. She can't even walk or talk, and she smells bad."

She felt consumed with anger, all the injustices accumulating in a giant pool somewhere at the center of her chest, in the place where her heart lived.

"You don't get to decide," she said angrily, scooping Lucy up into her arms, as if Peyton had threatened her physically. She pressed Lucy against her chest, covering her ear with the soft cup of her palm so she wouldn't hear what she was about to say. "You don't get to choose. She's your *sister*. She will always be your sister." Her voice broke as the anger spilled forth.

"She's weird," he insisted. "And stupid. Her eyes look like a China-man and her tongue is always sticking out."

Before Ginny could stop herself, she had used her free hand to push Peyton backward onto the bed and taken a swat at his bottom. "Shut up!" Ginny yelled.

The moment her hand contacted Peyton's skin there was a stunned silence. Then Lucy began to wail, Peyton cried out in alarm, and Ginny felt that swell of anger and sadness and disbelief overwhelm her. Tears ran down her cheeks as she shook her head. She had never spanked Peyton before. Never once laid a hand on him in anger, despite her mother-in-law's insistence that all bad behavior could be halted with a swift slap to the bottom. Ab had been the disciplinarian, though he needed to do little more than raise his voice to nudge Peyton back into line. Ginny had never so much as *threatened* a spanking before.

Her own capacity for violence terrified her. The fact that she'd wanted to hurt her son felt unbelievable. Incomprehensible. It was as though every instinct she had to protect Lucy made her capable of trespassing into a place she'd never thought she'd go.

She set Lucy down on the next bed and went to Peyton, but he shrank away from her, still crying.

"I'm sorry," she said, the words catching in her throat like spiny burs. "Pey, I didn't mean to hurt you. But your words hurt *me*. They hurt Lucy. Still, I shouldn't have hit you."

Her heart was beating hard and fast in her chest.

"Pey?" she said.

He slowly reached for her, and she scooped him up into her arms. Cradled him. He was so big now, but still just a baby, too. His body fit neatly against hers, and she stroked his hair, wiped his tears with the edge of her T-shirt.

"Goodnight stars?" she offered, her throat feeling thick.

"Goodnight air," he said and hiccupped.

"Goodnight noises everywhere."

His willingness to accept her apology was so easy. That sort of power, the power of being a parent whose children's love is unconditional, felt dangerous. Ginny worried that this sort of easy forgiveness could make one reckless, and she vowed that she would never take advantage of this. Not again.

She searched the room for something to tie to the doorknob so Marsha could find them, eventually settling on one of Peyton's grubby socks. She peeked her head out the window, and when the walkway was vacant, she quickly affixed it to the door and slammed it shut again, securing the dead bolt. She gathered both children into the bed, though she was too afraid to pull back the comforter, and she lay between them as they each drifted off to sleep in her arms. She stared at the ceiling, hoping that

Marsha would be back soon, that they could get to where they were going. That they could stop running.

The banging came just as Ginny was drifting off into a troubled sort of sleep, the kind that feels restless, just skimming the surface of consciousness. She shot up, gripping both children, terrified that the man who had been peering into the room earlier was now trying to get in.

"It's me!" Marsha said, and Ginny scrambled out of bed to let her in.

Marsha slammed the door shut behind her, breathless. Ginny could only see the silhouette of her now.

"What's going on?" Ginny asked.

Marsha shook her head and started grabbing her things. She clicked on the lamp on the battered table by the door, illuminating the room in a sickly yellow glow. Her hair was a mess, and she had mascara smudged under each eye; in the strange jaundiced motel light, she looked somehow *bruised*. Ginny felt her stomach turn. Her heart sank.

"What happened?" she asked.

"Let's go," Marsha said. "Please don't ask any questions."

Ginny got out of bed and started to gather her things into her bag. She felt dizzy, unsteady on her feet, as though still moving through a dream.

"The keys should still be in the car, over at the shop. We're only about ninety miles from Savannah." Marsha was suddenly clearheaded and purposeful. "We'll get the car fixed there."

Ginny silently followed Marsha's lead, figuring she'd get answers to her questions when they were finally on the road again.

"The room's paid for, right?" Marsha asked.

"Yeah," Ginny said. She'd used the credit card again. It was only ten dollars for the night, but she figured she'd better use the card whenever she was able, to save her precious cash.

"I'll carry Peyton," Marsha said. "You get Lucy."

Laden with their bags and the kids, they quickly exited the motel, circumventing the quiet pool area and the nearly empty parking lot. The main street through the town was empty as well, no cars at all except for an idling semi. The air was thick with humidity, a hazy mist hanging low. Mosquitoes buzzed and bit.

They quickly made their way across the street to the service station, where the Dart sat waiting like a patient in an emergency room.

"Stay here," Marsha said, setting a waking Peyton down. He rubbed his eyes and leaned into Ginny's legs for support.

Marsha hopped into the car and, as hoped, found the keys still in the ignition. She started the engine, and, thankfully, there was no smoke. No flames. No sign of trouble, for now anyway.

"Buckle yourself in," Ginny said, gently nudging Peyton into the back-seat and loading her bag into the trunk. She put Lucy in the backseat as well, and she didn't stir as Ginny strapped the safety belt across her. Ginny climbed into the passenger seat, and Marsha peeled out of the garage lot and onto the road.

In the dim light of the dashboard, Ginny could see the black trails like watercolors running down Marsha's cheeks.

"Hey," she said, reaching for Marsha's arm.

Marsha was trembling, her foot shaking so badly that it came off the clutch and the car stalled out.

"Are you okay to drive?" Ginny asked. She could smell booze on her, coming off in faint vaporous waves.

Marsha pulled over to the side of the road and shook her head.

Ginny had no idea what had happened with Jesse, but she did know she'd never seen Marsha rattled like this. Never seen her so much as shed a tear, not once in all the years she'd known her.

"I'll drive," Ginny said, surprising herself.

"You don't know how," Marsha started, but Ginny had already thrown the car door open and was coming around the front to the driver's side. Marsha scooted over to the passenger side and wiped furiously at her tears.

Ginny, in the driver's seat, realized this was the first time since Ab had once tried, and failed, to teach her to drive that she'd been behind the wheel.

She looked at the shifter, the dash, mystified as to where to begin.

"It's three on the tree," Marsha said, trying to explain the mechanics of it all, the clutch, the brake, how to put the car in first gear and how to shift. But Ginny struggled, the car jerking then stalling, jerking then stalling, with Marsha nervously checking the rearview mirror as Ginny kept attempting to achieve some forward momentum.

Finally, she managed to get the car moving, and Marsha said, "Now!"

Ginny depressed the clutch and shifted the lever to second before releasing the clutch and pressing on the gas. They tore down the road, Ginny gripping the wheel so tightly her knuckles ached. She was sure she hadn't breathed for at least a full minute when they climbed onto the highway, and Marsha talked her through another gear shift into third and then fourth. She was *driving*. Driving a car! Marsha rolled down the passenger window and the cool night air rushed in, making Ginny tremble. Marsha leaned her head out the open window and closed her eyes.

Ginny wanted to reach out and touch her, make sure she was okay, but she was too afraid to let go of the wheel. Instead, she studied that empty highway, trying hard to focus on staying on her side of the road, and trying not to panic when cars and trucks passed her.

Finally, Marsha rolled the window up.

"You okay?" Ginny asked.

Marsha took a deep, shuddering sort of breath and sighed.

"There was another one, you know," she said softly.

"Another what?" Ginny asked, feeling her stomach twist. "Another man?"

"No, no," she said. "Another baby. I never told you."

Ginny looked away from the road for a moment, but Marsha was staring straight ahead. Not at her.

"When we were in high school. Junior year."

"*What?*" Ginny managed, flipping through her memories of high school like Ab's Rolodex. Struggling to find that lost card. That missing piece. She and Marsha had spent nearly every waking hour together as teenagers. How could there have been a pregnancy? A baby?

"Remember Jimmy?"

"Sure," Ginny said. Jimmy Artelli was a year ahead of them in high school. But Marsha had never dated him. Never even went out.

"I tend to get myself into situations," Marsha said. "Situations I shouldn't be in."

Marsha stretched out her hand and examined a fingernail, its blood-red polish chipped.

"I drove myself to Boston. Some nurse there, worked out of her apartment. I paid her two hundred dollars and she took care of it. I even drove myself home."

The realization of what Marsha was telling her hit Ginny.

"I swore I would never ever allow myself to be in that position again. If my mother knew what I'd done. If *you* knew what I'd done. I couldn't bear it. But now, here I am again."

"Are you going to get another . . ." Ginny started, but couldn't bring herself to say the word.

"I don't know," Marsha said. "I don't know what to do."

"Why didn't you tell me?" Ginny asked. Her heart was beginning to ache in a remote sort of way. Like a remembered pain instead of a new one. "I could have come with you."

Marsha laughed, and it sounded like the crack of a whip. Like something violent. "Really?" she said.

Ginny nodded, even as she wondered if she was telling the truth. She thought about what it meant, what Marsha had done and might do again. She also recalled thinking in those awful days after Lucy was born that it would have been so much easier if she *were* dead instead of just gone. That sort of grief, at least, was absolute. It had edges. She'd even allowed herself to imagine what she would have done if she knew she would give birth to Lucy only to lose her again. Would she have gotten an abortion? Would she have preempted this loss if she could?

"You don't trust me" was what Ginny said instead. "You thought I'd judge you."

Marsha turned to her again and smiled sadly. "It's not your fault. You're a good person, Gin. You *should* judge people like me."

Ginny thought of the sting of the slap she'd given Peyton at the motel. She thought of all the times she'd dreamed herself out of that house in Dover, of leaving Ab behind. She thought of her capacity for rage, and worse, her inability to express it. She was *not* good. She was only playing the part she'd been given. Reciting the lines scripted for her.

"Did that man, Jesse . . . did he hurt you?" Ginny asked.

Marsha slipped her shoes off and put her bare feet on the dash. She leaned back and rolled her head toward Ginny and smiled a weary sort of smile.

"Somebody told me once there are only two kinds of men in the world: assholes and dumb-asses. I have a soft spot for the assholes," she said and smiled sadly.

"You don't believe that," Ginny said, yet still tried to think about which category Ab might fit in.

"I *believe* that all men, in the end, want the same thing. Some work for it, some bargain or beg, and some just steal."

"What about Gabe?" she asked. "He doesn't sound like an asshole *or* a dumb-ass."

Marsha sucked in a breath and nodded. "He's definitely a good one. The kind of guy who always does the right thing."

"Does he know about the baby?"

"No." Marsha's eyes glistened in the light of the dashboard. "Because if I told him, he'd want to marry me."

"And . . . ?"

"Nobody should get married because they have to," she said.

Twenty-four

❦

Summer 1964

Ginny and Ab had wanted a small wedding, just a quiet affair, maybe even in the little chapel on Amherst's campus. She didn't want a white gown, a veil. She thought she might wear yellow, with flowers in her hair.

When Ab first proposed, she hadn't expected that Mr. and Mrs. Richardson would even attend the ceremony. But the baby changed everything. Ab had been right. Despite their open disdain, they were indeed relieved that Ab wasn't going overseas. The pregnancy, the wedding, was perhaps (in the end) simply the price that had to be paid to keep their son home.

But there would be a price for Ginny and Ab to pay as well in exchange for their reluctant support. First off, the wedding would not be a small affair but a large one. At the Cathedral of the Holy Cross in Boston, where Mr. and Mrs. Richardson themselves had gotten married. The dress (despite Ginny's "predicament") would not be yellow but a virginal white.

There would be bridesmaids: his cousins, and Marsha as her maid of honor. The bridesmaids' dresses would be lime green and ugly to highlight the bride's own most attractive attributes. ("You have such a pretty face," Sylvia had said, the unspoken *for a chubby girl* implied by the quick head-to-toe scan she made with her eyes.) There would be a reception at the country club the Richardsons belonged to in Wellesley, and there would be a five-tiered cake and a live orchestra playing the music from Ab's mother and father's generation. It would be elegant, for sure. It would be the exact opposite of what either of them wanted.

But if they complied (with the gardenias and peonies, with the prime rib and live band), then his parents would not only foot the bill for the wedding but send them on a lovely honeymoon. Perhaps even a little help with a down payment on a home?

"You can't exactly raise a child in a rooming house," Sylvia had said to Ab.

Ginny should have known there was a hitch, of course. But between the exhaustion brought on by the pregnancy and willful ignorance, she didn't ask questions. And Ab slipped that little snag into conversation as though she might just miss it.

"The house is just a starter, of course," he said. "Two bedrooms. One for us and one for the baby. But it's got a certain charm. A little stoop out front, and a backyard. I thought we could maybe have a garden."

Ginny was trying to read. *Peyton Place* was the book of choice, given her inability to focus on much of anything for longer than a few minutes. It was trashy and delicious.

"What?" she asked, looking up from a page she had to have read at least a half dozen times.

"It's also close to school," he said.

"The baby hasn't even been born yet," she said, shaking her head. "You're already worried about school?"

"Not for the baby," he said, smiling. "For me. The house is in Cambridge."

Suddenly everything was clear. Like the letters at the eye doctor's office sharpening with each click of the lens.

"Law school?" she said, feeling queasy. She'd been feeling queasy pretty much every hour of every day for a couple of months, but this was different. It felt as if her heart was sick.

Ab sighed, his shoulders slumping.

She set the book down. "We don't need the house. The wedding. Any of it. Not at the cost of your future."

"My future?" He laughed. "There's not much of a future in delivering zucchinis. Zucchinis are not going to put a roof over our head."

"No, your *parents* are. God. This is so ridiculous."

"So, I'm ridiculous?" he asked, his face reddening. "Is that what you think?"

"Oh, Jesus," she said. "Some kind of lawyer you're going to make with that sort of reasoning."

"Please understand, Gin," he said. "I have no choice."

And so it was not with joy but with a sense of impending doom that she woke up on the morning of her wedding day, as she pulled on the panty-hose that nearly cut off her circulation. As she slipped her swollen feet into the pointy-toed shoes. As she affixed the pillbox hat and veil to her stiff hair.

Still, she went through the motions. Walking down the aisle alone, feeling her father's absence like a ghost at her side, the wedding march like some sort of death knell. The only comfort was that despite everything, at the end of the long walk was Ab. Ab, who couldn't stand up to his parents but who made her laugh and loved her despite every flaw she had. Ab, with his dimples and charm and quick wit. What was life but a series of compromises, anyway? She'd be a fool to think otherwise.

When she recited her vows, she meant them, and when Ab peered into her eyes and squeezed her hand, she was overwhelmed with happiness, even as that flashy ring cut into her neighboring finger.

They even enjoyed themselves at the reception. She didn't drink any champagne, but she felt as drunk as Marsha, whose dance card was full the whole night. And when Abbott Senior asked for Ginny's hand and led her to the dance floor, she thought for a moment that perhaps everything would be okay. That she'd been paranoid. That he truly only wanted the best for his son, ultimately Ab's happiness trumping all else. Abbott Senior held her as the band played, and she could see where Ab had gotten his moves on the dance floor. She even felt herself beginning to relax and smiled as he pulled her closer.

"Ginny, dear," he said, as he swept her across the floor.

"Yes, sir?"

"I hope you are enjoying yourself," he said.

"I am," she said, telling the truth. "It's a lovely party. Thank you so much."

"No, really now," he said and pulled back for a moment to look at her. "I should be thanking you."

"Whatever for?" she asked, laughing a little.

"For showing my son how the other half lives. It only took a few months of living in squalor before he changed his tune about law school."

"Excuse me?" she said, feeling her stomach bottom out.

"My son has ambitions," he said. "And you, dear, are simply a rather large bump in the road."

She'd been stunned into silence but said nothing to Ab.

But when they plowed through the corridor of guests chucking handfuls of rice to the waiting limousine, Marsha clutching the odorous bouquet Ginny had hurled in her direction earlier, she realized that this had been a terrible mistake. The music trailing behind them no longer sounded like a celebration but a dirge.

Later, breathless in the backseat of the limousine, when Ab kissed her and said, "I love you," into her hair, she feigned happiness, ignoring the queasiness, the uneasiness. But Ab knew something was wrong.

"You okay?" he asked.

She nodded quietly; she knew if she spoke she would burst into tears.

At the door to their honeymoon suite, he motioned as if to lift her up over the threshold, but her mouth twitched and she shook her head. "Lord, no, you'll put your back out."

"Come here," he said, reaching for her hand. He led her into the most beautiful hotel room she'd ever seen and then out through a set of French doors to the balcony. It was nearly midnight, and the city was aglow. Together they stood peering down from ten stories above.

The moon punctuated the sky, a thin white comma.

"You know Emily's poem about her?" he asked, nodding at the moon. "The moon was but a chin of gold / A night or two ago, / And now she turns her perfect face / Upon the world below."

He absently touched her belly in the way that had become habitual in the last couple of months.

"Well, what about your beloved Bobby Frost?" she asked, and he cocked his head. "The moon for all her light and grace / Has never learned to know her place." She wasn't angry, and it wasn't an accusation. It was just a simple fact.

She didn't belong here: not in this expensive hotel looking down at the world below. Not in that country club with its crystal glasses and its twelve pieces of silver at each setting. She was accustomed to margarine in a tub, not fancy pads of butter atop beds of crushed ice in silver chalices.

"The only reason I'm here is because of this baby."

Ab looked stunned. Hurt.

"I would have married you without the baby," he said. "I would have married you if there would never ever be babies. I would have married you if you hated babies."

"Who hates *babies*?" she asked, but felt something inside her softening.

Ab was smiling now, too.

"What should we name it?" Ginny asked, feeling tears welling up again.

"I was thinking Peyton," he said and grinned.

"Peyton? Is that a family name?"

"No," he said and laughed. "Peyton from *Peyton Place*. The book you've been reading. It's actually good for a boy or a girl," he continued.

She shook her head and closed her eyes.

"Hey," he said, holding his finger in the air. "Why don't we sleep out here? It's a beautiful night."

She shrugged. She was certain there wasn't any place she'd feel comfortable right now; might as well have a nice soft breeze.

He pulled the two chaises that were sitting there together, then disappeared into the room behind them and came back with an armload of blankets. Like a kid making a fort in the living room, he assembled a makeshift bed, and they both climbed in. He took her hand, the one with that enormous diamond, and kissed her fingers.

"Ginny Richardson," he said, "I love you." And as he nodded off to sleep, Ginny studied the sky and watched the moon disappear behind a cloud.

Twenty-five

༄

September 1971

After a while, Ginny could hear the soft sounds of Marsha snoring and the sleepy sighs of Peyton and Lucy in the backseat. She felt sleep trying to take hold of her as well, so she rolled the window down a bit to let the night air in and turned the radio on low. There was the crackle and hiss of static between stations, and then she locked into a gospel station. The music was deep and haunting, the harmonic voices like instruments all playing together: both music and prayer. Ginny looked at Marsha to make sure she was still asleep and glanced in the backseat at her sleeping children and turned the volume up a little higher. *Oh, they tell me of a home far away . . . they tell me of an unclouded day.* The lament, a sort of melodic keening, moved something inside her, as though there had been a rock, a large rock blocking out the light, and each chorus pushed it a little farther, made things a little brighter.

Something up ahead caught her eye. For miles and miles, the landscape had been barren and black. No signs of life. But there was something glowing orange in the distance. She could also smell, through the cracked window, the scent of smoke. She had to roll the window up, it was so strong. And then she could see that it was a house on fire, a farmhouse standing completely alone, engulfed in flames.

Her instinct was to wake Marsha up, to say, "Look at that! That house is on fire!" But something stopped her. There were no people, no cars. No fire trucks or ambulances, no neighbors clutching their robes, watching as the house burned.

She thought about its inhabitants coming home later from wherever they had gone to find nothing but the charred remains of their lives. She slowed as she passed, feeling oddly reverent, the gospel song crescendoing and then fading as she rolled past the fiery wreckage.

She hadn't realized she was weeping until the fire was just a faint amber glow behind her. The road ahead of her stretched on endlessly, but after a while, the road behind her was hardly visible anymore.

Twenty-six

❧

September 1971

At dawn, in Savannah, they brought the car to a repair shop just as smoke was beginning to bloom from under the hood. The mechanic told them that they'd gotten there just in time; they could have done a lot of damage to the engine if they'd driven even a mile farther.

As Ginny got out of the driver's seat, she realized that every muscle had been tensed as she clutched the wheel, her body aching in the aftermath. Still, she had *driven*. A vehicle. All by herself. The time Ab gave her a driving lesson had left her in tears. She'd felt foolish and incompetent as the car bucked and stalled down their street in Dover, the neighbors coming out to watch her failed attempts, standing in their respective driveways, pretending they were tending to their roses or checking their mail. When she finally did get some traction, she'd accidentally driven up over a curb and hit one of the neighbor's lawn jockeys. She'd gotten out of the car, slammed the door, run past that fallen statue back to their house, and told him she never wanted to drive again.

"I never thought you were capable of a hit and run!" Ab had teased. "That poor lawn jockey didn't see it coming."

She'd hated that he was making fun.

She wished he could see her now. She wished he'd seen her on that highway, the needle on the speedometer rising to forty, fifty, even sixty miles an hour.

"There's a Laundromat over that way," Marsha said, gesturing across the street. "We can do a couple of loads and then get some breakfast while they fix the leak."

They grabbed all the dirty laundry from the trunk, including the dirty cloth diapers that Ginny had been washing by hand and drying by hanging them out of the car, window rolled up pinching the edges to keep them from flying away. They'd bought a pack of Pampers in Virginia, but they were all gone now, and they'd been so expensive. It didn't make sense to Ginny to waste her money just for the convenience of the disposable diapers.

The only clean clothes any of them had were the ones they were wearing. Even then Ginny could smell the faint scent of her perspiration on her blouse. They say the scent of stress sweat is distinct from the smell of exertion, and this was the smell of stress.

"Hey, did you notice that car that pulled in behind us at the gas station?" Marsha asked as they entered the Laundromat.

"What car?" Ginny asked.

"That green one," she said, gesturing out the window across the street. An olive-green Duster was pulled up next to the gas pump, and an attendant was lowering a dipstick into the engine. The sun was reflecting off the driver's-side window, making it impossible to see inside.

"I swear I saw that same car back at the motel," Marsha said.

She was right. Ginny had seen it, too. Ginny felt her heart thunk. They both peered out the window, waiting to see if the driver would get out of the car. But the sound of a child screaming pulled her away. Lucy was sitting on the floor, happily playing with a pile of toys that had been left to occupy the Laundromat patrons' kids: wooden busy beads and one of those blocks with the pegs and a hammer to push them through. Peyton, however, had opted to use the shiny linoleum floor as a skating rink, having somehow managed to remove his shoes and slide himself right into the corner of one of the machines.

The egg on his head appeared almost immediately.

"Come here," she said, scooping Peyton up from the floor and sitting down with him in one of the plastic seats, ignoring the raised eyebrow of the attendant and the muttered complaints of the older woman who had her laundry spread across one of the folding tables.

Snot was streaming down from each of Peyton's nostrils. She grabbed one of the stiff cloth diapers from their pile and dabbed at it.

"I'll go grab some ice," Marsha said. "There's a Krystal restaurant right next door."

Ginny nodded and cradled Peyton, shushing him softly until his cries turned into an occasional hiccup. All the while, she studied the car across the street, wondering if the driver knew that she and Marsha were over here. The gas station attendant filled the Duster's tank and then used a squeegee to wash the car's windshield. When the driver rolled the window down to pay for his services, the attendant was blocking Ginny's view so she couldn't see inside.

She hadn't checked in with her mother since Atlantic City, choosing ignorance in case the school had sent someone after her. But if someone *was* following her, someone sent by Ab, or worse, by the police, or FBI even, it would probably be best to not remain in the dark.

They hoped to get to Weeki Wachee that night. Just one more day on the road. She'd call her mother once they got settled. Hopefully, she and Marsha were only being paranoid. Perhaps the driver in the Duster was just somebody taking the same route as them; they were on the main interstate, after all.

On the TV hanging overhead, a newscaster was talking about a riot that had just broken out at Attica, a prison in upstate New York. A thousand inmates involved. She stood up and walked to the TV, turning the channel to *I Love Lucy*. When Ricky Ricardo hollered "Lucy!" Lucy looked up, startled to hear her own name coming from the television. Ginny smiled.

Marsha returned with a paper cup full of ice as well as two soft-serve ice cream cones for the kids. Hardly a good breakfast, but if it kept Peyton from crying, she was game.

They loaded the soiled clothes into one large industrial-size washer, purchasing a small box of powdered soap from a vending machine.

"Peyton," Marsha said, "come help me?"

Marsha lifted him up and let him shake the soap into the machine. She handed him the coins. Because of the Magic Fingers, he knew exactly what to do and deftly put the coins in the slot. He squealed with delight as the mechanism returned empty and the water began to fill inside the machine. Marsha gave him a high five and asked for a lick of his cone.

Ginny was delighted when Peyton held the cone out to Marsha. For a child who found sharing a sort of affront to his nature, this counted as progress as far as Ginny was concerned.

She tried to imagine Marsha with her own child. When they were in high school, Marsha had always said she never wanted kids. Unlike most girls their age, she never babysat. Found no allure in babies. But watching her with Peyton, Ginny could almost imagine her with her own child. Her own son.

Ginny had been terrified when the doctor told her that she'd given birth to a boy. She didn't have brothers. And after her father passed away, there hadn't even been a man in the house. She would never have admitted it to anyone, but she'd been praying for a girl. When she imagined being a mother, it had always been as the mother of a daughter. As the baby grew inside her, she entertained thoughts of ballet lessons and piano lessons and the quiet talks they'd have when she became a teen. She would be the confidante her own mother had never been. She would be her best friend. And so, when Peyton had come out screaming bloody murder and the doctor had announced his sex like she'd won a prize, she'd felt tremendously let down. She never told Ab, but she'd been deeply and profoundly disappointed when Peyton was born. It made her ashamed, filled her with guilt.

Of course, over time, this sense of disenchantment eventually gave way to a new sort of happiness. She did, indeed, take pleasure in Peyton as he grew. The small milestones truly thrilled her: his first laugh had brought tears to her eyes, and his first steps had made her feel inordinately proud. She'd realized after not too long that he too loved to be read to (even if the books were not the ones she would have chosen herself as a child). She comforted herself with the idea that there was always time. That perhaps the next child would be a girl. And how lovely for her to have such a sweet older brother to care for her. It was what got her through the grass stains and wild streaks. It was the place she went when Peyton and Ab wrestled in the living room and broke the coffee table. When she sat in the hospital emergency room waiting for the X-rays to confirm a broken bone. When Peyton and she seemed to communicate in an entirely different language, she dreamed of the girl-child that would one day come. That placid beautiful creature that would understand her on the most primitive level. She waited for the kindred spirit.

She watched Lucy now as she played with the painted wooden beads, sliding one then another over the twisted wires, delighting when they were all stacked up on one side. Her heart trilled as Lucy looked up at her for approval. She nodded, tears filling her eyes as she reached out and stroked Lucy's soft curls. The lice, thankfully, were gone now, and the mayonnaise method had left her hair shiny and soft to the touch.

"Good job!" Ginny said.

"I'm going to go check on the car," Marsha said.

While the clothes spun in the dryer, Ginny read a *Cosmopolitan* magazine, the cover promising all sorts of things inside: THE STRANGE HAPPY LIFE OF A WOMAN WHO SUPPORTS HER HUSBAND and HOW SEXY DO YOU SEEM TO MEN?: A QUIZ. She flipped ahead instead to AN EXCERPT FROM *THE BELL JAR*, AN

IMPORTANT NEW NOVEL. Ginny had read *Ariel,* one of Sylvia Plath's poetry collections, a couple of years earlier. She had always felt a certain kinship with Plath, yet another troubled Massachusetts poetess. But her suicide, that horrific domestic drama that played out in her kitchen while her children slept, was something she could barely comprehend.

Ginny studied her children. Peyton was occupied with a toy dump truck, which he was running across the rows and rows of washers. Lucy was still contentedly playing with the busy beads.

"It's fixed!" Marsha said as she zipped back in. "Just like Jesse said, a pinhole-size leak in the radiator. They repaired it and said we're good to go. I called Theresa and told her we should be arriving tonight. I figure we've got about five and a half hours to Weeki Wachee, not including stops. We can stop in Gainesville for lunch and then try to power through the rest of the way, get there by the time she's getting off work tonight."

"Was that guy in the Duster still over there?"

"I didn't see him," Marsha said.

"Do you think he's following us?" Ginny asked.

"Do you know anybody who drives a green Duster?" Marsha asked.

Ginny shook her head. Her father-in-law drove a Lincoln, and Ab drove the same baby-blue Galaxie convertible he'd had since they started dating.

She wondered if she should call Ab once they finally arrived in Florida. So long as she didn't speak to Ab, she could imagine that he had simply just continued on with his life. Like a worm whose head has been cut off; it just keeps on wriggling. (She knew this because Peyton had demonstrated with one of the fat night crawlers he insisted on keeping in an old Chock Full o'Nuts can in his room.) But if she were to speak to him, this fantasy might very well be shattered. Facing Ab meant facing whatever consequences might arise from all of this. She wasn't sure she was ready for that. Wasn't sure she'd *ever* be ready for that.

The fact that someone appeared to be following them, even if it was just a paranoid delusion, reminded her of the very real possibility that

Ab would not just let her walk out of his life. Certainly not with his son in tow. It was only when she thought of Peyton that her heart snagged. What would she do if the situation were reversed, and Ab took off with her son without a word? She'd lose her mind; she knew this. She probably would get in the car herself (despite having exactly three hours of driving experience as of this morning) and chase them down.

She and Marsha folded the clothes quickly and stuffed them into Ginny's bag. They were hot and smelled so good and clean. There was a certain familiar comfort in the scent of the soapy detergent and fabric softener, but also a sort of sentimental longing for normalcy, for home.

They waited for the traffic on the now much busier street to wane before they ran across the road to the garage, each of them carrying one of the children. What a motley crew they must seem to the people who had emerged and were now filling the shops and restaurants on this small strip.

Ginny offered the garage manager her credit card, saying a silent prayer as he disappeared into his office. She knew that at some point the credit would be used up, though she had no idea when. He was gone for a long time. When he failed to return, Marsha looked at Ginny, eyebrows raised.

Ginny felt her pulse quicken. Peyton was restless, fiddling with the gumball machine in the waiting room.

"Can I have a penny?" he asked, tugging at her shirt.

She shook her head. "Not now." She jostled Lucy on her hip when she started to rub her eyes and fuss. The room was smoky, the other waiting patron an older gentleman who was chain-smoking Lucky Strikes, reading a ragged issue of *Field & Stream*.

"What is he *doing* back there?" Marsha whispered, leaning and stretching her neck to catch a glimpse.

"I don't know," Ginny said, feeling her heart rising into her throat. She moved a little to the left where she could see the man through a smudgy window, holding the card up and speaking into the phone.

She tried to recall if Ab's number was anywhere on the card. Was it possible he was calling to make sure it wasn't stolen?

Another minute passed. The paperwork, detailing the repairs made on the car, was sitting on the counter, along with Marsha's keys. Marsha gestured with her chin to the keys, and, feeling queasy, Ginny nodded.

Marsha grabbed the keys, motioned for Ginny to follow. Lucy on her hip, Ginny took Peyton's hand and hurried them all out through the door, the electronic bell announcing their departure. The man with the magazine didn't even look up.

They ran to the waiting car and leapt in. Marsha started the engine as Ginny threw both kids and the laundry bag in the backseat, and as the manager emerged from the building, Marsha peeled out of the parking lot and onto the road.

She raced through a flashing yellow light and then accelerated so fast, Ginny felt like she'd left her stomach behind. They climbed onto I-95 South, and Marsha kept accelerating.

"Whee!" Peyton squealed from the backseat.

"Whee!" Lucy mimicked. Ginny turned around to see them both gleeful in the backseat, and despite the sheer terror she felt at what might happen next, a small part of her felt absolutely and unequivocally happy.

"We're going to need to take some back roads," Marsha said. "If that guy at the garage called Ab or the police, they'll be looking for us on I-95."

The momentary rush of adrenaline, the hot liquid feeling that had coursed through Ginny's body as they made their getaway, had now pooled into a sort of molten dread in the center of her chest.

Both kids had fallen asleep again in the backseat, the narcotic effect of the engine's lullaby something they both seemed to suffer from, and Ginny took this opportunity to verbalize her fears.

"Abbott could have us arrested," she said.

"Well, he's definitely going to shit a brick," Marsha said.

Marsha had met Abbott Senior exactly three times. The first time had been enough for her to make her assessment of him. That he was a Class A Jerk. The kind of man who felt entitled to whatever it was he wanted. Money, power, women. Marsha said she knew the second he shook her hand, holding on too long, assessing her even as he wouldn't let her hand go, that he was somebody who saw the world as his for the taking.

Twenty-seven

‰

1965–1968

Peyton was born in February 1965, while Ab was in the throes of his first year of law school and he and Ginny were living in the little house in Cambridge. By the time Ab headed into his second year of school, they learned the news that one of those boys sent over to Vietnam by the IVS had died, killed in an ambush in the Mekong Delta. He was a Wesleyan graduate, of all things, and just a year older than Ab. It could have been him, she thought. Her pregnancy had simply been fate's way of keeping Ab away from harm.

And she enjoyed motherhood more than she had thought possible, though it did feel a bit as if their lives were on hold until Ab finished school. She knew that as soon as he had his degree they'd have much more freedom to forge the life they truly wanted. First of all, she wanted to move to a place where they could raise this child in nature. She'd never pictured herself raising a family in the suburbs with a husband who disappeared into the city each day only to come home bedraggled and weary each night. She knew she wasn't the only one who felt this way; there had been a virtual exodus from many of the urban areas on the East Coast, people of their generation fleeing the city for simpler lives. *Getting back to the land.*

Ab shook his head sadly. "How would we live?" he asked. "How would I make money? We have three mouths to feed, Gin."

They were sitting at their small kitchen table eating dinner. Ab's textbooks were next to his plate. He gripped one of the fancy forks they'd gotten for the wedding in his left hand. She used their good china and silver for every meal because she had neglected to register for everyday dinnerware, having difficulty imagining needing two whole sets of dishes.

"It's *communal* living," she argued. Marsha had told her about a friend of theirs from high school who had joined one such community. "Everyone works, and everyone shares. You raise your own food, live off the land."

Ab set his fork down and picked up his gold-rimmed goblet of iced tea. "I don't know the first thing about farming, Gin. I grew up in Dover, for God's sake."

"How hard can it be?" she asked. "You loved working for the produce company!"

"I don't think that counts," Ab said, grinning.

"It's a simple life," she said, staring at the ridiculous china upon which her miserable attempt at chicken cacciatore sat. "A good life. It's what you wanted, Ab. What *we* wanted."

Ab reached across the table and took Ginny's hand in his, ran his fingers across her dimpled knuckles. "Just let me finish school, pass the bar. Then I'll at least have my degree, something to fall back on. Maybe I can start my own practice."

Ginny sighed and reached for her own glass of iced tea. But it was bitter, and the ice had melted.

"I don't want to raise this baby here," she said softly.

"Well, of course not, we'll get a bigger house eventually. We'll outgrow this one after a couple of years."

She shook her head and gestured stupidly at Ab's fork.

"No," she said. "I mean here. In this world. Where a fork costs more than the weekly grocery bill for some families."

Ab removed his fork from his mouth and it hovered in all its delicate, ornate glory in the air before him before he settled it onto the plate.

"You knew," he said. "You knew this is how I grew up. That my family . . ." he trailed off as though he couldn't bring himself to say whatever he was thinking.

"But I thought you rejected all of this. That you hated it."

Ab wiped at his mouth with his napkin thoughtfully.

"Seriously," he said, smiling a bit sadly, "I think you are the only girl in the whole world who wants less instead of more."

Ginny felt her heart lighten some, though the cacciatore was making it burn a little beneath her ribs.

"I don't want or need anything other than you. And this baby. It's simple, really. Consider it *permission*," she said.

"Permission?"

"Yes. Carte blanche. Permission to leave all of this. I don't need any of it. I don't want any of it. What I want is a garden and a little sunny kitchen and a warm bed. But more than that, I want a happy husband."

"A happy husband, hmmm?" he asked, standing up from the table.

"Yes," she said.

He reached for her hand and pulled her gently to her feet and into his lap. "You already have a happy husband," he said, nuzzling her neck.

"That so?" she asked.

"Yep," he said. "But I see your position, counselor. And you've made a very good case. I'll take all of this into consideration in my deliberations," he said, grinning and pulling her close.

"I hope you do," she said. He smelled like something musky and sweet, cologne and chicken cacciatore.

Then he promised, promised in her ear in a whisper so soft, she had to strain to hear.

"I will follow you anywhere you want to go."

But when Ab finally graduated, a year later, they did not go to the woods. Instead, they moved to Dover, into a much grander house than their crowded row house in Cambridge. Abbott insisted on providing the down payment, and Ab insisted (to her, anyway) that it was only temporary, that he needed to get his toes wet in the law, and what better place to do so than at his own father's firm. He'd get some good experience and be able to save some money. They couldn't flee the city, their lives, without a *nest egg*, a term that made Ginny imagine an actual sterling silver egg. The magical, beautiful egg that would make their future possible.

And, to be truthful, there was something sort of lovely about their lives now. The house was beautiful, their son was beautiful (everyone said so). The neighborhood looked as though it belonged in a movie: the tree-lined street and singing birds. Once a week they put their shiny silver trash can out in front of their home (instead of in an alley Dumpster) and by ten o'clock in the morning, when she took Peyton out for a walk, it was empty. A gardener came weekly as well, to trim the hedges and mow the lawn in the summer. When snow fell, the walkway and driveway were shoveled and sprinkled with salt so that no one ever slipped and fell. They did not have a housekeeper; Ab had offered to hire one, though she declined. She was home all day with Peyton, what else was she supposed to do with her time?

She had traded in the old life in Cambridge for this new one, consumed by the demands of the house: ironing, folding, and vacuuming. The endless string of chores Peyton provided: tiny clothes to be laundered, toys to be picked up and put away, again and again and again.

She didn't socialize with the other mothers in the neighborhood. She imagined all of them, her compatriots, each living out their respective lives inside their lovely homes, each life quietly identical to the other. What on earth would they talk about? Their Frigidaires and their colicky infants? The price of ground beef or the best way to remove stains from the toilet? Besides, this was only temporary; she'd made the mistake of getting attached to their neighbors in Cambridge; leaving them behind had been difficult.

Thankfully, there were books. There had always been books. She missed the library, but she had her own personal library she'd built over the years, and she returned to those books again and again whenever she thought she might die of boredom inside the house. There were entire days when she neglected household chores in favor of hours spent reading on the couch. Once, when Peyton had some childhood illness or another, she was blessed with three straight hours of peace and quiet in which she read and reread *Ariel*, that collection of Sylvia Plath's poems Ab had given her for her birthday, from cover to cover. It made her feel guilty, of course, but she'd been slightly irritated when Peyton had woken up the next day healthy and energetic and as demanding as could be again.

And so her life moved forward in circles, in cycles, for the first year in Dover as Ab got his toes, then his knees, then his waist wet in the law. By the time Peyton turned three, Ginny knew that if she didn't pull him out soon, he'd be fully submerged.

"Let's drive down there," she'd said one Saturday morning, as she set Ab's usual Saturday morning soft-boiled egg and two pieces of buttered toast in front of him.

"Where's that?" he asked absently; he was reading something he'd plucked from his briefcase, the promise to leave work at work on the weekends long forgotten.

"The Cape. Let's go to the cottage."

She'd given up the idea that Ab and she would join one of those communes. The creature comforts of having their own home—privacy, for one—were things even she wasn't willing to sacrifice. But that didn't mean they couldn't live more simply. Move into his family's cottage. She dreamed of the woods, the ocean, a life in which her husband didn't spend seventy hours a week in the city.

Ab smiled, but the little spark was gone. He sighed and reached for Ginny's hand. "My dad has asked me to be a partner," he said.

Ginny's throat constricted.

"A partner?"

"Yes. It would take me seven years at any other firm to move from associate to partner."

"What does this mean?" she asked, knowing already and fully well exactly what it meant.

"Richardson, Richardson & Associates," he said, taking a deep breath, his chest filling with air, his shoulders broadening.

Overhead a large bird flew, casting a shadow, which for a fleeting moment cast a shadow over them all.

"Ginny, I want this. For us. For *me*."

Twenty-eight

۲

September 1971

I picked up a Florida map at the last gas stop. It's more detailed than the atlas. Can you grab it?" Marsha said, and Ginny reached toward the glove box, remembering for the first time that there was a loaded firearm inside.

Ginny located the key under the mat, unlocked it, and reached in, her fingers grazing the cold metal of the gun. She pulled the map out and closed the door, not bringing up how uncomfortable having the gun made her feel. This was Marsha's vehicle, one she'd essentially hijacked. Who was she to start making the rules?

"Gabe made me get it," Marsha said.

"What's that?"

She nodded her head toward the closed glove box and mouthed, *the gun*. She whispered, "He worries about me on the nights I work late. Remember that guy in Chicago a few years ago who raped and killed all those student nurses?"

Ginny nodded and thought about Marsha coming out of the hospital after her shift, the dangers lurking in the parking lot. She thought about how vulnerable they all were, how fear had lived inside her since she was old enough to understand the dangers of being a girl in this world.

She spread the map across her lap and studied the northern part of Florida, which they were set to enter in about a hundred miles if they stayed on I-95. The exit for State Route 301 was coming up.

"I think you want to go that way," Ginny said, motioning to the sign they were approaching.

Marsha, without using her blinker, pulled over to the right lane, taking the exit.

"It'll take longer this way," Ginny said, nervous now about taking a detour that would keep them on the road any longer than necessary. But really, what other options did they have?

The terrain here was much as it had been throughout Georgia, lots of trees and green on either side of them. Though she wondered if they'd have to wait for sunshine until they crossed the border into the so-called Sunshine State. Overhead the skies were gray and ominous, the air thick with a sort of buzzing electricity.

"When did they say that storm was supposed to hit the Gulf?" Marsha asked and reached for the radio knob, turning to the AM station, perhaps hoping for a weather report. Nothing but static and warbled music.

"The news last night said that it was coming up from Central America, expected to hit the Gulf of Mexico in the next day or so," Ginny said. It didn't seem like they'd have anything to worry about, even with this detour. Now, if they'd planned to drive to Louisiana or Texas, that might cause a problem, but as far as she knew they were still headed to Weeki Wachee, where Theresa would be waiting for them with a place to stay. She couldn't imagine that Ab would ever think to look for her in the Florida swamps. She didn't think she'd ever even mentioned Marsha's older sister to him.

"Oh, shit. Is that the car you saw?" Marsha asked, raising her eyes to the rearview mirror.

Ginny turned slowly in her seat and looked behind them. In the distance, there was a car, approaching quickly. It appeared to be green, but it was difficult to tell, the skies were so dark. She felt her hands begin to tremble again, and she turned back to face the road ahead of them.

"I don't know," she said. "But maybe go a little faster?"

Marsha gripped the wheel and accelerated; Ginny held on tight.

The car kept gaining on them, though; it had to be going at least twice as fast as they were. Ginny twisted in her seat to watch as it approached. Soon it went from being a speck in the distance to being nearly upon them. When it roared past in the passing lane, Ginny could see it was the green Duster.

"What the hell?" Marsha said.

The car had passed so quickly, Ginny hadn't been able to catch a glimpse of the driver, or of the passenger if there had been one. It was going so fast that she only caught the last couple of letters of the license plate, which was yellow with blue numbers. *Massachusetts.*

"I should see where that motherfucker is going," Marsha said, gunning the accelerator again.

"No," Ginny said.

But Marsha was racing ahead now, determined. Ginny felt queasy.

"Slow down, Marsh," she said. "If he was following us, he wouldn't have passed us, right?"

"He's screwing with us," she said.

It must have been true, because as they rounded a small bend, they could see the Duster parked at the side of the road. A man was leaning against the open driver's-side door. Marsha pressed her foot on the brakes and slowed.

"Roll down your window," she said.

"What?"

"Roll down your window!" She leaned across Ginny's lap and reached for the window handle. Lucy, who had been napping in Ginny's arms, stirred.

"Keep your eyes on the road! I'll do it." Ginny rolled the window down, and Marsha slowed the car to a crawl.

As they approached the Duster, Ginny took the guy in. He was nondescript. Not tall, not short. Anywhere from thirty to forty years old. Dark hair, pale skin, a thick beard.

Lucy peered out the window as Ginny did, saw the man, and started to wail. Of course, another *beard*.

With the window down, Marsha leaned across Ginny, extending her middle finger dramatically.

The man returned her gesture by tipping an imaginary hat, and as Marsha sped up and blew past, he calmly got into his car. Ginny turned to watch as he closed the door and started the engine. Ginny studied him in the side-view mirror as she tried to comfort Lucy, who, once again, was trembling and weeping. She also felt her lap suddenly warm and damp. A soaking wet diaper. But there was no way in hell they were going to pull over now.

"Who do you think he is?" Marsha asked, glancing in her rearview mirror.

Ginny shook her head. She didn't recognize him. The car was from Massachusetts. Could he be someone that Abbott Senior had hired to follow them? Someone from Willowridge? Or maybe an undercover police officer. But all the way from Massachusetts? And if that were the case, why not just pull them over?

"Well, whoever that asshole is, we need to lose him," Marsha said.

"That's a bad word," Peyton chimed in from the backseat. He hadn't said anything in nearly an hour. "You say a lot of bad words."

"Sorry, buddy!" Marsha said brightly into the rearview. To Ginny, she said, "Get out the map again?"

Ginny studied the map. There were about ten main arteries that would get them to Weeki Wachee, and about a hundred smaller veins threading from where they were now to the Gulf Coast of Florida. But choosing one seemed arbitrary, and depending on how far behind this guy was, potentially lethal. Lucy had finally stopped crying, but Ginny's blouse was damp with tears, her lap soggy with pee.

"We could go this way," Ginny said, deciding that perhaps a capricious decision would, in the end, be less predictable than one backed by any sort of reason or logic. Let fate decide.

The billboard, tattered and faded, loomed ahead. A beleaguered-looking alligator under the words GATORS GALORE: A REPTILIAN ADVEN-TURE. 161 MILES AHEAD.

Peyton perked up, pointing at the sign. "Like the crocodile in *Peter Pan!*" he exclaimed, climbing between the two front seats to study the antiquated sign. Ginny didn't have the heart to tell him that Gators Galore might not even exist anymore. But his enthusiasm seemed to be a sign.

"That will bring us almost to the Gulf," Ginny said, studying the map. "Then we can just hug the coast all the way down to Weeki Wachee."

Marsha nodded once and took the exit advertised on the billboard. Ginny said a silent prayer that whoever that man was wouldn't think to follow the signs for a reptilian roadside attraction.

Ginny had hoped that once they got on the new road, they'd see a place where they could pull over and she could change Lucy's diaper, but there was nothing as far as the eye could see except for orange groves. It was raining a little as well, and the prospect of trying to put a dry diaper on a wriggling child in this sort of drizzle seemed counterintuitive.

"Hey, Marsh, can we stop soon? Lucy's really wet."

"I thought it kind of smelled like pee," Marsha said. "My nose is finely tuned these days. I swear I can already smell the ocean."

Ginny recollected the heightened sense of smell she'd had when she was pregnant with Peyton and Lucy as well. She seemed to be able to smell everything; her world was a palette of conflicting odors. Ab had once gone out to lunch and eaten fried clams. For three days afterward she still thought he smelled like the bottom of the ocean. She'd made him gargle with Listerine, but the minty smell made her eyes water.

Finally, in the distance, through the drizzle and haze, Ginny saw an orange dome. It loomed in the distance like an odd beacon. As they approached, she could see that it was a citrus stand, shaped like a giant orange, complete with a jaunty stem nearly two stories up. She marveled at how enormous it was. Peyton perked up, too.

"Wow! That's a big peach!" he said.

"It's an orange," she said. *They were in Florida.* "I'll take the baby inside to see if they have a restroom. Can you watch Pey?"

"Sure," Marsha said. She pulled around behind the building, parking out of sight of the main road just in case the man in the Duster had somehow managed to track them down again.

Ginny grabbed a change of clothes for each of them from the laundry bag as well as a fresh diaper. Inside the shop, she was greeted by not only rows and rows of citrus bins, but also aisles of souvenirs. Key rings and plastic visors, T-shirts and flip-flops and beach towels and snow globes. For a moment, she allowed herself to imagine that she was just a tourist, that this was, indeed, just some lengthy road trip. A family vacation. What might she pick up to serve as a reminder? She even thought of what sort of postcard she might send home. "Wish You Were Here"? "Greetings from the Sunshine State"?

Home. It was Thursday, still less than a week since she'd taken Lucy from the school. Since her world systematically began to fall to pieces. She hadn't spoken to her mother since they were in New Jersey. She knew she should check in with her again, though she feared that Shirley would confirm her darkest fears. That Ab and his father were going to send someone after her; maybe they already had. That Willowridge had gotten the FBI involved. That she was on a road trip that would end not in Weeki Wachee but in losing her children. When her mind began to wander to those dark places, she had to pull herself back. Keep from opening those doors to all the awful possibilities.

As she made her way through the maze of colorful tchotchkes toward the overhead RESTROOMS sign, blinking lights to guide the way, she felt dizzy. She clung tighter to Lucy and rushed past a rack of tacky T-shirts (SEND US MORE TOURISTS, THE LAST ONE WAS DELICIOUS, said the grinning cartoon gator) and an entire display of coconut monkeys, feeling tears starting to spill from her eyes. What was she doing? This, all of this, was insane. The coconut monkeys seemed to mock her with their buck-toothed grins.

She rushed into the restroom and quickly changed Lucy first, noting that the diaper rash was looking angry again. She took care to clean and dry her bottom, using extra ointment and powder. What she needed to do was to just let her go without a diaper for a day. When Peyton had gotten a rash like this, she'd simply spent an afternoon in their back-yard, letting him run around naked. The fresh air had been the best medicine.

She set Lucy on the closed toilet lid and quickly changed out of her own damp clothes, considered just leaving them there. Once they got set-tled, she could get new clothes. Start over. But what did that even mean? Starting over. What was she doing? Did she really think she could keep running like this forever? So what if they finally reached Weeki Wachee; that was nothing but a momentary refuge. It wasn't as if being there would change anything about the fact that this little girl in her arms, this baby with her soft skin and tawny eyes, with her curls and tiny fingers, did not belong to her. This truth was one she'd been keeping behind a locked door, in its own room. She could not go inside. Would not.

"*Mum mum.*"

Ginny stopped.

She looked at Lucy, who was peering at her with an intensity that made her body soften, warmth pooling like something liquid at the center of her.

"Mumma," she said again and reached her chubby little arms up to Ginny, clasping her fingers.

The tears that Ginny had wiped furiously away returned, and she shook her head.

"Yes, baby?" she asked.

"Mumma," Lucy said again, and Ginny thought she could stay here forever. Inside a cramped bathroom stall in an orange-shaped souvenir shop, in some Florida swamplands. She could live inside this orange orb, subsist on tangerines.

Ginny picked Lucy up again and held her tightly. She smelled clean and sweet, and, at least for this moment, she knew nothing mattered but this.

Because she'd left her credit card at the body repair shop back in Savannah, she was starting to worry about money. She was down to her last fifty dollars. She'd seen a pay phone behind the giant orange when they pulled in. She'd get Lucy situated in the car and then call her mother collect. Ask her to wire some money to the Western Union closest to Weeki Wachee.

But as she and Lucy exited the store and moved around the back to the parking lot, Marsha came running up to her.

"Is Peyton with you?" Marsha said, her eyes frantic.

"What?"

"Peyton," she said. "You don't have him?"

"*No,*" Ginny said, and her heart started to pound in her ears and throat. "Weren't you watching him?"

"I told him to sit at that picnic table, and I went to get some snacks from the vending machine over there, but when I came back he was gone."

"You left him alone?" Ginny said in disbelief.

"I thought he went inside to find you. I was just headed in to look. I thought maybe he needed to use the restroom."

"Oh, my God," Ginny said. She felt Lucy stiffen in her arms. "It's okay, it's okay," she said, though she wasn't sure whom she was comforting: Lucy or herself.

"I'll go look in the store. Why don't you look for him back here," Ginny said and motioned toward the groves behind the shop, the endless identical rows of orange trees.

It was starting to rain now, and the air was oppressive and humid.

Still carrying Lucy, Ginny ran back into the store and went straight to the clerk, who was ringing up a customer's purchases. The middle-aged woman had bought six snow globes, and the clerk was wrapping each of them carefully in butcher paper.

"Excuse me," Ginny said, trying to keep her voice level.

The clerk, a wrinkled gentleman with wobbly jowls, barely looked up from his task.

"I'm looking for my little boy. He's six years old. He has brown hair. He's wearing a white shirt and blue shorts? With white stripes?"

He shook his head. "Haven't seen any kids," he said.

Ginny walked briskly up and down the aisles, searching for something that might have caught Peyton's attention. He wasn't a kid who generally wandered off, but then again, she'd never taken him somewhere he might be tempted. Aisle after aisle, there was no sign of Peyton. She walked back to the restrooms at the rear of the shop and looked at the men's room door. Maybe he had just needed to go to the bathroom. Usually, Ginny brought him in with her to the ladies' room, but he hadn't complained about needing to go potty.

She knocked tentatively, and when no one answered, she pushed the door gently open, saying, "Peyton? Pey?" Feeling her heart climbing up into her throat, she walked past the urinals to the stalls, and peered under each, looking for Peyton's sneakers. "Peyton!" she said more firmly now. As if he were only playing hide and seek.

When she saw a pair of boots beneath one of the stall doors, she gasped and started to back away. When the man emerged, Ginny gripped Lucy tightly and rushed toward the door.

It was the man from the Duster, the guy with the beard.

"Hey," he said, seemingly as startled as she. A slow grin stretched across his face even as Lucy began to quake. "Wait, are you—"

"Just leave us alone," she said. "Please!"

She ran through the aisles of seashells and back outside; she could see the Duster parked cockeyed at the far end of the lot. But she didn't see Marsha anywhere, and she felt like she might faint from the heat and the fear. Where was Peyton? Finally, when she thought her legs might not even hold her up for another moment, Marsha emerged from one of the grove's rows.

Peyton was riding piggyback on her back.

Relief flooded her; she wanted nothing more than to run to him, hold him, yell at him, and embrace him all at once. But when she looked behind her, she could see that the man was exiting the building, looking left and right. Looking for them.

"Let's *go!*" Ginny hollered to Marsha, and Marsha, seeing the Duster and the man, started to jog toward the car.

Ginny ran to the car as well and got in, still holding Lucy. Marsha backed out to turn the car around toward the parking lot exit just as the man was climbing into his own car.

"Jesus Christ!" Marsha said. "Who the hell *is* this guy?"

She peeled out of the parking lot and onto the road, the rain coming down in hard sheets now.

"Don't you ever, ever run off again," Ginny said to Peyton as she leaned between the rear seats. Peyton looked at her angrily, his arms crossed. "Where was he?" she asked, whipping her head back to Marsha, trying to keep her anger from blooming.

"He was picking oranges," she said. "I'm so sorry. I should have kept a better eye on him—"

"That man, that man could have taken him," Ginny burst out, verbalizing every fear she had entertained while he was missing. "What if Ab sent him to get Peyton? To take him home?"

For the first time, she began to think that this was, indeed, exactly what Ab would want most. His son. His perfect, beautiful son. She was disposable, replaceable. But he would never give up Peyton.

"Wait! Brownie! I left Brownie!" Peyton said, his eyes wide and stunned by the realization that he'd left his bear behind.

Crap.

"We can't go back," she said, feeling guilt overwhelm her. He'd slept with that bear every night since he was born.

"Oh, Pey, honey," she said. "We can't go back. I'm so sorry."

Ginny felt like crying herself as he burst into tears.

"I want my daddy," Peyton said. "I hate this car. And I hate that stupid baby."

Ginny's sorrow turned to anger and she seethed, but before she could lash out, before she could say the words that could never be taken back, Marsha said, "Holy shit." That was when Ginny realized that the steam coming off the hood of the car was not humidity or fog; it was smoke.

They drove until the engine cut out, then Marsha veered off the road and along the shoulder. It was raining hard now.

"Oh, my God," Ginny said. "What do we do?" She turned around and saw the Duster's headlights through the mist. He was coming after them.

Marsha leaned over, grabbed the key from under the floor mat, and unlocked the glove box. The door fell open, and she reached across Ginny and pulled out the gun.

Ginny was still holding Lucy on her lap; she clung to her tightly.

When Peyton saw the gun, he said, "Mama!" Just a single exclamation filled with terror and dread.

Ginny turned to Peyton, reaching into the backseat for his hand. It was clammy and warm in hers. "It's okay," she promised. "Everything is going to be okay."

"Lock your door," Marsha said. "And the back."

Ginny twisted backward to reach and depress the door lock behind her, while Marsha got Peyton's. When the man approached, Ginny felt like she might vomit. He tapped on the driver's window, and Marsha whispered, "What do I do?"

Ginny shook her head and held tightly to Lucy, who had buried her face in Ginny's chest.

He tapped again and signaled for her to roll the window down.

Ginny could see the gun in Marsha's hand, but she wasn't sure if the man could see it as well.

Marsha rolled down the window and turned to him. Ginny felt woozy.

The bearded man leaned into the window, resting his elbows on the window frame. He was chewing gum, delight dancing in his pale eyes.

"So, it looks like you've got a little something that doesn't belong to you," he said. His accent was thick. Boston Southie thick. Ginny sucked in her breath, thinking, No, no, no.

"What are you talking about?" Marsha asked.

"Pretty sure this cah's not from Virginia," he said, smirking.

The tags. This was about the stolen plate? Ginny let out a breath, just a little, but still, she was terrified. This guy had followed them all the way from Atlantic City to track down a license plate? Was he a police officer?

"Are you a cop?" Marsha asked, shoving the gun beneath her bottom.

"A cop?" the guy said quizzically, still grinning.

"Yeah," Marsha said defiantly. "Can I see your badge?"

Ginny waited. Here it was, the moment the world fell apart. She squeezed Lucy so tightly, she could feel her ribs expanding and contracting. Lucy was trembling with fear, though this time she didn't cry out.

"I ain't no cop." The guy laughed.

"Well, then, I think we'll be on our way. Have a nice day," Marsha said and started to roll up the window.

But the man's muscular forearm held the window firmly open.

"Listen, buddy," Marsha said, and Ginny watched as she eased the gun out from under her. "I don't know who the hell you are or why you're following us. But you are starting to piss me off."

At the sight of the gun, the man lifted his hands in surrender and backed away.

"Hey, you got this all wrong," he said.

Marsha was pointing the gun at him now, and Peyton was leaning between the seats as though he were watching an episode of *The Lone Ranger*.

"Sit back," Ginny said and gently pushed him back into the backseat.

"Who are you?" Marsha said.

"You don't recognize me?" he said, chuckling.

Marsha scowled.

"People used to say we looked like twins," he said. "Irish twins, maybe. Too bad we're Italian."

He leaned down again, gingerly leaning in, looking right at the barrel of the gun.

"You ladies pretty much had me on a wild-goose chase. He must really love you."

Ginny flinched. Here it was, someone Ab had sent?

"Holy shit!" Marsha said, lowering the gun. *"Lorenzo?"*

"Who's Lorenzo?" Ginny asked.

"Gabe's brother. Jesus H. Christ."

Gabe?

The man's smirk broke into a full grin. "Listen, he didn't want me to come at first. Figured you had your reasons for leaving. But then when your aunt told him you were pregnant, he asked me if I could keep an eye out. Make sure you got down here safe. Maybe even convince you to come home. I drove all night from Boston and caught up with you not long after you killed that deer."

He'd been following them since *Virginia*?

"Why didn't you tell us who you were?" Ginny chimed in.

"Gabe didn't want me to scare you, figured you might not even notice me tailing you. I was planning to tell you once you finally got to where you were going."

Marsha rolled her eyes. "Why didn't he come himself?" she asked. "If this is so important?"

"He woulda, but he was working back-to-back shifts over the holiday weekend. I'm currently *between jobs,* so I offered to help out. He's my baby brothah. Never mind that there'll be my nephew or niece." He gestured with his chin toward Marsha's stomach.

Marsha, stunned into silence, lowered her gun.

"What the fuck, Lorenzo? You scared the living shit out of me. I coulda shot you!"

"That's a bad word," Peyton chimed in from the backseat, and Ginny finally let out the breath she'd been holding.

"Well, you should be thanking your lucky stahs I've been tailing you ladies," Lorenzo said as he opened the driver's-side door for Marsha. "Looks like you might need a ride."

The engine had stopped smoking, at least, but the air stank of burned oil and gasoline.

"And long as you don't make a fuss, I won't tell Gabe about that guy I saw you with at the bahbecue joint back in Georgia."

Defeated, they got out of the car, and as Lorenzo tried to assess the damage under the hood, Ginny stood at the side of the road trying to keep the kids dry under one of their beach towels, which she held over them like a canopy.

"Well, it looks like the old Dart finally shit the bed," Marsha said. "What the hell are we gonna do now?"

"I can get you to where you're going, on one condition," Lorenzo said.

"Yeah, what's that?" Marsha challenged.

"Call my brothah. Talk to him. He's beside himself over you taking off. About the baby. I help you, you call him. You owe him that much."

Apparently, not only did Lorenzo have investigative skills, but he also knew his way around an engine. After a cursory look under the hood, he said, "Whoever you had work on the radiator did a pretty shitty job. There's a six-inch crack in the plastic tank. I can fix it with some epoxy. I hope you didn't pay for this."

Ginny thought about the man in the shop, the one where she'd left the Master Charge. They'd been totally scammed. Probably saw two easy marks the second they walked in the door.

"We're just thirty miles from Weeki Wachee," Marsha said. "If you can give us a ride, we'll leave the car here. Get it towed later."

"I've got Triple A." Lorenzo nodded. "I can meet them back at the cah and get it towed to wherever you are. It shouldn't take me more than an hour to fix it. I just need someplace dry to work on it."

Lucy had calmed some, enough for Ginny to get herself and the two kids piled into the back of the Duster, which smelled like cigarettes and bubble gum. Sure enough, the ashtray was full, and the floor was littered with Bazooka wrappers. Ginny wasn't sure how Marsha's delicate nose and sensitive stomach were going to take it. Marsha loaded their bags into the trunk and got in the passenger seat.

Apparently, when Marsha didn't show up at work at the hospital on Monday night, Gabe had called the apartment and her little sister had answered. Melanie (who, according to Marsha, couldn't keep a secret if her life depended on it) told him not to worry, that they were just in Virginia visiting her aunt. She'd given him Pepper and Nancy's number, even. But Pepper—from whom Melanie had inherited her loose lips—had spilled the beans about the pregnancy and told him that they were headed from Virginia to Florida. He'd called his brother, Lorenzo, in Boston and asked him if he could do him a favor.

"Where are you girls headed, anyway?" Lorenzo asked. "You haven't exactly been taking a direct route. I practically got whiplash followin' you."

"Weeki Wachee," Marsha said. "You know, the place with the mermaids? My sister lives there."

"Huh," Lorenzo said. "I'd have thought you might be taking the kids here to that new Disney World."

At this, Peyton perked up again. "We're going to see Mickey Mouse."

The man looked in the rearview mirror, and Lucy started to cry again.

"Something wrong with her?" he asked.

"She's afraid of men with beards," Ginny said.

"No, I mean she's retahded, right? Gabe and I got a mongoloid cousin. Name's Eddie. Slow as syrup, but a real sweet kid."

Ginny flinched, feeling anger bubbling up at the word. *Retarded*. It was a word she'd used herself before, but now it seemed inappropriate.

"She's got Down syndrome," she said.

Lorenzo shrugged and kept driving. Ginny knew that this was the way the world would see Lucy, but for the last week, she'd managed to avoid thinking about it. About how cruel people could be, even without trying sometimes.

"She's very bright, actually," Ginny said. "She said 'Mama' today. Just a week ago, she didn't have any words at all."

"She said 'Mama'?" Marsha asked, spinning around in her seat to face the back. "You said 'Mama'?" she said to Lucy and touched her tiny hand.

"Mumma," Lucy said in the affirmative.

Peyton scowled and kicked his feet against the backseat.

"What's the matter?" Ginny whispered.

"You're *my* mama."

"Of course I am. I will always be your mama," she said gently. But he was clearly enraged now; this was the face she'd seen when Christopher stole his Matchbox cars, his trike, his G.I. Joe.

"No. You're *her* mama now."

Ginny shook her head, guilt flooding her senses, shorting out the sort of electric buzz she'd been feeling when she sprang to Lucy's defense.

"Hey! Let's put on some music," Marsha said, reaching for the knob. "Maybe we can find the bullfrog song?"

Ginny shook her head. She reached for Peyton's hand, but he yanked it away at her touch.

"I want Brownie, and I want my daddy," he said, his face red, his chin quivering. "I just want to go home."

Twenty-nine

❦

1968–1969

It wasn't so terrible, this life. Most girls like Ginny dreamed of this: a handsome, successful, sweet husband, a beautiful son and a lovely home, a pristine kitchen and a growing savings account. She had to remind herself so many times when Ab was late coming home from work or her mother-in-law stopped by to expound her vast wisdom regarding decorating or impose her various and controversial methods on child rearing.

He's too old for a bottle. He's too young to give up his naps. He needs a spanking, Sylvia suggested more than once when Peyton acted up in the way that toddler boys are prone to do. All the while, Sylvia was perched at the edge of Ginny's sofa as if it were a public toilet she didn't want her bottom to touch.

When Ab came home with Arthur as a Christmas gift when Peyton was three, Sylvia had tsk-tsked herself into a tizzy.

"Animals are meant to live outside the house, not in it," Sylvia had said, shaking her head as poor Arthur tried to nuzzle against her.

"You grew up on a farm, didn't you?" Ginny had asked. "You didn't have any pets?"

"My father didn't believe in pets," she said. "Animals serve one purpose only, and that is to provide food."

It took all Ginny's imaginative powers to picture Sylvia growing up on that farm in Vermont. She was the kind of woman who wouldn't say *shit* if she had a mouthful (as Ginny's father might say); when Ginny tried to imagine Sylvia's former life, she could only conjure an image of her in her delicate kitten heels stepping over cow patties as though they were land mines, Chanel purse dangling from one bent elbow.

"Don't you ever miss it?" Ginny asked her once. "Living in the country? It's so beautiful in Vermont."

Sylvia had seemed startled by the question.

"Of course not," she'd said, gesturing as though this home (Ginny and Ab's) was her own. "*This* is what one aspires to, Virginia." And Ginny realized she meant a home like this in general terms: gleaming floors and luxurious drapes and candlesticks and linen napkins and brand-new appliances.

"What about the city, then?" Ginny had persisted, wanting desperately to understand this woman. "New York? Ab said you were a singer on Broadway? That must have been thrilling. I've never even *seen* a Broadway show."

Again, Sylvia clucked her tongue as if in disdain of the woman she once was.

"I was a girl, Virginia," she said. "Foolish."

Ginny couldn't help but think that this word was aimed at her as well. Perhaps Sylvia saw a bit of herself in Ginny: the poor girl who somehow navigated her way to this elegant suburban life. A girl who was always studying the teeth of this gift horse, looking for decay.

Despite the creature comforts of this new world, however, there were times when Ginny dreamed her way back into the stacks at the Converse, back into her old life. It was an odd nostalgia she had for those years in which her life had still felt like something on the other side of a window. There had been such exquisite pleasure in the anticipation of what her future held for her. But it seemed now that each decision, each choice she made, had narrowed those possibilities down, until there was but one solitary fate.

Of course, she knew she was not the only person who had felt this narrowing, this closing in. It was, in every way, the way that life tricked you into believing in destiny, when in fact she had been the one to determine everything. You could drive yourself crazy with what-ifs. She'd watched her mother do it after her father died. What if she hadn't sent him out for that gallon of milk? What if she had made the long trek to the market on foot? What if she'd kissed him good-bye? Would those two seconds of affection have been enough to prevent the seemingly inevitable collision? Ginny tried not to entertain such foolish unraveling. What if she hadn't accepted Ab's tickets to JFK's convocation and instead camped out with Marsha for a spot to see the president? What if they hadn't forgotten the condom, and she hadn't gotten pregnant that first time—Ab would have gone off to Vietnam with the IVS. Though this was one part where she hesitated. They hadn't known then what Vietnam had in store for them. For the boys of this country. Had he not gone to law school as his father had always planned, he might have wound up in Vietnam anyway—but as a soldier this time. He might not have come home at all, and then where would she be? A single mother, a widow. Exactly like her mother.

No, it was best not to try to untie the knots of a life. It was best to simply accept responsibility for what her life had become and make all future decisions carefully. Here was one such decision.

Still, a pervasive sharp pinch plagued her. *Regret*. That was what it was. The sense of having done the wrong thing, made the wrong choice. It was what niggled at her those nights when she lay awake alone waiting for Ab to come home, the times when she was so exhausted and lonely she just wanted to walk out the front door of that colossal house and keep walking. The times when she longed for a different future. A second chance.

Thirty

❧

September 1971

The storm coming up through the Gulf of Mexico was a full-blown hurricane now, according to the AM radio station they managed to tune in to, though what this meant for the Gulf Coast of Florida was simply rain. Lots and lots of rain. The sky was thick with it. The trees and foliage at the side of the road bowed under the weight of all that water. The windshield wipers on Lorenzo's car could barely keep up. Several times they had to pull over and wait for it to let up enough for them to see the road ahead. There were cars parked all along the side of the highway doing the same thing; even when they were back on the road, the slow procession of vehicles seemed almost funereal.

It was only thirty miles to Weeki Wachee from where the Dart had broken down, but for nearly an hour they drove along the highway in fits and starts. Both children were soggy and restless, and Ginny wanted nothing more than a hot shower and a clean bed to fall into. She planned to call her mother as soon as they got settled in. She'd ask her to wire some money, to help hold them over, and then she knew she'd need to deal with Ab. Her hope was that with this week to think about everything, with her gone, he'd realized that she was serious. That if forced into a choice, she'd choose the safety of her children. *Both* of them. This is what she told herself; however, she felt the sharp sting of the truth. While Lucy was no longer in that horrific place, was she really safe? She thought of Peyton slumped over in the backseat, holding his arm after they hit the deer. She thought of him slipping away from her, nearly disappearing at that roadside citrus stand. She thought of Marsha clutching the gun as that man leaned in. What if it hadn't been Gabe's brother? And what about the car, nearly bursting into flames with them still inside it? She'd done nothing but endanger not only Lucy but Peyton as well. If Abbott Senior had any idea what they'd been through, the dangerous situations she'd put them in, he'd likely make Ab take both children away from her. Argue that she was unfit.

And perhaps she was. Perhaps she was only competent within the safe confines of the house that Ab had given her. Perhaps she could only function effectively as a mother when her environment was one of his making. She thought of the way he doled out her allowance each week, she thought of the daily, weekly, monthly chores she was expected to fulfill (though of course he never said so in words, this was her end of the exchange). She thought of that pervasive hiss, the one that whispered at her ear, that gnawed at her spine as she ironed, and folded, and scrubbed, and shopped. As she cooked and coddled. As she sewed on loose buttons and affixed Band-Aids. All the mind-numbing hours spent pacing like a caged tiger inside those same four walls, wondering what the point was. Looking for a crack, a fissure, a weakness through which she might escape. Perhaps that was what Lucy had been. Just a week ago, she had been so numb she could hardly feel her own misery. And then she'd seen the opening and pushed herself through.

But to what end? To the swamps of Florida? With no money and only a bag of laundry? What had she been thinking? She felt like she was an animal escaped from the zoo, wandering through an unfamiliar city. A hostile place. Perhaps she would have been better off to stay confined. At least in that cage, she was safe.

"Here we are!" Lorenzo said, pulling off the road. The Weeki Wachee Springs sign was less showy than the billboards advertising the mermaids for the last thirty miles.

Lorenzo pulled into the parking lot, and as they gathered their things, he reached into his glove box and pulled out an envelope.

"Gabe asked me to give this to you," he said to Marsha.

Marsha looked at him for an explanation, but he only shrugged.

"Thanks," she said as she took the envelope, then leaned over and kissed his cheek. He seemed startled by the gesture but broke into a grin.

"I'll let Gabe know I found you. But please give him a call yourself after you open that up."

Marsha nodded and clutched the envelope tightly.

"Speaking of which, I need to find a pay phone to get ahold of Triple A. You guys gonna be here for a while?"

Marsha nodded. "Not going anywhere until you get back here with the car. You sure you can fix it?"

Lorenzo nodded. He shook off the rain and climbed back into the Duster. As he drove away, Ginny, Marsha, and the kids walked toward the Weeki Wachee Springs entrance. The rain was coming down hard now and the wind was tugging at the trees, pummeling the battered red arrow-shaped sign for the park that promised 9 LIVE SHOWS TODAY, RAIN OR SHINE.

"What's in the envelope?" Ginny whispered, though Lorenzo was long gone by then. "A letter?"

"Oh, who knows," Marsha said dismissively, but Ginny noted she was still clutching it in her hand.

"Does Theresa know we're coming today?" Ginny asked.

"The last time I talked to her was back in Savannah," Marsha said. "I was going to call her on the road, but we got a little sidetracked."

Ginny held tightly to Peyton's hand. She'd warned him that if he ever, ever decided to wander off again, she'd have his hide. She wondered if it would be cruel to put a leash on him. With her other arm, she held on to Lucy, who had found a comfortable spot on Ginny's hip. Her back was aching from only a few days of lugging around the extra thirty or so pounds. At least Lucy had finally calmed down in the car when she realized that Lorenzo was harmless. Ginny still shuddered whenever she tried to imagine what was causing such a visceral reaction to every man who wore a beard.

"Are you sure they're even open?" Ginny asked.

The parking lot had been nearly empty, save for a few cars.

Marsha didn't answer, which was Ginny's signal to stop asking questions. Marsha marched forward, and Ginny quietly followed behind.

The man at the ticket booth seemed surprised to see them, apparently the only show-goers in sight. He ran his hand across his thin hair, combed over a bald pate. Adjusted the collar of his Hawaiian shirt.

"How many tickets y'all need?" he said. "Kids under three are free."

"I'm actually here to see my sister? Her name's Theresa Malone?"

The man let out a loud laugh and said, "You mean Terra?"

Marsha had mentioned to Ginny earlier that Theresa had changed her name when she moved to Florida, though Ginny thought Terra was an ironic name for a mermaid.

"Yeah," she said.

"Shoulda known from that hair! You come to be a mermaid, too?"

"Nah," she said. "I don't even like to swim."

"Then Florida seems like a crazy place to come!" he said, chuckling. "That's like saying you don't like cheese and heading off to Wisconsin! What about you?" he asked, turning to Ginny. "You could get a job here. Pretty girl like you."

"I suppose it's one of my *many* prospects," Ginny said.

He scowled. Apparently, men didn't like it when their compliments were met with sarcasm.

"Well, isn't she a feisty one," he said to Marsha. "Usually it's the red-heads that are made of piss and vinegar."

Feisty was not a word anyone had ever used to describe Ginny. Some-thing about that made her smile. Just a few hours in Florida, and she was already becoming someone completely new. Maybe she would change *her* name, too.

"Listen, it's been real quiet because of the storm," he said. "But like the sign says, the show goes on rain or shine. How about I go ahead and give y'all complimentary tickets for the next performance. Come back here after and I'll make sure you get backstage to see your sister."

They made their way down a long sloping hallway and into the the-ater, which consisted of several rows of seats facing a curved wall of glass. The seats were hard and uncomfortable, and there was something nearly suffocating about the muggy air.

They got the kids situated, and not long after, lights illuminated an underwater stage. It was as if they were peering into a giant aquarium, complete with sunken caverns. She turned to Peyton, whose eyes wid-ened at the spectacle.

The "mermaids," beautiful girls in shimmery swimsuits and flippers, performed a sort of water ballet. Taking periodic breaths of air via long rubbery tubes hidden behind the rocks, they held their breath for min-utes at a time until bubbles tumbled from their lips. Peyton and Lucy were both rapt.

Lucy's chest rumbled, and she coughed again. This damned muggy air. Ginny hoped she wasn't coming down with a cold.

"You okay?" she asked, and Lucy leaned into her. Ginny rubbed her back.

Music was piped in through speakers overhead, and it was mesmer-izing.

"There she is!" Marsha said, squeezing Ginny's arm and gesturing to a dark-haired mermaid who had just emerged from one of the caverns.

She wore a bejeweled emerald bikini top and a shimmery tail, and her hair, like Marsha's, was a wild tangle of dark curls.

Ginny's memories of Theresa were of a sullen teenage girl with glasses and hunched shoulders. Theresa was five years older than Marsha and rarely came out of her bedroom. How funny to see her now, this glamorous, otherworldly creature. It really was possible, she thought, as she watched Theresa—*Terra*—navigate the waters as though she truly were part of that underwater habitat, as though she had become someone else.

When the brief show ended, they filed out, and as promised, the man from the ticket booth led them to the backstage area, where he left them. "Dressing rooms are down that way. Little fella, you'll cover your eyes, won't ya?" he said to Peyton.

"Yes, sir," Peyton said.

Marsha knocked on the battered dressing room door, and someone inside hollered, "Hold on!"

Marsha shrugged and smiled.

It was Theresa who answered the door, though it seemed to take her a moment before it registered that her sister was standing there.

"Marshmallow!" Theresa said. "You made it!" She hugged Marsha and then pulled back, still holding on to her shoulders, studying her face. Then she noticed Ginny, who was standing behind. "And *Ginny*! Come in, come in. Oh, my God, it's so nice to see y'all." Not only did she have a new name, but an entirely new accent. Smooth and southern, sweet as peaches. "These must be your sweet babies?"

Ginny nodded. She was carrying Lucy, as always, and Lucy reached out to touch the sparkly green strap of her costume.

"Ain't it *pretty*?" she said to Lucy.

Ginny waited for Theresa to notice Lucy's disability, but she didn't. Instead she continued talking to her.

"I like how it sparkles, too. A girl can never have too many sparkles."

"Spaw-kul," Lucy said.

Ginny caught her breath.

"And what did *you* think of the mermaids?" she asked, leaning down to Peyton. Peyton was suddenly, inexplicably shy, hiding behind Ginny's legs. Then again, he'd never met a real-life mermaid before.

"Let me get changed, and then we can all go get something to eat across the way. Figure out what's next."

Theresa emerged from the dressing room just five minutes later with another girl. They'd both traded in their sparkly mermaid costumes for T-shirts and bell-bottom jeans, only their wet hair remaining as evidence of their underwater exploits.

"This is Brenda Hopkins," Theresa said. "My roomie. At least for now. Her boyfriend Tony's stealing her away, though. Convinced her to go to Vermont, of all the godforsaken places."

Vermont! How funny. Sylvia's old haunting grounds. What were the chances?

Brenda was strikingly beautiful. Tall, with impossibly long legs and golden hair, like walking sunshine. Sleepy, doelike eyes. She was the kind of girl that mystified Ginny: flawless, nearly gilded skin. Not an unwanted pound on her body.

She smiled. "Tony's mom was a mermaid at Weeki Wachee, too. She took off when he was just a kid. He came down looking for her but found me instead."

"She left her son?" Ginny asked in disbelief. The idea of leaving her children to pursue a dream, any sort of dream, seemed unfathomable.

Brenda shook her head sadly. "I know. He was just a baby still. Like your little one," she said, smiling at Lucy.

"Wow," Ginny said.

"Not much work for mermaids in New England, I imagine?" Marsha said.

Brenda sighed. "Well, there may not be much work down here for us, either, what with Walt Disney World about to open. They're predicting all the roadside attractions are gonna suffer. I figured I'd jump ship before it sinks."

They walked en masse across the road to the Holiday Inn, which had a small café inside. Theresa and Brenda were friendly with the waitresses, Theresa explaining that many of the mermaids picked up shifts at local restaurants when they weren't performing.

"So, I think Terra told you, y'all are welcome to come down and stay at the orchard," Brenda offered. "We've got plenty of room. Me and Terra stay there with my folks. There aren't any more rooms in the big house, but there's plenty of space in the old pickers' quarters. Nothing fancy, but a warm, dry place to stay until you get your feet on the ground."

"Or your tail in the water." Theresa winked.

"We don't have much money," Ginny said. "But I'm going to call my mother tonight and get some wired down."

Brenda waved her hand dismissively. "Don't y'all worry about that. Those cabins would just be sittin' empty anyways. You take all the time you need."

They waited at the Holiday Inn for only an hour or so for Lorenzo to show up with the tow truck and Marsha's car. The mermaids went back to the theater for the next show, but Ginny and Marsha stayed, nursing their cups of coffee and sharing a slice of key lime pie with extra whipped cream. Rain pelted the glass of the restaurant window as they watched the tow guy unload the Dart under the carport of a defunct gas station next door, and, as promised, after just about an hour under the hood, Lorenzo had repaired the cracked radiator.

"Good as new," he said, as he joined them at the table.

Marsha thanked him again and offered to pay for a room for him at the Holiday Inn.

"That's okay. I'm going to head over to see a buddy in Orlando tonight and start back north tomorrow. I did what Gabe sent me down to do."

"Can I do anything to thank you?" Marsha asked. "Buy you some dinner? Pay for your gas, at least?"

Lorenzo winked. "Just remember your promise. Call Gabe."

Brenda's family's orange groves were about a half hour drive south of Weeki Wachee, just north of Tampa. Brenda drove an old woodie station wagon, which Marsha followed closely behind in the resuscitated Dart. They arrived just before nightfall at an old white farmhouse with a wraparound porch, coming into view as a silhouette. Brenda and Theresa drove past the house and down a short dirt road, where, as promised, there were a series of old cottages, each with its own porch.

Brenda parked the car.

"Let me show you around. We'll unload the car when the rain lets up."

They followed her into a dark little one-room cottage. "There's a little cook stove," Brenda said, gesturing like a tour guide or a realtor. "A mini-fridge. There are bathrooms and showers out back, but you can come to the big house for all that. I asked my mama to put some clean sheets on the beds. She also has an old crib we can bring down from the attic for the baby."

Peyton went straight to the bed and appeared to be searching for something.

"Did you lose something?" Ginny asked.

"I'm looking for the Magic Fingers!" he said.

Theresa let out a howl. "What kinda places you been staying, sis?"

she asked. "Let's go up to the house and you can get cleaned up and make whatever calls you need to make. We can get you settled down here later."

Brenda's mother, Lois, greeted them inside with coffee and hugs. Ginny was taken aback by her warm and seemingly indiscriminate affection. The house was bright and cheerful. Feminine touches everywhere: frilly curtains and doilies and ruffled lampshades. Lois, an older version of her golden daughter, smelled like soap and citrus. *The Carol Burnett Show* was on a small television in the dining room. The same show she'd been watching when Marsha called to tell her about the exposé just a week ago. She could hardly fathom all that had happened in the last week.

"If y'all have any dirty laundry, you just bring it up here, and I'll throw in a load. I bet y'all could use a nice warm bath, too," Lois said.

Ginny wanted nothing more than to sink into a hot tub. She hadn't had a bath since they left Massachusetts. But she also knew that she needed to call her mother, let her know they'd finally arrived safely. And the kids needed baths more than she did.

"You look like somebody who might like chocolate chip cookies?" Lois said, bending down to Peyton.

He nodded, grinning.

"Terra, hon, can you bring that starving child into the kitchen and get him some cookies?"

Theresa smiled, took Peyton's hand, and led him into the kitchen.

"Let me take the baby," Marsha said, reaching for Lucy. "I'll get her cleaned up down here. You go on upstairs and take a nice hot bath."

"I really need to call my mom," Ginny said.

"Take a nice soak first. Wash the road off."

Ginny wanted to cry. All this kindness. All these women caring for each other. As she climbed the stairs, warm towels fresh from the dryer in her arms, she felt her eyes fill with tears. She found the bathroom at the end of the hallway as promised. It was clean and bright, with a deep porcelain tub. When she ran the water, it nearly steamed with heat. She even found a box of clumpy Calgon, which she tipped into the water, creating sweetly scented bubbles that she sank into up to her chin.

For the first time in a week, she was alone. Blissfully and completely *alone*. Still, while her body relaxed, her mind raced. She'd been so intent on the journey, she hadn't given much thought to the destination. They'd arrived, but to what future? She was penniless. With two children. And worse, one of those children did not even legally belong to her. She was a fugitive. An outlaw. Lorenzo, thankfully, had not been sent by the FBI or Ab, but that didn't mean they weren't still being followed. They might have reached their destination, but that didn't mean they were safe.

For the first time in a week, Ginny allowed the emotions she'd been keeping inside to spill out. She cried big hiccupping sobs, tears running hot down her cheeks and into the water. She allowed the sorrow to rush over her in waves. She slipped under the water and wished she *could* simply grow a tail.

She recalled the Hans Christian Andersen story "The Little Mermaid"— her father had gotten her an illustrated collection of fairy tales when she was a girl. Even as a young child, she'd thought that the little mermaid was no more than a foolish fish who gave up her voice, her magical life under the sea, just for a man. She could have stayed in her watery home with her sisters, but the temptation of love was too much. And at what cost? She was rendered mute, the prince fell in love with another girl, and even when she was given the chance to return to the sea by taking the prince's life, she was unable to do so, and instead hurled herself into the water. What a fool, she'd thought. She'd never sacrifice herself for a man.

But then, here she was. Living a life she'd never planned to live. Making sacrifices she would once never have dreamed of making. Maybe she, too, was a fool. Maybe they all were.

She stayed in the tub until the water grew cold, and afterward wrapped herself in the fluffy robe that Lois had offered her. Her fingers were wrinkled into prunes, but at last her heart had slowed. Outside, the wind had calmed, and when she peered through the window, there was no rain falling. Perhaps the storm had passed. Still, the idea of making the trek back to the sleeping quarters seemed impossible.

Downstairs, Marsha had cleaned Lucy up and put her in a pair of fresh pajamas. Peyton was watching TV, eating cookies, and slurping from a tall glass of milk.

Ginny entered the kitchen to find the women sitting around the kitchen table drinking coffee. There was a man there as well, which startled Ginny, and she pulled the robe more tightly around her.

He was maybe in his midtwenties, but his face was damaged with scars that made his features look like melted wax. She sucked in her breath and then caught herself. Isn't this exactly what she'd abhorred about taking Lucy out in public: other people's instinctual shrinking away?

"Ginny!" Theresa said brightly. "This is Brenda's boyfriend, Tony."

He stood up and reached his hand out. "You can call me Brooder," he said. When he smiled, only half of his mouth rose. Brenda had mentioned at lunch that he'd been in Vietnam, she wondered if this was where he'd gotten burned.

"Nice to meet you," Ginny managed. No wonder Brenda hadn't even flinched when she'd met Lucy.

"Now that the storm's passed, I think we're all gonna go out for a drink," Theresa said. "Maybe some dancing?"

"You wanna come?" Brenda asked Ginny. "I'm sure Mama wouldn't mind watching the kids."

Ginny shook her head. "Oh, no, thank you. I need to call home. I'm exhausted."

Marsha said, "Yeah, we should probably just get some sleep."

"No," Ginny said. "You should go. Have fun."

"Well then, why don't you sleep in my room tonight," Brenda said. "I can sleep on the couch when we get back, and we'll get you set up in the cottage tomorrow."

"That sounds wonderful," Ginny said, relieved not to have to go out again. "Thank you."

"You sure you don't mind if I go?" Marsha asked. "I could really stand to blow off some steam."

"Absolutely. Go have fun. I am dead tired."

After they were gone, Ginny asked Lois if she could use their phone to make a collect call, and Lois pointed her to a back room where she found a telephone and a comfortable chair. It seemed to be an office of sorts. Theresa had explained that Brenda's brother, Bobby, was the one who ran the orchard now that Brenda's father had passed. Bobby lived down in Tampa, drove up each day for work. It was just the women who lived there: Brenda, Lois, Theresa, and any other mermaids in need of a place to stay while they got on their "feet."

Ginny dialed her mother's number, asking the operator to reverse the charges. There was a pause after the charges were accepted, but it was a male voice on the other end of the line.

"Gin," he said.

Ab? Her skin grew hot, and she felt sweat rolling down her sides. Her chest ached: with loss and anger. Relief and fear. Why was he answering her mother's phone?

"Ginny?" he said again. She hadn't spoken to Ab in nearly a week. His voice felt both remarkably strange and oddly familiar.

"What are you doing there? I called for Mama," she said. "Is something wrong?"

"No, no, she's fine. Oh, my God, I can't believe it's finally you. You're okay? How is Peyton?"

She needed to hold firm, to not crumble under the weight of whatever he might have to say. "I called for Mama."

He coughed softly. "I'm sorry. I've been, we've just been so worried. I've been staying on your mother's couch for the last few nights, hoping you'd call. How's Peyton? Are you okay? Peyton?"

"Ab, aren't you going to ask about her, too? About Lucy?" she asked, feeling her shoulders stiffen, her back straighten with purpose. With resolve.

"Yes, yes, of course. Is the baby alright?"

"She's not a *baby*. Not anymore. She's two years old."

There was silence on the other end of the line. She wondered where her mother was.

"Where *are* you?" he asked. When she didn't answer, he said softly, "I just need to know you're safe. You don't have to tell me."

"I'm safe," she said, but even as she did, the branch of a tree scraped against the window, startling her, and the wind howled an awful lament.

"I got a call from a repair shop in Savannah, Georgia," Ab said. "He said you and another woman had come in with a car from Virginia that was overheating. Who are you with? Is Marsha there with you?"

She thought of everything that had transpired on the road, the miles and miles between them now.

She shook her head. "Please don't ask any more questions."

"Okay," he said. "Okay. I am so sorry, Gin. But this is crazy. You took our child, our son, and ran *away*. In the eyes of the law, you *kidnapped* her. Do you realize the danger you put everyone in? This is the most selfish thing you've ever done. This isn't you," he added, clearly exasperated.

"What do you mean, not *me*?" she asked.

"I just . . . I feel like I can't trust you anymore."

"*Trust*? You can't trust *me*?" She snorted and thought about slamming the phone down on its waiting cradle. "Do you realize how ridiculous that sounds? I trusted you that our daughter was going to be taken somewhere safe. I trusted you when you said it was the best thing for her. I trusted you when you promised me this. But you lied about everything. That place is a freaking hellhole, Ab. And you and your father are defending it. Those children are human beings. They are daughters and sons, and they are being treated like animals. The fact that you refuse to even consider this is beyond belief. You say you don't know me anymore, but I'm starting to think I never knew you."

There was nothing but silence on the other end of the line.

"Gin," he said finally after drawing a deep breath. "I've been in touch with the school. I pleaded with them not to do anything drastic. They're giving us until Sunday evening to return her. I can wire enough money for you to fly home from wherever the hell you are. But if you don't come home, there is literally nothing I can do. They'll send out a warrant for your arrest. They'll notify law enforcement in all fifty states. Your phone calls here will be traced, and they will find you. Do you have any idea what this means? Do you even care?"

"What does your *father* say?" she asked venomously.

"My father?"

"Yes. I know he's behind all of this. He' s behind everything. I love you, Ab. I really do, but this has made me lose respect for you." The words came forth in a rush, a dam let open followed by a flood of thoughts she hadn't articulated since the first time that Abbott Senior commandeered their lives.

"Well, if you really want to know," he said, "he doesn't even know I've been in communication with the school. To negotiate. If he did, I'm pretty sure he'd have me packing up my office. This is a huge case for the firm. There are thousands and thousands of dollars at stake."

Ginny balked. "So there it is," she said bitterly. "It's about *money*. The bottom line that would have you separate a child from her own family. That would damn a little girl to hell. For a *job*."

"Gin," he said. "My *job* is what keeps a roof over your head. It pays for the food on your plate. The clothes on your back. It's what keeps you from peeling potatoes in some cafeteria."

This felt like a slap, a bite. She thought of her mother, who since Ginny was ten years old had toiled away in the Amherst cafeteria, cooking for all those ambitious men. For all those other mothers' sons. She had arthritis in her fingers from peeling potatoes. The work had *crippled* her.

"Do not bring my mother into this," she said and then remembered it was her mother she had called. Her mother she had wanted to speak to.

"I'm sorry, Ginny. I didn't mean—"

"Where is she? I need to talk to my mother."

Ab was quiet. In the other room, she heard Lucy cry out, the rumble of that awful cough she'd been battling since they crossed over from Georgia into Florida.

"She's downstairs at your aunt's. She's not feeling well," he said. "She's torn up about all of this. Just so you know. I told her what could happen to you. That what you've done could get you arrested. Could cause you to lose your son."

Ginny felt a surge of sadness flood her senses.

"Is she okay?" she asked.

"Bonnie's taking her in to see the doctor in the morning. Her heart's been skipping beats. Arrhythmia?"

Ginny felt nauseous.

"Ginny, please just tell me where to send the money. Bring Peyton home. Bring *her* back."

"You can't even say her name, can you?" she said in disbelief.

"Please, Gin. God, please just do what's right."

What was *right*? There was no moral ambiguity here, if that was what he was suggesting. The fact that her husband insisted on defending a virtual prison to save a few dollars was morally corrupt. The fact that after all that she had been through, he was still just a ventriloquist's dummy, his father's hand up his back, his father's words coming out of his mouth, was what was *wrong* here.

"I'm sorry, Ab," she said. "I'm not returning her to the school."

She heard him sigh in frustration. But just as he was about to protest, she said firmly, "Ab, please. *You* just do what's right."

She was trembling as she slammed the phone down onto its cradle.

There was a small knock at the door, and Lois poked her head in. "Hey. I'm worried your little one might have a fever," she said. "She's got a pretty bad cough, too."

"Thank you," Ginny said. "I'm almost done. And thanks for letting me use your phone. I need to make one more quick call. Tell the kids I'll be right out in a second. Oh, wait—can you tell me where the closest Western Union is?"

"There's got to be one down in Tampa," she said. "There's a Yellow Pages in the desk drawer." She closed the door again.

She called her aunt Bonnie's house this time and asked the operator to reverse the charges.

"Mama," she said when Bonnie put her on the phone. "Are you okay? Ab said your heart's skipping beats?"

"Oh, honey," she said. "I'm fine. Are *you* okay?"

"I'm fine. But listen, I need you to wire me some money. I'll pay you back as soon as I can. And you have to promise you won't tell a soul where I am."

"Of course," she said.

Thirty-one

ॐ

September 1971

Peyton had fallen asleep on the couch, but Lois was holding Lucy, cradling her more like an infant than a toddler.

Ginny went to pick Lucy up, but just as she reached for her, Lucy began to cough again. It was explosive, a croupy wet cough. Her face was red with the effort. She'd had just a small cough in the car; when had it turned into this?

"Oh, my goodness," Ginny said, holding out her arms so that Lois could transfer her into them.

Her body was emanating heat.

"Oh, honey," she said, brushing Lucy's curls off her face to feel her forehead. She was burning up. Ginny looked up at Lois. "Do you have a thermometer?"

"Yes," she said. "You think you can get her to hold it under her tongue?"

"God, I don't know." The idea of having to use a rectal thermometer on Lucy was so daunting. She avoided it at all costs with Peyton. "I'll try."

She was only able to get Lucy to keep the thermometer in her mouth for about thirty seconds before she began to shake her head and cry. But even in that short period of time, the mercury crept up to over 101 degrees. If she had to guess, she'd say that Lucy was approaching 104 or 105.

"I need to get her cooled down," Ginny said, trying not to panic. She wished desperately that Marsha were here.

"I've got some rubbing alcohol; that'll cool her off," Lois said.

"I think maybe just a cool sponge bath?" Ginny said. Marsha had told her once when Peyton was running hot that it could be dangerous to try to bring a fever down with alcohol. At the hospital, Marsha had seen a little boy go into a coma after his mother tried to reduce his fever with an alcohol rub. It seeped from his skin into his bloodstream and poisoned him. She remembered aching at the thought of that poor mother who had caused so much harm just trying to help her child.

She carried Lucy up the stairs to the bathroom where she had just taken a steaming bath and filled the tub with cool water. She undressed Lucy carefully and started to lower her into the water. Lucy was shivering violently, so much so, Ginny nearly dropped her. Her eyes were heavy lidded, and for the first time, Ginny started to feel panicked.

Ginny picked her up, naked, and pressed her body against her own as she made her way back down the stairs. The lights flickered once, and she heard the wind howling at the windows.

"I think she needs to see a doctor," she said to Lois, who was rifling through the freezer in the kitchen.

"I was just looking for some frozen veggies to put on her forehead. That always used to help with my little ones."

"She's really, really sick," Ginny said, her voice catching in her throat. "Do you know where everyone went? Is there someplace I could call to find Marsha? She's a nurse. She'll know what to do."

"I'm sorry, sweetheart. I have no idea. The closest town is Odessa, but they could have gone anywhere."

"Is there a hospital close by?" Ginny asked. "Someplace with an emergency room?"

Lois nodded quickly. "There's one in Tampa. That's the one where I had my kids. It's about twenty miles from here. But you don't want to go out in this weather. It's started to rain again. I really wish Brenda and the others had stayed home, too. This storm's not over yet."

Lucy coughed again, and her whole body convulsed with the effort.

"It's okay. I can drive," Ginny said. "Marsha taught me."

Ginny thought about how empowered she'd felt when Marsha let her take the wheel, but that seemed like eons ago. And Marsha had been talking her through every step, plus, there had been clear skies then, not a brewing hurricane.

"Would you be able to stay here with Peyton?" Ginny asked. "I know it's a lot to ask, but I hate to wake him up. He can sleep down here on the couch. He probably will sleep right through the night." She wanted nothing more than to stay inside, to crawl into bed with both of her babies, to sleep and sleep and sleep.

"Of course, sweetheart," Lois said, but her eyes were filled with concern. "You sure that car of yours is fixed up? Theresa told me you broke down earlier. Maybe you should just wait until the kids get back. Maybe have Tony drive you?"

It was only ten o'clock; they might be out for hours still.

"Can you hold her while I put on my shoes?" Ginny asked.

Outside, the rain was coming down hard again, but the air was remarkably warm. Muggy, even. She navigated her way across the muddy drive to the parked Dart. Lois followed behind her, carrying Lucy. As Ginny climbed into the driver's seat, Lois put Lucy into the backseat, where she immediately curled up into a ball. Lois covered her with a crocheted afghan, bent over, and gave her a little kiss on the forehead.

"She's such a sweet girl," Lois said, closing the rear door. She came around to the driver's side, reached in through the open window, and squeezed Ginny's shoulder. "She's going to be okay. Just drive slow and safe. You got the house phone number?"

Ginny nodded. Lois had scratched it on a paper napkin for her along with directions to the hospital.

She pressed her shaking foot down on the clutch, her other foot on the brake, and turned the key. The car didn't start right away, and so she tried again, feeling a cry of relief crawl up her throat when the engine finally turned over and sputtered to life. She located the lights and the wind-shield wipers and turned on both. As the rain started to pour down in sheets, Lois made a dash for the house. Inside the lights flickered again, as though the house were illuminated by a candle.

Ginny put the car in reverse and slowly released her foot from the brake, the Dart lurching backward. She held her breath and cranked the wheel so that she was facing in the right direction. She depressed the clutch again, put the car in first gear, and repeated the process, until she was rolling forward. She was trembling so hard—cold and wet and terrified, but when she turned to see that Lucy had fallen into a fitful slumber, her chest whistling, her breaths frighteningly shallow, she shifted into sec-ond, turned onto the main road, and then gave it gas and said a prayer.

Thirty-two

ॐ

December 1951

She was ten when her father died.

They'd been out of milk, and her mother was making Christmas cookies. The entire kitchen table was covered with rows of cooling racks, all her specialties hot out of the oven: oatmeal lace cookies, chocolate crinkles, gingerbread men.

Ginny was old enough to help now. She was busy at one end of the table decorating the gingerbread men: tiny silver balls for eyes and red cinnamon buttons. Her fingertips were pink from the bleeding candies.

"Well, you can't have cookies without milk," her father said, peering into the refrigerator. "That would be unconscionable!"

"Oh, dear," her mother said as she reached into the cupboard. "I'm nearly out of vanilla, too. If you go to the market to get milk, could you pick me up some extract?"

"Yessirree," her father said. "Come on, Ginny girl. I need you to drive me to the market."

244   ⌐♦ T. Greenwood

That was what her father always said. He didn't mean it, of course, it was just his way of inviting her along. She loved to accompany her father—it didn't matter where they were going. He made even a trip to the gas station an adventure. He was filled with stories. Jam-packed with information and gossip and speculations, too.

They left her mother busy in the kitchen, loading the next batch of thumbprint cookies into the oven. As she piled into the passenger seat, he wiped off the snow that had accumulated on the windshield. It had been snowing for three days straight. He had spent almost the entire weekend shoveling the drive. He'd also made her her very own snow cave—a sort of makeshift igloo. It had been magnificent. Every kid on the street had wanted to come sit inside its cold walls. Marsha had gotten the idea to charge admission. Ginny had fifty cents in nickels in her pocket—her cut from the entry fees.

As the sun had started to go down that night, while her mother was busy inside baking, she and her father had climbed up the small hill behind their house. He'd carried the sled, an old Sky Plane, an artifact from his own childhood, and together they had sped through the shimmering darkness, him whooping into the night and her clinging to his rough wool coat. They must have made a dozen trips up and down the hill. By the time they made their way back to the house, her cheeks were on fire and her boots were filled with snow, her ankles raw with cold. She had never felt so blissfully happy. A warm kitchen filled with cookies, the scent of wet wool as their socks dried on the radiator in the kitchen, the soft sounds of the radio playing "O Come, All Ye Faithful."

Now, her father tuned the car radio to the same station, the one that played round-the-clock carols this time of year, and began to sing along, "It's beginning to look a lot like Christmas!"

They pulled out of the driveway and onto the street, the windshield wipers furiously beating time like the metronome that tick-tocked on top of the small upright piano her mother played.

Her father reached over and turned the radio off as they approached

Emily Dickinson's home. Softly, he recited: "It sifts from leaden sieves, / It powders all the wood, / It fills with alabaster wool / The wrinkles of the road."

She thought of her mother in the kitchen with her tin sieve, cranking the dry ingredients through, the sifted flour and baking soda and salt becoming snow filling a bowl.

He slowed as they reached the Dickinson homestead, decorated for the holidays. He put his hand across his breast as he always did, such a reverential gesture, she thought.

They didn't speak; they didn't need to. She understood her father's silences. And he, hers.

"What did your mother want again? From the market?" he asked, breaking the silence and beginning to turn back onto the main road. He was looking at her, grinning.

But before she could remind him of the milk, the vanilla, there was the terrible sound of brakes squealing and ice breaking and glass, all at once, accompanied by the surprised expression on her father's face when he realized what was happening.

The snowplow slammed directly into the driver's-side door. In quiet disbelief and the strange place before the horror set in, she recalled looking up at the sky at the snow falling and dreaming it was only flour, sifting down from her mother's sieve. And she'd looked at that yellow house and wondered if Emily's ghost had been looking out the window when her father died.

Thirty-three

ꙮ

September 1971

She was terrified, her hands gripping the wheel tightly as she navigated the wet highway. Thankfully, there were no other vehicles on the road except for an occasional eighteen-wheeler. Each time one approached to pass her, she clutched the wheel and held her breath. She was weeping, she realized, but soundlessly.

Lois had said the hospital was about twenty miles away. It was only ten thirty, but the lights in the local businesses were all out. It took only a moment to realize that every building along the road was dark as well. The power must have finally gone out.

For a moment, as a gust of wind shook the Dart and she had to clutch the wheel even tighter, she thought that maybe this was crazy. Maybe she should just turn around and go back, wait until Marsha and the others got home. Wait until the rain stopped. But when she reached into the backseat and touched Lucy's head, it was even hotter than it had been before, and Ginny felt like she might vomit. Her body was so tense, she could barely breathe.

Maybe Ab was right. Maybe they all were right. She wasn't equipped to care for this child. This poor little girl. Lucy had been perfectly fine less than a day ago, and now her body was aflame. If Ginny had functioning maternal instincts toward her, wouldn't she have intuited that something was wrong?

The rain slowed for a moment, allowing her to stop holding the wheel so tightly. She saw a sign for Tampa, only fifteen more miles. She adjusted the rearview mirror and turned on the overhead light to check on Lucy, but she hadn't moved.

"Lucy," she said, hoping she'd stir. She reached behind her and touched her leg. "Lucy, baby. It's okay."

The next cough sounded like something inhuman, and Ginny's foot instinctively pressed the gas pedal. Outside the rain began to come down hard again. The wipers could barely keep up, their sweeping arcs seeming both futile and somehow desperate. Ginny leaned closer to the dash, as though she would be able to see the road ahead better this way.

On either side of the highway, giant palm trees bent as if in supplication to the wind that rattled and shook the car.

Another sign. Ten miles to go. She hoped there would be signs for the hospital so she wouldn't have to pull over to look at Lois's directions.

When the lights first appeared in her rearview mirror, she thought it was an ambulance. Red lights and a blaring siren. There must have been an accident. She expected at any moment she would stumble upon the wreckage. But when she pulled over to the shoulder of the road to let the ambulance pass, the vehicle stopped behind her, and her throat began to close.

The police.

Had she been speeding? She hardly knew. Her heart rattled in her chest like a can filled with dry beans, and she broke into a sweat. She tried to

248 ～ T. Greenwood

conjure the explanation that she could give that would get her out of this, send her on her way.

I have a sick child, she thought. *I need to get to the hospital.*

But if she revealed that she had Lucy with her, this stolen child, he could arrest her. Ab had said they hadn't put out any sort of warrant yet, but could she trust this to be the truth? And what about Abbott Senior? He could have called law enforcement himself.

No, best to not mention Lucy. Best to apologize, claim ignorance, say that she was so worried about the storm she didn't realize the speedometer was creeping upward.

She heard the cruiser door slam shut like a fist to her chest. It was raining so hard now, she knew that if she were to roll her window down, she'd be soaked. Still, she didn't want to show disrespect, so she reached for the handle and started to roll the window down just enough so when the officer leaned in, she could see his face. His handlebar mustache. Thank God, he didn't have a beard.

"Pretty bad night to be out on the road," he said.

She nodded and turned to him, smiling weakly.

"Do you know why I pulled you over, ma'am?"

"I'm sorry, sir. I didn't realize I was speeding. It's the rain. I was so focused on staying on the road." Her words tumbled out of her mouth, like a child caught in a lie.

"You weren't speeding, ma'am. Actually, if anything, you were going below the limit."

"Oh?" she said, surprised.

"Where are you headed so late?" he asked.

Now, maybe now she should just tell him she was taking her daughter to the hospital. That the little bundle in the backseat was burning up. No, no. Too dangerous.

"I'm headed home from a friend's house," she said. "Tampa?"

"Well, can I see your license and registration, sweetheart?" he asked.

Ginny felt herself grow hot, as though she were the one with the raging fever.

She had no license. And the car was registered in Massachusetts. And if she were to open the glove box, then he might see the gun.

"It's not my car," she blurted out.

"Well, honey," he smirked. "I know that. I pulled you over because your tag belongs to a 1970 Dart. This here's a '67. I called it in when I saw you swerving all over the road back there. You want to explain how it is you wound up in a car with a stolen license plate?"

Ginny felt tears coming to her eyes. Then Lucy coughed. The sound was animalistic, primitive. And the bundle moved.

His hand flew to grip his holstered gun, and he backed up a few steps.

"Who's that in your backseat?"

Ginny was crying now, her hand over her face. She reached into the backseat and the officer barked, "Keep your hands where I can see them!"

Her hands flew up in surrender, but Lucy was sitting up now, still coughing. The officer moved to the rear of the car, slowly drawing his gun from his holster. He opened the rear passenger door with his free hand and Ginny held her breath, her heart pounding.

"Please, no," she managed.

At the sight of the man, Lucy let out a howl unlike anything Ginny had heard in her life.

"She's afraid!" Ginny pleaded, desperate for him to put his gun down. "She's just a baby."

The officer lowered his gun but lifted his flashlight and shined it into the backseat. Lucy squinted and cried, covering her eyes.

"Jesus Christ, lady. You should have told me you had a kid back there," he said, lowering his firearm. "Wait, is there something wrong with her?"

"Yes," Ginny said, sucking in a sob. "She's sick."

"No, I mean, she's . . . *handicapped*?"

Ginny felt rage replace all the fear she'd been feeling. For a moment, she considered reaching over and getting Marsha's gun from the glove box, of pointing it at him the way he'd just pointed his at her child. For a moment, she wanted to turn all of this around. To be the one in power as he cowered.

Instead, she felt a certain calm descend upon her. She would not lose sight of the goal here. Of what she needed to do.

"I borrowed the car from a friend. I don't know anything about stolen plates. I'm on my way to the hospital," she said. "I think she has pneumonia. She's burning up. I just need to get her to the hospital."

The officer nodded one short nod.

"Listen," he said. "I don't know what your game is, lady. But I'm also a little more concerned about your baby than I am about the rest of that right now. I'll get you to the hospital in my squad car, but after we get her help, you're going to have some explaining to do. Deal?"

Ginny was exhausted. She felt like she'd just run ten miles rather than having driven them.

She nodded. "Yes," she said. "Whatever you say, Officer . . . ?"

"Marley," he said.

Officer Marley got them situated in the backseat of the cruiser, which smelled heavily of cigarettes. Lucy was still crying, though not wailing like she had been before. But her fever was raging. Ginny could feel the heat all the way through the afghan.

The rain was still coming down hard, making visibility terrible. But the officer seemed unfazed by the storm. He periodically glanced in the rearview mirror at her, through the mesh that separated them.

They pulled up in front of the ER, and the officer accompanied her into the brightly lit hospital. Under the glare of the fluorescent lights, it felt as if she'd walked out of a dark theater into the sunlight.

She sat down with Lucy in an uncomfortable yellow plastic chair in a waiting area while the officer spoke to the women at the front desk. He returned to her and said, "They'll take her in a couple of minutes. You're going to need to go give her your information. You got insurance?"

Ginny nodded. They had Blue Cross at home. Though she had no idea if the insurance would work down here or if it would cover Lucy. She fumbled in her purse and pulled out her insurance card.

"You want to maybe give your husband a call?" he asked. "Let him know what's going on?"

"I don't . . ." she said, and felt her heart snag. "We're . . . we're separated," she said, which made her think of the chasm between them, that growing sinkhole like the one she'd seen advertised on a billboard along the highway.

Ginny carried Lucy, following the nurse who called them.

"I'll be right here," the officer said. "We'll have a little chat when you get out."

The nurse took them to a small room where she unwrapped Lucy from the blanket, took her temperature, and listened to her heart with a stethoscope. She jotted down notes on her pad and then brusquely said, "We'll take her for a chest X-ray in a minute."

After the X-ray, she and Lucy returned to the ER to wait for the doctor.

When the doctor finally arrived, he examined her briefly and said, "Did she have an accident recently?"

Ginny shook her head, confused, but then thought of the accident back in Virginia. She'd seemed fine.

Ginny nodded, her eyes flooding with tears. "We had a little car accident. I didn't know . . ."

"Looks like she broke a couple of ribs at some point. A few months ago? They're mostly healed, but that's likely what compromised her."

Ginny's eyes widened. She nodded. How on earth had her ribs been broken while she was still at Willowridge?

"Children with Down syndrome are prone to infections. Their im-

mune systems are weakened by the disease, and their muscles are un-
derdeveloped; that's why her lungs are working so hard to get the phlegm
out. We're going to need to admit her. Get the fever under control."

Ginny nodded. Anything. She'd do anything at this point.

"Y'all aren't from around here, are you?"

Ginny shook her head. "No," she said. "We're from up north. We came
down to go to the new Disney World that's opening soon. My friend, her
sister works at Weeki Wachee?" She didn't know why she was spilling
all of this to the doctor. Maybe because he reminded her of Peyton's pediatrician, Dr. Little, back in Dover. Friendly and gentle.

"She needs antibiotics, some fluids, and lots of rest. I'd like to admit
her, keep her a couple of days, do a few more tests."

"But she's okay?"

"She's in good hands," he said.

Lucy looked up at Ginny, reached her tiny hand out to touch Ginny's
face. Her fingers were hot.

"Mumma," she said.

Ginny felt her throat thicken.

"She looks like you, you know," the doctor said. "Two real beauties."

After they had admitted Lucy and gotten her set up in a room shared with
a little boy who had apparently broken both of his legs leaping off a garage roof, Officer Marley knocked on the door.

The sun was just coming up, the storm having weakened. Ginny pulled
the curtains shut so that Lucy could get some sleep. She'd called Lois collect and let her know that Lucy was okay, but that she'd be at the hospital
for a while. Lois told her not to worry. That she'd take care of Peyton for
as long as she needed.

"I'm technically off duty now, heading home in a few. But I thought I'd
get some breakfast first. The cafeteria here's got some pretty decent coffee.
Can I buy you a cup?"

Ginny looked at Lucy, who had fallen asleep. The IV was dripping medication and fluids into the back of her tiny hand, and her cheeks had lost that red flush of her fever. Ginny was reluctant to leave her in case she woke up, but she was also starving, feeling weak in the knees. Hollow. However, as he stood there in his uniform waiting, she also knew she ultimately didn't have much say in the matter.

"Why don't you start at the beginning and end with me pulling you over," Marley said as they sat down with their trays. He'd treated her to a cup of coffee and a blueberry muffin, and it wasn't until the sweet smell of the muffin reached her nose that she realized how long it had been since she'd eaten. "I can't promise anything, of course, but my ear and some advice."

Ginny nodded, knowing that whatever she said now could seal her fate. Part of her wondered if she should make up some elaborate story, to placate him enough that he would simply go away. But as he sat there, peering at her intently, kindly, even, she knew the jig was up.

She reached into her purse and pulled out the newspaper clippings that had started this whole mess. She smoothed them each out and set them in front of him. She hadn't looked at them for nearly a week, could hardly bear to recall what she had seen for herself inside the walls of Willowridge.

Officer Marley cocked his head quizzically and began to read. Ginny unwrapped her muffin from its paper cup, but despite being so hungry, she struggled to swallow. She watched him as he scanned each article, each smudgy photo.

"She was taken away from me right after she was born," Ginny said when he looked up at her. "My husband promised that she would be safe there. That she would be cared for."

"This is horrifying," the officer said softly.

"I went to see for myself last week, and it was just as awful as the reporter said. She was being neglected. They are all being mistreated. Ignored. I couldn't leave her there. I just couldn't. So I took her out for a visit. I had permission to have her for the weekend. We took her to see the ocean." She thought of Lucy sitting on the beach, the delight in her eyes at the warm sand, the way she marveled at the waves tickling her tiny feet when Ginny dipped her into the water. "I didn't know, I didn't realize that my husband had given up our parental rights."

One of Marley's heavy eyebrows shot upward.

"You don't have custody?"

Ginny shook her head, and as she did, she felt a fat tear roll down her cheek. She wiped it away. She needed to stay strong for this.

"But I never signed anything. It was all my father-in-law's doing. He's a big lawyer in Boston. His firm, my husband's firm, is representing the school in the class-action lawsuit filed by a group of the residents' parents."

"Damn," Marley said.

She nodded. "My husband says he convinced the school to give us a few more days. But his father is threatening to contact law enforcement. Claim I kidnapped her. My own daughter."

She took a sip of coffee, feeling lighter for finally having gotten all of this off her chest.

"How did you wind up all the way down here? This place, Willowridge? It's in Massachusetts, right?" he asked, motioning to the Massachusetts newspaper.

Ginny rubbed her temples. "Very long story. My friend's sister lives down here. She's a mermaid." She smiled.

"At Weeki Wachee?" he asked.

Ginny nodded. "She lives at one of her friends' orchards not far from here. That's where we are staying. Until I figure out what to do."

Marley nodded. She waited for him to read her her rights. To take the handcuffs she'd seen dangling from his back pocket earlier and arrest her, right here in the hospital cafeteria.

But instead, he simply took a deep breath and lifted his chin.

"The doctors tried to convince us to send our daughter away, too," he said.

Ginny caught her breath.

"Cerebral palsy. They told us she wouldn't walk, talk, use the bathroom. That she'd have the mental capacity of a toddler."

Ginny thought of the doctor offering her the same grim outlook for Lucy. Through the ether haze, she recalled his prognosis sounding like a death sentence. How any of what he said that night connected to this beautiful, happy child was beyond her.

"We even arranged a tour of a facility in Gainesville. But we couldn't do it. My wife said she would never be able to look me in the eye again if we sent her away. That she wouldn't be able to live with herself, either."

Ginny thought of her pleas to Ab, the same sense of guilt of shame. She nodded.

"Honestly," the officer said, "if I were you, I would have done the same thing." He took a swig of his coffee and set it down on the table. He nodded sharply, and Ginny felt her eyes filling with tears again.

"You said you could give me some advice?" she said, feeling emboldened by his compassion. "Legally?"

Marley nodded. "Well, I think the first thing you need to do is let the school know exactly where you are. The hospital can notify the school, let them know that she cannot be transported while she's still sick. Then, you need to get your husband to fight like hell to get your custodial rights back."

Ab. Of course, it would all come down to Ab.

"As for everything that happened on the way over here? Let me see what I can do." Marley unwrapped his own muffin and took a big bite. A crumb stuck in his mustache, and as she motioned to it to let him know, she got an idea.

❧

Marsha and Theresa arrived at the hospital with Peyton around 11 A.M. Peyton was carrying a stuffed alligator in one hand and a white balloon in the other. Lucy's eyes widened at the balloon.

"Moon?" she said, and Ginny smiled.

"No, honey. It's a balloon."

"Is that a new stuffy?" Ginny asked Peyton.

He nodded. "Marsha bought it for me because I lost Brownie."

"Thank you," she said to Marsha.

"But she can have it," he said, pushing it toward Lucy.

Lucy seemed surprised but reached for the offering and held the gator close to her chest, cuddling it. "Pey," Lucy said softly. "Pey-ton."

Peyton's chin dimpled a little, and his lip quivered. He looked to Ginny, eyes wide. "She said my name!"

Ginny felt a surge of hope.

Lucy coughed again, her face reddening with the effort.

"Oh, my God," Marsha said to Ginny, reaching for Lucy's little hand. "I am so sorry. I should have never left you alone last night. I feel so awful."

Ginny shook her head. "No," she said. "*I'm* sorry. For all of this. I should never have put you in this position."

"Did you talk to Ab yet?" Marsha asked.

"Not yet. I'm waiting on something from Officer Marley first."

Before Marley left, Ginny had asked him if he could call the police department back home and have them do a little research on one of the employees at Willowridge. Look into an attendant who worked in the children's ward. Guy with a beard. Ginny knew it was likely a shot in the dark, but she was so desperate now, she would try just about anything.

Now Marley poked his head into the room. "Mrs. Richardson? Can you come with me a minute?"

Out in the hall, he pulled her over to a waiting area and had her sit down.

"Listen, turns out I am in a pretty serious bind here. The stolen plates alone; that's a felony—" He glanced around to make sure no one was listening to their conversation. "—but you add on a concealed *weapon*?"

The gun. Dear God, he must have gone back to the car and found Marsha's gun in the glove box.

"Never mind that you removed a minor from a care facility. A minor that, let's face it . . . you've got no more authority over than I do. A minor you took across state lines. You'd be looking at somewhere between five and ten years in prison, and that's if the DA is feeling gracious. If he decides to go federal, you could go down for twenty-five years."

Ginny was stunned. She had no idea that she was putting herself, her children, her future in this sort of jeopardy. That it could come to this. Lucy was her daughter. Every inch of her body, of her heart, knew this to be true. But in the eyes of the law, she was no one to Lucy. She had given up any rights the minute she allowed Ab to put her in the institution.

"What do I do?" Ginny managed at last.

"Well, in terms of the plates, I plan to write up that I found them dumped at a rest stop. As for the rest of this . . . I'm calling it a medical assist. I came across someone experiencing a medical emergency who needed an escort to the hospital. Everything else will be between us."

She nodded. She'd do anything he said at this point if it meant not going to jail.

"Why are you doing this for me?" she asked.

"Well, you might not have a license, and you might not have custody of that girl, but you've got some mighty fine maternal instincts," he said.

Ginny held her breath.

"I called up north like you asked and had the folks there do some digging. It appears that one Robert Hanson, the man who works as an aide in the facility, has quite a criminal background."

Ginny felt her heart sink. This was exactly the information she'd wanted, needed. But the reality of it was that her worst suspicions were true.

"Seems he has a pretty extensive history of domestic violence. Against girlfriends, his wife. Once against his own kid. Broke his son's arm in three places. I wouldn't be surprised if that's why your little one is so afraid."

"How the hell did he get a job at Willowridge?" she asked.

Marley shook his head. "That is a question your lawyer husband should be asking the school."

Robert Hanson must have been the one who broke Lucy's ribs. Her own ribs felt cracked and sharp at the thought, puncturing her heart, which rose like a helium balloon toward her throat.

"My God. What do I do?"

"Well, I can suggest they send someone over to the school. Clue them in to this guy's background. I would think that with all the hot water they're in with the class-action lawsuit, it's not going to help their case to have a convicted felon on their staff."

She nodded.

"But this was *not* the way to do things," he said. "You really need to get your husband to intervene. Does he have any friends at the DA's office?"

Ginny reached deep into her memory, trying to recall the dinner parties she'd attended. All those men Ab talked about: the lawyers in high places wearing expensive suits.

"I'll find out," she said.

"I also disposed of that firearm for you," he said, his voice hushed.

"Thank you. I'm sorry. About all of this. I appreciate everything. I know you're probably taking a real chance by helping me."

"Well, I have never seen a mother risk so much for her child."

Ginny felt the tension that had been building in her chest beginning to release.

"You're a good mom, Mrs. Richardson. I hope you get to keep your daughter."

Ginny returned to the hospital room to check on Peyton and Lucy. Marsha said she was just about to take Peyton to the park near Weeki Wachee Springs to see if they could spy a real-life alligator. Lucy was clutching the stuffed alligator from her brother.

"Goodnight stars," Peyton said, leaning over to hug Lucy. "Then *you* say, 'Goodnight air.'"

Ginny's eyes filled with tears

"Goodnight noises everywhere," Ginny said.

Thirty-four

❧

September 1971

S he made the call from the pay phone outside, borrowing a cigarette from Marsha. She rarely smoked, but she thought it might calm her jitters. Unfortunately, it made her insides feel jumbled up even worse than they had been before. Her heart raced, her knees trembled, and she felt nauseous. She tossed the cigarette onto the pavement after only one puff and extinguished it under the toe of her sandal.

"Hi, this is Ginny Richardson," she said to Sissy. "Is Abbott available, please?"

"Junior or Senior?" Sissy asked.

She paused.

"Senior."

"One moment, please."

She could have hung up. Put the receiver back on the cradle, walked back through the electronic doors and upstairs. It would have been easier putting this off. But she knew that, in the end, Abbott Senior was the one who would decide her fate. As much as this troubled and angered her, it was the truth.

"Virginia," he said. His voice was like smoke and dirt.

"Hello, Abbott," she said. "I'm sorry, I don't have long. I'm at a pay phone. I am just hoping you'll hear me out."

He coughed. "Go on," he said.

She could picture him, sitting in his leather club chair by the window in his office. Belt loosened beneath his thick waist. Freckled hands and graying hair. His glasses would have slipped down the bridge of his nose. Outside the window there would be the blazing fire of a hundred-year-old maple tree.

"I understand that my marriage to Ab was never what you wanted for your son. And right now, you're probably thinking that if he'd only done what you and Sylvia had expected, none of this would be happening. But he *did* marry me. It had nothing to do with you, and it's probably the only decision in his life that he has made on his own."

She could hear papers rustling in the background. She squeezed her eyes shut.

"And while Ab seems okay with you calling the shots for him, I am not. What you did was unforgivable. You stole my daughter from me."

Still he said nothing. She wondered if this was his way in the courtroom as well, allowing the witness to spin his tale while patiently listening, hoping they might hang themselves with it. She wondered if he was using this time to formulate his counterargument.

"I know that you thought you were doing what was best for us. For our family. For Peyton. For Lucy, even." Here, she knew she needed to coddle his ego. To make him believe she didn't think his intentions were cruel.

"But the so-called school you sent her to is everything those parents are claiming it to be. It's filthy, understaffed. The children, including my child, are being neglected."

"Now, now, this is all speculation," he interrupted.

"It is not *speculation*," she said, feeling her words beginning to hiss. A steam iron heating up. "When I picked her up, she had parasites in her stool. She had lice. She is malnourished and hasn't reached any of the milestones she should have reached at this age."

"She hasn't reached those milestones because she's retarded. That is what it means, dear. Her development has been delayed. *Retarded*."

Ginny's eyes stung. The word seemed so cruel to her.

"Please let me finish," she said. "There was no record of a heart condition in her files. She's a healthy little girl."

"You are calling from a hospital, dear. I would hardly say this is evidence of her good health."

She took a deep breath. If this didn't convince him, then she didn't know what would.

"Listen, I understand your livelihood depends upon defending those accused of terrible things. But this time, you are defending the indefensible. There is a man, a man named Hanson, Robert Hanson, who's been working at Willowridge since before Lucy was committed. He's been arrested three times for assault. For child abuse. He broke Lucy's ribs, which made her vulnerable to pneumonia. That is why she is sick. Because a man charged with her care *hurt* her, and if you think there is any way in hell I would bring her back there, you are clearly no better than the so-called school you are defending."

She sucked in her breath, realizing that she hadn't stopped talking once to breathe. She continued. "You can do with this information whatever you will. I plan to share this with Ab as well. But regardless of what you decide to do, you should know I am prepared to reach out not only to the parent group, but to their legal counsel, to the school itself, and to the reporter who wrote the exposé."

"Are you threatening me?" he asked, almost laughing.

"Not at all. But I will tell the truth. And I will use my real name. Everyone will know what you've allowed to happen to my child. To your own grandchild. However, if you are so inclined, you could, perhaps, speak to someone at the district attorney's office about this. You could figure out a way to return the custody of my child to me."

"What does your husband have to say about your little plan to blackmail me?"

"I haven't spoken to Ab yet. I plan to call him when we finish. He's a good man, though, and so I suspect when he understands the scope of what has happened, he'll agree with me. If not, then I suppose he's not who I thought he was."

"I doubt he's going to be thrilled with the idea of you disappearing with his son. Even if you regain custody of Lucy, you could still be charged with kidnapping Peyton."

Ginny felt that same sharp pain under her rib. This was the one bargaining tool she had known he was bound to throw down.

"Well, I think the reporter of that exposé would be very interested in that twist. Imagine that, Ab married to a felon. I can't imagine that will help much in his campaign for assistant DA. It might create, what would you call it? A rather large bump in the road."

Abbott coughed again. When he finally spoke, Ginny felt like she might vomit. She wished she had someplace to sit down.

"I underestimated you, Virginia," he said. "Perhaps *you* should have gone to law school instead of your husband."

Ginny leaned against the wall, her legs suddenly feeling too weak to support her.

"Here is what I am going to do," he said firmly. "I will go through the necessary channels to get custodial rights reverted to you. But you—you will return to Massachusetts with my grandson. And you will *not* go to the press."

"But . . . the other residents. You can't expect me to just keep quiet?"

Abbott Senior paused, cleared his throat.

"It seems to me you have a decision to make, Virginia. Perhaps you should speak to your husband now, so you can discuss our arrangement."

❦

Ginny wiped at the tears that were spilling hot down her cheeks. She waited for Sissy to patch her through to Ab, feeling spent, her body like a rag that had been wrung hard.

"I'm sorry," he said, before she had time to speak. "For everything. I was wrong. I just want you to come home. I'm going to talk to my father and get this straightened out."

"I already did," she said.

"You talked to my father?"

"Yes. He's going to take care of the custody issue. But he won't drop the school as a client."

Ab was silent on the other end of the line.

"Ab, why didn't you believe me? Why wouldn't you listen?"

Ab was quiet. "I don't know, Gin. I was afraid. I *am* afraid. I don't know the first thing about raising a child like Lucy. I am afraid that it will change our family. That it will change our marriage. All those things the doctor said, the things my father said? They terrify me."

"Well, I need you to be brave," she said. "And I need you to get down here to meet your daughter."

Thirty-five

༇

1969

"He's ours?" Ab had said the moment he held Peyton in his arms.

Ginny had smiled and nodded.

"Forever?" he said, but he was talking to the infant in his arms now.

Ab was a good father, and he loved Peyton with a ferocity that Ginny rarely saw in him. He'd had no real passion for his studies, and definitely no passion for the law. Most of his life until then had been spent going through the necessary motions. And it was taking its toll. But *fatherhood*. With Peyton he was joyful, bubbling over with plans. He took little Peyton everywhere with him. He bought a camera to document every moment. His pride at even the smallest milestone was infectious. *Did you see that?* he'd say to anyone, everyone. *He's only eight months old and already walking!* Peyton's first word had been *Dada*, of course, uttered in the middle of the night when Ginny went to feed him a bottle. She'd leaned over the crib to pick him up, and clear as a little silver bell, he'd chimed, "Dada."

When she returned to bed and told Ab, he had whooped with delight, nearly waking up the entire neighborhood.

"You are going to have a very important job," he had said to Peyton, when they explained Ginny's growing belly to him. "You're going to be a big brother. Do you know what that means?"

Peyton was only four; he had no idea why his mother was swelling up like a balloon.

"A baby," Ab had whispered conspiratorially to him. "Maybe a baby brother."

Peyton's eyes had widened at the news, though they had also filled with tears. "Does Mommy *have* to have a baby?" he'd asked.

"Well, here's the thing, little man," Ab had said, hoisting Peyton onto his lap. "This baby is not for us. Not for Mommy, and not for Daddy. This baby is for *you*. He'll *belong* to you. Your brother. Your very own."

Ginny had felt her own eyes dampen as Peyton smiled.

"You'll need to take care of him and keep him safe. You'll need to teach him everything you know and help him do things. And someday, when you are both grown, he'll be your very best friend."

Ginny's heart cracked as she thought of Ab's brother, Paul. Ab had told her the story after they got married, one night in their house in Cambridge as she tried and failed to make the meat loaf that Rosa usually made for him. (Ginny had inherited none of her mother's culinary gifts.) He'd been matter-of-fact as he relayed the details: the fever, the race to the hospital in the middle of the night, Sylvia's empty arms when she left the hospital the next morning. He told her that no one ever spoke of Paul and that sometimes, he wondered if he'd only dreamed him; as an only child, he sometimes wondered if maybe he'd simply wished him into existence.

As he'd relayed the story, his cool demeanor had changed to that of someone who had been storing a lifetime of sorrow.

"I didn't wash my hands," he said. "At school. My father told me I must have brought the flu home from school. That if I'd just washed my hands before I held Paul's hand, then he would still be alive."

"That is a horrible, horrible thing to say to a child," she'd said, stunned.

"But it was true," he said. "I did forget. There was a little girl at school who was sick. She wound up in the hospital, too. But I was too busy. I didn't listen."

"You will protect him," Ab said to Peyton. "It is your job to keep this baby safe."

But three days later was the baby shower at Sylvia's, and the next day Sylvia explained to Peyton that his baby sister was with the angels now. Peyton had never even gotten a chance to meet her. And Ginny, so mired in her own sadness and loss, hadn't even begun to think what sort of damage this lie might do to her son.

She also had not considered the damage that Abbott had done to Ab all those years ago when he blamed him for his brother's death. She had not stopped to consider the enormity of the guilt that Ab must have been carrying that caused him to give in to his father. Again and again and again. She didn't consider that it was this crushing culpability that made Ab relinquish control of his own life. That it was this that had, in the end, enabled him to relinquish his own child.

Thirty-six

❦

September 1971

That afternoon Ginny lay down next to Lucy in the hospital bed. Lucy was watching *The Guiding Light* on the TV that hung suspended from the ceiling, clutching the stuffed alligator from Peyton. Her fever had come down some, but her body was still toasty as Ginny curled up next to her and rested her cheek against her soft back. Lucy touched Ginny's hair, absently playing with it. It made Ginny feel drowsy, and she soon found herself drifting off to sleep.

"Mrs. Richardson?"

As the doctor entered the room, Ginny jolted upright, heart pounding like an alarm in her ears. She swung her legs over the side of the bed and stood up.

"I'm sorry; I didn't realize you two were sleeping."

She looked to the bed, and Lucy had, indeed fallen asleep, her legs splayed open the way they did whenever she succumbed to slumber's pull.

"Can we chat for a minute?" the doctor asked.

Ginny nodded.

"Normally, I'd like to speak to both parents, but I understand your husband isn't here yet?"

Ginny nodded but did not elaborate.

"Well, then, hopefully you can relay all of this to him. I'm also happy to give him a call if you prefer."

"That won't be necessary," she said. "What's going on?"

"Well, as you know," he said, "Lucy's condition means that she's got some issues to contend with. For *you* to contend with. Delays in gross and fine motor skills. Speech. The lack of muscle tone can make all these things more challenging than with a typical child. You have a son as well?"

Ginny nodded. "Yes. He's starting first grade soon."

"Well, raising Lucy will be quite different than raising your son."

"Of course," she said.

"I also understand that until recently she's been institutionalized?"

Officer Marley must have spoken to him.

"Did your doctor advise you to send her away?"

Ginny's head fell to her chest, pulled by the weight of her shame, by the memory of the doctor who first delivered Lucy and then the news of her disorder. His warnings and condemnation. That was exactly it; he had *condemned* her

Ginny looked up again. His eyes were apologetic.

"Yes," she said. "He did."

"Well, a great many of her delays can be attributed to her Down syndrome. However, many others simply have to do with the lack of stimulation she's likely to have experienced at the facility where she's been living. Children with Down syndrome need attention: physical activity, interaction. They need to be held. And they need to be loved."

Ginny's eyes pricked with tears.

"But all these things, all these challenges, are something I suspect you are willing to take on. Or, perhaps, you wouldn't be here?"

"I am," she said. "I mean, I understand the challenges."

"Good, good," he said. "But listen, I need to give you a clear assessment of her health as well, before you make any decisions about her future."

"You said she was going to be okay," Ginny said, looking toward Lucy, who was snoring softly, her chest rising and falling with each breath. "She's already getting better; her cough is better."

The doctor took a deep breath. "I heard something a little concerning when I listened to her heart, a bit of a murmur. There were also some suspicious ventricular markings when we did the chest X-ray of her lungs."

Ginny felt her stomach bottom out, the same way it had when they rode the Ferris wheel in Atlantic City. Her heart? There was nothing in her file about her heart.

She shook her head.

"I thought at first it might be benign, but I also knew we needed to be extra cautious given her disability. While we were running tests, we did an echocardiogram and have confirmed the presence of a moderate ventricular septal defect."

Ginny scowled, confused. "What is that?"

"It's a congenital defect, very common in children with Down syndrome," he said and paused. "It's essentially a hole in her heart."

She felt a hole in her own heart beginning to open. A chasm deep in her chest.

"What does that mean?"

"Well, smaller defects will often repair themselves as a child grows older. Or, if they are small enough, they can be managed with medication. But Lucy's defect seems to be growing, which will eventually require surgery to repair."

Ginny nodded. "But she'll be okay if she has the surgery?"

The doctor smiled a little sadly. "Hopefully. But to be completely candid, had this diagnosis been made when she was born, the prognosis would have been much clearer. The defect has gone both undiagnosed and untreated for two years. The later the surgery is conducted, the riskier it is. There can be complications, the risk of permanent pulmonary hypertension. Her lungs could be compromised."

Ginny felt dizzy and gripped the bed rail to keep herself upright.

"What happens then? I mean, if it can't be fixed? Will she . . . could she die?"

"I don't mean to scare you," he said carefully, his voice measured. "And I am not a cardiologist. You'd need to take her to a specialist, ideally a pediatric cardiologist. You have a wonderful children's hospital in Boston. My recommendation would be to have her seen there. They can give you a much more thorough diagnosis and prognosis. Of course, this all depends on whether you decide to keep her in your home. If she is returned to the institution, the medical team there will determine her treatment plan. But this is an important decision, one that should not be taken lightly. If you decide to care for her on your own, there will be tremendous demands: emotional, financial. A child with extreme medical issues can put a strain on a marriage, on a family."

She felt as though she were swimming through that ether haze once again, the fog she'd found herself in after Lucy was born. Though back then the doctor had been condescending, insensitive. And her response hadn't mattered one bit.

The doctor reached out and put his hand on her trembling shoulder.

"Mrs. Richardson, I only want you to be aware of the risks, but in the end this is your decision to make. Your choice."

Thirty-seven

༄

Autumn 1969

She had left, once before.

Fall arrived early that year she was pregnant with Lucy, the heat of summer gone overnight, frost lacing the windows like Mother Nature's curtains. She'd woken early as she always did, her enormous belly angrily growling with hunger. She hadn't been able to eat more than a few bites in the last two weeks. The baby was so high up, she could barely even swallow, and when she did, the heartburn was unbearable. But now, it seemed like gravity had won, and the baby had sunk lower, opening her chest. She felt free. And starving.

It was a Sunday, the one day each week when Ab didn't set the alarm clock on the nightstand. He slept soundly next to her, fists under his chin, more boy than man in this moment. She felt tenderness toward this sleeping man-boy, and she leaned over and gently kissed his cheek before quietly rising from bed and pulling her robe on, though it would no longer close over her belly.

She tiptoed down the hall, noticing that her usual stealth was compromised by her tremendous weight. Still, she managed to get past Peyton's room, where he, like his father, slept soundly and sweetly.

What exactly had she wanted, if not this? The sense of loss, that palpable regret, consumed her at times, but she could never seem to figure out a solution. What would the remedy be? It wasn't as though she could walk out of this life and into another. She had cemented herself in this house, in this family of Ab's, in this world of country club brunches (glancing at her watch, she noted that they had exactly three hours until they were to meet Abbott Senior and Sylvia at the club for postmass eggs Benedict and golden toast) and afternoon bridge (though she still hadn't gotten the hang of the game) and evening charity meetings (so many causes, so many unfortunate souls—none of them with this tremendously good fortune that Ginny had been proffered).

She set the coffee to brew and thought she might take her book (*My Life with Jacqueline Kennedy*) out onto the back porch, lose herself for an hour or so until the boys rose. Grab a piece of toast or a banana from the bowl, something to tide her over until they got to the club later. But suddenly, she was overwhelmed by hunger. Insatiable. She wanted pancakes, bacon, creamy scrambled eggs, and she wanted them now.

Not wanting to risk waking either Ab or Peyton up, she went to the laundry room, where she found the one pair of pants she was still able to fit into and a blouse that fit so long as she didn't button the bottom four buttons. She put on a jacket and her shoes, though tying them proved impossible given her girth (she'd been shuffling around in her slippers for the last week), so she slipped on her Dr. Scholl's wooden sandals right over her socks. Then she walked out the front door. Just like that. Twist of the knob, a little push, and she was outside, staring at the kaleidoscopic view of the trees' autumn leaves. She found a sudden lightness in her step as she made her way down their street to the next block and finally to the street that led to downtown Dover.

It was the strangest feeling being out and about without anyone knowing where she was. Both liberating and terrifying. She entered the little diner, and no one even looked up at her as she made her way to a booth near the back and grabbed a newspaper someone had left there.

She had ten dollars in her pocket from her last outing to the market, and so she ordered enough food to feed an entire small family. She gorged herself on waffles and sausages. Even a small hot bowl of oatmeal with swollen sweet raisins. She read the newspaper from cover to cover. She could hardly believe all the things that were happening in the world. She felt like a time traveler who'd just realized they had zipped ahead into the future. Nuclear tests were being conducted by both Russia and the U.S. The Soviets were also busy launching spacecraft. Of course, that sort of news felt far away. Hardly affecting her life here in Massachusetts. It was easy to keep your head in the sand, she thought, when there were no waves crashing against that shore. But then she read the news article about the riots in Springfield and felt as though there was sand in her eyes as she read about the so-called Days of Rage in Chicago. Her woes seemed suddenly so small, her sense of injustice almost silly in the face of this. It (as well as the mountains of waffles) filled her with tremendous shame. What was wrong with her? Who was she to lament this life, this gift she'd been given?

Trying not to cry, she paid her bill and didn't stick around for her change. She pulled her coat on and left. She walked until her legs ached and she felt her ankles beginning to swell, then she sat down on a bench in the park and allowed herself to weep.

As she made her way home, she thought about the time she'd threatened to run away as a little girl. She could hardly remember the reason anymore, but she recalled the same distinct need to flee.

It had been winter then, and she'd packed a backpack and put on her boots and her winter coat. Affixed her own scarf.

"I'm running away," she'd announced to her mother, who shrugged and said simply, "Okay. Take this apple in case you get hungry."

She'd opened the front door to a blustery twilit afternoon and walked

across the small front yard to the front gate that separated her from freedom. She'd sat down at the gate, not quite ready to commit to her departure. She removed her mittens and pulled the apple out of her pocket. It
was a perfect Red Delicious. Not one bruise on it and shined to a high
gloss. She pictured her mother at the market, carefully selecting the apple from a bin, inspecting it for flaws. She imagined her rubbing a cloth
towel across each piece of fruit before assembling them in the wooden
bowl on the counter. Recalling this small gesture filled Ginny with re-
morse and sadness. How could she run away from this woman who, in
her own small way, brought beauty to the world? A woman who nurtured
her, who fed her when she was hungry?

She'd returned to the house, knocking on the door like a visitor, and
thrown herself into her mother's arms.

When she returned home and opened the door that autumn morning in
Dover, Ab was waiting for her. He had poured her a cup of coffee and
handed it to her, smiling. "Just needed some fresh air?"

And she threw herself into his arms as well, saying, "Thank you."

Thirty-eight

⸙

September 1971

Outside the pickers' cottages, Peyton happily stomped in the endless mud puddles. Lois had found an old pair of galoshes that once belonged to her son, Bobby, when he was little as well as a tiny yellow rain slicker. Peyton hadn't been this content since they left Dover; he'd been out there for over an hour already.

She looked at her watch. Ab's flight was due into Tampa in two hours, and Marsha was set to fly out in three. A changing of the guard, so to speak. They'd need to get on the road soon. Marsha had offered to drive this time, but Ginny said she could handle it. Marley had helped her procure a set of temporary *legal* plates for the Dart, and Marsha had given her driving lessons on the dirt roads that threaded through the groves. Ginny was legally allowed to drive so long as she had a licensed driver in the car with her, and eventually she'd just need to take a road test to get her license.

Marsha was sitting on the bed in the cottage they had shared for the last week while they waited for Lucy to stabilize enough to be discharged, the open envelope discarded on the threadbare chenille spread. Marsha had finally opened it, expecting a letter, and found, instead, three crisp one hundred dollar bills and a letter.

"What does it say?" Ginny asked.

Marsha had shaken her head, two fat tears rolling down her cheeks.

"He wants me to come home," Marsha said. "He wants to marry me."

"He proposed?" Ginny asked. "Is that what the letter says?"

Marsha nodded her head.

"Well, why *not*? He loves you, obviously. Sending his brother all the way down here just to make sure you got here safely. You said he's a good man, Marsh."

Marsha took a deep breath and studied the bills in her hand, the letter.

"What else does it say?" Ginny asked again, confused.

"It says there's enough here for a plane ticket home," Marsha said. "Or to pay to have the procedure done."

"What?" Ginny asked, stunned.

"It's legal in North Carolina. He gave me the name of a doctor, an address."

Ginny had no words. The idea that Gabe had given her this gift of a decision rendered her speechless.

They walked out onto the porch and sat down in the two cane rocking chairs. Peyton had stopped puddle stomping and was making mud pies out of dirt and water in some old pans that Lois had given him.

"What's it like?" Marsha asked. "Being a mom?"

Ginny felt her chest swell. "It's amazing. It's awful. It's too much, and it's too little."

"That is not helping things," Marsha said.

"It makes me feel completely powerless," Ginny added, thinking of her empty arms as she left the hospital that morning after Lucy was born. "But also more powerful than I've ever felt before."

When she'd hung up the phone with Ab that night at the hospital, her body had been electrified. That pervasive hum and hiss inside her now. Buzzing. For nearly an hour, she'd felt as if she were carrying a current. She felt illuminated, everything suddenly somehow clarified and bright.

"So I should say yes?" Marsha asked. "Keep this baby?"

"That is your decision to make," Ginny said. "Just like Gabe says. Your choice."

Thirty-nine

ᷙ

September 1971

"Y ou sure about this?" Ginny asked as she hugged Marsha good-bye
at the curb, where the Dart idled.

"Yes," Marsha said.

"Call me when you get home," Ginny said, tears stinging her eyes.

"I will," she said.

Marsha had bought the airline ticket to Boston with the cash Gabe had
given her. No stopping in North Carolina. No procedure. Marsha wasn't
entirely sure about the marriage proposal, but she figured she had plenty
of time to decide on that.

"Thank you for everything," Ginny whispered into her curls. "I love
you."

"Love you too, Gin," she said. She leaned over into the back window,
offered Peyton a high five. Then she stepped away from the car and
grabbed her suitcase. "Okay, kiddos! Catch you on the flip side!" she said
cheerfully, despite her tears, and slipped through glass doors.

Ginny got back into the driver's seat and wiped at her eyes. When she looked up again, Ab was emerging through another set of doors. He looked bedraggled in a pair of wrinkled trousers and a button-down shirt, tie and hair askew, as though he'd been sleeping in his clothes since Ginny left.

He spotted Ginny right away, and a smile spread across his beleaguered face. In the backseat, Peyton was leaning out the open window, waving and hollering, "Daddy!"

Ab jogged to the curb, set down his suitcase, and threw open the back door, hoisting Peyton up into his arms. Ginny's chest felt tight, her heart heavy.

Ab leaned into the open passenger window and said to Ginny, "Do you want me to drive?"

Ginny shook her head and smiled. "It's okay. I can do it."

"All right, back in you go," he said, delivering Peyton to the backseat again, along with his suitcase, before opening the passenger door and climbing into the car.

"Hi," he said as he settled in.

"Hi."

He reached over and took her hand, kissing her knuckles, and Ginny released the breath she'd been holding since she'd spotted him.

"You ready?" she asked, pulling her hand away to grip the wheel. A Cadillac was behind her, impatiently trying to inch into her spot at the curb.

She parked at the visitor lot at the hospital and led the way as Ab and Peyton straggled behind. Peyton was talking Ab's ear off, stopping to show him all the various amusements afforded by the hospital along the way: the ambulances parked out front, the gift shop with its balloons and rows and rows of candy, the elevator with its glowing buttons.

But once the elevator doors closed and Ginny pressed the button for Lucy's floor, Peyton grew quiet.

Lucy's roommate, the little boy with the two broken legs, had been sent home, and so Lucy was, for now anyway, alone in the room. Still, the curtain dividing the two beds was drawn, though Ginny could see the silhouette of a nurse on the other side, hear her cooing at Lucy, who had, in only a week, become one of the favorite patients in the pediatric ward.

"Oh, Mrs. Richardson!" the nurse said, her hand fluttering at her chest as she emerged from behind the curtain. "You startled me. Well, hello, Big Brother!" she said to Peyton and then smiled at Ab. "And you must be Lucy's father?"

Ab's face betrayed his surprise at the ease with which this association had been made. But he nodded.

Ginny tried to think what must be going through Ab's head. She'd had two long weeks with Lucy, with their daughter. And in that time, she'd become familiar with every aspect of her personality. But Ab had not seen her since that night nearly two years ago; he had never even held her. Never smelled the milky scent of her breath or touched the silky curls on her head.

Surprisingly, it was Peyton who spoke first after the nurse excused herself.

"Come see Lucy," he said, grabbing Ab's hand. "Come meet my sister."

Ab stood at the foot of the bed where Lucy was sleeping, her dark lashes brushing the tops of her round cheeks.

Ab ran his hand across his face and looked anxiously at Ginny.

Ginny nodded. *Go ahead.*

Ab sat down in the chair by the bed, facing Lucy, and slowly, he reached for her tiny hand. At his touch, Lucy's eyes fluttered open.

Ginny held her breath, hoping she wouldn't be afraid. Ab's cheeks were shadowed by neglect; he clearly hadn't shaved in a couple of days. Not quite a beard, but still.

Lucy tilted her head and studied him as he smiled at her. Remarkably, she didn't seem afraid. "Mumma?" she said, looking to Ginny, as if to ask her permission or maybe just for her assurance.

Ginny nodded. "This is your daddy, Lucy."

Lucy smiled and coughed, though the rumble in her chest wasn't nearly as deep and ominous as it had been when Ginny brought her here. But Ab visibly tensed and then leaned over and touched her hair. Ginny watched everything in him soften, the hard plane of his shoulders, the severe furrow of his brow. All of it, melted. Like cold, hard butter left in the sun. This was the effect Lucy had, Ginny thought. She softened people. She took away their sharp edges. She made people, Ginny included, *better*.

Ab and Ginny left Peyton sleeping in the cottage after he had fallen asleep that night and walked out into the orange groves. The air was muggy and dense, and everything smelled of citrus.

Ab's hands were deep in his pockets, his shoulders slumped forward. He didn't seem defeated, exactly, but *humbled*.

"Your father wants us to just go home," she said. "To forget about the school."

"I know," Ab said.

"He's still planning to defend Willowridge in the lawsuit."

Overhead, the skies had cleared, the hurricane now sweeping west-ward across the Gulf. Wreaking its havoc elsewhere. Above them, a swirl of constellations.

"He only agreed to help us regain custody if I promised not to go to the press about the school," she continued. "About what I saw with my own eyes. About the way those children, *our* child, are being treated."

Desperate and scared, she'd agreed to Abbott's terms, but with each day that passed, each hour, she felt the guilt of this becoming a heavier and heavier burden. How many parents had relinquished their rights to their children? How many did not have the financial resources she and Ab had? How many had no luxury of choice?

"You need to choose," she said, summoning the courage, the words she'd been too afraid to say for years now. "Between your father and your family. You've done your penance, Ab. He may never stop blaming you, but you need to stop blaming yourself."

Forty

༡

October 1, 1971

The gates to Walt Disney World opened at 9 A.M.

Theresa and Brenda worked with a girl at Weeki Wachee who'd gotten a job as a Disney "hostess" nearly a year earlier, leading tours of the Walt Disney World Preview Center. Now that the park was opening, she'd been asked to stay on and work as an ambassador. She was able to procure free passes for opening day.

Ginny had caught a ride to Disney World with Brenda and Tony, who were planning to start the long drive north but figured they'd go too and see what all the fuss was about before heading out.

Ab had returned to Dover while Lucy finished up her stay at the hospital. She was there for another week after she had a bit of a relapse, and they'd had to start back at square one with treatment. Ab had offered to stay, but he had clients waiting, his father waiting. He called each night to check on Lucy. On Ginny. And he felt something shifting, tectonic plates slipping. Little by little.

After they parked, the group took the monorail from the parking lot to the park entrance. Ginny held her breath nearly the whole way, Lucy on her lap, Peyton peering awestruck out the window, looking at the world below as it whizzed by. When the monorail cut through the Contemporary Resort Hotel, they were delighted as guests peered up at them, pointing and waving.

At the park entrance, she purchased two caps with mouse ears: a plain black one for Peyton and a Minnie Mouse one with a red-and-white polka-dot bow for Lucy.

"We'll meet you back at the castle at five o'clock?" Tony said. "Maybe grab some supper, and then we can head to the airport." Marsha had given the old Dart to Brenda and Tony to make their trek to Vermont. They would drop Ginny and the kids off at the airport before starting their long journey home.

"Sure," Ginny said.

Ginny studied the map they'd given her at the ticket booth. Peyton and she peered at all the places on the map: Frontierland, Fantasyland, Adventureland, Cinderella's Castle, Tomorrowland.

She put Lucy in a stroller to make things easier, and she seemed content, her eyes wide as she took in the elephant-shaped topiaries and the bodies of water around them. It really felt magical, she thought. This world made for children. Devised of children's dreams.

When they got to Tomorrowland, Peyton pointed to the Skyway that would lift them high above the earth, carrying them over the park to Fantasyland, where the map promised that there would be a *Peter Pan* ride.

They climbed inside the bucket, like a gondola, really, and lifted up into the air. Both children were thrilled as they lifted off—though Ginny's heart stuttered in her chest.

"Mama!" Lucy said, pointing one chubby finger at the sky, though there was nothing there, not even a cloud. "Moon," she said with certainty. And just as she was about to correct her, Ginny realized that Lucy somehow understood, even without being able to see it, that the moon was there. Would always be there.

Forty-one

𝓮

October 2, 1971

When they stepped off the red-eye flight, bleary eyed and exhausted, Ginny didn't see Ab anywhere. She squinted into the bright lights of the airport, straining to see his face among those waiting for her fellow passengers' arrival.

Where was he? When she'd called him and told him she was ready to go back to Massachusetts, he'd purchased the tickets, sent them overnight to her at the orchard, promised he'd be there to greet her at the airport. She'd stayed in Florida while Lucy was released from the hospital, not wanting to risk traveling until she was well. She'd needed the time, too, to think about what she should do. She and Ab had a lot to talk about still.

Her heart stopped when, in the distance, she spotted the pale pink Chanel suit and matching lipstick. A distinct scowl on her powdered face. Not Ab but *Sylvia*, waiting for them at the gate.

Ginny hoisted Lucy onto her hip and gripped Peyton's hand tightly.

She had half a mind to turn around and get right back on the plane, take it wherever it was going. Instead, she marched up to Sylvia, filled with a rare resolve.

"Where's Ab?" she asked, figuring if she wanted a direct answer she'd better be direct herself.

"He asked me to come get you," she said. "Hello there, children."

"It's Saturday. Is he at *work*?" she asked, feeling suddenly duped, infuriated that while everything in her world had changed, nothing in his had. Perhaps agreeing to this was a terrible, terrible mistake.

"Just come along," Sylvia said tersely.

They followed Sylvia and her clickety-clackety heels to baggage claim, where they retrieved their meager belongings.

As far as Ginny knew, Sylvia didn't drive, yet there was no taxi waiting outside. They made their way to the parking garage and to a Lincoln she recognized as Abbott Senior's.

"Is Ab at the house?" Ginny asked as she loaded her bags and kids into the car.

Sylvia took a deep breath and motioned for Ginny to buckle her seat belt.

"Have the children had breakfast?" she asked. "Rosa made some muffins. They're in that bag."

With that, she started the car and they made their way out of the parking lot and onto the road.

"I didn't think you drove," Ginny said as Sylvia navigated the heavy Boston traffic.

"I started driving a tractor when I was ten years old," she said, lips pursed. "Just because I *don't* drive doesn't mean I don't know how."

Ginny imagined the worst-case scenario. That Sylvia was going to drive them straight to Willowridge, to hand-deliver her criminal daughter-in-law to the authorities. That Lucy would be ripped from her arms and

returned to that awful place. She thought that Abbott Senior had lied to
her simply to get her home. That despite everything, Ab had been com-
plicit in all of this.

But as she studied the road signs, she realized that Sylvia was not
headed to Willowridge.

"Sylvia, I think you missed the exit," she said, watching as they blew
past the ramp. They weren't headed to Dover either. Instead, they were
hurtling south.

Sylvia gripped the wheel tightly and sighed. "Aren't you tired?" she
asked impatiently. "Maybe you should just take a little nap. There's a blanket back there you can use as a pillow."

"Sylvia?" she said, but it was clear that Sylvia was not going to offer
any answers for the million questions running through Ginny's head. And
she was exhausted, the humming of the engine lulling her to a dreamy
sort of state as she tried to keep her eyes open.

"Are we going to the Cape?" Ginny asked. She thought of the little
weathered cottage at the shore. The place where she and Ab had made
love for the first time, where he had proposed. Why on earth was she
bringing her there?

Sylvia stared at the road, scowling. "It's in terrible shape, falling down,
really. I could never understand why Ab loved it so much. Though he's
always been able to see the potential in things, I suppose."

The idea then struck Ginny that perhaps Abbott Senior had changed
his mind. That the police were coming. Was Sylvia offering her a place to
hide out? This was crazy. She couldn't keep living like this. Abbott Senior had promised. He'd given her his word. She'd agreed to keep quiet
in exchange for her daughter. For her son.

"Sylvia, I think maybe we should go back home. Let me talk to Ab . . ."

Sylvia turned to her suddenly, and she looked almost angry. "You
think you know me? That you have me figured out?"

Ginny shook her head. Startled by the sharpness of her words, an
accusation.

"We're the *same*, Virginia. You and I. I spent my whole girlhood wishing myself away from the life I'd been given. The moment I turned eighteen I took off, went to New York. Became someone else. But when I met Abbott, he swept me off my feet. He offered me the world that I thought I wanted all this time."

Ginny's throat felt swollen.

"It's not without its blessings," she said. "Our sons. Our beautiful home, of course. I don't mean to sound ungrateful. But just because a husband provides financial security does not mean he provides love."

Ginny felt a sudden urge to touch Sylvia, to hold her. But Sylvia was still gripping the wheel tightly.

"Women of my generation," she continued, "did not have the choices you have. The opportunities."

Choices. There was that word again. Did Ginny really have choices? She'd felt as though she had no say, no sway. This was how she'd wound up where she was for the last month.

"When I lost my son," Sylvia said, "I almost left. Abbott didn't want to talk about him. He wanted to pretend that he'd never existed. It was too difficult, too shameful. He saw Paul's death as a personal failure."

Ginny wondered if this was how Ab felt about Lucy. If he felt culpable for her disability. She knew she had blamed herself, but had he also felt that impossible burden of guilt?

"I wanted to leave him. I wanted to take Ab and go. But where would I have gone? I had a child to care for. I had no choice."

"Why are you telling me this?" Ginny asked as Sylvia put on her blinker and began to exit the desolate interstate.

"Because the sins of the father need not belong to the son."

The dirt road was riddled with bumps. Both children were jostled about in the backseat.

"Where are we going, Grandma?" Peyton asked.

Ab was outside the cottage when Sylvia pulled into the grassy drive. He had an ax and was splitting a thick log, one of a hundred in a pile by the back door.

Ginny's heart swelled as he stopped what he was doing and looked at them. The sorrow, the *sorry*, in his eyes.

Peyton threw open the back door and ran toward his father, Ab scooping him up in a bear hug, ruffling his hair. Arthur came bounding out of the woods that bordered the property.

Ginny got out of the front seat and moved around to the back, opening the door and reaching in for Lucy.

Lucy, as always, clung to her, burying her face in Ginny's chest.

Ab lowered Peyton down to the ground, and Peyton took off running with Arthur to a pile of leaves Ab had clearly raked up for the sole purpose of jumping into. Sylvia got out of the driver's-side door and moved to the trunk, which she popped open. From the trunk she withdrew two grocery bags Ginny hadn't noticed before and disappeared into the house.

Ginny stood by the car, holding Lucy tightly as Ab made his way slowly toward them.

"Hi," he said, his mouth twitching.

"Hi," she returned.

"Hello, Lucy," he said. At the sound of her name Lucy lifted her head.

Ab's eyebrows raised. His chin quivered like his son's so often did, and he looked like he might cry. He held out his hand tentatively, reaching for her small one.

She accepted his hand, and Ginny saw Ab trembling as he studied her tiny fingers. Lucy gripped his hand tightly.

"What's going on, Ab?" she asked. "Why are we here?"

He looked up at Ginny. "I quit the firm."

"What?" she asked.

"I told my father that if he insisted on defending the school, I would resign."

"He's going forward?"

Ab nodded. "But I've reached out to the parent group. Offered my legal assistance. Pro bono."

"Really?" she asked. "What did he say?"

He shook his head. "Let me worry about my father."

"But what will you do? For work?" Ab had been immersed in the law for seven years.

"I've spoken to the folks at Legal Aid here. They're always looking for attorneys. I'd like to sell the house in Dover. We can use the equity to winterize the cabin here. Add on if you like? There are over two acres of land. We could have a garden. Also, there's a library in town; I'm sure with your experience you could get a job if you want one."

Ginny's eyes filled with tears.

"We're just an hour from Boston, from Children's Hospital. They are so appreciative of Mother's philanthropy; they promised Lucy will get the best care. And *your* mother spoke to her cardiologist, who recommended a wonderful pediatric cardiologist at Children's to head up her team."

"But what about school? Where will Peyton go to first grade?"

"There's an elementary school here. And even better, there's a school for Lucy. When she's older. In East Sandwich. It's called Riverview."

Ginny felt her shoulders stiffen. Another "school"?

"It's a boarding school, but they also accept day students. It's for children like Lucy. The teachers are trained to help children with special needs."

Ginny searched for something in Ab's eyes, some sort of hesitation or reluctance. But she saw nothing but earnestness.

Arthur came tearing around the corner again, tongue hanging down in sheer canine bliss.

"Besides, Arthur loves it here!" Ab said matter-of-factly.

"Really, Ab? Live *here*?" she asked, still stunned. As if her whole world had suddenly cracked open like an egg, and inside was a shimmery golden possibility.

"Isn't that what you've always wanted?" he asked. "Just a simple life?"

She thought about want. About need. About how humble her wants were, but how hard they had been to fulfill.

Peyton and Arthur came running and tumbling, both covered with brittle leaves and dirt. Lucy giggled and looked up at the sky. Ginny and Ab followed her gaze, looking for that guidepost, that beacon. Sure enough, there was a tiny sliver of a moon still in the sky. Just the memory of a moon.

"Moon," Lucy said.

"Well, not only are you a great beauty, but so smart, too!" Ab said.

"I'm scared, Ab," Ginny said.

"Me, too." He nodded, reaching for her. "But it'll be okay."

"*My* moon," Lucy announced.

"Yes, it is," Ginny said, her chest swollen with pride. With love. With hope. "It's all yours."

Acknowledgments

To all the cooks in this crazy kitchen, I am so grateful.

Thank you to my early readers and friends, Jillian Cantor and Amy Hatvany, who never say no to reading those early terrible drafts and helping me navigate revisions and other sundry crises. To Neal Griffin, who answers the call whenever law enforcement steps into the story, to Carlene Riccelli for all things Massachusetts, and to Tabatha Tovar, who helped bring Lucy to life on the page.

I am indebted beyond repayment to my agent, Victoria Sanders, and her team: Bernadette Baker-Baughman, Jessica Spivey, and Allison Leshowitz. I am also brimming with appreciation to all the incredible people at St. Martin's: George Witte, Sally Richardson, and Lisa Senz. To Jessica Zimmerman, Alex Casement, Sarah Grill, Erica Martirano, Brant Janeway, Mara Delgado-Sanchez, and Jordan Hanley. To my editor April Osborn, whose editorial advice changed everything, to Greg Villepique, who tidied it all up, and to Olga Grlic for another stunning cover. And with special gratitude to Alexandra Sehulster, who took on this project with generosity and enthusiasm. Thank you.

Thank you as well to the librarians, booksellers, and readers for continuing to carry, promote, and read the books I write.

Lastly, my heart, as always, expands and contracts for those people who love me no matter what: my parents, my sister, my extended family, Patrick, and our girls, Mikaela and Esmée.

Reading Group Gold

KEEPING LUCY
by T. Greenwood

About the Author

- A Conversation with T. Greenwood

Behind the Novel

- Author's Note
- Bonus Chapter
- Photos from the Author's Visit to Belchertown

Keep On Reading

- Recommended Reading
- Reading Group Questions

A
*Reading
Group Gold
Selection*

Also available as an audiobook
from Macmillan Audio

For more reading group suggestions
visit www.readinggroupgold.com.

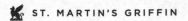

ST. MARTIN'S GRIFFIN

Could you tell us a little bit about your background, and when you decided that you wanted to lead a literary life?

I began writing when I was a little girl. I grew up in rural Vermont with few neighbors, and I wrote stories to entertain myself. In school, I had a series of teachers who encouraged me to continue writing. In almost every grade, there was a teacher who allowed me to explore poetry and fiction. Even all these years later, I can still remember the stories I wrote and the things these teachers said to me.

Nevertheless, I never really considered being a writer when I grew up (other than a brief dalliance with the idea of being a reporter after a school trip to our local newspaper). I had my mind set on one day going to medical school; I had my whole life mapped out. But math and science were more difficult, and certainly less joyful, than reading and writing. (I also didn't really like blood all that much.)

All through middle school and high school, I kept writing, but it wasn't until my senior year that my AP English teacher read a short story I had written and responded with a note that said I was meant to be a writer. That two-sentence note changed the entire trajectory of my life. I went to college as an English major, followed by two master's programs in English. I saved that note and sent it to him when my first novel came out.

*Is there a book that most influenced your life?
Or inspired you to become a writer?*

Right about the time that Mr. Porter (that AP
English teacher) turned my life upside down,
someone recommended *Writing Down the Bones*
by Natalie Goldberg. The summer after my senior
year, I must have read it twenty times. It was as if
my world had suddenly opened up, and here was
someone telling me that what I most loved to do
could be a way of life, not just a hobby.

In terms of fiction, my early influences were John
Irving and Tom Robbins (for their marvelous
imaginations and plots). I was mesmerized by Toni
Morrison's novels, which felt like puzzle boxes to
me: full of secrets. And I gravitated toward writers
like Anaïs Nin, whose language was so beautiful it
seemed almost *edible*.

*How did you become a writer? Would you care to
share any writing tips?*

At a book signing last summer, my eighth-grade
English teacher, Mrs. Lacroix, showed up. After the
reading, someone asked her if she knew back then
that I would be a writer. She said, "She already *was*
a writer."

I tell my students that writers *write*. Yes, I studied
English and writing, but studying doesn't make you
a writer. Writing does. As for tips for becoming a
published writer, I always say it's the three P's that
will enable you to survive: passion, patience, and
perseverance.

What was the inspiration for this novel?

This novel was inspired by a fascination (and horror) I have always had for the institutions that warehoused people with special needs in the days before the Americans with Disabilities Act. It was also inspired by the misconception that in the early 1970s all women one day threw off their bras and fought the patriarchy. I wanted to write about a woman in that time who is at the cusp of self-discovery. A woman who must find her voice in order to save her own child. This was how the two ideas ultimately merged.

Can you tell us about what research, if any, you did before writing this novel? Do you have firsthand experience with its subject? Base any of the characters on people from your own life? What is the most interesting or surprising thing you learned as you set out to tell your story?

I read a lot about institutions like Willowridge, which was based on the Belchertown State School for the Feeble-Minded in Belchertown, Massachusetts. I also watched several documentaries. I do not have any firsthand experience with children with Down syndrome, and so I asked a student of mine whose daughter has DS to read for authenticity. It was critical to me that I do justice to these tremendously special children. The most surprising thing for me was that Belchertown did not officially close until 1992 despite the lawsuits filed against it. Last summer, after the publication of *Keeping Lucy*, I was able to visit the campus. The buildings are all still there. It was one of the most haunting experiences of my life.

*Are you currently working on another book? And if
so, can you tell us what it's about?*

I have recently completed a suspense novel about
a group of mothers with daughters aspiring to be
professional ballerinas.

Author's Note

In March 1971, *The Lowell Sun* ran a multipart series of articles exposing the horrific living conditions at the Belchertown State School for the Feeble-Minded, a state-run institution in Belchertown, Massachusetts. The articles revealed an understaffed facility, ill-equipped to manage the needs of its residents. Living in filth and squalor, the residents were treated more like animals than humans. The photos that accompanied the article are haunting, daunting. At Belchertown, the most vulnerable members of society were no more than criminals in a virtual prison.

Because of this exposé, parents of the residents at the so-called school were galvanized to file a class-action lawsuit against the institution. This effort was led by author Benjamin Ricci, who had relinquished his own six-year-old son to the school in 1953 when he was denied access to a public education. Ricci would later write about this ordeal and the atrocities his son suffered at Belchertown in his book *Crimes Against Humanity: A Historical Perspective*. The Riccis, like many parents, were forced to surrender their custodial rights to their son, committing rather than admitting him to the school. The Belchertown parents had no idea they were condemning their children to a life of agony and neglect, even abuse, by those charged with their care.

This was at a time when civil rights for African Americans were at the forefront of the country's consciousness. And this struggle for human rights and human dignity began to filter into other factions of society, the so-called mentally defective being one of them. However, it was still often the case that parents were encouraged to relinquish

their mentally disabled children at birth "for the sake of the family." And so, this is where *Keeping Lucy* begins, with the birth of such a child. A child who is deemed a burden rather than a gift.

Keeping Lucy is a work of fiction, and Willowridge is a product of my imagination, but Ginny Richardson's fight to save her daughter is grounded in the struggle of each of those Belchertown parents who fought tirelessly for the rights of their sons and daughters in a time when children with special needs were considered less than human. It is also about Lucy's mother, Ginny, a woman, like so many women at that time in history, fighting for her own rights. Finding her own *voice* in a world not yet ready to listen.

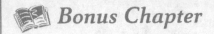 ## Bonus Chapter

Epilogue

Cape Cod, Massachusetts
July 1972

A hush. This was what the world sounded like now: the peaceful *shhh, shhh* of the waves. The sound of a child's soft sighs in sleep. The reassuring murmur of the breeze.

From the patchwork quilt they'd spread on the sand, Ginny could see Peyton, who was playing in the waves, and Lucy, who was diligently digging a hole in the sand with a bright yellow plastic shovel.

Marsha had fallen asleep practically the moment she'd handed the baby to Ginny; she said she'd been sleepwalking through most of her days since Gio was born two months ago. She lay flat on her back now, a sun hat covering her face. Only the soft *shhh* of her sleepy exhalations escaped. Ginny noted how pregnancy had transformed Marsha. Her body was now soft and yielding, her breasts swollen, her tummy tiger-striped with stretchmarks. (Though she hadn't bothered with one of those horrid skirted bathing suits, opting for a brand-new red bikini. *I'm a mother, not a nun*, she'd said.) But motherhood had changed her in other ways, too. Where she'd once been restless, she now seemed somehow subdued. Where she'd once been grasping, she was now content.

Since Ginny and Ab had moved to the Cape, Ginny felt herself changing, too. Caring for Peyton and Lucy occupied much of her time, of course,

but now that Ab was home more, there were times when she could actually *leave*. Take a break from it all. When she could walk down the grassy path to the beach and just sit, listen to the waves, to their comforting *shhh, shhh*.

She worked a couple of mornings a week at the local library as well, leaving Lucy and Peyton with a neighbor girl. In that peaceful place, she'd started to write, just a few lines of poetry scribbled here or there on stray catalog cards, nothing of significance, but there was something pacifying about the soft brush of the pencil against the paper.

Shhh, she said now to baby Glo, who fussed and rooted in her arms, likely looking for his mother's breast.

She reached over and gingerly touched Marsha's golden wrist.

"The baby's hungry," Ginny whispered.

Marsha lifted the hat from her face and smiled as she sat up, reaching for Glo and removing her breast from the bikini top. They were alone out here on the beach. There was no one to judge or condemn.

"I'm going for a dip," Ginny said, suddenly inspired.

She stood up and pulled off the white embroidered kaftan she always wore over her swimsuit.

The shock of the sun and the breeze against her bare skin nearly took her breath away. But as she jogged toward the water, she didn't think about the way she might look to passersby. She didn't worry about the thickness of her thighs, the soft flesh at her middle; she felt no shame. Instead, she felt the pride that this body had brought these two children into the world. That this flesh had made her a mother, and being a mother had given her this flesh.

Lucy looked up at her and said, "Mama go swimming?"

Peyton also looked surprised to see her heading toward the water but then quickly hollered, "Come swim, Mama!" and motioned for her to join him in the waves.

The shock of the cold water lasted only a moment before she finally allowed it to fully enclose her. She closed her eyes and plunged deeper, the only sound now the reassuring *shhh* of the sea whispering in her ears.

Photos from the Author's Visit to Belchertown

Behind the Novel

Recommended Reading

Beloved by Toni Morrison

This novel is about a mother making the ultimate sacrifice to keep her child from living a life in captivity.

Anywhere but Here by Mona Simpson

A beautiful and heartbreaking novel about the complicated relationship between a single mother and her adolescent daughter.

We the Animals by Justin Torres

This is a gorgeous little novel about family: about mothers and fathers and boys.

Little Fires Everywhere by Celeste Ng

This book wonderfully elucidates the various definitions of "motherhood."

White Oleander by Janet Fitch

One of the most gorgeously written mother-daughter stories I have ever read.

The Memory Keeper's Daughter by Kim Edwards

Like *Keeping Lucy*, this is about an "unwanted" child and a woman's fight to save her.

Discussion Questions

1. How do you think being a mother allows Ginny to never give up on her daughter, in a way that her husband can't understand?

2. How do you feel about Ab's change at the end of the novel? Do you think he is committed to the new life they have built? Will he ultimately find it too hard to leave his old way of life behind?

3. How do you feel about Ginny's initial willingness to send Lucy to Willowridge? Are you surprised by her level of trust that this was the right move? Given the time period, could you see yourself initially believing this was the best place for Lucy?

4. Talk about Ginny's transformation of character. What kind of woman is she at the beginning of the novel? Who is she by the end?

5. Put yourself in Ginny's shoes. How would you handle the situation once you found out about Willowridge? Would you follow the same path Ginny did? Pursue legal options? Involve Ab?

6. Discuss the role of friendship in the novel, particularly in relation to Ginny and Marsha.

7. Examine the larger dynamics of Ab's family at play, and what that means for Ginny and Lucy. Is there any way in your mind Ab's family would have acknowledged Lucy?

8. Did you at any point blame Ginny for what happened to Lucy?

9. Do you think Lucy will remember, or be affected in some way, by her time at Willowridge? In your opinion, does she have the chance to only experience a life filled with love?

10. Which relationship is the most complex? Ginny and Lucy? Ginny and Ab? Ginny and Marsha? Why?

11. Did you place current-day expectations on the characters? How did this affect how you felt about them?

Reading
Group
Gold

Esmée Stewart

T. GREENWOOD's novels have sold more than
250,000 copies. She has received grants from the
Sherwood Anderson Foundation, the Christopher
Isherwood Foundation, the National Endowment
for the Arts, and the Maryland State Arts Council.
Her novel *Bodies of Water* was a 2013 Lambda
Literary Award finalist, *Two Rivers* and *Grace* were
each named Best General Fiction Book at the San
Diego Book Awards, and *Where I Lost Her* was
a *Globe and Mail* bestseller in 2016. Greenwood
lives with her family in San Diego.